The Nightmare Kingdom

Also by Rob Bauer

Fiction

The Long Way Home

Darkness in Dixie

The Buffalo Soldier

The World Traveler

My Australian Adventure

Nonfiction

Outside the Lines of Gilded Age Baseball: Alcohol, Fitness, and Cheating in 1880s Baseball

Outside the Lines of Gilded Age Baseball: Gambling, Umpires, and Racism in 1880s Baseball

Outside the Lines of Gilded Age Baseball: The Origins of the 1890 Players League

Outside the Lines of Gilded Age Baseball: The Finances of 1880s Baseball

The Nightmare Kingdom

Rob Bauer

This is a work of fiction. Names, characters, places, and incidents either are the product of the author's imagination or are used fictitiously. Any resemblance to actual persons, living or dead, events, or locales is entirely coincidental.

For any inquiries regarding this book, please contact Rob at Rob@robbauerbooks.com.

No part of this book may be reproduced in any form or by any electronic or mechanical means, including information storage and retrieval systems, without written permission from the author, except for the use of brief quotations in a book review.

For Lucas & Irene

My favorite two young people.

Contents

Chapter 1

Frankenhausen, Thuringia, Holy Roman Empire

May of 1525

In the patchy sunlight of the overcast dawn, Sofie Gresbeck stared across the smoldering, charred fields. The gray-black smoke billowing heavenward in the distance was Sofie's only reminder that her home village had ever existed. Nearby, the Wipper River flowed placidly, its waters no longer stained crimson.

With her free left hand, Sofie pulled her ragged, dirty linen shirtsleeve over her mouth and nose. On the field before her, blackened corpses lay amongst the ashes of what had been, just two days ago, a beautiful wheat field. Even today, the day after the great battle, the reek and overpowering stench of burnt human flesh filled her nostrils. She tasted the smell when she swallowed. Sofie fought down the urge to vomit even as she felt the dizziness claw at her mind. The nausea was so overpowering, she thought she saw the skeletons of those slaughtered yesterday come back to life. For a moment, their soot-encrusted, bony limbs seemed to dance and sway among the gray ashes and stubble of the wheat field.

With her right hand, Sofie squeezed her little sister's hand tighter while she fought down the dizziness. Sofie was eleven, but Hilde was just five years old, and she'd cried ever since they'd arrived at the scene of the battle. Sofie had, too, for a while, but now the sobs were just sniffles. Because she was older, she wanted to look strong for her sister. Hilde's fingers trembled in hers. How long ago they'd locked hands together in silence, Sofie couldn't remember anymore.

Suddenly, Hilde pulled free. She turned to Sofie and their Uncle Heinrich and said, "We've got to look for papa."

"No, little one," Heinrich responded quietly. "I don't believe you will find him." He stooped over and pulled Hilde back to him. Although he stood behind her, Heinrich put his hands upon Hilde's tiny shoulders, in case she tried to run. Sofie saw that her uncle's hands shook, and he had a nervous twitch in his right arm.

Then Sofie looked at Uncle Heinrich's face. He was about as old as her own father, thirty or so, with light brown hair and deep brown eyes. Unlike her father's face, which was rough and worn from working outside on his farm, Uncle Heinrich's had fewer lines and creases. She hadn't seen him cry today. But she'd never seen him be this quiet, either.

She'd never met Uncle Heinrich until a week ago, but the day he arrived at their cottage, Sofie's father told her Heinrich was his brother, and she and Hilde must do whatever he said. Every night since then, she, Uncle Heinrich, and Hilde had hidden in the forest, huddled and shivering beneath wool blankets in the damp night air because Uncle Heinrich said they must not make a fire. He'd told stories to Sofie and her sister, stories about what it was like to live in the city, while they sat amidst the sighing, creaking branches of the trees. He laughed often, but last night, Sofie heard no laughter. Had he known what would happen in the battle?

"But why not look for papa?" Hilde asked in her thin little voice. "We have to see if he's out there." Then she coughed, choking on the acrid smell.

"We need to leave soon, my children."

Uncle Heinrich's deep, soothing voice wasn't angry, Sofie noted. But he spoke in a sad monotone, and his gaze searched the ground as he spoke. Although her heart pattered quickly, Sofie wanted to stick up for her little sister, so she said, "Why can't we look, Uncle Heinrich?"

"Your mama and papa are here, somewhere, but we'll never find them. The soldiers burned all the bodies. No one can tell them apart now."

He coughed into the loose sleeve of his gray doublet, which he held to his face just like Sofie. She remembered Uncle Heinrich's clothes had been finely tailored cloth, very clean and new, when he arrived at her father's farmhouse. By now, however, they looked stained and worn, just like hers, from sheltering in the forest. While he spoke, he pulled a weathered, brown cloth riding cloak over his shoulders with his free arm.

"But how do you know?" Hilde whined. "Did they die in the battle?"

"Yes, they did. Everyone in the village died in the battle," Uncle Heinrich said even more quietly, his eyes still downcast. "I'm so sorry, Hilde. That's why you've been in the forest with me all week. So that you and Sofie would be safe, and the soldiers wouldn't find us."

"Is that why you came to stay with us?" Sofie asked. "To keep us safe?"

"Yes. I told your papa I'd protect you, and I will. I'm going to take care of you girls from now on. But we're in danger as long as we stay near Frankenhausen. We must travel to my home in Münster, and we must start today."

Heinrich picked up Hilde and walked to his horse, which he'd tethered to a solitary fencepost that somehow survived the flames of the battle.

"Where are the soldiers now?" Hilde asked in between coughs as Heinrich set her on the horse's back.

"I can't say for sure, Hilde, but probably not far off. They looted the clothing and valuables from the bodies and houses after killing all the people yesterday, but they may return today to see if they missed anything. That's why we must begin our journey immediately, my children."

"Why must we travel? Why can't we go home?"

"See all that smoke billowing into the sky?" Heinrich asked Hilde as he pointed to where the village had been.

"Yes." She coughed again.

"The soldiers burned your village. All of it."

"But why?" Hilde asked plaintively. Her shining young eyes looked to Uncle Heinrich and then to Sofie.

Heinrich coughed, too, and tried to clear his throat. "The peasants of Thuringia were angry, Hilde, and decided to take up weapons and fight. Our emperor became upset at the farmers and sent his army to kill them. I'll explain more someday, my child, when you'll understand."

"How come you didn't fight like papa?" Sofie asked her uncle. Her head kept spinning from the charnel stench, but the question seemed important.

"I would have. But your father, my brother, told me to hide, instead, and watch you children, in case the battle went ill for the peasants. Because I live far away, no one will suspect I'm in league with the peasants. Like I told your sister, I'll explain more when you're older and will understand. Are you ready, Sofie?"

Heinrich cupped his hands and bent at the knees. Sofie put her bare foot into his hands, and Uncle Heinrich boosted her onto his horse. Heinrich mounted the horse last. He had Hilde in front of him while Sofie rode behind.

Sofie admired the great strength of the large horse. She felt so tiny in comparison, especially today. Its brown hair felt sleek. She gave the animal a nice pat as Uncle Heinrich nudged it into motion with his feet.

"How far away is your home?" Sofie asked her uncle once they'd started, her nausea finally subsiding as they left the battlefield behind.

"Many days ride to the north. Münster is in Westphalia. It's a peaceful country, Sofie, with no war. You'll be happy there."

Although Sofie appreciated her uncle's encouraging words, he looked down at the dirt path when he spoke, and he still spoke very quietly, like he didn't really believe his own words were true. But if Münster was a peaceful place, that sounded good to her.

As the horse walked, Sofie's teary eyes scanned the windswept countryside without seeing anything. She'd never been more than a few miles from her father's house. Although her heart thumped in her chest, it was fear, not excitement, that made it do so. What would she and Hilde do without their parents? Sofie hoped that one day she'd understand why they had to die.

Chapter 2

Münster, Westphalia, Holy Roman Empire

November of 1530

"Have you heard, Sofie? Bernard Rothmann will preach at St. Tilgen's today!" Rudolf Schweren said to his neighbor when Sofie appeared at the door of her uncle's home.

"Bernard Rothmann? You mean the blacksmith's son?" Sofie questioned as she swept dust out the door and into the cobblestone street with her straw broom. The dirt mixed with the mud and animal droppings pushed to the gutter.

"He's not a blacksmith anymore. Rothmann is back from the University of Strasbourg, and I hear he's brilliant. We must go and hear him." Rudolf bounced on his toes while he spoke.

"I don't know, Rudolf. I already went to church once today, at St. Lambert's with my uncle and sister. I've got too many chores to go again."

Rudolf held out a loaf of fresh barley bread he'd held behind his back. "I'll share if you come with me. You always tell me how good my father's baking is."

Sofie gave him a polite smile, but on the inside, her blood churned, and she tried not to let her cheeks flush. Somehow, Rudolf always seemed to find her, or be in the same place she was, at the exact moment she wished he were somewhere else, which was most moments. So, instead of replying right away, she looked down at her sleeves.

Her woolen shirt had seen better days, it was true. The original dull gray had given way to the brown of the constant dirt one dealt with in the autumn in Westphalia. Sofie could almost see through to her thin, pale arms in a couple threadbare spots.

Rudolf interrupted her self-inspection. "Do you like my newest doublet? It's silk-satin from Bruge, with hose to match."

Reluctantly, Sofie looked up and studied her neighbor's appearance. Although the shirt was indeed of fine fabric, she believed it looked ridiculous. The left side of the billowing doublet had gray and white vertical stripes, while on the right side the stripes flashed pale yellow and bright green. Because the doublet was open at the neck, Sofie could see that Rudolf also wore a white undershirt with a frilled, lacy collar that went halfway up his neck. Rudolf's hose, tight-fitting, looked equally ridiculous on his spindly legs. When he stood with his feet close together like he did now, Rudolf resembled a triangle balanced on one of its points.

"Are you ready to come with me?" Rudolf asked again while looking into her eyes. His assuming tone made it as much a statement as a question.

Then Sofie heard her stomach grumble. Loudly. "I guess my chores can wait a little longer," she said with another forced smile as she set down the broom. "Give me a moment to grab my bonnet. I'll ask Brigitte to keep an eye on Hilde while we're there."

Rudolf nodded while he broke off a chunk of bread and nibbled. A smug smile slowly spread over his face.

A moment later, Sofie knocked on the door to her neighbor Brigitte's home. Unlike Sofie's, it had two stories and a shingled roof. She noticed that Brigitte's children had made a hopscotch course in front of the door using tiny rocks as the borders. Brigitte did her work as a seamstress on the bottom floor, so she answered quickly.

"Good afternoon, Brigitte," Sofie called when the door opened. She strove to sound happy and chipper.

"Sofie, darling, good to see you. What can I do for my excellent neighbor's niece?"

"Rudolf and I are going to hear Bernard Rothmann preach at St. Tilgen's. Will you check on Hilde while we're gone?"

"She's still working on her weaving?"

"Yes. Ever since our Aunt Liese died, Uncle Heinrich wants my sister and me to learn weaving."

"Your aunt was excellent at it, let me tell you. Good afternoon, Rudolf," Brigitte called nonchalantly to the young man who stood just behind Sofie.

"Good afternoon to you, too, Miss Brigitte."

"My, that is an impressive satin doublet, my boy."

"Thank you, Miss Brigitte. It's silk and satin, actually," Rudolf answered while pinching the fabric between his thumb and index finger, although from the touch of color Sofie saw come to his cheeks, she guessed he didn't care to be called "boy." Sofie didn't know his age, but she guessed Rudolf was two or maybe three years older than she was.

"Are you in a hurry, or may I speak with Sofie just a moment?" Brigitte asked. "I've got something for her uncle."

"I think we've got a few minutes, but no more. I'd like to get seats in the front aisles of the church."

"Of course. We'll be brief. Come with me, my lass."

Brigitte laid her hand on Sofie's shoulder and directed her away from the door and into her sewing room.

"What do you have for my uncle, Brigitte?"

"Nothing, of course. I just wanted to talk to you away from that pompous boy Rudolf for a moment."

"I don't think he liked it when you called him a boy."

"Precisely why I did it. I know he's your neighbor, our neighbor, for that matter, but I wanted to warn you to steer clear of him as best you can. He fancies you, you know."

"I thought as much. Rudolf has a way of showing up whenever I'd rather he didn't."

"I take it you don't fancy him back?"

"Not at all. I find him arrogant, and I often hear him late at night, singing vulgar songs in the streets after a night of drinking."

"Although I have no proof yet, I suspect he's up to something he shouldn't be, Sofie."

"What do you mean?"

Brigitte lowered her voice. "Do you ever wonder how the son of a baker affords the gaudy clothes he always wears? Especially one who seems to do as little baking as Rudolf does?"

"His father is the best baker in the town. His two older brothers help. I'd guess they have lots of business at their bakery."

"Maybe, my girl, maybe. Still, I fear something more is afoot. Perhaps he gambles on games of chance in the taverns at night? Something about him doesn't seem right to me."

Sofie nodded. She felt the same but like Brigitte wasn't sure exactly what made her so uneasy about Rudolf.

Brigitte went on. "If you don't approve of Rudolf, do you have someone you do fancy, Sofie?"

She blushed a touch. Brigitte was her neighbor, and Sofie trusted her, but Sofie was sixteen, and the question unnerved her a little.

"I don't know for sure," she stammered, "but Kurt Boetmester is nice. You know Kurt, right?"

"Of course. His father works with your uncle in the cabinet shop. I think he's a good choice, for what it's worth, Sofie. He's got manners, he's humble, and he gives every appearance he'll grow into a fine young man."

"I just want to be married happily someday, Brigitte, like Uncle Heinrich and Aunt Liese were. The right man will come along when it's time. Don't you think so? I very much look forward to my wedding day. And having a big family of my own."

"And I can't wait to come to your wedding, Sofie, my dear. To Kurt or, well, whoever is the lucky man."

Sofie blushed, more than ever, and smiled bashfully. "Where are your own children today?"

"Oh, who knows? Playing hide-and-seek somewhere behind the house, I suspect."

"And how old is Rolf, your oldest, now? I saw him yesterday, and my, has he grown."

"He turned nine in September."

"Nine! My goodness. He'll be an apprentice to a tradesman soon."

"I'm afraid so, young Sofie."

"And have you found someone who fancies you yet?" Sofie asked her older friend to turn the tables.

Brigitte's husband, like Sofie's aunt, had died when the Black Plague struck Westphalia the year before. The ugly sickness carried off many people despite Münster's effort to enforce a quarantine. Brigitte's husband had been among the best tailors in Münster, so Sofie knew Brigitte had some money saved, but Sofie thought her neighbor deserved to have a husband again. She couldn't be much past thirty, if any, and Sofie believed Brigitte to be the wisest person she knew, other than her Uncle Heinrich. Not only that, Sofie thought Brigitte quite pretty, with her sandy hair, fair complexion, and light blue eyes.

"Not yet, my dear. Not yet. Someday, perhaps," Brigitte answered. "But now, you'd better return to go with Rudolf. Just keep your eyes open when he's around."

"What'll I say when he asks about the item for my uncle?"

"Tell him I wanted to show you my progress and see if you approved," Brigitte answered with a laugh and a grin. "Oh, and here, take these."

Brigitte reached into a wicker basket on her table and produced three apples. "In case the sermon goes long," she said with a knowing smile. "Don't worry, I have plenty more."

Sofie smiled back while she took the apples. "Thank you, Brigitte," she said as she walked back to the front door.

While Brigitte watched her young neighbor walk toward St. Tilgen's, she bit her lip and sighed. In fact, she'd given Sofie the last three apples she had. Brigitte was saving them for her three children, but when she'd seen how thin her sixteen-year-old neighbor's arms had become and how loosely Sofie's clothing hung on her shoulders, pity had overtaken her.

Seated in the third row of pews at St. Tilgen's, Sofie gazed up at the figure of Bernard Rothmann while he addressed the assembly. At first, Sofie wondered how he'd gotten permission to preach a sermon at St. Tilgen's. Then she recalled the church was a collegiate church. Rothmann must have used his connections to the church in Strasbourg to arrange his appearance.

The man himself was tall, a bit gaunt, and wore a brown mustache that blended into his beard. Sofie thought he was about thirty-five years old. His dark robes of plain black cloth posed a stark contrast with the vibrant biblical scenes in painting and sculpture surrounding him as he stood in the pulpit. St. Tilgen's, like the larger churches in town, had holy icons of Christ, the apostles, Old Testament figures like Abraham, and scores of others. Chin thrust forward, Rothmann spoke with a firm, melodic voice Sofie found very pleasant. As he preached, she looked over at Rudolf sitting next to her. His eyes never strayed from the figure of his admiration.

"Today, good people of Münster, I wish to preach on a matter of greatest importance. We live in a time of upheaval. You all know this to be true."

Nods from the congregation.

"All know that God is angry with His people. All are sinners. This we know. All fall short of God's glory. This we also know."

More nods.

"But it is not mere sin that angers God. No. What angers God is that His people have fallen away from the true tenets of the faith. Whether through improper teaching or willful disobedience, mankind denies God and therefore forfeits God's grace and its own salvation."

Sofie glanced over at Rudolf again, but he took no notice of her.

"And who can complain of the righteousness of God's wrath or deny that the consequences He visits on the sinful are altogether just and proper? Only last year, He sent the plague, the Black Death that laid low our ancestors of yore, among us in Westphalia. Many died. Although saddened to lose neighbors I'd grown to manhood with, some who died had fallen into the blackest of sin. Yet, others whom God saw fit to take led outwardly Christian lives. But who can know what lies in the depths of the human heart? Who but God can judge the inner, private self? Only He knows our true desires, deeds, and feelings."

Sofie noticed several of the congregants look down while these rhetorical questions drifted in the air, although whether in self-contemplation or in acknowledgment that it could have been them, she couldn't tell. Rothmann's words also made her think about her aunt and Brigitte's husband. She'd thought highly of both, yet both had died in the plague.

As Rothmann went on, his voice rose, and he spoke louder. "But, like Pharaoh of old, the people of Westphalia hardened their hearts when the plague struck. Instead of repenting and begging God to forgive their iniquities, their pride and vanity led them, not to obedience and submission, but to still greater pride and defiance. And what was the consequence?"

The question hung for several moments. Then, more quietly, Rothmann said, "We know the consequence. All too well do we know the consequence. The Lord punished the defiance of His people with famine. Late frosts came among us, and then heavy spring rains to decimate our wheat and barley crop. And then early frosts followed in the fall to claim much of what remained. This is the price of defiance. The price of pride. The price of turning our backs on God!"

The slap of Rothmann's hand on the wooden pulpit echoed through the silent church. After a moment, he calmed himself and continued.

"Yet that was not the end of our tribulations. No, it was not the end. For at the same moment that the Black Death ravaged our people, those most infidel Turks invaded the Holy Roman Empire. Indeed, even as our brothers and sisters lay dying of plague on the plains of Westphalia, the good Christians of Vienna suffered the onslaught of the Sultan's barbaric hordes."

Many in the audience crossed themselves at the mention of the Sultan of the Turks, although Sofie didn't even know his name and suspected that few of the others assembled did, either.

"And although God saw fit to relieve the Christian city of Vienna from the ravages of the Ottoman host, the war brought suffering even here, in the far corner of the Empire. For who paid the taxes needed to supply our Christian armies? On top of those already paid, those taxes that leave so heavy a burden on our town, who had to pay a special tax to support the soldiers who dealt death to the infidel? The people of Münster. The sinful people of Westphalia."

As Rothmann made this last point, Sofie looked again at her thin, scrawny arms and heard her belly rumble. She hoped Rothmann was near the end of his sermon, for she wanted to eat one of Brigitte's apples. He didn't lie about the hard times suffered in Münster over the past two years. Sofie went to bed hungry many nights, partly because she often shared her food with Hilde.

"But it's not too late. No, good people of Münster, it's never too late with God. Just as He punishes, He forgives a penitent people. Forgiveness is yours. Simply reach out your hand and take it!"

Sofie heard many sighs of relief. She also noticed she'd been holding her own breath as Rothmann preached. Slowly, inaudibly, she let it out.

"But how? I hear your hearts beg the question. How do we regain God's mercy? We must return to the true teachings of our faith. And that's what I'd like to speak about now. I want to explain to all our brothers and sisters in Christ how to find the path back to God. It begins with the correct observance of the Lord's sacraments. Let us consider holy Communion and the Lord's Supper, one of the two true sacraments."

At this last remark, a gasp went up from several in the audience, followed by a confused babel. Sofie turned to Rudolf and whispered, "Did he just say *two* true sacraments?"

Rudolf grinned. "Yes, he certainly did."

"He's a follower of Martin Luther, then!"

"Yes."

"And you knew this when you brought me here?"

Before Rudolf could answer, a commotion in the back of the church drew Sofie's eyes. A pushing and shouting match had broken out in one of the back aisles. Rough-looking, bearded men in peasant woolens bumped chests with others in linen hose and doublets like what Rudolf wore. When the shouting grew louder still, several of the more well-dressed men stormed from the church. They threw open its tall, wooden double doors and stomped down the stone steps beyond. Sofie stifled a laugh. Anywhere else, the men would have fallen into fisticuffs. But not in a church.

As things quieted down, all eyes looked to Rothmann for his response. Sofie knew his declaration in favor of the Reformers was brave. Her own sympathies, as far as she'd thought about the question, also lay with the Reformers, as did Uncle Heinrich's, although Sofie didn't claim any proficiency in theology. She wasn't sure why people got so angry over questions like whether God had two real sacraments or seven. Sofie had always felt people should focus on trying to act like Jesus had. Jesus was God's son, after all, so of course God would love people who tried to act like His own son. However, her uncle had cautioned her to never say as much in public. A Catholic bishop governed Münster, after all.

Besides that, she didn't mind Rudolf thinking he'd done something of which she disapproved by bringing her here. So, Sofie sat and watched to see what happened next.

Far from appearing disturbed by the argument, Rothmann also smiled. When silence had fallen once more, he scanned the congregation, slowly, and then spoke again. "I will pray for God's mercy for our misguided brethren. I'll pray for mercy and for them to turn from the darkness of sin to the light of God's grace. Because grace begins with the teaching of Holy Communion. John the Evangelist, the most revered Church Father Paul, and many other of the ancient commentators understood the Lord's Supper as a meeting of the community of true believers and those who wished to commemorate Christ's sacrifice. This was the way of the early Church. Communicants prayed together, read scripture, and attempted to correct their own errors and those of the Church."

Once more the audience listened in rapt silence. Sofie wasn't sure how many sympathized with Rothmann and how many remained simply to see what outrageous thing he might say next.

"But that is not all. The early leaders of the Church also used Communion for two other purposes. One was to learn who in the community of believers was in need, and to see to their support. The other was to deny the Lord's Supper to the enemies of the Church, those who practiced evil and lived sinful lives, willfully disobeying Christ's teachings. That is how things must be once again if we are to show God we deserve His mercy and love once more."

Rothmann opened his mouth to continue, but once again the audience interrupted while people murmured and whispered. Just as Sofie turned to see if any new arguments would begin, she saw a side door to the sanctuary open. Timen Kemner, the rector of the church, scurried through.

Sofie believed Kemner a distant relation of a weasel. His long nose, heavy eyebrows, and long limbs were obvious to all as he scuttled toward the pulpit. It was common knowledge that he was St. Tilgen's rector because he purchased his position from the bishop who ruled Münster, Frederick of Wied. Sofie once overheard her uncle say he believed Kemner simply the bishop's spy, a man of weak religiosity who held his office to report on the doings of the town. She had little trouble believing the assertion.

While Sofie reflected on Kemner's character, he reached the pulpit and tried to push Rothmann aside. Then he spoke in his high, nasally voice. "Citizens of Münster, the Lord recognizes seven sacraments, as all here know—"

Simultaneously, Rothmann resumed preaching. "As I was saying, friends, let us continue our examination of one of the two sacraments, that of Holy Communion—"

"—and these seven sacraments are communion, baptism, marriage, confirmation, penance, anointing the sick, and ordination—"

"—which the Church Fathers believed was a time for identifying both those in need and the ungodly whose actions befouled the Lord's teachings—"

"—and that there can be no deviation from these teachings—"

While the two men preached at the same time, their voices rising to outdo each other, to Sofie's surprise, most of the audience started laughing. She couldn't remember the last time she'd heard such laughter in a church.

Looking over at Rudolf, however, a frown burned its way across his face while he watched Kemner try to shout down his latest idol. This made Sofie even happier. She giggled.

Finally, this got Rudolf's attention. "What's so funny?" he growled at her.

Sofie said nothing but jerked her head toward the pulpit.

"The swine," he whispered while the two men continued their verbal sparring. "Everyone knows Kemner is the bishop's lickspittle."

Meanwhile, the laughter in the congregation had grown louder because now Kemner began gesticulating, and he turned red in the face at the same time. Rothmann, meanwhile, continued to smile as he spoke louder.

Then, the double doors of St. Tilgen's Cathedral banged open, and a handful of soldiers marched through. Instantly, silence reigned.

Their leader, a man with a metal helmet, strode down the center aisle, his hard leather boots echoing on the marble floor. His right hand rested on the pommel of his sword.

"In the name of Count Frederick of Wied, Bishop and ruler of Münster, I ask you to step down from the pulpit and come with us," the man said while pointing at Rothmann.

The soldiers arrived so fast, Sofie thought to herself. *Did the bishop know this would happen?*

Frederick of Wied was both a prince and the bishop of Münster. Sofie knew that the bishop was unpopular, however. He'd bought his church office, for one thing. That cost him considerable money, which he'd tried to recoup by taxing the laity of the town and selling lower positions to men like Kemner. Being the bishop, Frederick was immune to taxation, thus, his vast unpopularity. He did, however, have military force on his side— for now.

Rothmann made no move to resist or flee. Instead, he smiled, folded his hands, recited a brief prayer, and then bowed to the leader of the soldiers and preceded him out of St. Tilgen's.

As soon as Rothmann and the bishop's soldiers departed, a confused babel ensued. Because she had no one else to speak to,

Sofie turned to Rudolf. "What will become of Rothmann? Would the bishop dare imprison him?"

"I think not," Rudolf replied smugly once his surprise at the arrest started to fade.

"How do you know?"

"You forget, my father is the head of the Bakers Guild."

"I haven't forgotten that, Rudolf. But why does that matter?"

"Before you came to stay with your uncle, the guilds clashed with the bishop during the Peasants' War. As soon as the peasants' revolt died, Frederick hired some of the mercenary soldiers in the south to come north and chastise the guilds here in Münster. None of the guilds have forgiven the bishop for that. If he imprisons Rothmann, it'd be a great excuse for the guilds to rise up and start trouble for the bishop."

"Why do the guilds support Rothmann? Because he's a Lutheran and Frederick is a Catholic? Are the guilds full of Lutherans, too?"

"I don't know if I'd use the word 'full,' but Luther has many sympathizers, yes."

"Do they sympathize because they believe Luther or because they hate the bishop?"

"Some of both, I think, Sofie. Who knows? Perhaps today is the stone that starts the avalanche toppling the bishop from his throne in Münster. And we were here to see it!"

Sofie sighed. She wasn't sure she understood everything her neighbor had just told her. If the people in the guilds didn't want to follow Luther because of his teachings, weren't they guilty of the things Rothmann had just preached were sinful? Once again, Sofie wondered if Rudolf had taken her somewhere she shouldn't have gone.

But Rudolf sat there with the loopy grin on his face that Sofie couldn't stand. "You really think it'll go that far? Just because of one sermon?" she asked him.

Another smug smile. "I know things, Sofie. Rothmann is friends with Bernhard Knipperdollinck."

"The head of the Clothmakers Guild?"

"The very same. I have a feeling Rothmann will be free before long."

Sofie wasn't sure about this news. She'd heard Brigitte talk about Knipperdollinck because her husband had been in the Tailors Guild. He was supposed to be deeply religious as well as a skilled clothmaker, but she couldn't remember if Brigitte had ever talked about what kind of a man he was beyond that. Sofie had never met him.

"Well, let's head home. I think the action is over, Sofie," Rudolf said to her. "I just have a feeling that changes are on the horizon. Soon, all the hunger and disease will be over."

As she finally bit into an apple, for once, Sofie hoped he was right.

Chapter 3

Münster

November of 1530

That evening, Sofie, Hilde, and Heinrich ate a dinner of onion soup and what remained of the bread from Rudolf. The coals in their foot stove glowed red, giving off heat to offset the chill of the foggy, misty evening outside. Sofie decided it was time.

"Uncle, can you tell me more about what happened when Hilde and I came to stay with you? Can you tell me more about the Peasants' War of 1525?"

His wooden spoon halfway to his mouth, Heinrich paused and sighed. "I had a feeling you'd ask me about that someday."

"Did it have anything to do with Martin Luther and his teachings?"

"Yes and no." Another sigh. "Yes, I suppose it's time I told you that whole story. Would you like to hear it too, Hilde?"

Sofie's eleven-year-old sister nodded excitedly, her spoon resting in her empty bowl.

"It isn't a story with a happy ending, as you girls know, but I suppose you two are old enough to hear it. In 1524, peasants in many parts of the empire rose in rebellion because they felt oppressed by their lords."

"How did the lords oppress them?" Hilde chimed, her bright eyes fixed on her uncle.

"The lords didn't allow the peasants to move away from the village where they were born, and the peasants couldn't marry a person unless that person lived in the same village they did. When people in the village died, they had to pay the lord a heavy tax to bury the body in the village cemetery."

"You had to pay when someone in your family died?" Sofie asked as her eyebrows rose.

"Correct. On top of that, people also had to pay to grind grain in the lord's mill, and the lords raised the fee even though the wealth of the peasants wasn't rising. Some peasants were unable to go into the forest to gather firewood because the lords claimed the forests, too. The last thing the peasants asked was the right to choose their own pastors. The freedom of religious choice, in other words."

"Just like what Rothmann preached at St. Tilgen's today," Sofie said. She wasn't sure if her uncle approved that she'd gone, but she'd been so late getting her sweeping and other chores done that she knew he knew she'd gone somewhere.

"So, you did go see him, as I suspected. I heard it was quite a scene at the end."

"Yes. The rector came out and argued with Rothmann, and then the bishop's soldiers came and arrested him. I thought it a bit comical, to be honest."

Instead of the expected rebuke, Uncle Heinrich laughed, too, which took Sofie by surprise. She still remembered how, for the first few years she and her sister lived with Uncle Heinrich, he'd laughed often. His wife, Liese, had had a marvelous sense of humor and a fine singing voice, and Sofie and Hilde had grown up in a house of music and mirth for several years.

But then Liese died in the Plague of 1529, and Sofie's uncle rarely laughed anymore. Now, whenever she visited him at work making cabinets, she observed that he worked steadily, and his craftsmanship seemed as good as ever, but he worked with his head down and rarely spoke. Even at home, Heinrich seemed to take little joy in anything. Instead, he trudged around the house and muttered to himself often, even during the bright summer days that brought Sofie so much joy. Heinrich rarely showed anger toward either Sofie or Hilde, but he rarely smiled at them, either.

Hilde interrupted her sister's thoughts when she asked, "Uncle, why weren't the people allowed to pick their own preacher?"

Uncle Heinrich grew somber once again. "Hilde, do you understand how in Münster, the prince who rules the town is also the bishop who decides things about religion?"

A nod.

"Some other places in the empire are like that, too, and in others, the prince and bishop are friends even when they aren't the same person. Sometimes, they're brothers from the same family. If our town became a Lutheran town, the bishop would lose his position and the privileges that go with being a bishop. There's a lot of money and prestige at stake. Does that make sense, Hilde?"

Another nod.

Uncle Heinrich addressed both girls again. "The village where your parents lived, Frankenhausen, saw some of the worst oppression. The lord was a villain who squeezed the peasants for every coin he could wring from them. So, the local peasants decided they had nothing to lose and rebelled. They even hired some professional soldiers to teach them military tactics, but they didn't work together well enough to overcome the army that Emperor Charles sent against them. They all died in the end. Including your parents. My brother."

"How many other people died in the Peasants' War?" Sofie questioned.

"I don't know. Some say tens of thousands. Others claim several hundreds of thousands. I suspect the truth is somewhere in between, as it often is."

"What did Martin Luther say about the revolt?"

"Luther condemned everyone. He condemned the lords for treating the peasants so poorly that they became desperate and revolted. However, he hated the peasants even more. Luther called them murderous, thieving hordes, and quoted them passages from the Bible about owing allegiance to their rulers." Heinrich sighed once more.

"Do you think the revolt might have turned out differently, if Luther had supported it?"

"It's impossible to say, Sofie. But remember this. The only reason Luther's teachings have spread so widely is that some of the princes in the empire protect him. Without their help, the emperor would have killed him years ago, and we probably would've forgotten his name already. Luther needed the protection of authority, so he wasn't going to say anything to put his benefactors at risk."

"I suppose that does make sense."

"Mark my words, girls. Whenever people mix religion and politics, the religious half of things suffers. Just look at our town. We're ruled by Frederick of Wied, who holds the title of Bishop. Taxing wealth from the townspeople to pay for buying his bishopric is what he cares for most. That, I think, is why Luther's cause has support here. Folks may not be convinced that Luther's teachings are perfect in a biblical sense, but they know that the way things are right now isn't very good. So, they look for change and hope it'll be change for the better. Doesn't always work that way, though. Just look at what happened to your parents."

"Is that why Papa sent for you? In case he was killed?" Hilde wondered.

"Yes, Hilde, it is. He knew that because I lived far away, no one would think I was helping the peasants. For the week I stayed with you in Frankenhausen, I pretended to be a traveler."

"How come you and Papa didn't live in the same village?" Sofie inquired. She'd thought about asking her uncle this question many times but never had. Most people in her village, she remembered, lived with their whole family, and Uncle Heinrich had just said that villagers couldn't move away from the village without permission.

He laughed again. "I was wondering when you might ask me about that, too, Sofie. The truth is, I ran away from the village when I was about your age."

"You ran away?" both girls gasped in unison.

"I did. One night, a merchant came through with a wagon of apples. He drank himself into a stupor in the village tavern, and when he did, I hid myself under the apples in his wagon. That's how I got out of the village and here to Münster. By hiding in an apple cart. When the merchant found me the next day, we were too far away for him to take me back, and I bribed him not to say anything with a promise of more beer at the next tavern. To my amazement, he kept his word, and he never did tell anyone how I escaped."

"But why did you go?" Hilde asked.

Uncle Heinrich still smiled, but now it was a thoughtful smile, perhaps even a rueful smile, rather than a happy one.

"I thought I would become a great traveler and see the world. That's what I wanted most, to see the world and not spend my whole life in a little village. But I only got as far as Münster before the money I had gave out, so I had to take up a trade. A local cabinetmaker took me in, and I became his apprentice. Then I met Liese, and my traveling days ended. I guess it turned out well, though. When I found out about the trouble in Thuringia and went to see if your father was safe, I arrived just in time to rescue you two girls and bring you here. Luckily, I'd been gone long enough that I could slip in and out of the village at night, and no one recognized me."

"I'm glad you did, Uncle," Hilde told him. Sofie nodded her assent. She'd had no idea her uncle was so adventuresome when he was her age, but she resolved to ask him more about it someday because a story that dramatic had to have more details worth hearing about.

In his cold, candlelit room in his father's house, Rudolf Schweren read the document again, his eyes still wide in wonder. He'd gotten it from Bernard Rothmann himself after Rothmann's release today. Just as Rudolf suspected, Rothmann hadn't stayed under arrest for long. The Peddlers Guild petitioned Bishop Frederick for his immediate release, and when a large group of town women marched to the bishop's residence to make the same point, he'd let Rothmann go on the condition he cease preaching in the town.

Rothmann agreed, of course, and then he'd visited his friends at the Bakers Guild, where Rudolf had gone after the abbreviated service at St. Tilgen's. That's where Rothmann had given him the parchment document now riveting his attention. He read the title again, out loud. "The Fifth Epistle of St. Clement." Enthralled, Rudolf barely noticed the vapors from his breath in the still, cold night air.

When Rothmann had handed a copy of the epistle to Rudolf, he'd explained that Clement was one of the early bishops of Rome. In fact, he'd lived in the first century after the birth of Jesus. Rothmann also explained that when the early Church Fathers debated which texts belonged in the Bible, they disagreed about which to include and which to leave out. The books of the Bible should've included the epistles of Clement, Rothmann claimed, but for some reason now lost to history did not. As he read the epistle aloud in a whisper, Rudolf began to understand why.

"Shortly after that, Nimrod began to rule and then whoever could manage it got the better of the other. And they started dividing the world up and squabbling about property. Then Mine and Thine began. In the end people became so wild, they were just like wild beasts. Each wanted to be finer and better than the other, in fact wanted to be his master. Yet God had made all things common, as today still we enjoy air, fire, rain, and sun in common, and whatever else some thieving, tyrannical man cannot get hold of and keep for himself.

"For the use of all things that are in this world ought to have been common to all men, but through injustice one man says this is his, and another says that is his, and so division is created among mortals." Rudolf continued whispering Clement's words as he read down the page. "In short, knowing these things to be so, all things should be in common amongst friends. And unquestioningly amongst 'all things' spouses are included. Just as the air cannot be divided up, nor the splendor of the sun, so the other things which are given in this world to be held in common by all ought not to be divided up, but really ought to be held in common."

Then Rudolf saw a hand-written notation at the margin of the text: "Acts, chapter four."

Opening the family Bible that he'd brought upstairs with him, Rudolf's fingers, nearly numb from the cold, turned to the fourth chapter of Acts. He saw that toward the end of the chapter, the text referred to the early Christian community of Jerusalem and how the Holy Spirit came upon them. Verse thirty-two described the teachings of the early Church about property: "And the multitude of believers had but one heart and one soul. Neither did any one say that aught of the things which he possessed was his own, but all things were common unto them." Verse thirty-four continued: "For neither was there any one needy among them. For as many as were owners of lands or houses sold them and brought the price of the things they sold, and laid it down before the feet of the apostles. And distribution was made to every one, according as he had need."

The words raced through Rudolf's mind, and he sat so quietly he could feel his pulse beating. What if Rothmann was right and Clement's words indeed belonged in the Bible? Was he living in sin, in the abhorrence of God, with his fine clothes, rich meals, and nightly drinking? His family was among the wealthiest in Münster, at least as far as the craftsmen who labored went. Were the souls of all his family in danger?

Heinrich Gresbeck looked up at the darkened rafters of his modest home. Although he'd snuffed out the candles long ago, he continued staring because sleep wouldn't come. Time and again, he ran through the conversation he'd had with Sofie and Hilde earlier that day.

Was he wrong for what he'd told them? Although Heinrich could honestly say he'd answered their questions, he hadn't answered them completely.

He *had* arrived in Frankenhausen in time to save them, but that wasn't what had drawn him to Thuringia and his old home in the first place. . . .

Heinrich had to admit that Thomas Müntzer's words were powerful. He still recalled the day in March of 1525 when Müntzer came to the town of Mühlhausen. On a bright, sunny morning, amidst the paupers lining his way and with a rag-tag band of followers at his back, Müntzer marched into the town square bearing aloft a red crucifix while one of his followers carried a naked sword at the front of his procession. Standing atop a horse cart in the center of the town square, the man with the wild hair began preaching.

"The godless rascals of the nobility have forfeited all claim to honor, obedience, and dominion. These henceforth belong to God's Elect alone. The will of God must be carried out by the observation of the law, it is true, but no law emanating from the nobility can be true or righteous, for those serve only to oppress the Elect. When the so-called great have mastery of the law, they twist God's word to take the property of the Elect and hoard it for themselves. The seed grounds of usury, theft, and robbery are our lords and princes, for they take all creatures as their property: the fish in the water, the birds in the air, the plants on the ground have all got to be theirs. Likewise, do they claim the trees of the forests and grass of the fields as their own.

"For it is written in the Book of Isaiah: 'Woe unto them who join house to house, who lay field to field, till there be no place.' The nobility publishes God's commandments amongst the poor and then tells them 'God has commanded, thou shalt not steal.' The princes oppress all people, and shear and shave the poor peasant and everything that lives, yet if the peasant commits the slightest offence, he must hang.

"And so, the peasant looks for leadership. But where can he turn? To Martin Luther? That wiliest of weasels? The wretched flatterer is silent about the origins of the great theft. By his lies, he has made sad the heart of the righteous man, whom God has not saddened, and thereby he has strengthened the power of the ungodly scoundrels, so that they shall continue in the old ways. Therefore, things will go with him as with a fox when it is caught.

"For the day of the Elect draws near. Soon, we'll see a time when the Elect wield the sword in righteousness. With it, they'll destroy the ungodly, who include all who call themselves great and lord it over the peasant. Then the people will become free, and God alone means to be Lord over them."

Müntzer continued in that vein for quite some time. He wasn't a demonstrative speaker with gestures or movement, Heinrich remembered, but achieved his hypnotic effect through modulating his voice. While he spoke, Heinrich took stock of the crowd gathered to hear him preach.

Most were, to be charitable, the hardscrabble sort. Grime-encrusted journeymen, unshaven young apprentices, a scattering of women with ill-clad young children in tow, and farm laborers in their threadbare linen shirts and with holes in the knees of their hose. Not surprisingly, considering the nature of Müntzer's message, Heinrich saw few of the town's guild merchants in attendance.

That's what he'd written in his report to the man who'd been bishop of Münster in 1525, Frederick of Wied.

While Heinrich hesitated to call himself a spy, the term wasn't that far off. Bishop Frederick had paid him to travel to Thuringia and report on Müntzer's doings out of suspicion that Müntzer, or someone like him, might appear in Münster someday. A reasonable precaution, given the storm unleashed by Martin Luther. Frederick needed a literate man for the job, and because Heinrich had gained a solid reputation as a cabinetmaker, and could also read and write, he'd accepted the offer.

This put Heinrich in a strange situation. His sympathies, even then, had been with Luther rather than the Catholic Church, but the pay was good, and he and Liese had needed the money. He'd not mentioned to Frederick, of course, that Thuringia was his home because he didn't want the bishop to have any reason to question his motives.

Soon, however, Heinrich realized that Müntzer was not a harmless itinerant preacher looking for followers. He truly meant to join the peasants and take up arms as part of the peasants' revolt. So, Heinrich had gone looking for his brother, to warn him and convince him to leave Frankenhausen, but his brother insisted he would live and die in his home village.

That's when Heinrich had promised to watch Hilde and Sofie, bringing them back to Münster to raise as his own daughters. Perhaps, someday, he'd tell the girls the whole story.

Chapter 4

Münster

October of 1532

Sofie Gresbeck ran through the stubble of the barley field. Her long auburn tresses trailed out behind her while she gave chase. Just as she caught up to Kurt Boetmester, he spun, grabbed her under the shoulders, and lifted Sofie into the air. Kurt carried Sofie for a short distance before collapsing to the earth, gently, with her beside him, laughing the while.

"Found you!" Sofie said while she panted to regain her breath. "You really should try hiding somewhere other than the barley fields next time, Kurt."

"Maybe I want you to find me," he replied while gazing into Sofie's eyes, his own chest rising and falling as he regained his wind.

"But the game's no fun when you make it so easy," she teased with a smile.

"Being around you is all the fun I need," Kurt replied as he pushed up to his feet and extended his arms to help Sofie to hers.

Jumping up with Kurt's help, Sofie inhaled the beautiful fall air. Although she felt a touch of cool on the breeze, heralding the deepening of fall and the coming of winter, the sunlight still warmed her body. Sofie relished days like this because she knew it would be many months before they returned. The smell of barley and wheat drifted to her on the breeze as she and Kurt walked back toward the city walls of Münster.

Kurt took Sofie's hand while they ambled along. "This sure beats an afternoon of sanding cabinets."

"Uncle says you've become a good journeyman, and you'll be in the Cabinetmakers Guild someday."

"If there's any work still to be done by that point. Between you and me, Sofie, perhaps I shouldn't have said what I just said. There just aren't many orders coming in for work because so few people in the town have money. It doesn't look as though this harvest has been much better than the last two, either, so I don't know when that'll change."

"My uncle says the same thing. He's worried."

Although he still held her hand, Sofie noticed that Kurt now walked with his head down. She found him very handsome with his long brown hair, green doublet, and floppy brown cloth hat, but Sofie hated to see him sad.

"What do you think, Sofie?" he asked without looking up. "Will things ever get better around here?"

"I think they will. I don't like to live my days worrying about everything, Kurt. Aunt Liese always said to look for the good in things, and I think that's smart advice."

"I don't know about that. I don't see much bright going on around Münster, do you?"

"Not today, maybe, but better days will come."

"Yeah, maybe," Kurt replied without enthusiasm.

Then he gave the ground a hard kick.

"What's the matter now?"

"I'm so sorry, Sofie. We were having such fun today, just running around and playing games like we were young again, and I messed it all up."

"But we're still young, Kurt. I'm not even twenty yet, and neither are you."

"How old was your Aunt Liese when the plague killed her?"

"Thirty-one."

"See what I mean? If we were to die at the same age she did, we've only got a dozen or so years left."

Kurt paused his stride and let go of Sofie's hand. "There I go again. I just can't shake the doldrums, Sofie. I'm afraid I'm ruining our afternoon together."

"Nonsense. It was fun. And when things do get better, I'll be there to say, 'I told you so,'" she teased with a smile, hoping Kurt would brighten up.

"You can't be serious."

Sofie blanched. "I'm so sorry, Kurt, I didn't mean it that way. You know I didn't mean it that way."

"No, not you. Look." He pointed toward a grazing pasture just outside the city walls. "What on earth is going on?"

Sofie followed Kurt's arm and saw what had caught his eye. Soldiers led cattle toward the city's New Bridge Gate. Other soldiers brandished swords and shouted to keep a group of townspeople at bay.

"Are they stealing those cattle from the townspeople?" Sofie asked.

"I think so. And look, those soldiers over there have commandeered those carts of cattle hides."

"But why, Kurt?"

"I'm guessing it's Bishop von Waldeck's doing. I hear through the older cabinetmakers that he's in another argument about Bernard Rothmann."

"Uncle Heinrich hasn't mentioned that to me. What are they arguing about now?"

"Rothmann demanded that the bishop abolish all Catholic ceremonies not explicitly found in the Bible. Von Waldeck, in response, demanded that the town council expel Rothmann and all other Lutheran sympathizers from the town permanently."

"But that hasn't happened, has it? Rothmann still preaches in Münster, doesn't he?"

"Yes. The town council doesn't like von Waldeck, so it refused to expel Rothmann."

"Because of von Waldeck's new taxes, right?"

"Partly, Sofie. I heard that every time the Church appoints a new bishop in Münster, he must pay Rome for the position. And it isn't cheap. But because bishops are immune from taxation, he wrings it from the brows of the townspeople. That's the main reason the town council clashes with whoever is bishop. But with von Waldeck, it's worse. He's not even an ordained member of the clergy. Von Waldeck is just a rich prince who bought his bishopric and leadership of our town."

"No wonder the council and the guilds don't like him."

"Exactly. And it appears von Waldeck's latest response is to seize the goods and animals of some of the townspeople in retaliation for them supporting Rothmann. We're right by New Bridge Gate, and the fields of St. John's Monastery are right inside that gate, so I'll wager these soldiers will lead the animals straight to the monastery."

"That doesn't sound good at all. I bet the council or the guilds will retaliate. What do you think, Kurt?"

"Seems likely to me. I imagine things will get worse before they get better."

Sofie wanted to frown at Kurt's latest bout of pessimism, but she had to admit that probably he was correct this time.

"Come on, Sofie, let's stay out of trouble and avoid New Bridge Gate. Let's use Cross Gate instead. From Cross Street, we'll be able to see if my guess about leading the confiscated cattle to St. John's is right."

Sofie took a deep breath and nodded. It all seemed like so much fuss over one man's preaching. Especially when all she wanted was to spend more time with Kurt.

Chapter 5

Amsterdam, Duchy of Brabant, Holy Roman Empire

December of 1532

Eleven men huddled in the room on the second floor of the Weary Traveler Inn on Wide Church Lane. Rain lashed the shutters, the musty smell of wet clothing strong in the close air. Had the men dared open the shutters, they would have seen the Old Church of Amsterdam looming over them, its great bell tower spiking into the murky, leaden late-afternoon sky. But this was too important to worry about the world outside. The future of mankind hung in the balance.

Melchior Hoffman stood first. He set his felt hat on the room's lone table and smoothed the fur-lined, brown leather vest he wore over his gray doublet with the white sleeves. His mud-stained riding cloak hung near the fire crackling behind him. Hoffman stroked his forked beard.

"My friends, fellow disciples, the year of our Lord 1533 is only weeks away. The time is at hand."

All present nodded. Hoffman continued.

"The Return of Christ is nigh. Soon, God will come back to Earth and gather up His children. The signs are unmistakable. The Age of Mankind is over. We stand upon the threshold of the nightfall of the world."

Several of those present grunted their affirmation. One listener, John Matthys, stood and faced Hoffman. "We believe you, of course, Teacher. Still, perhaps you should explain the signs for all present. I've brought two young apostles with me from Haarlem, my apprentice from my bakery, Hans, and his best friend. They are true in the faith but have never heard you explain the mysteries of Revelation before."

"A fine idea, Brother John," Hoffman replied with a kindly smile. Matthys, a burly, blond man with a beard, folded himself back into the plain wooden chair that was far too small for his hulking, six-foot-four frame.

Hoffman hefted a Bible. "Friends, I've traveled all the lands north of the Alps preaching the Word of God. I've been as far north as Stockholm and Reval on the Baltic, and as far south as that great city, Strasbourg. I've met many true Christians, and I've met wolves clothed as sheep. These travels and people inspired me to a deeper reading of the Bible and a more thorough examination of the Christian faith, especially the teachings of Christ's great disciple, Thomas Müntzer. This is what I've discovered.

"Fellow apostles, the Bible is the Word of God and must always remain the center of our faith. For this truth, we owe our brother, Martin Luther, although since his courageous stand for God in 1517 he's fallen into error. There exist, however, certain other books and commentaries not included in the Bible that nonetheless help illuminate the meaning of Holy Scripture. Methodius of Patara, who wrote in the fourth century, authored one such book, although the Romans martyred him for his faith.

"In it, he predicts the return of the Ishmaelites from the deserts into which Gideon drove them. Methodius wrote of how the Ishmaelites will hold sway over all the land from Egypt to India, from the Nile to the Euphrates and beyond, even into the darkest corners of Ethiopia. Christians dwelling in these lands will face death and the defilement of their holy places. Some, their hearts hardened in selfishness and clinging in vain to the pleasures of this life, will even renounce their faith for that of the Ishmaelites. This swells the pride of the Ishmaelites, who brag to all that the Christians will be subject to them forever."

"And so it has proven," Matthys, the baker from Haarlem, broke in. "For centuries, the Arabs and Turks have ruled our great holy sites—Jerusalem and the Holy Sepulcher, above all—just as Methodius predicted."

"Yet, that is not all, Brother John," Hoffman answered. "The Book of Daniel makes clear that the end of the Age of Mankind will last for seven years, beginning in 1526."

"How do you know the end began in 1526?" Bartholomew Bookbinder broke in. His intent eyes shone as he looked Hoffman in the face, but then he looked down at the simple wooden table, his face flushed. "I'm sorry to interrupt, Teacher, but John Voelkerts said nothing of 1526 when he baptized me a year and a half ago."

"The year 1533 marks the fifteenth century since Christ's death on the Cross. Therefore, the seven preceding years must begin in 1526. The first three and a half years will witness the appearance of God's saints to gather the faithful despite horrid oppressions. The second three and a half years will see judgment visited upon the wicked. We know this from verse twenty-five of the seventh chapter of Daniel: 'And he shall speak words against the High One, and shall crush the saints of the most High, and he shall think himself able to change times and laws, and they shall be delivered into his hand until a time, and times, and half a time.' Then, later, in Daniel's twelfth chapter, verses eleven and twelve tell us, 'And from the time when the continual sacrifice shall be taken away, and the abomination unto desolation shall be set up, there shall be a thousand two hundred ninety days. Blessed is he that waits, and cometh unto a thousand three hundred thirty-five days.'"

Although Bookbinder continued looking at Hoffman, he squinted and leaned his head to one side.

Hoffman decided he must help the young apostle understand. "The first time referred to in chapter seven is the 1,290 days of desolation. Three and one-half years. This period began when the accursed Turks defeated the Christians of Hungary at the Battle of Mohacs in 1526."

Several of the men crossed themselves in memory of the tragedy.

"However, in 1529, right in the middle of the fourth year, the same Turks laid siege to Vienna but were beaten back. This was the turning point, the sign that the second time had come. The second time is the 1,335 days, another three and a half years, when God shall visit the wicked with judgment. After that comes the dividing of Time and the Third Age of the World."

Hoffman paused a moment. "God's judgment will begin in 1533. It is nearly at hand.

"Also consider the other signs given us by Daniel. In chapter two, he writes of four kingdoms, and in chapter seven, he describes four beasts who stand against God's people. The first beast was like a lion, but with the wings of an eagle. Can the reference to the Roman Empire be any clearer? The second beast, the bear, was Charlemagne. The bear had three rows of teeth in its mouth, just as Charlemagne's three grandchildren divided his empire at Verdun. The third beast, the leopard with wings of a fowl, stands for the Ottonian emperors of our own Holy Roman Empire. The first ruler of that line was Henry, known as 'the Fowler.'

"Which brings us to the fourth and greatest beast of Daniel's vision. The beast with ten horns that devours with teeth of iron. The Holy Roman Emperor who rules over us now, Charles, was in his tenth year as emperor in 1529. What European monarch controls more lands than Charles? He rules the Empire, Spain, and the Americas. Charles is the great beast who makes war without end, the Roman Catholic servant of Antichrist. All the signs are clear. Christ's return, and the opening of the final Age of the World, will begin within a year."

"Then what happens?" Hans, the baker's apprentice, questioned breathlessly.

"Do you know the teachings of Joachim of Fiore, young Hans?" Hoffman asked patiently.

"No. What did he teach?"

"Joachim was an abbot from Calabria, in southernmost Italy. He unraveled the mysteries of the Book of Revelation. You see, Hans, the entire history of the world consists of three ages, each ruled by a member of the Holy Trinity. The First Age was the age of God the Father. The faithful lived under the commandments sent down by God to Moses on Mount Sinai. It was the age of the Old Testament when men both feared and loved God.

"Then came the Second Age. This was the age of Jesus, the Christ, and the New Testament. Christ revealed the Gospels, and the faith spread throughout the Roman Empire as people submitted to Christ's truth. But the first two ages were only the beginning, the winter and spring before the arrival of summer.

"Summer is now at hand. The reign of the Holy Spirit is at hand. In the Third Age, God will reveal His truths directly to the hearts of all believers. It will be an age of love where hunger, property, and want are no more. Indeed, the earthly Church, the clergy, and even the Bible itself will no longer have meaning or value. All believers will know God and sing His praises.

"But before the changing of the age, the true believers must make the path straight. Joachim also predicted that a new order of monks would arise. According to the seventh chapter of Revelation, they will be 144,000 in number. Each of these servants will have a seal, their baptism, and over these true believers will be twelve Elders who will return the Jews to the true faith they renounced when they denied Christ. Two prophets, Enoch and

Elijah, will arise to lead the host, each having the power of prophecy for 1,260 days. Finally, at the end of that time, the Second Coming will dawn, and the Time of Judgment will arrive."

"And Joachim predicted the Third Age would begin in 1533 as well?" Hans exclaimed.

"Not quite," Hoffman stated as his smile faded momentarily. "According to Matthew, forty-two generations passed between Abraham and the appearance of Christ, which signaled the end of the First Age. The Second Age, then, must likewise have forty-two generations. If a generation lasts thirty years, that puts the end of the Second Age at the year 1260."

"How are we still here, then?" Hans asked. A few other members of the gathering nodded or murmured.

"Although Joachim's explanation of the Book of Revelation is without question, his predictions lacked one thing. They were not so much wrong as incomplete. Here, we must return to the writings of Methodius. You see, an event did happen near the year 1260 that seemed to confirm Joachim's writings. In 1228, the Emperor Frederick II embarked on his religious pilgrimage to the Holy Lands, the sixth of the Great Crusades for Christ, and in 1229 he entered the city of Jerusalem where the people proclaimed him King of Jerusalem. He did all this without fighting a single battle of note. Only the Anointed of the Lord could have done so. Thus, it appeared that Joachim's writings were on the verge of coming to pass.

"But then," and here Hoffman's gaze fell to the plain wooden table all his auditors had gathered around, "but then, something happened which Joachim did not foresee. Antichrist revealed himself, and the Beast came forth."

"Who?" Bartholomew Bookbinder asked.

"Jealous of Frederick's achievements and desirous to steal from Christ's glory, Pope Gregory IX quarreled with Emperor Frederick and placed the Holy Roman Empire under interdict, so that no one in the empire could give or receive the Holy

Sacraments. Then, at the Council of Toulouse in 1229, Gregory declared that God's people could not possess the holy scriptures. Thus, was Antichrist known to all, his plans laid bare at last. The Roman Pope is Antichrist, the Holy Roman Emperor his dragon, and the monastic orders of the Catholic Church are the false prophets Revelation warns of.

"When Frederick died in 1250, men reported seeing visions of dragons, and others claimed that blood rained from the sky, blood that nothing could expunge from their clothing. New enemies appeared from the East, and soon, the earthly Kingdom of Jerusalem was no more. Gregory's successor as pope, Innocent IV, had not lifted the ban of excommunication on Frederick, thereby taking up the mantle of Antichrist after his predecessor died and plummeted into the deepest dungeons of Hell. They, and all the popes since that time, have continued to show their wickedness through their oppression of the poor and their perversions of Holy Scripture. Martin Luther knew this to be true, although he failed to understand the importance of the prophecies I've described."

"What does all this have to do with the prophecies of Methodius? You said you'd get back to that," Bartholomew asked Hoffman.

"Indeed, I did. This is the rest of Methodius's prophecy. When life on Earth reaches its most terrible state, God's people will cry out for salvation. Who can doubt that that time is now? The plague, war, and famine have all struck the Holy Roman Empire in the past seven years, just as chapter six of Revelation predicts. At this time, Methodius tells us, a great emperor will arise from the past. Throwing back the Ishmaelites with the righteous fire of the Lord, he'll repay them for their persecutions of God's people with a persecution one hundred times greater. So, likewise, will he do to those Christians who renounced God and turned away from Him."

"Who will this emperor be? Will it be Frederick himself?" Hans interrupted once more.

Still, Hoffman responded with a gentle smile to the young man. "Only God knows. He has not revealed His choice yet, but the time nears. It won't be long, young Hans. This emperor will bring in a period of peace and plenty, although none can say how long that time will last. But it will not last forever. Antichrist will unleash the unnumbered hosts of Gog and Magog to overwhelm and destroy God's people, but the emperor will triumph nonetheless, wielding fire from the sky with the Sword of Judgment.

"Next, the emperor will go to Jerusalem to meet Antichrist himself and the Beast in the form of a great red dragon with seven heads and ten horns. The emperor will place his crown upon the True Cross on Golgotha, and the crown will rise to Heaven, destroying the Beast as it does.

"But the power unleashed thereby will also destroy the emperor, thus paving the way for the final coming of Satan himself, the great horned serpent emerging from the innermost bowels of the Earth. Thus begins the final reign of evil. In God's own time, however, he'll take pity on his children, and Christ Himself will appear from the clouds to vanquish Satan and evil forever. Then, and only then, the Third Age of the World will last forever. Brothers, we stand on the brink of this final battle with evil. It will begin at Strasbourg within one year."

When Hoffman finally concluded, everyone in the room exhaled, although their countenances remained deathly serious.

Finally, when several of the men fidgeted and looked around, Matthys arose and spoke. "Teacher, thank you. Although many of us have heard you preach before, I don't know if any have heard the Great Mystery explained with such clarity and utter surety as what you've given us. I think I speak for all, then, when I ask the question in my heart. What must we do now? What must God's Elect do to make straight the path?"

"It is time to fulfill the prophecy of Revelation and baptize the 144,000 new apostles. We must resume adult baptism, come what may, in the months to come."

"Adult baptism is punished by death in the Holy Roman Empire," Bookbinder stated amid the grunts of affirmation of several others. "The civil authorities of The Hague beheaded my own baptizer, John Voelkerts, just one year ago."

"It is punishable by death, yes. But do you doubt for a moment that the Lord will shield His Elect from harm? Can the laws of man and the servants of Antichrist avail against God's Word?"

Bookbinder said nothing.

"My Brothers," Hoffman continued, "adult baptism must commence immediately. Baptism is only valid when the baptized accepts God's forgiveness with the conscience of true belief. Adult baptism is the seal, the sign of the Elect, described in Revelation. We must resume the practice, for the time has come to anoint the Lord's messengers and send them forth.

"Tomorrow, at daylight, I leave for Strasbourg. On the way, I shall proclaim the good news to all true believers. I, the prophet Elijah who has returned at last, will reveal my true name to the People of God and offer baptism to all who desire salvation."

"What of those who resist?" Matthys interjected. "What of those who seek to thwart our efforts to prepare the Way of the Lord? Surely, we must answer them. With violence, if necessary. The consequences of failure are too great to do otherwise."

"No, Brother John, we must not turn to violence of our own account. Have faith that the Lord will deliver us from our enemies. For what weapon can pierce the seal set upon the faithful? Who can stand against God's wrath? It may be that He shall use the enemies of Christ to eliminate the false believers from among us, as the Lord did at Mohacs.

"For understand, Brothers in Christ, Revelation tells us that God's two witnesses will have the power of prophecy for 1,260 days. And thus have I preached for the past three years. My time as Elijah, one of the Lord's two final prophets, nears its conclusion. Before the year 1533 ends, a great council held by the Beast in the human form of Emperor Charles shall arrest me. Then he will come and lay siege to Strasbourg, but the Beast shall not prevail."

"How do you know that Emperor Charles will lay siege to Strasbourg next year?" Hans asked quietly.

"It is revealed in scripture. There will be unrest and insurrection throughout the world. Charles will lead an army to widen the insurrection, but the Elect will throw back this army and destroy it. Only then can the earthly Jerusalem become a heavenly one.

"Rest tonight, fellow apostles, and tomorrow, we set out to fulfil the scriptures. We shall do no harm to others, but trust in the Lord to guide and lead us on the path He's laid out for us.

"I leave for Strasbourg. Bartholomew, you shall go to Münster and spread the news there. One of our Brothers who couldn't be here today, William de Cuiper, will travel with you. The rest of you have your destinations as well. Now go, my Brothers. Go and make straight the Way of the Lord."

Chapter 6

Münster

April of 1533

"Victory! We have victory!"

Sofie heard Rudolf's voice at her uncle's front door, and then his fist pounded on the door.

"Sofie, open the door! We've won!"

She rolled her eyes, sighed deeply, and then rolled her eyes again, but decided she should see what the fuss was about. The sooner she spoke with Rudolf, the sooner he'd stop shouting and leave her alone.

While Sofie got up, Brigitte called out from next door, "Rudolf, why must you make all that racket in the streets, young man?"

Sofie couldn't help but love Brigitte. She always brought a smile to Sofie's face at just the right time.

"Yes, Rudolf, what is it?" Sofie said while she opened the door, trying to keep the smile in place. "What have we won?"

"Bishop von Waldeck has tipped over his king," Rudolf said, bouncing on his toes while a smug smirk grew on his face.

"I don't know what that means."

"It was a joke, Sofie. You don't get it?"

"No," Sofie replied as she tried her utmost to keep up the smile.

"Oh, that's right, you've probably never learned to play chess, have you, Sofie?"

"When would I have learned to play? I'm a weaver. Rudolf, would you just get to the point?"

"In chess, when the opponent knows he's beaten, he tips over his king and admits defeat. That's how gentlemen play. I learned it from my father's friends. Plus, I thought the whole bishop-king chess reference was rather clever, even though you didn't see it."

"Rudolf, just tell me what's happened! Why are you banging on my uncle's door?" Sofie grabbed Rudolf by his doublet, which today was field blue on the left side and bright orange on the right, and then shook him in frustration.

"Relax, Sofie, it was only a joke." The smirk never left Rudolf's face, even when Sofie shook him. "Anyway, here's the news. Bishop von Waldeck has agreed to leave the city. Münster will be Lutheran at last!"

"He has?"

"Absolutely. You remember when his men tried to steal cattle from the citizens last fall?"

"Yes. I was there. Kurt Boetmester and I watched them do it one day."

Finally, Sofie had found words to take the smug grin off Rudolf's face. A distinctly ungentlemanly hue of red replaced it. Perhaps she shouldn't have mentioned Kurt around him, Sofie thought, but she couldn't help it. At least her smile was genuine now.

"Anyway," Rudolf mumbled after a moment, "it was the guilds who led the opposition to the bishop after that. I rode with the men who ambushed von Waldeck's delegation to Emperor Charles at Telge." Then, Rudolf straightened once more, and traces of his grin returned. "However, I don't recall seeing Kurt in the party. I guess he wasn't considered reliable enough to go along."

Now, it was Sofie's turn to blush while her insides churned. It wasn't a fair comment. She couldn't remember ever talking about religion with Kurt, other than about how it influenced town affairs. Besides that, he was too busy working to go riding after some delegation formed by the bishop.

Finally, Sofie managed to stammer, "I thought the town council and von Waldeck came to an agreement after that. The parish churches would be Lutheran, but the city cathedral was still Catholic."

"Not anymore. In the town elections last month, the Lutherans gained a majority on the city council. This morning they voted to expel the bishop. Bernard Rothmann is now the pastor of St. Lambert's Cathedral!"

"That *is* big news, Rudolf." St. Lambert's was the largest church in Münster; it sat atop a slight rise in the square at the center of the city.

"Just like I told you. Now, I've got to go spread the good news. Excuse me, Sofie."

"Yes, of course you do. Don't let me stand in your way," Sofie exclaimed with all the politeness she could muster.

That same evening, Sofie and Hilde sat at Brigitte's table for supper. They dined on bread, a few soft apples left from last fall, and a block of cheese. Sometimes they ate fish when the young women visited Brigitte—cod, mackerel, or perch—but not this evening. Sofie sat next to Rolf, Brigitte's oldest child. When he'd been younger, Sofie played with him by making shadows on the wall with her hand in the candlelight. Today, she'd shown him how, so he could do the same with his brother and sister.

"Your uncle isn't joining us this evening?" Brigitte asked Sofie.

"No. For once, he had quite a bit of work to do today."

"Business is picking up for him, then?"

"I don't know, but he doesn't talk like it. Today just happened to be busy, I think."

"But you've told him the news about the town council's decision, right?"

"I'm sure he knows."

"Is that what Rudolf was shouting about this morning?"

"Of course. He mentioned something I hadn't heard of, though. Rudolf claimed he rode in an ambush of the bishop's men at Telge. Do you remember what that's about?"

Brigitte just laughed. "Ambush? Well, I suppose he might call it that, although it's not the word I'd choose. From what I've heard, it was more of a payoff than an ambush. The guilds tried to buy off some of the bishop's messengers to Emperor Charles, so they'd reveal what their messages were about. It didn't work."

"Why did Rudolf make such a big deal of it, then, if it didn't work?" Hilde asked Brigitte.

"Soon, Hilde, you'll understand that some people try to make their accomplishments seem grander than they are, so they can impress other people with their own importance." She raised an eyebrow at Sofie while she said it, and then winked.

"Yeah, I see that sometimes, too," Hilde replied. "Like when Sofie tells everyone how she's better at weaving than I am."

Everyone laughed, Sofie included. She might not have been guilty of doing what Hilde said, but she loved her little sister enough to let her get away with making that up. Besides, what Brigitte said was a good lesson for Hilde to take to heart. She was a very pretty young lady who was nearly fourteen, her brown hair almost as long as Sofie's. Hilde also had rosy cheeks and a heartwarming smile. The only thing that worried Sofie about her sister's good looks was that it wouldn't be much longer before the young men of Münster took notice. Sofie just hoped she'd draw the attention of men like Kurt rather than men like Rudolf.

"Well, ladies," Brigitte said to her young friends while she stood to clear the wooden plates from the table, "I suppose you'd better go home soon. Your uncle will be worried if he comes home to an empty house."

"But he knows we come over here all the time, Miss Brigitte," Hilde said.

"Which is why we mustn't upset him, so he'll keep letting you visit so much."

While Hilde got up and prepared to leave, Sofie helped Brigitte by stirring the coals in her iron foot stove. Although today had been sunny and clear, a decided coolness was in the air. Sofie tossed a few more hunks of coal into the stove, and then went back to showing Rolf how to twist his fingers to make shadows in the candlelight before standing to leave.

"Thank you, Sofie, you're such a dear," Brigitte said. "I don't know how I'd manage all these children without your help."

In reply, Sofie smiled and waved as she passed through the doorway.

As Sofie and Hilde departed, Brigitte smiled fondly. What she'd told Sofie was true. That young lady was always around to help Brigitte manage her children, keep an eye on them, and help her keep her home clean. Usually, she did so without Brigitte even asking for help. Whenever Sofie found a husband and moved in with him, Brigitte wasn't sure what she'd do.

Perhaps it was time to find a husband of her own again. Although Sofie was far too demure to ever say it aloud, Brigitte knew she would be thrilled if Brigitte would wed her uncle. They'd been neighbors for years, both had lost their spouse in the Black Plague of 1529, and she knew Heinrich was a decent and hardworking man.

But things she didn't know about Heinrich worried her. Brigitte knew about how Sofie and Hilde had come to stay with him, of course. Heinrich had told her the story of how he'd been in the employ of Bishop Frederick in Thuringia and that the girls were his nieces. He'd even hinted about how they'd become orphaned. But how had an apprentice to a cabinetmaker become literate so that he could write reports to the bishop? And even before that, before he'd married Liese, Heinrich had disappeared from Münster for nearly a year before returning. Brigitte had no idea why. Perhaps she should look for a way to find out.

Chapter 7

Münster

November of 1533

"Uncle, I've seen a great number of people whom I don't recognize in Münster lately," Hilde said at the family meal after Sunday church services. "Some of them speak funny, too."

"Yes, it's true, Hilde. We've had many new arrivals in Münster lately. I think most of them come from the Duchy of Brabant."

"Where's that, Uncle?"

"It's to the west of us. In the area of the empire also known as the Netherlands."

"Why are they here? Most of them looked rather ragged to me," Hilde said while she fidgeted in her chair.

Heinrich gave a slight nod. "It's true that many of them seem down on their luck. I can't speak for all of them, but I suspect the preaching of Bernard Rothmann has drawn them hither."

"But wasn't Rothmann thrown out of town again last month?" Sofie asked. "Back in July he'd become the preacher at St. Lambert's, but then he angered the city council, and they banished him to that parish church outside the city walls."

"Why is the council angry with him?" Hilde questioned. She glanced quickly at Sofie and then looked away.

"Have you ever heard him preach, Hilde?" Heinrich responded.

"No. You told me he was dangerous, so I guess I'm glad he's gone."

As he often did when he was about to give bad news, Heinrich sighed and took a deep breath. "Remember, girls, a while ago when I told you that when religion and politics mix, the religious half of the mix always suffers?"

Both girls nodded.

"Something's afoot in Münster, but I haven't learned all the details yet. I don't think it's going to be for the best, however. It's true that Bernard Rothmann became the head pastor at St. Lambert's a few months ago. But it wasn't long before he began preaching that adult baptism was necessary for salvation."

"Why is that important?" Hilde wondered. "Both Sofie and me were baptized when we were tiny."

"As was I," Heinrich replied. "But Rothmann preaches that baptism only counts if done to a consenting adult. We call he and his followers Anabaptists. Trouble is, it's against the laws of the empire to perform adult baptism. It's punishable by death, in fact."

"Death? Then how come he does it?"

"Because the town isn't under the control of Bishop von Waldeck anymore, Hilde. When he left the city, Rothmann and others grew bolder. They believed the city council would protect them."

"Does that have something to do with all the recent immigrants, Uncle?" Sofie wondered.

"I think so. That, and a pamphlet he wrote. I'll show it to you after dinner if you want, Sofie, so you can read it for yourself. But I think it's no coincidence his teaching has brought outsiders to our city, and outsiders of a not always savory nature, at that."

"Why doesn't the city council expel them, too?" Hilde asked.

"It's complicated, Hilde, but it goes like this. This March, when Lutherans dominated the city council, they expelled the bishop. That made the Catholics still on the city council very angry. But since then, some of the Lutherans, like Bernhard Knipperdollinck, have embraced Rothmann's Anabaptist teachings. As a result, the Lutherans no longer have a majority on the city council, so they can't vote Rothmann banished from the town."

"And the Catholics won't cooperate with either the Lutherans or the Anabaptists?" Sofie guessed.

"I suspect they would cooperate with the Lutherans against Rothmann but only at the price of bringing back the bishop, and the Lutherans judge Rothmann a lesser evil than von Waldeck."

Without much more to say after that, Sofie and Hilde chewed their bread and finished their cabbage soup.

After they finished and left the table, Sofie took her uncle's arm and asked softly, "May I see the pamphlet you mentioned before I start my chores, Uncle? I'm curious why it's such a big deal to people."

"Yes, I suppose you're old enough. I didn't want to show it at the table. Partly because the table is for eating, and partly because I'm not sure Hilde would understand its contents. But I think you can handle it. I'll fetch it."

Momentarily, Sofie stared at a printed document titled *Confession of the Two Sacraments, Baptism and Communion.* She sat down to read by the window. Sofie wished it were nice enough to read outside, but an early November chill was in the air, and rain had threatened all day.

"I've got to go out to get some firewood," Heinrich told Sofie while she settled in by the window, gray light coming through the open shutters. "I'll be back in a few hours if the rain holds off and doesn't turn the road to mud."

Sofie nodded and began reading.

The *Confession* began with Rothmann's proclamation that the Church consisted only of believers and that belief must be based on Holy Scripture, true baptism, and the Lord's Supper. It wasn't much different from what she heard the Lutherans preach each Sunday, Sofie thought.

But then, she read farther. "There is no other gate to eternal life" than baptism, Rothmann wrote, yet baptism was the key not because of the words spoken or the use of water but because of the believer's "covenant of a good conscience with God." He then quoted various pieces of scripture—Romans, chapter six; Colossians, chapter two; Galatians, chapter three; and Acts, chapter two—to make his point that repentance, faith, and commitment to God formed the basis of Christian baptism.

Rothmann found no examples of infant baptism in the Bible and denied the apostles ever did so. He wrote that people who did baptize infants had committed a sin and described how the Lord would punish them for their false belief.

In the section on the Lord's Supper, Sofie read more things that seemed different from what she'd learned in church. Rothmann claimed that Paul, John the Evangelist, and other early followers of Jesus understood Communion as done in memory of Christ, but also that it must be accompanied by prayer, Scripture readings, correction of errors within the Church, excommunication of the unrepentant, and support for believers in need.

Such had been the practices of the early Church, Rothmann wrote, yet false teachings had shown themselves very early in Christianity's history. Foremost among these had been attributing salvation to the act of baptism rather than to the commitment to God required for baptism to be valid. Likewise, the misuse of common property by bishops and other Church leaders had corrupted God's Church from its earliest days.

He closed with the declaration, "We are not now under the Old Testament, but under the New." God's Old Testament covenant with Abraham no longer applied. The Christians of today were not the literal descendants of Abraham, only figurative ones, and thus the only people who would enter God's Kingdom were those who believed and accepted baptism of their own volition.

Sofie had to admit this was a lot to think about, and she didn't understand all of it. She had just resolved to ask her uncle to explain certain things to her when she heard the shouting begin in the street outside.

At first, it sounded like no more than a dull roar. Before long, however, Sofie realized the crowd responsible for the noise was moving in her direction.

"Sofie, what's happening?" Hilde cried as she ran over to look out the window where Sofie read. Sofie could see that her sister's lips trembled as she blinked rapidly.

"I don't know, Hilde, but the cries are getting louder." Sofie felt her pulse speed up. She looked around for her uncle before she remembered he'd gone to purchase some firewood after their afternoon meal. She and Hilde were on their own.

"What do we do?" Hilde cried, her hands on the sides of her face while her eyes got wider.

"Listen, Hilde. The crowd seems to be chanting something. Can you tell what it is?"

Both young women stopped and listened. The chants and shouts sounded like "A new baptism for God's elect!" The crowd was now in the street right outside their door.

Then Sofie looked at the door. She hadn't locked it! Just as she leapt for the door, it opened, and three strangers barged inside.

The strangers wore threadbare clothes, and scraggly beards hung from their faces. One had no shoes. Of more immediate importance, however, all three bore weapons, wielding a hatchet, an iron rod, and a pitchfork, respectively. They advanced on the two girls.

Two of the men spoke quick words to each other, but Sofie couldn't catch them. The third intruder simply asked her, "Are you among the Elect?" When he leaned forward to ask the question,

Sofie noticed that a copper token hung from a string around the man's neck.

Sofie wasn't sure what he meant or what would happen if she said yes or if she said no. She staggered backward while she tried to stammer an answer to buy time, but as she did, Sofie slipped on her uncle's copy of Rothmann's *Confession*, which had fallen to the floor.

As Sofie fell on her backside, the paper soared into the air before descending back to the floor in gently curving arcs. Just before it landed, the man who'd questioned Sofie snatched it. His companions continued holding their weapons at the ready.

He looked at the document, at Sofie, and then at the paper again. Then, he held out his right hand to help Sofie from the wooden floor. "You must come with us," he told her, the challenge gone from his voice. "God's Elect are gathering in the cathedral square. Come," he continued, turning to Hilde, who'd backed herself against the opposite wall while her whole body trembled. "Come, my friends. You belong with us."

Sofie thought she detected something vaguely familiar about this man, but she was far too frightened to place what it was.

"How do you know these women are among the Elect? They have no coins, and they wear no wimple," one of the other men growled.

The first man brandished the paper he held in his friends' faces. "It's Rothmann's *Confession*," he told them. That seemed to be good enough, for both men lowered their weapons at last. Next, the leader turned back to the young women and said, "He's right, though. You really must remember to have your copper coin around your neck all the time. We almost mistook you for Lutherans. But there's no time to find your coins now. Come with us. My name is Jaspar Gelgoter. I'll guide you to the square and see that no harm comes to you."

"Come on, Hilde," Sofie said to her sister, although her own voice shook so much, she barely got the words out. She held out her arm to Hilde, but it shook visibly.

Hilde tiptoed to Sofie, making as wide an arc as possible away from the Anabaptists who'd broken into their home, and took her sister's hand. Both women knew how badly they trembled, but the comfort of togetherness helped Sofie calm herself a little. She decided to play along as best she could. Sofie was no Anabaptist, but she hoped that after just reading Rothmann's writings, she could fake it.

"Let me do the talking," Sofie whispered in her sister's ear while pretending to brush a stray lock of hair from Hilde's face.

Hilde gave no sign in return, but when she looked intently into Sofie's face, Sofie knew she'd understood.

"There's nothing to fear from us," Jaspar said when he saw that Hilde's body still shook every few seconds.

"We're not scared of you," Sofie said on her sister's behalf. "My sister is just worried that our uncle will miss us when he gets home."

"I'm sure you'll find him at the cathedral," Jaspar countered. "Now, let's get going. The gathering will begin soon."

When he turned to walk through the door, Sofie finally remembered. The argument that broke out at St. Tilgen's so long ago. That's where she'd seen Gelgoter before today. He'd been among those arguing in the back of the church when Rothmann announced his Lutheranism by stating only two sacraments existed. Apparently, he'd followed Rothmann into the Anabaptist ranks as well.

It didn't take long for Sofie and Hilde to reach the cathedral square. The city of Münster was home to about ten thousand souls within its double walls, and St. Lambert's Cathedral was right in the center of the city. Uncle Heinrich lived in the residential area to the south of the city square. They followed the crowd north on St.

Ludger's Street. Sofie knew their route would take them to the city marketplace and that they'd enter the cathedral square from the southeast.

As they walked, the crowd jostling around them, Sofie noted that Jaspar Gelgoter stayed behind them, fingering his iron bar. When she looked at Hilde's face, she saw her sister flinch whenever the crowd chanted its slogan. Hilde also had her arms pressed in at her sides, like she wanted to shrink herself and disappear. Then Sofie noticed she was doing the same and that she was sweating even though it was November, the weather was quite cool, and a moderate rain fell intermittently.

"Keep calm," Sofie said softly to Hilde. "And follow what I do."

After a few minutes they reached the square, and to her astonishment, Sofie realized hundreds of people had gathered under the darkening skies. Maybe even one thousand, although she had no way to count. To her, the crowd seemed a mix of the newcomers and established residents, although again, that was just her guess.

In the square, someone had overturned several carts to serve as a makeshift stage, and already, several speakers, all men, stood atop them, taking in the crowd.

Sofie recognized one of them. It was Bernhard Knipperdollinck, the clothmaker. He wore heavy, deep red robes for this occasion, with a white linen shirt beneath. Like many men in Münster, his brown beard, although trimmed, encircled his mouth and spread up the side of his cheeks to join with his hair. Sofie thought he was in his mid-forties. Next to him, however, was a man she'd never seen before.

Regardless, the crowd was in a surly mood. Around her, Sofie saw faces with scowls twisted in anger. Nearly everyone had a makeshift weapon of some kind. Again, she wanted to shrink into herself and disappear. But only for a moment. Then, Sofie summoned her courage.

"Mr. Gelgoter," Sofie asked her abductor, "who is the man who stands next to Knipperdollinck? I've not seen him before."

"You haven't met Brother Albert Wiemhave before? How can that be so?"

"My sister and I weave in our home," Sofie explained. "Our uncle does not like us to leave our looms."

Just as Gelgoter opened his mouth to respond, Wiemhave shouted a greeting to the crowd from the improvised stage.

"Peace be upon God's Chosen!" he shouted in a clear voice.

"And peace be with you!" the crowd shouted back. To Sofie, it seemed terribly incongruous for the crowd to yell such a thing, given that nearly all carried weapons.

"Brothers and sisters in Christ, I've called you here today to counter a most heinous threat to God's Elect. You all know of Brother Rothmann's banishment outside the city. Woe unto those who have sent God's prophet into exile!"

Some in the crowd roared to encourage Wiemhave, while others hissed their displeasure at Rothmann's fate and shouted accusations and curses against Münster's city council.

Wiemhave continued. "It is as God's prophet, our Brother Rothmann, foretold. Soon, the Lord will place the Sword of Vengeance into the hands of His true believers. We will reveal the wicked and make the path of the Lord straight!"

The mob cheered once more.

Then Knipperdollinck, who was half a head taller than Wiemhave, held his arms aloft. The noise subsided.

"Brothers and sisters," he called, face tilted to the sky and arms still raised as if calling down God's approval from Heaven, "the time has come when such abominations shall be no more. Adult baptism is the way to salvation! Join me upon the way. The Clothmakers Guild, and several other guilds of our great and righteous city, shall stand Rothmann's banishment, this denial of God, no longer. Today, we march to recall Bernard Rothmann, the

Prophet of the Lord, from his wanderings in the wilderness. Today, we make straight the path of the Lord!"

As if on cue, thunder boomed mere moments after Knipperdollinck's exhortation, and then the section of the crowd in front of Sofie parted. When it did so, she saw the people standing nearest the stage, in the outfits of the various guilds of the city, turn and march toward Hilde and her. The cathedral square had three entrances—to the northwest, the southwest, and the southeast—but because the city council building was located on the eastern edge of the city marketplace, almost due east from where Sofie stood, the militant procession bore down on the sisters as it headed for the southeastern entrance.

Sofie looked at Hilde and saw she'd frozen, unsure of what to do. Sofie felt so much compassion for her younger sister. Hilde was only fourteen. How could anyone expect her to cope with being torn from her home by strangers and marched into a scene like this? Grabbing Hilde by the sleeve, Sofie tugged her out of the way. Just when she'd gotten Hilde into the fringes of the crowd, a horn blew.

Looking toward the sound through the thickening raindrops, Sofie saw several men in the regalia of the city council stride into the square. They wore brown satin doublets, and their sleeves billowed out where the clothmakers had cut slits in the upper arms. Likewise, their white hose and brown leather hats were new and in good trim. It made quite a contrast with the shabby clothing worn by most of the people in the square.

Their leader, whom Sofie didn't recognize, stepped forward and called, in a strained voice that Sofie could barely hear over the crowd, for everyone to halt. Instantly, the crowd in the square shouted hisses at him.

"Come on, Hilde, follow me," Sofie said as softly as she could while being sure her sister heard her. Hilde nodded and took Sofie's hand as the pair slinked and snaked through the angry mob, trying to get near the southwest entrance to the square.

When Sofie heard the exchange of shouted words begin behind her, and the volume of the crowd rise still higher, she pulled Hilde close and commanded, "Run!"

She and Hilde bolted. Sofie heard surprised shouts behind her but put her head down and didn't look back.

They'd almost reached the edge of the gathering when an unknown member of the crowd tore Hilde's arm from Sofie's grasp.

She looked ahead. The exit to the square was only a hundred feet away. When Sofie looked back, though, she saw her sister reach out for her, even as another member of the mob knocked Hilde to the ground and into the mud. Sofie had to go back.

Hilde tried to rise, but another member of the crowd pushed her back down, and she lost her footing, sprawling on her face.

Finally, Sofie reached her sister and pulled Hilde up. Hilde was crying, and her entire body shook now in her wet, muddy clothes.

"Come on, Hilde, let's go home," Sofie suggested.

Hilde nodded mutely and took Sofie's hand once again, clinging to her sister. The pair stumbled toward the southwest exit to the cathedral square when, suddenly, Sofie looked up to find the exit barred by a handful of soldiers with swords. Their leader, Sofie realized after a moment, was the same man who'd come to arrest Rothmann at St. Tilgen's three years ago. Now that she could see him up close, she noticed his scarred face and that his left hand was missing a finger.

The soldiers showed no sign of advancing. Neither, however, did they show any sign of stepping aside to let the sisters through.

One of the soldiers, a younger man, looked to his captain and asked, "What do we do with this pair, sir?"

The captain fingered his beard. "Well, girls, what do you have to say for yourselves?"

Sofie felt Hilde inch away but held on and pulled her back, so she wouldn't face separation from her sister again. "We just want to go home, sir. We never meant to be here. Some of the mob took us from our home and dragged us here, in fact."

"A likely story," the young guard grunted. "Look, the little one's all muddy. She's shaking, she's so angry. They've been in the fighting."

"But, but . . ." Hilde stammered.

"We have not been fighting. Look at us. We have no weapons." Sofie held out her free hand, palm upward, as evidence.

"You mean you lost your weapons," the soldier corrected.

"We did not! We—"

Before Sofie could finish her response, the captain held up his hand for silence. "That's enough, Reinhold. We're here to observe what happens and report to Bishop von Waldeck, not detain the townspeople against their will. Look in the little one's eyes. If that's not fear, then I'm not a soldier. Step aside, men."

Nearly an hour after she and Hilde had left, Sofie and her sister crept back onto St. Ludger's Street, having crossed over from King's Street by St. Ludger's Gate. The street was quiet, even though it was the middle of the afternoon. Whether that was because of the action in the cathedral square or the steady rain falling all around her, Sofie couldn't say.

She looked at Hilde. They'd stopped to wipe away most of the mud from Hilde's clothes, but cleaning them would require a lot of work tomorrow. "Are you hurt, Hilde?"

"I'm not quite as frightened anymore. I'm just cold now. Very cold. Can we go inside?"

Instead of going inside her Uncle Heinrich's house, however, Sofie pulled Hilde toward Brigitte's front door instead. Tentatively, she knocked and then waited.

"Why are we going here?" Hilde asked.

"I don't think Uncle Heinrich is home yet. The house is dark. His wagon for hauling firewood must've gotten stuck in the mud. And I want to speak with Brigitte about something."

In a few moments, their friend came to her door. "Sofie! Hilde! What's happened to you? Please, girls, come inside and out of the rain."

Before long, both young ladies huddled in front of Brigitte's brick fireplace, wool blankets draped over their shoulders. Sofie told Brigitte everything that had happened, both at home and at the cathedral square, with Hilde offering the occasional addition while she tried to calm her chattering teeth.

Brigitte nodded gravely. "This Anabaptist nonsense isn't likely to end well, mark my words. I was no supporter of von Waldeck, but this is worse. How come you girls didn't call for my help when the three men came to your door?"

"I was too frightened to think of it," Sofie admitted. "I've never had something like that happen before. When Gelgoter asked me if I numbered among the Elect, I had no idea what to say, and it was all I could think about."

"Well, here's one more thing you probably should know," Brigitte told the young women while she patted both on the shoulder. "Knipperdollinck and the bishop are mortal enemies."

Sofie raised her eyebrows. She hadn't known that.

"Last year, shortly after von Waldeck bought his way into office, he had Knipperdollinck arrested on some bogus charges. He didn't stay in prison for long because his guild friends put pressure on the city council to secure his release, but he's never forgiven the bishop."

"So, do you think he was leading the crowd today out of conviction or from a desire for revenge, Brigitte?" Sofie wondered.

"I can't say. Possibly both. Regardless, I'm worried about the future of Münster, and I'm worried about the two of you. Do you want me to talk with your uncle about things?"

"It's probably for the best," Sofie conceded. "There's no other good explanation for how our clothes got all wet and dirty on the same day a mob gathered in the cathedral square. But there's something else I came here to ask you about, Brigitte."

"What's that, my darling?"

"What's the big deal about adult baptism? Why do the Anabaptists insist on it, even when the law says it's punishable by death?"

"You've read Rothmann's writings?"

"I did. Just today before the mob showed up and threw everything into chaos."

"You know his arguments, then, so I won't bother repeating those for you. But the Anabaptists think they're copying the actions of the Church in its earliest years. Whether that's true, only God knows. I don't, at least." Then, Brigitte paused and sighed, like Uncle Heinrich did whenever he had bad news.

"What is it? What's wrong?"

"To finish the story, well, that will take explaining some things that might be hard for you to hear. Do you want me to go on?"

Sofie looked at Hilde, but when Hilde nodded, she answered, "Yes, go on."

"Very well. Another thing that Rothmann sometimes preaches is that people should hold their goods in common and that all should have access to what they need."

"You mean people should share everything they have with everyone else?"

"That's a simple way of putting it, but yes, that's what he means. Again, Rothmann claims that's what the Book of Acts says to do, and the Book of Acts is supposed to have a record of the early teachings and actions of the Church."

"I think I can see why that would be upsetting to some people," Sofie told her friend. "Just look at the difference between Rudolf and his brothers. They work hard all the time while he dresses in fancy clothes and gets drunk in the evenings. If Rudolf wasn't their brother, I'm sure they'd resent him living like that with the money they help make. Maybe they resent him, anyway."

Brigitte nodded. "That's one way to look at it, but there's more. And here's the hard part. About eight years ago, another man who taught similar things traveled around the empire preaching to people. His name was Thomas Müntzer. Has your uncle ever mentioned him?"

"No," Hilde said, speaking out. "Uncle has never mentioned him to us."

"He lived, or at least at the time of his death he was preaching, in Thuringia."

"That's where we're from."

"Yes. One of the things that Müntzer preached is the same as what Rothmann does. That people should hold things in common. The lords of Thuringia hated him for that, just like the Lutherans and Catholics on the city council hate Rothmann when he does it."

"Because holding things in common means they'd have to give up some of their wealth to everyone else?"

"Yes, Hilde, that about sums it up. Throughout the empire, whenever the lords and bishops hear people preaching about sharing their wealth, they get suspicious and remember what happened in the Peasants' War of 1524 and 1525. They fear these preachers mean to start a new round of the Peasants' War, so they crack down on them right away. And because the same people who preach about sharing goods often preach about the importance of adult baptism, the laws of the empire forbid adult baptism on the penalty of death. The lords see adult baptism and the community of goods as two sides of the same coin."

Sofie wasn't sure how her neighbor knew so much, but her words made sense. She said nothing for several moments.

"Thinking about your parents?" Brigitte asked her.

"Yes," Sofie admitted. "I was just wondering if they knew all that back in 1525."

"That's why I wasn't sure if I should tell you the whole story. I didn't know how much it might hurt you to remember your parents."

"It does hurt some. But I'm glad you told me. It helps me understand things a little better. Now it makes sense why adult baptism matters so much. I'm scared of something else, though."

"Like what'll happen between the Lutherans and Anabaptists in the days to come?"

"Yes, Brigitte. After today, I'm scared even to stay at home. I won't forget to bar the door again, that's for sure, but living behind locked doors all your days is a frightening thought."

Chapter 8

Münster

January of 1534

Fingers entwined, Sofie and Kurt shuffled through their third dance in the main room of the Boetmester household. With the fire burning high in the hearth and mugs of ale waiting for them at the table, they pranced around while Kurt's parents played a lively tune on their wood flutes.

While Sofie and Kurt circled the room, they jumped out of the way of Hilde and Conrad, Kurt's ten-year-old brother. The Boetmesters had asked Hilde to come with Sofie because Kurt had no other siblings, and Conrad wanted a dancing partner for the New Year's Day celebration. Neither he nor Hilde had much practice at dancing, though, so they kept crossing the path of Sofie and Kurt. Sofie barely noticed and just laughed it off when Conrad tripped over his own feet for the second time.

"You're going to skin your knees bumbling around like that. Try not to be an oaf," Kurt scolded Conrad.

Conrad's smile disappeared.

"But the only way to learn is by trying, so keep going," Sofie added. She smiled as some light came back into Conrad's eyes.

"Sorry," Kurt whispered in Sofie's ear when the tune ended. "That came out wrong."

"Maybe you should tell Conrad and not me," she whispered back. "I know you didn't mean to hurt his feelings, but I'm not sure that he does."

"That's why I'm lucky to know you, Sofie. You always look to bring out the best in me."

"Go tell him, then."

Kurt gave her the slightest of frowns.

"I know, I know," she chided gently. "You're Conrad's big brother, and you aren't allowed to admit you were wrong around your little brother. But just this one time, go tell him you're sorry. For me. It's New Year's Day, after all."

"Well, just this once," Kurt replied as a grin broke over his face. "But tomorrow I get to go back to being his big brother."

"Fair enough."

When Kurt shuffled off to find Conrad, Hilde sat down by Sofie in his place. "That was fun, although I suppose I looked foolish," she told her older sister.

"You did fine. It just takes practice."

"Kurt didn't seem to think so."

"He just likes giving Conrad a tough time. It's what big brothers do. He didn't mean anything by it."

"But you don't tease me like that."

"Everyone is different, Hilde. I try to see the best in people. Kurt happens to be more serious, and his words don't always come out the way he means them to. But look, he's over giving Conrad a hug right now."

"Will you show me how to dance?"

"Of course," Sofie exclaimed as she stood. "Give me your hand, Hilde. First, we shuffle left, and then we shuffle back to the right. Spin once, then twice," she said while holding her right hand up, so Hilde could twirl beneath it. "Don't go so fast, Hilde! You'll get dizzy and fall over doing that!"

"Sorry for being such an oaf."

"Come now, none of that kind of talk," Sofie said as both young ladies grinned. "You're far too beautiful to ever be an oaf, Hilde."

On January 5, 1534, Bernard Rothmann stood in the cathedral square of Münster once again, a small crowd around him. Rudolf Schweren, the baker's son, was among the onlookers.

Rothmann nodded to the two apostles beside him, Bartholomew Bookbinder and William de Cuiper. "It's time." Rothmann fell to his knees.

Bookbinder stood over him. "Brother Bernard Rothmann, I baptize you in the name of the Father . . ." Water fell from Bookbinder's hand onto Rothmann's forehead as Bookbinder spoke, ". . . and the Son . . ." Again, Bookbinder's hand dipped into the font, cupped the blessed water, and released it onto Rothmann's face. ". . . And the Holy Spirit. Rise, Brother Bernhard, as one of the Elect of God."

Before standing, Rothmann folded his hands and said a quick prayer. Then, his eyes opened, and he stood to address the small crowd.

"Fellow believers, I repent for my indecisiveness in undergoing adult baptism. Too long did I live in fear of the consequences. For as some of you know, that servant of Antichrist, Bishop von Waldeck, has decreed the death of all Anabaptist preachers, along with the citizens who protect them. Even those who tolerate adult baptism are liable to arrest. This is, indeed, a serious development, and one designed to strike fear into God's Elect and make them question their faith.

"You may also have heard the rumors that von Waldeck plans to gather an army and retake our city. For so shall Antichrist attempt to take by force what is God's by right. Ever shall the Lord's enemies attempt to persecute His faithful people.

"But, far from being a dangerous development, this is, in fact, a blessing. The greater the persecution of the Elect, the nearer God's return to Earth. The hour is at hand. Indeed, the final days have begun. I've cast aside my fears. For who need fear when the Lord is their shepherd?

"Brothers and sisters in Christ, I'll not keep you here long today. For today is not about me, but about God and His return in glory. Brothers, step forward."

With a gesture from Rothmann's hand, Rudolf saw nine men step to the font and kneel, heads down. One by one, de Cuiper and Bookbinder baptized them, repeating the same words they used with Rothmann.

All the time, Rudolf stood, transfixed. Energy pulsed through his body, and he found himself bouncing on his toes even though he was only a silent onlooker. He'd followed Rothmann's teachings ever since Rothmann returned to Münster, and he had no intention of backsliding now, no matter what Franz von Waldeck might threaten.

The baptisms complete, Bookbinder addressed the gathering. "Ten new apostles of the Lord. Jesus himself had twelve, but one betrayed our Lord and Savior, leaving eleven. We are but poor instruments who fall short of Christ's glory, so today we baptize ten men in humble recognition of our lesser status as a fallen people.

"Eight shall remain here in Münster to preach the Word of God. Just as God sent two of his apostles here to Münster, Brother William and me, so shall two of this gathering go forth and spread the good news throughout the lands. Now, let us say a prayer and depart in peace."

As Bookbinder prayed aloud for humility, fortitude, and courage, Rudolf knelt and listened. His heart stirred with each word. At last, God would reveal Himself in glory. And Rudolf would get to witness all of it. His only hope now was that someday he'd be among the chosen to bring God's Word to the world.

Chapter 9

Leiden, Duchy of Brabant, Holy Roman Empire

January of 1534

Bartholomew Bookbinder entered the candlelit room at the back of the house. He laid aside his soaking wet riding cloak and accepted the mug of ale offered by the owner, John Bockelson. Bookbinder sat next to the warm fire on a wooden stool and sipped from the pewter mug while checking to see that all had arrived. Seven men, including himself.

"Bartholomew, thank you for riding all the way from Münster. What news do you bring from Westphalia?" John asked his guest.

Instead of answering immediately, Bookbinder panned the room with his eyes. His host, John Bockelson, stood out. Known to most as John of Leiden, he was a very tall man, well over six feet, but gaunt, with a great black beard and intense eyes. John brewed ales and, from the taste of what Bookbinder held in his hand, was good at his trade.

John Matthys was present as well. Like John of Leiden, he was very tall, but was a huge, ursine man with blond hair. He had the same type of eyes, however, intense and fanatic. Bookbinder had met him before, slightly more than one year ago. John Matthys had been at the meeting in Amsterdam where Melchior Hoffman commissioned Bookbinder to go to Münster. The two young men who'd been with Matthys at that meeting, Hans, the baker's apprentice, and his best friend, were in attendance today, too, along with two others who must've joined the Elect while Bookbinder was in Westphalia. Their clothing, expensively tailored vests over satin doublets, marked them as prosperous members of the merchant class.

Finally, Bookbinder cleared his throat and answered. "Much has happened in the last few weeks. Some of the news is good, and some less so."

"Tell us the good first," John of Leiden requested.

"Adult baptism goes on as planned. I personally baptized Bernard Rothmann just two weeks ago, along with nine other preachers. Since then, we've sealed hundreds of the townspeople with Christ's love, and they've accepted rebaptism. Our numbers grow daily. I estimate that close to 1,500 adults in the city have received baptism by now."

"For that, you must thank the work John has done here in Leiden," John Matthys interjected, raising his mug to the host. "Leiden is the home of many who yearn for salvation, but the churches and town authorities have turned their backs on the people."

"It is true," John of Leiden stated. "The poor and downtrodden here are legion, but the authorities squash them underfoot rather than extend Christian fellowship or practice the community of goods described in the Book of Acts. I, and the others here," John nodded toward the two wealthy men Bookbinder didn't recognize, "encourage them to go to Münster to live as Christ would have it. We provide them with what money we can to make the journey."

For the first time, Bookbinder noticed John of Leiden's deep, resonant voice. Ideal for speaking in public, he thought. Then, Bookbinder resumed. "I'm grateful for that. The number of God's

Elect in Münster has grown to the point where the Elect now have more influence than either the Lutherans or Catholics separately."

"Is that so?" Matthys asked, his eyebrows going up.

"It is. Here's the proof. Two days after I baptized Rothmann, the town council tried to expel him from the city and ban him from preaching yet again. However, the Peddlers Guild gave Rothmann a building to preach from, and hundreds flocked to hear him each day. The city council finally granted Rothmann's freedom to preach because the guilds back him and, furthermore, announced that it would not enforce Bishop von Waldeck's decree condemning Anabaptists to prison and death."

"Things are as I hoped, then," John of Leiden announced. "The bishop has persecuted the people of God so badly in the past the Lutherans fear him more than they fear us. Just as our great prophet, Melchior Hoffman, predicted, Christ will use his enemies against themselves, clearing a path for the righteous."

Bookbinder nodded. "Yes, it is so. And I have one more desirable development to report. Several groups of believers have formed who live in accordance with the acts of the early Church. They've accepted rebaptism and now share their goods in common. They shun nonbelievers but associate with others of the Elect with goodwill and charity."

"Excellent," Matthys announced. "All these developments are welcome news. However, you said not all was well."

"William de Cuiper is dead."

"Dead? How?"

"Killed by the bishop's men for baptizing people in a village near Münster. He and I set out to convert the nearby villages and bring them into the fold, but von Waldeck's men captured and hung Brother William. I only escaped because some villagers gave me warning of the approach of the soldiers. The rumors that Bishop von Waldeck is preparing a large army to retake the city are true, I believe."

"Again, this is as Father Hoffman predicted," Matthys claimed. "All is going as he foretold. The persecution of the Elect by the ungodly. The gathering of armies for a final battle. God's true kingdom is at hand."

"What has happened to Melchior?" Bookbinder asked. "I've not had news of him since our meeting in Amsterdam."

"He was arrested in Strasbourg, just as he foresaw that he would be," John of Leiden told Bookbinder. "He languishes there in prison."

"Then is the prophecy flawed?" Bookbinder asked, eyes darting from John of Leiden to Matthys and back. "He said the end would come in Strasbourg and that Emperor Charles would lay siege to the city in 1533."

"He was wrong only in the location," Matthys countered as he stood up to pace the room, his massive frame casting deep shadows on the walls in the frail candlelight. "The people of Strasbourg did not heed his message. They turned a deaf ear to the teachings of the prophet Elijah, so God rejected the city for its unbelief. It's now clear that the Lord means for Münster to be the New Jerusalem, not Strasbourg. Münster is where the Elect will gather to witness the nightfall of the world and God's return to Earth."

"The end has been delayed by our failures as God's prophets," John of Leiden added. "As God's people, we must make straight the path. All other parts of the prophecy are in place. It's time for us to take the last step. Bartholomew, you will not return to Münster. Matthys and I will go in your stead. You stay here and rally the people of the Netherlands. Baptize as many as you can and implore them to come to Münster.

"We can delay no longer if we are to save mankind. The salvation of the world will begin at Münster. It is the New Jerusalem, and all roads now lead thither. We *will* make straight the way of the Lord before it's too late. With the sword if the ungodly leave us no other choice."

Chapter 10

Münster

February of 1534

"Confess and repent! Confess and repent! Confess and repent! God is going to punish you! All who would save themselves from the Lord's Judgment, confess and repent!"

Thus rang the cry summoning Sofie, Hilde, and Heinrich to the street in front of their door in the gloaming of the late afternoon on February 8, 1534.

When Sofie stepped outside to see what the shouting was about, her feet crunched on the snowy, frozen mud of the gutter, and her breath puffed into clouds in front of her face. She pulled her drab wool shawl tighter around her shoulders and neck while the pair of men ran down her street again.

To her amazement, the men were none other than Bernard Rothmann and Bernhard Knipperdollinck. To Sofie's still greater surprise, both ran barefoot through the frozen snow coating the cobblestones of St. Ludger's Street. They seemed oblivious, even immune, to the chill while they shouted and exhorted all who could hear them.

On the third time they'd run shouting through the street, Rothmann stopped near the Gresbeck home and stood still, arms out to the side, palms up, face to the sky.

"Confess and repent! Confess and repent! Confess and repent!" Rothmann shouted as he repeated his litany. Slowly, he sank to his knees but with his neck bent back and his face toward the heavens even as tiny snowflakes fluttered around him. In the dying light, Sofie could see his flushed face and rapid pants for breath.

Sofie looked to her uncle for a sign of what to do, but as she did so, she saw other residents of her street emerge from their homes and take up the chant. "Confess and repent! Confess and repent!"

Standing still, looking around helplessly at the surreal scene unfolding before her eyes, Sofie was unprepared for what happened next. A group of women marched south on St. Ludger's Street toward her. But not just any women. Sofie recognized them as nuns from the convent of the Church of Our Dear Lady, which was north and west of the cathedral square. And who was at their head but Rudolf Schweren, of all people.

"Let's go inside Hilde, Sofie," Heinrich whispered while tugging on the sleeves of his nieces. As they retreated toward the door to their home, Sofie saw Brigitte wave them over from the corner of her eye.

Heinrich saw it, too, and guided the two women into their neighbor's house. "I'm glad you're here," Brigitte said breathlessly as they gathered around her. "What on earth is happening, Heinrich?"

"I don't know," he confessed while bolting Brigitte's door. "I've never seen anything this strange before. What are the nuns doing here? They belong in their convent, don't they?"

"Let's watch from upstairs," Brigitte suggested. "We can see better up there. All these people chanting in the street frighten me."

The four climbed the solid wooden stairs to the second floor of Brigitte's home, where they found Brigitte's three children already looking out the window at the street below. Snowflakes swirled through the opening. Sofie peered through the window in time to see that Knipperdollinck had returned to join Rothmann, who still hadn't risen from his knees, and then to see Rudolf stop in front of them and bow. The nuns of the Church of Our Dear Lady, or about twenty of them, at least, stopped behind Rudolf, and the townspeople who'd entered the street encircled the three men and the nuns. Their chant of "Confess and repent! Confess and repent!" never ceased. The vapors from everyone's breath shrouded the scene in mist.

Rothmann rose to his feet, and the chant stopped. "Have you come to repent and confess?" Rothmann asked the women.

"We have," said the nun who stood at the front of her sisters. "We've come to cast aside our sinful past and join the People of God."

"Then cast away those clothes that are an abomination in God's sight!"

One after another, the nuns took off their habits and discarded them into the snow and frozen mud at the side of the street. Soon, the only clothes that remained were the white robes the nuns wore underneath their habits.

"Brother Rudolf, see to it that these old clothes are cast into the bonfire in the cathedral square. No more shall the teachings of Antichrist stain the lives of these women, and no more shall these clothes befoul their bodies or remind them of what they've chosen to leave behind. Their souls will soon shine out with the pure light of God! For God is merciful to those who seek His love. He will forgive your past transgressions if you but put your faith in His true teachings."

Sofie could see Rudolf stoop and begin to gather the discarded black garments, as instructed, draping them over his left arm. She noticed that her arms trembled while she watched. Brigitte's arms trembled, too.

In the street below, Knipperdollinck stepped forward to address the women. Although he was barefoot, in other respects his dress reflected his station as the head of the Clothmakers Guild. Knipperdollinck wore rich robes over his linen shirt. The robes featured alternating crimson and gold stripes and fell loosely over his arms. He wore a low-profile hat of white cloth and a gold chain around his neck.

"Are you prepared to accept God into your lives as true believers? Are you willing to submit to baptism and thereby gain God's seal of righteousness and live amongst God's Elect, forever forsaking your past?" he asked the women.

All nodded or mumbled something in agreement.

"Then God will have mercy on your immortal souls. No longer need you take refuge in a secluded convent and live apart from the rest of God's Elect. Rather, from this moment forward you shall live in the freedom of the light of God and join hands with the rest of His people! Do not fear that you have few possessions, for in the New Jerusalem, all will share in common."

At that moment, the waning sun broke through the clouds and fell upon Rothmann, Knipperdollinck, and the former nuns. It shone directly into their faces, illuminating them in gold as the whole street grew blindingly radiant with sunlight reflecting off snow.

Just as suddenly, all grew dark once more as clouds swallowed the sun. The contrast from the blinding sunlight made Sofie blink repeatedly to get her vision back in focus. As the spots cleared, she saw Rudolf gesture below.

"Look at the sky!" he shouted, pointing upward. His face beamed with a look Sofie couldn't remember ever seeing before. His left arm held the nuns' former clothing while his right hand pointed, and his mouth was wide open. "See the dark flames descend on the whole city!"

Although it had indeed become quite dim very suddenly, Sofie could see no flames in the sky, dark or otherwise.

"I don't see them," Hilde muttered at her side. "Where?"

"Shh," Heinrich whispered.

Soon, Rothmann and Knipperdollinck pointed, too. "See! In the sky!" Rothmann shouted. "God's blue flame covers the entire city, but look above! See the figure on the white horse! In his right hand he wields a sword to kill the unrighteous! The Lord favors us!"

"Yes!" Knipperdollinck bellowed. "So shall the Lord ever provide signs to the Elect. The hour is come for the New Jerusalem to rise!" As Knipperdollinck held his arms aloft, giving his body the shape of the letter Y, he spun slowly, as if to embrace all the heavens.

Sofie looked toward the former nuns for their reaction. A few pointed, too, but others shook their heads as if unsure what they were supposed to see.

Then, one of the women near the back of the group fell to the ground. She screamed and writhed, and although Sofie wasn't sure at her distance, she could have sworn the woman began foaming at the mouth.

In moments, the woman's companions gathered around her, with Rothmann barging his way forward to see what had happened for himself. When he reached the fallen woman, he knelt and folded his hands in prayer.

After a few more wrenching twists of her body, the woman slowed her contortions and sat up.

"O Father, grant mercy!" she shouted, and then her body fell back to the ground. Mud and dirty snow caked her white robes.

Rothmann extended his arm to the woman and commanded, "Hold fast! Pray truthfully!"

Once again, the woman sat up, only this time, she looked around with her eyes wide and her mouth open, as if seeing the rest of the crowd for the first time. "Where? Where is he?" she said in a loud voice.

"Where is who?" one of the other former nuns asked.

"The angel of God. I saw him. Right over there." She pointed north, in the general direction of the cathedral square. All eyes followed her index finger.

"The Lord appeared to you?" Rothmann questioned.

"One of his angels. The angel said to me, 'Begone, and trouble this woman no more!' At that moment, I felt a weight leave my body, and when I looked down at myself, I saw my soul glowing within me with a golden light. A black cloud, shaped like a bat, slowly drifted away from me, but faded into nothing and disappeared when it approached the angel."

Again, Rothmann extended his hand. The woman took it, and Rothmann helped her back to her feet even as the setting sun shone out again. "See?" he called to the assemblage. "Not even demons can stand against the pure light of God. All the old sins shall be washed away, and God's Elect will shine forth as an example for the world!"

The crowd surrounding him cheered various exclamations exalting God's goodness.

"Need you further proof?" Knipperdollinck addressed the women in front of him. "The Day of the Lord draws near, and He shall number you among his Elect."

"We need no further proof," the spokeswoman for the nuns replied. "We are ready."

"Then follow us to the cathedral square. There, you shall be baptized and marked with the Lord's seal forever."

While the nuns moved northward, accompanied by the crowd in the street that had seen the whole bizarre scene, everyone in Brigitte's house turned to face each other.

"What do you make of that, Heinrich?" Brigitte asked.

"It's completely out of my experience."

"Really?"

"I've never seen nuns abandon the Catholic Church, or people fall to the ground, or claim to see men with swords in the heavens. Did any of you see any signs in the sky?"

All shook their heads.

"What happened to the woman? The one who fell in the street?" Hilde wondered. "She looked like she was in great pain, and then an angel healed her. I didn't know that could happen."

"It appeared rather marvelous, it's true," Brigitte told her. "But, Hilde, those things can be arranged ahead of time."

"You mean you think the nun faked it? And the signs in the sky, too?"

"I'd give good odds that she did. Have you ever looked up at the sky and saw things in the clouds that look like animals or faces, Hilde?"

"Yes."

"Then you know how easy it can be. The twitching on the ground seems harder to explain away, but I'll bet there's a reason for that, too."

"Speaking of, I'm going to follow behind this procession and watch what happens in the city square," Heinrich informed the others. "Sofie, Hilde, you stay with Brigitte until I come back. I want to know what all of this is about. If nothing else, I want to know what our fool neighbor Rudolf has gotten himself involved in this time. His father will want to hear of this if he hasn't already."

"Don't go, Uncle," Hilde pleaded. "I'm scared that something bad will happen."

"I think you'll be safe with Brigitte. The crowd is gone, and the street is empty now."

With that, Heinrich descended the stairs and let himself out the front door.

Once he'd left, Sofie asked, "Brigitte, why did you ask my uncle two times whether he'd seen that happen before?"

"What do you mean, Sofie?"

"You asked him if he'd seen that before, and then you asked him again."

Brigitte's face looked tense, and she bit her lower lip.

"Is there something about him I don't know?" Sofie asked her friend.

"Has your uncle ever told you about how he came to Münster, Sofie?"

"Yes. He said he hid in an apple cart because he wanted to travel, but once he got here, he married Aunt Liese and stayed here."

"Well, I don't know how fully he explained everything," Brigitte said cautiously, "and I don't know everything about your uncle, Sofie, but he did travel over much of the empire to get here from Thuringia as a young man. And then he traveled again when he went south and east to find you during the Peasants' War. I just figured he might have come across something like this on his travels, that's all. He's certainly seen more of the world than I ever will, so it seemed likely he might understand what just happened in the street. But I guess not."

"When is all this going to stop, and things go back to normal?" Hilde asked plaintively.

"Soon, I think," Sofie told her younger sister. "Things can't get much stranger than what we just saw, can they?"

"Let's go downstairs and get a little food. Sound good?" Brigitte told the young women.

Sofie noticed that Brigitte didn't say if she thought Sofie was right about things getting stranger.

It was about three hours after nightfall when Sofie, Hilde, and Brigitte heard Heinrich knock at Brigitte's door. When Brigitte ushered him inside, Sofie could see her uncle was out of breath, and his cheeks were red. He bent over, hands on his knees.

"What's happened?" Brigitte asked him. Then, she saw the bloodstains on Heinrich's arm and took two steps back, hands on her cheeks. "What happened?" she repeated quickly.

Hilde noticed it as well. "You're bleeding, Uncle. Were you attacked? Who did it?"

"Oh, that. It's not bad, girls. I'll live." Heinrich panted without looking up.

"But what happened?"

"There's been fighting on the city walls between the Lutherans and the Anabaptists."

"Is that where you got hurt? You were on the Lutheran side, right?" Hilde interrupted.

"Hilde, calm down a moment, young lady. Let your uncle tell the story," Brigitte said while she placed a hand on Hilde's shoulder and gave it a reassuring pat.

"I know you're worried, Hilde, but trust me, my wound isn't bad. It barely hurts. Let me tell you what I saw, though. The Anabaptists held a huge rally in the cathedral square. They baptized hundreds of people, including those nuns we saw. They had seven or eight preachers baptizing people in lines, including Rothmann and Knipperdollinck."

"And all the baptized were adults?" Sofie asked, giving Heinrich a moment to catch his breath and stand up straight.

"Yes. Every single one. The Anabaptists only believe in baptizing adults because only adults have knowingly accepted God into their lives. It was an eerie scene. But what happened next was stranger still. Two men stood in the center of the square. I've never seen them before, but they were very tall, and one had a great black beard." Heinrich made his palm flat and held it at the middle of his chest to show how long the beard was.

"The one with the beard had a normal frame, but the other, who was blond, was a huge bear of a man. The one with the long beard kept referring to the blond one as Enoch. I gather it's the name of a biblical figure from the Book of Revelation."

"I'll check while you go on," Brigitte announced as she took a few steps to locate her family's Bible. "But how do you know Enoch is from Revelation?"

"Just a guess. The bear kept on talking about the rise of the New Jerusalem and the duty of the Elect to make straight the way of the Lord. Apocalyptic stuff. So, that'd be my guess of where to start looking."

Brigitte nodded as she thumbed the pages of the large, leather-bound book and began to scan its contents. Not every family had its own Bible, Sofie knew. Only the wealthier ones could afford the cost of printing and binding a book that long. Perhaps Brigitte and her husband had been even more prosperous than she'd thought. At one time, anyway, even if it wasn't true now.

Meanwhile, her uncle continued. "The two men took turns speaking for a while, but to me they sounded more like military commanders trying to rally their troops than preachers offering an outdoor sermon. They went on at some length about how Münster was the New Jerusalem, and how a great battle would take place between the Elect and the ungodly at the New Jerusalem. The two men mentioned a siege by the forces of Antichrist followed by the victory of God's chosen people, a victory that would spread over the entire Earth. All of this was destined to happen within a year."

"Then what happened?" Hilde asked her uncle, eyes fixed on his.

"That's when the fighting began. The two leaders called on the assembled Anabaptists to take control of the city walls and prepare for the siege of Antichrist. Like they'd planned it ahead of time, each of the eight preachers who'd been baptizing people in the square led an armed group toward one of the city gates."

"The city is under siege?" Hilde cried, the worlds coming out rapidly.

"When they said that, I followed one of the groups to the city wall to see for myself. I've heard the rumors that Bishop von Waldeck is gathering troops to storm the city, of course, but I couldn't believe he'd arrived without anyone being aware of it, so I went to the walls to know what was really going on. What I saw was that the Anabaptists and Lutherans fought briefly, but everything took the Lutherans by surprise, and they gave up their positions on the walls without much of a fuss. A few people suffered wounds, but I saw no one die. I can't say what happened at the other gates to the city."

"Is that when you got hurt?" Sofie asked her uncle.

"Well, sort of," he replied with a little laugh. "I gave myself a little cut by scraping my arm lightly against some bricks."

"Why?"

"After the Anabaptists had control of things, I pretended that I'd helped and showed them my 'wound' as proof that I'd engaged the enemy. If the Lutherans had won, I'd have done the same to them."

"But why, Uncle?"

"Sofie, it's just a tactic. Things today were stranger than anything I'd ever seen. But if the Anabaptists control the walls and gates of the city for good, it'll be helpful if people think I contributed to their success. Plus, I noticed that the Anabaptist leader in our section of the city walls was Engelbert Eding."

"Who is that? I don't recognize his name."

"Eding has lived in the city for years. He's a brewer. He's also, well, I'll be charitable and say he's gullible. Eding will believe about anything if you say it convincingly enough. I'm thinking that's how the Anabaptists converted him to their cause in the first place. But when I showed him the blood, he hailed me as a true apostle of God. I didn't bother to correct him. Then I walked back here."

"So, we're not under siege?" Hilde said, her breathing calmer.

"I saw no troops when I got to the parapet on the walls. Perhaps the Anabaptists meant that in a symbolic way, Hilde. It's possible they just wanted to fire up their supporters. There's no danger right now."

For several moments, everyone paused and just looked at each other, as if they were all asking themselves what would happen next.

"I haven't found anything so far," Brigitte suddenly broke into the silence. "I've scanned all the chapters of Revelation and haven't found the name Enoch anywhere. However, I did find this in chapter eleven. Listen while I read some of the verses: 'And I will give unto my two witnesses: and they shall prophesy, a thousand two hundred sixty days, clothed in sackcloth. These are the two olive trees and the two candlesticks that stand before the Lord of the earth. And if any man will hurt them, fire shall come out of their mouths and shall devour their enemies. And if any man will hurt them, in this manner must he be slain. These have power to shut heaven, that it rain not in the days of their prophecy: And they have power over waters, to turn them into blood and to strike the earth with all plagues, as often as they will. And when they shall have finished their testimony, the beast that ascendeth out of the abyss shall make war against them and shall overcome them and kill them.'"

"You think these men believe they are the prophets of Revelation, Brigitte?" Sofie asked her friend.

"It sounds similar to what you saw today, doesn't it, Heinrich?"

He nodded, his face drawn and brow furrowed.

"But, in what you just read, the prophets die," Sofie pointed out.

"Not for good, though, Sofie. A few verses down the page, it reads, 'And after three days and a half, the spirit of life from God entered into them. And they stood upon their feet: and great fear fell upon them that saw them. And they heard a great voice from heaven, saying to them: Come up hither. And they went up to heaven in a cloud: and their enemies saw them.' Not a bad way to go, if you ask me."

"Brigitte, try the book right before Revelation. Try the book of Jude," Heinrich requested.

"I guess I can do that. The whole book is only one chapter, anyway."

After looking for a few moments, Brigitte's eyes opened wide. "Now of these Enoch also, the seventh from Adam, prophesied, saying: Behold, the Lord cometh with ten thousand of his saints to execute judgment upon all and to reprove all the ungodly for all the works of their ungodliness, whereby they have done ungodly, and for all the hard things which ungodly sinners have spoken against God. These are murmurers, full of complaints, walking according to their own desires, and their mouth speaketh proud things, admiring persons, for gain's sake. But you, my dearly beloved, be mindful of the words which have been spoken before by the apostles of our Lord Jesus Christ, who told you that in the last time there should come mockers, walking according to their own desires in ungodliness. These are they who separate themselves, sensual men, having not the Spirit.'"

"Brigitte, this could be very serious," Heinrich said after a moment. "How many people live in Münster? Ten thousand or so, would you say?"

"That sounds about right. And that's just the number that verse fourteen mentions."

"The Book of Jude also mentions the ten thousand will execute judgment upon all, and the last verse you read stated that people will separate themselves into those with the Holy Spirit and those without."

"The Anabaptists executing judgment on the rest of the world," Brigitte said gravely.

"What does it all mean?"

"I don't know, Heinrich. What do you think?"

"I think I'd better pay another visit to Engelbert Eding and see what he knows about the plans of these two new arrivals in Münster."

Chapter 11

Münster

February of 1534

"Is the time right, brothers? Has the hour come?" John of Leiden asked the assemblage in Münster's City Council chamber. Daylight streamed through the glass windows of the second floor's meeting hall.

"I believe the hour has come, Brother John," John Matthys stated flatly. His huge frame dwarfed his wooden chair. "Since taking control of the walls and gates of the city yesterday, we now control Münster. The Elect in the city outnumber the godless. I believe we should allow two more weeks for the ungodly to see their sinful errors and accept baptism. We must make straight the way of the Lord. After two weeks, we shall put to the sword all those who remain in a state of sin. The ungodly must be exterminated, root and branch, for the New Jerusalem to rise."

For a moment, no one else ventured to speak. Bernhard Knipperdollinck looked from one man to the next. Besides Matthys, John of Leiden, and himself, six others were present. Bernard Rothmann sat nearby, along with the Kerkering brothers,

John and Christian. John was the Baumeister of the city, its Building Master, who had the responsibility of preparing the city walls for the coming siege of Antichrist. Also present was John Deventer, the Second Baumeister, who assisted John Kerkering. Henry Redeker, the strongest and most loyal Anabaptist member of the city council, sat between Deventer and Herman Tilbeck, the Burgomaster, or Master of the City of Münster.

After Matthys's statement had hung in the air for some time, finally, Knipperdollinck cleared his throat. "Brother John, I believe you are correct. We must purge the city of the ungodly. But perhaps that time has not yet arrived. I do not think the people of Münster are prepared for such a step."

"And why would they not be prepared?" Matthys answered, his voice rising a touch. "We will continue to show them the path of true belief. Soon, it will be time for all to hold their goods in common. It is inevitable. It is God's will."

"I still don't think the population is sufficiently ready for such a drastic change."

"Do you dare to doubt the Lord's prophet? Will you, too, cast aside His messenger, Bernhard?" Matthys's voice rose another notch.

"It will turn the whole empire against us in an instant, Brother John. The army of every prince within one hundred miles will be on our doorstep before Easter. My spies in Wied and Paderborn tell me that even as we speak, the forces of Bishop von Waldeck muster."

"It will avail our enemies nothing, no matter how many troops they bring to Münster. This is the New Jerusalem. Our people have the seal of baptism, and no host of the unrighteous, no matter how great, can avail against us. Five of our people can stand against one hundred nonbelievers, and ten can stand against one thousand! Have you lost your own faith already, I wonder, Brother Bernhard?" It was both a taunt and a question, Knipperdollinck knew. He must respond with care.

"Nothing could be further from the truth. Was it not but yesterday that I ran through the streets calling on the Elect to repent, and then baptized them by the hundreds? I simply meant, Brother John, that I'm not sure all the population is secure enough in the faith. Perhaps we require more time to educate them and make sure their belief is true before putting them to the test?"

"I believe Bernhard speaks truly, Brother John," Herman Tilbeck stated, although Knipperdollinck noted hesitancy in his voice. "No one here doubts your leadership, of course, or that we are indeed living in the New Jerusalem, on the brink of the Second Coming of Christ. But, as you and John of Leiden have said, we must make straight the path. I agree with Bernhard that we should bring the people along more slowly and build their faith. Even if we teach the Elect to recognize and shun the ungodly as they should, only yesterday these people were neighbors. Killing the unrighteous after living beside them for so many years might be too stern a test for many of our followers this early in their faith."

"What you say seems like wisdom, Brother Herman, but I am doubtful," Matthys informed the gathering. "Already we fall behind. The Last Days were to have begun last year, and they did. The prophecies have begun. When we stand before God to answer to Him, what shall we say? That we meant to lead the Elect to Him but fell short because of our lack of faith and timid resolve? That we cowered in fear because we believed our enemies too numerous?"

"May I make a suggestion, Brother John?" Knipperdollinck interjected.

"Do you wish to plead for the ungodly once more, Brother Bernhard?" Matthys replied with a harsh glare.

"No. I wish to suggest a compromise that will give us time to build the confidence of the faithful without betraying our purpose of raising up the New Jerusalem."

"Speak, then."

"What if we banish the ungodly from the city rather than killing them? If they have not repented and joined us within two weeks as you propose, why not simply expel them? This solves two problems at once. It removes the ungodly from the presence of the Elect. And if the ungodly face an eternity of hellfire, does it matter if we send them to that fate in two weeks, or in two months when the battle is over, and we've triumphed as God's Chosen People? They face an eternity of torment in either case, so of what consequence is it whether that torment begins in February or in April?"

As Knipperdollinck spoke, Matthys's glare faded somewhat. He bit his lower lip thoughtfully. "I hear you, Brother Bernhard. What is the second benefit you foresee?"

"This will give the newly baptized time to grow in their faith. We'll have the chance to preach to them and teach them more about God's plan for His Elect. We've baptized many. But it's another matter to help them understand the purpose of the Elect, and how they are meant to help usher in the third and last era of history. Without that, I fear, many will backslide and fall into the ranks of the damned."

At this point, John of Leiden stood, his gaunt figure unfolding to its full height. Through his great beard, he spoke calmly but firmly. "Brother Bernhard, you claim that Bishop von Waldeck has not been idle since his expulsion from the city. What have your spies told you of his plans?"

"He's in the process of mustering mercenaries to storm Münster. How many is unknown, but rumor holds the number could be as high as five thousand men. Don't forget that von Waldeck's brother, Herman, is the Archbishop of Wied. Between the two, they have substantial resources."

The rest of the gathering murmured in surprise at Knipperdollinck's estimate. Five thousand!

"It's true," Knipperdollinck confirmed. "These are seasoned fighters, not mere townsmen given pikes and told to stand their ground. Some are veterans of the Peasants' War. Others fought against the Turks at Vienna."

"Baumeister Kerkering, what is the state of the city's defenses?" John of Leiden asked the city's chief engineer.

Kerkering cleared his throat and spoke for the first time. "Brother Deventer and I made a full tour of the walls yesterday. They are sound and in good repair. The city of Münster has, as you know, ten gates by which an outsider might gain entrance. An outer moat protects each gatehouse to deter assailants, and each gatehouse can raise its bridge over the outer moat. Our exterior walls connect all the gatehouses, and we have catapults mounted atop each gatehouse. It would be a simple matter to position arquebusiers atop each gatehouse as well."

"The city will hold, then, against this rumored horde of mercenaries purchased by the bishop in the service of Antichrist?" John of Leiden asked the Baumeister.

"Without doubt, as long as we have defenders enough. Besides our outer ring of defenses, we have the inner ring as well. Behind our first line of gatehouses and walls is our second moat. Wooden bridges span the inner moat just as they do the outer. The inner walls of the city also have ten gatehouses, and these gatehouses can raise the bridges over the second moat. The inner walls are likewise sound and in good repair. So long as we have sufficient defenders, we have little to fear from von Waldeck. The only way he can take the city is by mustering an army of tens of thousands. Or by a siege and through starvation."

Knipperdollinck expected Kerkering's statement to hang there for quite some time. All knew, of course, that even the best prepared and perfectly defended city could succumb to hunger, given enough time, and Münster was no exception.

Immediately, however, John Matthys slapped his palm on the table. "We have nothing to fear, regardless of the condition of the walls. The Lord is on our side, and He will deliver us from Antichrist long before hunger can set in. And even if it takes some months, still, fear not. Do we not read in chapter eleven of the Book of Revelation that God will give power to his witnesses, and that they will have the power of prophecy for 1,260 days? If I would, I can turn cobblestones to bread! No, we have no reason to fear."

"Since we have no reason to fear, I'll send word to Bartholomew Bookbinder back in the Netherlands," John of Leiden informed the others. "I'll instruct him to send all to Münster whom he can persuade to undertake the journey. This is the New Jerusalem. We must welcome as many of our fellow believers as we can."

Bernard Rothmann, who had uncharacteristically sat silent through the whole conversation, finally raised his head and spoke. "What is the will of God's prophet, then, Brother John? What is to be the fate of the nonbelievers in Münster?"

Matthys looked Rothmann directly in the eye. "I will pray to the Father for guidance, Brother Bernard."

A soft knock at her door awoke Sofie from her daydream. While she'd watched the gentle snowflakes drift down from the iron-gray clouds and land silently on the windowsill, she hadn't even seen the quiet figure come to her uncle's door.

Shaking herself back to the moment, Sofie called out, "Who is it?"

"It's just me. Can I come in?" answered a reassuring voice.

Sofie's face brightened. Kurt had come for a visit! She jumped up and let him inside. "Kurt, I'm so happy to see you! Wait, you don't look happy at all. What's just happened?" Sofie took two steps back. Kurt didn't come inside.

"Haven't you heard today's news, Sofie?" he said very quietly, barely raising his head enough to look at her.

"No. I've been weaving all day. I just stopped for a moment, and then you knocked. Please, though, Kurt, come inside. There's no need to stand outside in the cold."

"I can't stay long, but thank you," he replied as he trudged through the door and closed it behind him. Kurt didn't sit or remove his dark leather overcoat or brown fur hat. The cold breeze that had come through the open door made Sofie shiver.

"Kurt, you look like you're spooked about something. Are your mother and father well? You said your mother had a fever the other day."

"She's recovering. I think she'll be fine."

"Then what's the matter?"

"Your uncle told you about the city council elections yesterday, right? About how the Anabaptists now control most of the spots on the council?"

"Yes, I know about that."

"They issued a proclamation this morning. All citizens of Münster have five days to accept baptism or leave the city."

"What?" Sofie nearly shouted because Kurt's statement took her by such surprise.

"Yes, Sofie. We have five days to either be rebaptized, or else face exile. That's it. Five days. Those who stay and refuse rebaptism face execution."

"What'll we do? What do you plan to do, Kurt?"

"That's part of why I came here. I don't want to be separated from you, Sofie."

Neither person said anything for several moments, until Sofie finally stated the horrible truth that hung over their decision. "If we stay, then we must be baptized. But adult baptism means we'll either hang or go to prison, should the Anabaptists lose control of the city. But if we leave, we'll have no place to go and be left to wander the countryside while winter still holds Westphalia in its grip."

"It's even worse than that, Sofie. If we choose to leave the city, we can only take with us what possessions we can carry. Everything else must stay in the city."

"So, we'd be without nearly all our clothes, food, and other items, too?"

"Yes. The Anabaptists have proclaimed that they will confiscate all worldly goods of the unbaptized and redistribute them to the Elect according to their needs. Since they now control all the gates out of the city, it's impossible to sneak things by them."

Another pause followed. Sofie and Kurt looked at each other with nothing to say because they had no good answers.

Finally, Kurt found his nerve. "Don't go somewhere that I can't follow, Sofie."

"Does that mean you've decided to stay?"

"I don't know. But you mean so much to me. I couldn't stand to lose you now or think you might be in danger without me to help you."

"Oh, Kurt," Sofie cried as she hugged him close.

"I know I get down too easily," he told her. "And I know I'm just a cabinetmaker who'll never amount to anything grand. But you can count on me to always be at your side and protect you. I'll never walk away from you."

Sofie hugged tighter. "I know that. Somehow, I've always known. You're the best man I've ever met, even if your words come out wrong sometimes."

"So, you agree that we must stay together no matter what?"

"I want to say yes, but I have to talk with Uncle Heinrich," Sofie said at last. "He's like my father, and if anyone knows what to do, he does."

Chapter 12

Münster

February of 1534

It was the worst storm Sofie had ever seen, especially given that February was nearly over. As she and Hilde looked through the window of her uncle's house at the forlorn line winding its way toward St. Ludger's Gate, the combination of snow, sleet, and stinging hail fell from the low-hanging clouds of iron without mercy or relent. In fact, Sofie could barely see the sky, so thick was the storm. As if that wasn't enough, the wind howled down St. Ludger's Street, whistling and whipping through every crack in her uncle's house. It froze the snow and sleet onto the sides of the houses.

After a few moments, Sofie turned away. The tears that had cascaded down her cheeks all day just wouldn't stop. Kurt was out there somewhere. His father had decided to leave Münster, and Kurt felt he needed to go with his parents and little brother. He'd asked Sofie to join him. But she couldn't. Her uncle couldn't leave Münster because he was a captain of the guards on the walls. That meant Hilde couldn't leave, either, and Sofie wouldn't go without

Hilde. So, Kurt and she had said their goodbyes last night. Sofie hoped she'd see him again someday, once everything was back to normal in Münster, but she had no certainty of that. She'd cried most of the night, and now, seeing everyone trudging through the arctic blasts of wind and snow outside, she put her head down and cried again.

Hilde put her arm around her sister's shoulder. "You'll see him again someday, Sofie. I know you will."

Sofie couldn't muster the heart to reply. Or even raise her head.

Hilde hugged her tighter.

Then, across St. Ludger's Street, Sofie heard the cry, dim through the angry wind: "Get out! Get out, you godless people! God's about to wake up and punish you! Get out, godless ones, and never come back, you enemies of the Father. Get out!"

She raised her head and peeked through the window again. Three Anabaptists, armed with a pike, a halberd, and an arquebus, yanked open the door of one of the houses across the street and stormed inside. They literally threw the occupants, an older man and his frail wife, out the door and into the driving snowstorm, and then one of the Anabaptists pushed the man in the back with the butt of his pike, knocking him to his knees.

Looking up and down her street, Sofie saw the same thing happening in other houses. Armed bands forced the "nonbelievers" from their own homes and prodded them toward St. Ludger's Gate with weapons.

Just as Sofie prepared to close the shutters, she saw a young child, a boy wrapped in a heavy wool blanket, slip and fall into the frozen mud of the street. When the child's mother picked him up, Sofie saw tears as his little body trembled and shook. At the same time, Sofie tried to keep her own tears from falling even faster. Finally, she tore herself away from watching the pitiful procession outside, and with Hilde's help, closed the shutters as tightly as she could.

When Sofie turned, she saw Brigitte add coal to the foot stove in the center of Uncle Heinrich's house. Brigitte and her children huddled around the foot stove, but even though it was full and the coals radiated heat, everyone shivered. Uncle Heinrich was absent. When he'd pretended to help win the walls for the Anabaptists earlier that month, he'd gained their approval, but that also meant he had to take turns on guard duty on the walls, and today was his day to patrol. Sofie hoped the wind didn't blow him off the wall altogether.

"How many would you say are leaving, Sofie?" Brigitte asked.

"I think I counted nearly two hundred people on our street who've decided to get out now. Some looked prosperous, but others looked ragged. A few looked exasperated or annoyed, like they probably have somewhere to go but are scared to leave behind their homes and friends. But most simply looked terrified. I doubt they know what they'll do," she managed to say through her sniffles.

"Well, the city has ten gates. If two hundred people pass through each one, that means almost two thousand have left Münster today. That's two out of every ten."

"Except we've had so many immigrants in recent months, I don't think the city's population today is any different than what it's been for years. All these newcomers from Holland seem to be Anabaptists, too, like it's all part of someone's plan."

"It's uncanny," Brigitte confirmed. "The Anabaptists declare that the so-called nonbelievers must leave the city, and on the very day declared for them to leave, we get the worst snowstorm we've had in years. To them, they probably think it's all God's doing and that He's showing His disapproval of the exiles by freezing them to death with this ferocious wind."

Sofie nodded grimly. She hadn't thought of that in her misery, but Brigitte had a good point.

"Brigitte, why are most of the people leaving today men and not women?" Hilde asked.

"What do you mean, Hilde?"

"Exactly what I said. When the people walked past just now, most of them were men. How come?"

On the inside, Sofie applauded her younger sister's perceptiveness. She hadn't noticed that. Sofie supposed her concern for Kurt and the other exiles outweighed her awareness of who was going and who was staying.

"I have to admit I don't know for certain, Hilde. Maybe the men feel more fit to make the journey to wherever they're going, and they plan to come back and get their wives, sisters, and daughters later? That's just my guess, though."

Hilde nodded, then asked another question. "Brigitte, why did you decide to stay in the city?"

"I've spoken at length with your uncle over the past five days, Hilde. We both decided to stay. Hopefully, everyone will shake off this madness and come to their senses soon. That, and we have nowhere to go. Neither of us have relatives anywhere nearby whom we can stay with or who can support us if we must leave our possessions behind. There's nowhere safe for us to go. Besides that, this is my home, and I don't want to leave it."

"Did my uncle ever speak with that man he knew, Engelbert Eding, to find out anything more about what the Anabaptists plan to do?" Sofie asked her friend, her voice still choked by emotion.

"He did, but Eding didn't know much. According to Heinrich, he only became a leader because he's a large, strong man who would've been imposing if the fighting on the city walls got serious. It doesn't appear he stands very deep in the councils of the Anabaptist leaders. Maybe Heinrich has learned something more during his time manning the walls today. We can hope so, at least."

Hilde opened her mouth to ask another question, but a powerful knock came at the door before she could speak.

"It's me. Open the door," Uncle Heinrich's voice called to them.

Once he was safely inside and the door shut to keep the scything wind at bay, Heinrich walked to the foot stove and held out his hands. Everyone waited mutely because his face looked so grim.

As was his custom, however, Heinrich looked down at the glowing coals in the covered iron basket, sighed, and took several breaths before saying anything. He flexed his fingers a few times, even after taking off his wool gloves.

"What a day to inaugurate the New Jerusalem," he stated at last. Then, looking from one expectant face to the next, he announced, "Münster is now under siege. Bishop von Waldeck's army arrived today. Tomorrow, or whenever the ground thaws enough to allow it, they'll start building earthworks around the town. I don't know how many men for certain, but the word is nearly three thousand mercenaries. Münster is now at war."

Both Sofie and Hilde shivered at the word. Sofie thought back to how the last war, the Peasants' War in which her parents fought, had turned out—every peasant dead. She wondered if Hilde was doing the same in her mind.

Brigitte put a hand on Hilde's shoulder. "It isn't the time to despair yet, Hilde. Not all sieges end in death and destruction."

Heinrich nodded. "It's true, girls. I'm sure the bishop will try to negotiate with John Matthys. That's normal in sieges."

Sofie noted, however, that her uncle spoke in the dull monotone he reserved for times when he was depressed. "But you don't believe that will change anything, do you, Uncle?"

Heinrich sighed again. "No. I guess I don't. Just from listening to the talk of the other men on the walls today, I doubt that Matthys will negotiate on any terms that von Waldeck will accept. Or that anyone in their right mind would accept."

"Why not?"

"Most of the watchmen are true believers. I heard them talk about how the appearance of von Waldeck's men fulfills the prophecies of Matthys. They believe the New Jerusalem will rise after a siege by the armies of Antichrist. To the Anabaptists, the arrival of the bishop with his army confirms the truth of what Matthys has said."

"But those rumors have been going around since last year," Sofie pointed out. "How can Matthys, or anyone, claim something fulfills their prophecy when they knew it would happen before they made their prediction?"

Heinrich nodded sadly. "Because that doesn't matter, Sofie."

"What do you mean, it doesn't matter?"

"When people's beliefs are strong enough, or when they want to believe something badly enough, facts don't matter. People want to feel right in their beliefs. For a lot of people, it's easier to imagine they're correct, regardless of facts, than to face the possibility they might be wrong. They'll look for any sign, however dubious, to prove they're right, at least to themselves."

"That doesn't make a lot of sense. Why would people act like that?"

"I have a feeling, Sofie, you'll get to find out the answer for yourself before everything is over."

"Why do you say that, Uncle?"

Heinrich grimaced. "I just don't like the direction things are going."

"Do you think we should've left with the others today?"

"A small part of me wishes we could, but since I'm a captain on the walls, I can't just go. Besides, like Brigitte and I have discussed, we have no place to go to. I like our odds better here than I do wandering the plains of Westphalia begging. Plus, I obtained this today."

Heinrich reached into his heavy wool coat and produced a printed letter. "I haven't been able to learn much from Engelbert Eding because he doesn't know much, but he did share this with me. It's a letter from Bernard Rothmann that he claimed Rothmann has had copied and sent to Anabaptist leaders throughout the empire."

Unfolding the letter, Heinrich handed it to Sofie. She scanned down the page. "Rothmann writes that all the Anabaptists in the empire should come here. The Anabaptists mean to 'restore the New Jerusalem and Zion and the true Temple of Solomon and worship of the eternal God, rejecting all idolatry.' That isn't very helpful, though. We could've figured that out for ourselves after today."

"Read farther."

"He mentions the prophet Elijah and says that Elijah told him, 'In Münster they have a prophet named John Matthys who is one of the witnesses of God. Münster will not be oppressed.' Who is Elijah, though? I remember that name from the Bible, but all the prophets in the Bible died a long time ago."

"Eding told me that Elijah is a prophet of God who used to be known as Melchior Hoffman. I'm not familiar with who that is, but I gathered from Engelbert that Hoffman and Matthys think they are Enoch and Elijah, God's prophets of the Second Coming." He frowned and exhaled sharply. "Now read what Rothmann writes at the end of his letter."

"The Lord has performed glorious works with us. He freed us from the hands of our enemies and not only freed us but also cast out our enemies. For they were stricken with some fear or another and streamed out in storms. The Lord has borne witness to us through His prophets that the saintly people of God will be congregated together in this city. For this reason, the prophets have ordered me to write to you that you should order all the brothers to come here quickly."

"You know what that means, don't you, Sofie?"

"It's the same thing we just finished talking about. Rothmann mentions that God has used the Anabaptists to do glorious works like causing their enemies to leave Münster, but that wasn't God's work at all. The Anabaptists made people leave by force, but then Rothmann claimed it was God's doing."

"I'm proud of you for figuring that out."

"But it's a lie, and lying is a sin. How can the Anabaptists claim they're following God and making the city pure when they're using lies to do it?"

Heinrich sat down with his head in his hands and then rubbed his cheeks and his forehead. "Ah, who knows what'll happen, Sofie? It may all blow over and amount to nothing. You know me. I tend to think about the worst. Maybe I should be more like you and hope for the best."

A long pause ensued while all in the room looked down and said nothing, contemplating their own thoughts.

"Did Matthys follow through on his promise to confiscate the worldly goods of those who chose exile?" Brigitte asked Heinrich to break the silence.

He stood once more and paced the room. "He did, or, at least, he's in the process of doing so. On my way back here, after watching the people pass through St. Ludger's Gate, I watched armed men carry goods from the houses of those who'd departed. Bedding, clothes, and food, for the most part. The word is that Matthys will appoint seven deacons to superintend public storehouses where those in need can go and get supplies."

"And all the new arrivals in Münster will be first in line to get them, I suppose."

"Agreed, Brigitte. Very convenient, isn't it?"

"What do you mean?" Hilde asked her uncle.

Sofie felt sorry for Hilde. She was still only fourteen years old, and all these complicated events and scary developments had to be hard for her to understand. Sofie was pleased her sister kept asking questions, however. That was better than just giving up and letting people tell her what to think.

Heinrich, meanwhile, bit his lip for a moment before he answered. "Hilde, you know how most of the new people who've come to Münster in the past year have been poor? Not all of them, but many of them."

"Yes, I noticed that."

"If you were really poor and didn't own many things, what would be your response if someone gave you things that made you less poor?"

"I'd be happy that I wasn't quite as poor, of course."

"And would you support the person who gave those things to you?"

"Yeah, probably."

"That's what's going on, I think. When Matthys and the other Anabaptist leaders decided to get rid of the people who aren't Anabaptists, part of the reason was to hand their possessions over to these new arrivals. Matthys wants to buy their support and loyalty. Does that make sense?"

"Yes, I think so."

"People who are desperate and down on their luck tend to make unreliable allies unless you give them a solid reason to support you, something to hold in their hands, and that's what I think the Anabaptists are doing. Buying support."

"You don't think Rothmann's words about copying the practices of the Apostles and the early Church have anything to do with it, then?" Sofie wondered.

"I think John Matthys is scheming enough to accomplish both at the same time, Sofie. I've not met him yet, but that's my feeling. I think he's just clever enough to bring the people of Münster along with him."

"Along to what end, Uncle?"

"Yeah, what's the worst that could happen?" Hilde asked.

"Like I said, don't listen to me," Heinrich said as he stood and embraced his nieces. "I tend to look on the dark side of things."

Then, a solid knock at the door interrupted Heinrich. All looked around. Who could it be? Had the Anabaptists decided to send them into forced exile as well?

"Stay back, everyone. I'll get it," Heinrich said in the breathless silence.

Slowly, he walked to the door, fingered the latch, and opened it. Frigid air blasted the room.

A hooded figure plastered with snow stood in the doorway. He took one step inside, and then threw back his hood.

Sofie ran to the door. "Kurt! It's you!"

He embraced her as Sofie jumped into his arms. "I've decided to stay. I won't let anything part me from you, Sofie."

After he set her back down, she asked, "But what about your parents and brother? I thought you'd made up your mind to follow them. Did they change their minds, too?"

Kurt shook his head. "My father told me I was old enough to make my own decision, and that he'd support me, either way. I choose to be with you."

Sofie looked in Kurt's face, her eyes beaming. "I really mean that much to you?"

"Absolutely," Kurt replied while pulling Sofie in for another hug. Maybe it wasn't appropriate with her whole family watching, but at the moment, he didn't care.

Chapter 13

Münster

March of 1534

"Sofie Gresbeck, I baptize you in the name of the Father . . ." the cold water cascaded down on Sofie's forehead, ". . . and in the name of the Son . . ." another splash, ". . . and of the Holy Spirit." After the third and final handful of holy water covered her face, Sofie opened her eyes, although she continued kneeling in the cathedral square. "Amen. Sofie Gresbeck, you are now among the People of God. Turn away from evil and do good, never forgetting your covenant with God."

As she wiped the water from her eyes and blinked her vision back into focus, Sofie watched the man next to the preacher record her name in a book. That man happened to be Sofie's neighbor, Rudolf. The Anabaptists had spent the past three days baptizing those who'd chosen to remain in Münster, recording their identities and where they lived.

The preacher who'd performed the baptism next handed Sofie a copper token with a hole punched in it for the leather band that went around her neck. The coin bore the letters "DWWF" on it. To the question in Sofie's eyes, the preacher said, "It stands for '*Das Wort Wird Fleisch*'." The Word Becomes Flesh.

Apparently, Sofie still had a blank look on her face because next the preacher said, "It's a reference to the first chapter of John, verse fourteen. Münster has become the Kingdom of God. The Word is made flesh in Münster."

While she walked away, Sofie remembered to wait for the preacher's voice baptizing the next person before she shook her head. All the same, she put the token around her neck.

At least the storm was over. The past two days had been just as sunny and beautiful as the preceding week had been snowy and stormy. Still cool, but sunny, at least. Sunny enough that Sofie felt almost her normal self. She held her uncle's hand while she waited for Hilde to kneel and receive her second baptism.

Then, she spotted a familiar face in the crowd. Kurt Boetmester made his way to her side and embraced Sofie.

She looked to Uncle Heinrich, who nodded.

"Kurt, come over here with me," Sofie said as she dragged her friend by the arm and dodged through the crowd of onlookers.

"What's the matter?"

"Rudolf. He's the one taking down the names of the newly baptized."

"He's still jealous of me?"

"More than ever, I think. I just hope he was too busy writing down names to notice you this time."

"And what about your uncle?"

"Come on, you know he likes you, Kurt."

"You're sure about that?"

"Yes, of course. Why wouldn't he like you?"

"I'm never sure, that's all."

"He's told you that you're welcome in our home about a hundred times, Kurt. Even after you hugged me in front of everyone last week. He likes you a lot more than Rudolf, anyway; I can tell you that much."

"Is that even a compliment?"

Sofie chuckled.

Kurt continued. "I wonder if Rudolf has any role to play in today's wedding."

"What wedding, Kurt? What are you talking about?"

"I've heard that John of Leiden is going to marry Bernhard Knipperdollinck's daughter Diana today, just as soon as the baptisms are over."

"He is? That's plain crazy, Kurt. John of Leiden isn't that much older than she is, but he's only been living in the city for a couple weeks, hasn't he?"

"I know, Sofie, I know. It isn't normal, but nothing is normal around here anymore, it seems like."

"Did God's prophet in Münster, Enoch, approve this holy bond?" she asked with sarcasm.

Kurt smiled, but only for a moment. "No. Word is he's spent the past three days praying to the Father over who to appoint as his seven deacons."

"The ministers meant to oversee the goods confiscated from the ungodly three days ago?"

"The very same, Sofie. He'll also announce their names at the wedding ceremony. Not only that, I hear that Matthys and his henchmen confiscated all legal contracts and accounting books found in the homes of the departed."

When Kurt said the word henchman, Sofie looked back at Rudolf through the crowd. She had no idea how he'd done it, but he'd weaseled his way into the favor of the Anabaptists. Perhaps Rudolf had convinced Engelbert Eding, the man her uncle said was so gullible, to help him. Sofie trembled on the inside at the thought of someone as vain and impetuous as Rudolf someday having enough influence that he could make decisions affecting other people. Other people like Kurt and her. With another shudder, Sofie considered that that day might be sooner than even her nightmares imagined.

When Sofie looked back at Kurt, for the first time she saw things that she didn't recognize in Kurt's body language. His eyes darted this way and that, and at times he turned his shoulders to look around, like he was afraid of someone sneaking up on him. She put her arm around his shoulder and squeezed.

"Sofie, whatever happens, don't go away from me," he suddenly blurted to her.

"I don't think I'm going anywhere. The city's surrounded. My uncle has been building earthworks behind the inner gates the past two days."

"That isn't what I meant, Sofie. You know me as well as anyone, and you know how it doesn't take much to make me worry about the future. But I'm more than worried right now. I'm scared, I admit it, and I need people I can count on to stand by me."

"I'm on your side, Kurt. You might not think so, but I still have faith that things will turn out for the best. Try not to see the devil around every corner, all right? Try not to see everything as confirmation of your fears."

"How are you so calm, Sofie? The Anabaptists, which I guess includes us now, just made you accept a second baptism."

"It's only water, Kurt. I don't pretend to speak for God," she paused for emphasis, "but I can't imagine He's angry with me for accepting one of His sacraments for a second time, can you?"

Kurt looked in her face for just a moment, but then looked down, ran his hands through his hair, and toed at the ground. Before he could speak again, however, trumpets blared, drowning out the murmur of the crowd and the words of the preachers finishing the last round of baptisms. The wedding ceremony was about to begin.

A feast began after the wedding. Baked bread, beer, cheese, and smoked ham. The Anabaptists' newest converts sat or stood as they talked about whatever came to mind. Sofie and Kurt huddled near the edge of the gathering, so they could talk apart from

Sofie's family for a little while. Kurt took his time to finish eating, his breathing was calm, and he smiled more often. Sofie had become more worried, however. She knew the taste of the bread well. It was the same bread Rudolf's family baked. That must be how he'd ascended to his current position of record keeper in the Anabaptist hierarchy. It was excellent bread at least—the Schweren family was among Münster's most respected bakers for good reason.

Rudolf wasn't the only worry on Sofie's mind, however. All through the wedding, she'd noted the thick swarm of guards stationed at each exit to the cathedral square. A few times, cannon fire from the besiegers interrupted John Matthys while he officiated over the marriage.

At the conclusion of the wedding feast, John Matthys stood. In Sofie's mind he looked how Moses must have looked to the Israelites when he came down from Sinai, with his long beard, flowing robes of silk, and eyes that seemed to pierce the soul of whomever he looked at.

After standing, Matthys raised his arms and called aloud to the great assembly of the newly baptized, his voice matching his great physical size. "Now, fellow children of the Father, let us rejoice and sing a hymn unto the Father in thanks for this wedding. The time of God's people is at hand, and today's feast is but a foretaste of the everlasting feast all will enjoy in the days that draw near. I sense that the Father shall raise up John of Leiden and he will become a great prophet. Let our voices praise the Father for this wedding."

Matthys lowered his arms, and the choir of women who had sung during the wedding now began the hymn "A Mighty Fortress Is Our God." Sofie supposed that was a natural choice for the situation Münster's people were in, even if Martin Luther wrote the hymn himself.

She was about to go home at the conclusion of the hymn when a commotion broke out in the northwest part of the cathedral square. Several guards with drawn swords, led by the newlywed John of Leiden, dragged a man to the stage in the center of the square where Matthys sat. One of the guards stepped forward and spoke to Matthys, although Sofie was too far away to hear the words.

The meaning of what he'd said was clear enough, however, when the guards forced their prisoner to kneel in front of Matthys. Soldiers gathered around him in a horseshoe shape, with the open end facing the crowd, so it could see what took place.

"It's Hubert Smit," Kurt whispered to Sofie. "He's a blacksmith who lives in my neighborhood. I wonder what he's done this time?"

"This time?"

"He's known for having a short temper. But he's also known as the most honest friend a man could ever have. I heard he'd disappeared from his blacksmith shop yesterday, though. Maybe he tried to escape the city?"

Matthys held his arms aloft and then spoke to the assembly. Like it had during the wedding, Matthys's voice boomed through the square so that even those on the periphery heard him clearly. "Hubert Smit, you stand accused of slandering the Lord's prophets. For this, we've justly arrested you, and now you must stand trial and plead for God's mercy."

Although the guards had forced Smit to kneel, he didn't bow his head. Rather, he looked Matthys straight in the eye and said, in a voice nearly as loud, "I spoke only the truth."

Matthys's face grew sterner while his brows pinched together. Sofie saw his hands clench at his side. "You do not deny your words at New Bridge Gate, then?"

"I do not deny them. Several witnesses here can repeat what I said, should that be necessary."

"And what did you say at New Bridge Gate?"

"I said that the prophets and preachers, they'll prophecy until they do us in, and they must have a devil in their body."

Even from her distance, Sofie saw the color come into Matthys's cheeks when Smit spoke.

"And do you repent of these words now?" his bear-like voice boomed.

"I do not."

A muffled gasp from the crowd. Now, Matthys's face was so red, Sofie thought he'd strike Smit without delay.

Instead, Matthys sank to one knee and prayed. He remained on his right knee for several minutes. The crowd waited silently. Sofie realized she'd been holding her breath and let it out.

At last, Matthys stood. "I have prayed to the Father. This man is worthy of death. He must die because he's angered God. His death is God's will. God doesn't want anyone impure in the New Jerusalem. He wishes us to be a holy folk. The Father has shut the door of mercy because He is outraged at the slandering of His prophets. He will take vengeance upon all unless we sever the ungodly from the presence of the Chosen. The door of mercy remains shut."

As soon as he'd finished, John of Leiden took a halberd from one of the guards and jabbed it into the kneeling Hubert Smit, the spearpoint at the end of the weapon sinking into Smit's chest. Smit cried aloud as the blade smote him, then began gasping like a fish on land. Sofie imagined the blow must've pierced his lungs.

But Smit didn't expire on the spot. Rather, he crumpled to his right and lay upon the stage. That's when John of Leiden hacked at him with the halberd's ax blade. This time, Smit screamed an unearthly howl when the blade struck his neck and blood sprayed. Sofie turned away, hands going to her face as she gasped.

"Let's go, Kurt. I can't watch anymore."

"Yeah, you're right, we should go. I don't want to see any more of this, either."

Just as they reached the edge of the square, Kurt and Sofie heard the gunshot behind them. Sofie turned just in time to see Smit fall on his back and lie still. Apparently, even the ax blade to his neck hadn't killed him. But when John of Leiden lifted one of Smit's arms and it fell back to the stage limply, it was clear a lead ball had.

Before either Kurt or Sofie could say anything else to each other, they heard Matthys speak from over their shoulders.

"Now, go, children of the Father. Trust in God's prophets, and the New Jerusalem will rise from the ashes of this fallen world. Soon, you shall rejoice when you stand over the bones of the ungodly, knowing righteousness while the unrighteous suffer everlasting torment. Be at peace, brothers and sisters. Let us sing another hymn to the Father's glory."

Numb, Sofie and Kurt stumbled from the cathedral square even as a new song began behind them. Finally, when they'd nearly reached Sofie's house, Kurt said, "We've got to stay together, no matter what happens, Sofie. I don't think this is the end of the scary things we're going to see."

For once, Sofie didn't contradict Kurt's pessimism.

Chapter 14

"Can't you see that I'm poor, Deacon? I make cabinets, but my patrons, the Mesmacker brothers, left last month with the other nonbelievers. I've had little business since that happened."

"All the same, Brother Heinrich, God's prophets require that God's people shall hold all money in common. That includes anything made from gold or silver. It's a sin for Christians to hold money on their own account. The Father wishes for His people to be pure, and so, we do as the Father commands through His prophets. I must search the house."

"And are the Father's people allowed to make money by dealing with nonbelievers, or are only the godly worthy of our work?"

"Soon, Brother Heinrich, the day will come when that question no longer has meaning. If you are in need, the common supply house near St. Ludger's Gate will provide for your sustenance, as it does for all the Father's children."

Sofie and Hilde listened from the back room of her home, crowded as it was with the looms and piles of wool thread they used when weaving. Sofie didn't recognize the voice of the man at her uncle's door, but from how Uncle Heinrich spoke, she gathered he was one of the seven deacons named by John Matthys. His voice was gruff, and he spoke German with an accent, the same accent as most of the other recent arrivals from the Netherlands. She heard her uncle sigh and continue arguing he had nothing.

"Unless I'm mistaken, Brother Heinrich, you're due to man the walls at the end of the hour, are you not?"

"I am. You can see my knapsack here by the door."

"Today, you'll find that the communal dining halls are in operation, so there's no need to bring provision of your own. You're welcome to break your fast before your turn on the walls comes. God's prophets have commanded that all who stand watch must eat communally, just as the apostles ate communally in the early days of the Church."

"I was not aware of this change, Deacon den Slotel."

"I have the decree of Enoch here, should you need to read it for yourself."

Accent or not, Sofie decided, this man was trouble. Although she couldn't see den Slotel's face, she could picture his haughty grin and knowing smile while her uncle perused the words of the prophet Enoch.

After a significant pause and the sound of papers shuffling, she heard Uncle Heinrich's footsteps approach the back room of the house.

"Sofie, Hilde, it seems I'm to dine communally this morning with the other watchmen. I'll see you this evening. Allow Deacon den Slotel to conduct his search undisturbed, even though we have no gold or silver to contribute to the New Jerusalem." Heinrich spoke the last line with a wink.

Sofie and Hilde winked back. It was true they hadn't much money, but they'd hidden what few coins they did have at the first

116

rumor that the possession of money was a sin. Some coins lay secure in the false back of one of their cabinets. A few others now rested within the thick leg of the stool Sofie sat upon while weaving. Their uncle's woodworking skills had many uses.

Then, Heinrich leaned in close to his nieces and whispered, "I don't think den Slotel is a threat to you, but be watchful all the same."

"Is he another of the immigrants who arrived earlier this year?" Sofie whispered back.

"Yes. It appears the prophets are using outsiders who have few friends in Münster to carry out their orders."

"Because the prophets are outsiders, too, and these men are loyal to them rather than to their friends in town?"

"Yes, I'd say that's correct, Sofie."

Then, Heinrich raised his voice for den Sloten's benefit. "Try to keep the foot stove heated, all right, Sofie? It's warmer since that snowstorm three weeks ago, but it's only the middle of March."

"Yes, Uncle," Sofie called back when Heinrich turned to leave.

Once den Slotel had rummaged through the house and made his notes of the family's possessions, he addressed Sofie and Hilde.

"It seems your uncle did not exaggerate his poverty. The Father blesses the honest man, however poor he may be."

"Is there anything else you require, Deacon den Slotel?" Sofie asked as demurely as she could. Now that den Slotel stood in front of her, Sofie saw he was probably in his fifties. He had the stout body of someone who worked with heavy items regularly, although he was on the short side. A stonemason, perhaps? No, probably not, she decided. A stonemason was unlikely to be literate, yet this man was. She reserved judgment on his former profession.

"Yes. One more thing. The prophets wish to summon you to the cathedral square today. The two of you are on my list of those who must heed the call to gather."

"Why do the prophets wish to see us?"

"They did not say, but I sense there will be a large crowd in attendance."

"Perhaps the prophets will clarify what is sinful about holding money, so that the Elect can serve the Father with a true heart?" Sofie suggested.

"Perhaps."

Sofie saw just a trace of a smug smile on den Sloten's face as he said it.

Sofie and Hilde arrived at the cathedral square hand in hand. They had no idea what to expect but resolved to stay together, come what may. Sofie's heart already beat quickly as she approached, however, and from the slight tremor in her sister's arm, she guessed that Hilde's did, too. A brisk breeze blustered through the cathedral square and puffy white clouds hurried past overhead.

A large crowd had gathered, as den Slotel had predicted. Soon, trumpets sounded, and John Matthys himself marched into the square at the head of a group of soldiers. When Matthys stopped at the makeshift stage he often used to address the people of the New Jerusalem, this time Sofie noticed he had his beautiful young wife on his arm, although he practically dwarfed the young lady with his great size. Sofie didn't know the woman, except that her name was Divara. At least, that's what she'd heard the woman's name was. Divara was another of the recent arrivals in Münster, and no one seemed to know more than that about her.

Still, Sofie couldn't deny her good looks. She had long, dark hair, like Hilde did, strong facial features, and, despite her short stature and youth, an impressively full figure. In fact, it struck

Sofie that in a few more years, Hilde would look about the same, except Hilde was taller.

It appeared, however, that age was of little importance when God's prophets married women. Matthys was easily a dozen years Divara's elder. Possibly more, if Divara was still a teenager like Sofie guessed she was.

Still, when the crowd cheered their arrival, Sofie did the same. She gave Hilde a nudge to remind her that she needed to, as well.

As the cheers died down, Hilde whispered, "Sofie, what are all the soldiers here for? They're all around us."

It was true. Sofie had barely noticed because she was looking at Matthys and his lovely wife, but while some of Matthys's guards stayed near him on his stage, others had fanned out around the crowd. Silently, she rebuked herself and pledged to pay more attention in the future. To Hilde, she just said, "Maybe because the city has been under siege for three weeks now and Enoch needs protection? I don't know for sure."

It was weak, and Sofie knew it, but Hilde already seemed scared enough, and she didn't know what else to say.

Matthys smiled as he held up his arms to speak. "Brothers and sisters in Christ, the building of the New Jerusalem continues. Though the armies of Antichrist assail us, soon the siege will be over, and God's people will issue forth to claim the entire world. This the Father has revealed to me, and so it shall be. By Easter, the Father shall deliver Münster from its foes!

"But the Father has also instructed me that the city can only be saved when it has purged itself of all sin and unbelief. The Book of Acts declares that the early Church, the original apostles, held their possessions in common. And so, it must be the same in Münster if we wish for God to save this city. Alas, some of our number have fallen and have resisted the call to hold money in common.

"Make no mistake, Elect of the Father, the time is at hand. The return of the Father is at hand. But we must make straight the path.

The distinction between Mine and Thine must end. We will end it."

"Sofie," Hilde nudged her sister's shoulder and whispered.

"What?"

"If the Father is as powerful as the prophet claims, why does He need people to do things for Him? Can't He do them Himself if He wants to, without our help?"

Sofie just stared. She looked to Matthys on his stage, waving his arms and exhorting the Elect to prepare the way for the Father, and then back to Hilde. What her sister had just said was perfectly true, of course. So true, and so obvious, that Sofie had no response. Just pride in Hilde for being smart and figuring that out on her own. Sofie put her arm around her sister and drew Hilde in for a hug.

Meanwhile, Matthys continued. "We must prove our worthiness to the Father by living as the Bible teaches in the New Testament. Likewise, we must prove our true belief by clearing the way for the New Jerusalem here and now. Only by living out the Father's will can we avoid the fate of the ungodly."

Even as Sofie turned to whisper the words "salvation by faith alone" to Hilde, she saw Matthys's visage change. Gone was the warm smile. His posture stiffened, his jaw tightened, and Matthys' fingers balled into fists, knuckles whitening.

"Some of you," he intoned solemnly, "have refused to renounce your wealth in defiance of the Father's command to me. Your actions put the stain of sin on the New Jerusalem, the blot of selfishness. You endanger the salvation of all. Shall Münster suffer the fate of Strasbourg, renounced by the Father for turning its back on His Word? Deacons, bring forth the faithless!"

On command, seven men, accompanied by soldiers, escorted seven townsmen to stand in front of Matthys just below the stage. Drawing himself to his full height and puffing out his great chest, Matthys stared at each of the hoarders for several moments, his stare burning into each in turn. Then, he nodded, and the deacons took their seven sinners to the west side of the stage.

"Fall to your knees and pray for forgiveness! Ask the Father for pardon for bringing sin to the New Jerusalem. Pray that the Father holds open the door of mercy," Matthys called to those singled out for clinging to their money.

Then, he turned to the rest of the assemblage, which Sofie guessed included between two and three hundred townspeople. Sofie expected Matthys to become calm once more now that he'd singled out the sinners and rebuked them. Instantly, she learned her mistake.

Still nearly rigid, Matthys pointed his index finger into the middle of the crowd. "The sinful must pray to the Father for mercy. But who among us is without sin? Many are weak in the faith. They doubt the Father and His prophets."

From the corner of her eye, Sofie saw the guard nearest Hilde and her stiffen and tense. She bit her lip and looked around as discreetly as she could. The handful of other soldiers in her vision had done the same.

"Unbelief deserves death at the hands of God's people," Matthys boomed to the crowd. "Weakness in the faith is a short step from unbelief. All of you here today, every one of you, waited until the third day to accept baptism. When the Father opened the gates of mercy, you hesitated."

Sofie had wondered how the deacons knew which citizens to bring to the cathedral square today. Now she understood. The recorders of baptisms must have noted who accepted their baptism on each of the three days that the preachers spent baptizing adults.

Matthys continued his jeremiad. "The Father is angry with you. Only those strong in the faith will be worthy to take up the sword and smite the ungodly in the days to come. Now you must prove your faith is true or perish with the unrighteous."

With these words, Matthys raised his arms once more, and the soldiers surrounding the crowd drew their weapons and advanced.

"To the cathedral with you!" the soldiers growled as they closed in and began prodding the crowd with the tips of their weapons, herding the people toward St. Lambert's Cathedral.

"Sofie?" Hilde whimpered, eyes wide while her hands shook and fluttered.

Sofie looked around, hoping someone would provide a distraction that she and Hilde could use to escape. But it seemed everyone in the crowd felt stunned at this sudden turn. No one knew what to do or even had time to think before the guards began pushing them through the cathedral doors.

"Just stay with me, Hilde, and hold my hand," was all Sofie could come up with. What else could she do? If she or Hilde tried to run on their own, the soldiers would catch them, for certain. Matthys had too many soldiers, and the people had no one to lead them.

Once inside St. Lambert's, Sofie soon realized that all the artwork of the church was gone. The paintings, tapestries, and everything else. The only art that remained was the things not easily removed—the marble sculptures and stained-glass windows.

Once everyone was inside, Matthys came and stood in the pulpit of St. Lambert's. Drawing himself up to his full height, the ursine man scanned the assembly as the light from outside streamed through the stained-glass windows, casting a rainbow pall over everyone. Some in the crowd wailed in fear while their neighbors trembled in place. Others put their heads down in prayer. Sofie and Hilde clung to each other, staring mutely at the man in front of them who now held their fate in his hands.

After what seemed an endless time, Matthys finally spoke. "The gates of mercy are shut. The Father offers no more mercy. God is angry. The Father will brook no doubts from His people. You hesitated to accept baptism and demonstrated fear that the teachings of the prophets were empty. The Father wishes you to be a holy people, a people without sin. But your belief is weak. When the Father called, you faltered and did not trust in His prophets.

God doesn't want anything impure in the New Jerusalem. The Father wishes a holy people who trust in Him and praise His name. You have failed the Father. For that, death awaits."

"O Enoch, what must we do to regain mercy?" a woman in the crowd behind Sofie wailed. Others all around her took up the pitiful lament. Some people extended their hands, clasped together in prayer, while others shed tears and begged for forgiveness from their knees.

Finally, one man near the pulpit stood and cried, "Enoch, intercede with the Father on our behalf! Tell the Father his children yearn for the light!"

Matthys replied sternly. "The Father is a loving Father but will stand no falsehoods from His people. The Father knows the hearts of all. Pray to the Father, and if God wills it, and if your hearts are true, perhaps the Father will open the gates of mercy once more, and you may remain in the New Jerusalem. But if your hearts are false, know that death and the everlasting darkness awaits."

With that, Matthys departed the cathedral, a train of guards in his wake. Some of the guards, however, stayed inside St. Lambert's and exhorted the prisoners. The one nearest Sofie and Hilde shouted out, "Pray, pray, pray to the Father truthfully!"

Again, Hilde looked to Sofie. Sofie could see the tears fall from her sister's eyes, and Hilde's entire body shook as she whispered, "What do we do, Sofie?"

"Pray," Sofie managed to stammer, although her own voice shook, and she barely got the word out. She felt hot tears stain her own cheeks. What had she or Hilde done to deserve death? Could God really be so angry because she'd waited a day or two before her second baptism?

Sofie had never regarded her faith as lacking. She attended services each week, observed the feast days and holidays of the Church, and believed that God was active in her life. She prayed the prayers of the Church and sang the hymns with enthusiasm, and asked God's forgiveness for her sins each night before bed.

She tried to live the life that she heard the preachers describe each week in their sermon. Had it been enough?

There must have been a mistake. That was the only explanation. But that didn't matter now. Mistake or not, she and Hilde remained trapped inside the cathedral.

"Take my hand, Hilde. We'll pray together."

Kneeling at first, and then lying on their chests, Sofie and Hilde prayed every prayer of forgiveness they could think of. Some they whispered aloud to each other, and some they said to themselves.

The time dragged. Soon, Sofie had no idea how long they'd been inside the cathedral, whether it had been twenty minutes or two hours. The sisters prayed again because they had nothing else to do.

At times, Sofie noticed that the shaking in her body had died down, and her breathing was calmer. As soon as that happened, however, she began to wonder if she'd prayed enough to receive the Father's mercy, and the shaking began again.

The people around Sofie and Hilde had a variety of reactions. Most prayed in silence or whispered to a neighbor as Sofie and Hilde did. One ragged woman nearby would pray silently for a time, but then sit up and shout, "O Father, O Father, O God, have pity on us and admit us to mercy!"

After a time, however, near the back of the cathedral, a group of people panicked. Mostly women and a few boys who were Hilde's age at most, they wailed and shouted incoherently for many minutes. Finally, the guards threatened them, and they quieted.

All except for one woman. When the guards tried to herd her back to her spot on the floor, she pushed back. "I demand to speak to Enoch."

"The door of mercy is closed. You cannot interrupt the prophet Enoch while he prays on your behalf."

"The prophet is a fool," she shouted at the guard. "And so are you."

Sofie saw the guard raise his sword to strike when, without warning, the doors to the cathedral swung open. All turned to see.

It was bright daylight outside, but dimmer inside the cathedral despite the stained glass, so at first all Sofie could make out was the dark silhouette of a figure against a blinding background. After a moment, though, her eyes adjusted, and then she saw it was Matthys. No one moved or spoke as he strode back to the pulpit, his long, black, fur-lined cape dragging behind him on the smooth marble floor of St. Lambert's.

For the second time that day, John Matthys ascended the pulpit and addressed the people of the New Jerusalem. As he did, the guard from the back of the church hurried forward. Matthys leaned down to hear what the man whispered in his ear.

"The Father has spoken to me, and I have heard His words," Matthys announced.

No one moved or spoke. The air in the cathedral was breathless.

"The Father declares that unbelief still exists among his chosen people, and the Father is abhorred. Nine of you must come with me while the rest ask the Father for his blessing."

Matthys descended from the pulpit and strode amongst the tearful, trembling prisoners. He walked to the back of the assembly, picking out five people on the way by tapping each one upon their shoulder. Some were men, but not all. The woman who'd called Matthys a fool was among those chosen as abhorrent to the Father. Then, Matthys began his path toward the cathedral doors, tapping more unbelievers as he walked.

Six.

Seven.

Eight.

Cries and sobs began from those chosen as guards pulled them away by their shirtsleeves, swords drawn.

Almost to the door, Matthys stopped and tapped Hilde on her shoulder.

Sofie's heart stopped.

"No!" Sofie shouted, jumping up. "Not Hilde! She's done nothing wrong! This must be a mistake!"

Beside her, Hilde cried while tears rolled down her face. Sofie clung to her sister's arm even as a guard pulled Hilde's frail body away. Another shoved the point of his sword into Sofie's chest, impressing the point in the fabric.

"The Father has spoken," he said in a lifeless monotone. "None may question the Father's will."

"No!" Sofie shrieked as she broke down in heaving sobs. "This can't be!" Then the words faded into wails of helplessness as Hilde's blurred form receded farther and farther away. Finally, the cathedral doors closed with a clang, and Sofie collapsed onto the cold marble floor, weeping inconsolably.

All around her, Sofie heard people praying once again. But she didn't. If a harmless soul like Hilde had angered God and He wished her death, she'd be happy to share her sister's fate.

Just as Sofie made this resolve, the gunshots exploded outside the cathedral. She put her head in her arms and wept again, chest heaving, oblivious to the rest of the world.

Sofie had no idea how much time passed before John Matthys entered St. Lambert's for the third time. Like the last two, he walked slowly to the pulpit. Silence followed in his wake. Sofie couldn't bring herself to raise her head and look at the monster who had just killed her sister for no reason at all.

When he reached the pulpit, the people in the cathedral began crawling toward Matthys on their hands and knees. They begged for mercy and forgiveness. All promised they would live only to follow the Father's commands from that moment onward.

"Dear brothers and sisters, I inform you for God's sake that you have mercy from God and are to remain with us and be a holy folk. The gates of mercy have opened for a time. Walk into the light as children of the Father! Go forth, strong in the faith, and sin no more!"

Sofie was one of the last people to leave the cathedral. She shuffled forward, trying to think of how she could ever explain to her uncle what had happened. Sofie also considered what she'd do without Hilde, and if the time had come to join her sister in death.

"Sofie!"

She raised her head at the mention of her name.

Hilde stood before her.

"Sofie," Hilde said again while she buried her face in Sofie's chest and squeezed her in a bear hug. "Sofie, it was terrible."

Sofie extricated herself from Hilde's arms and said, "What do you mean, it was terrible? I thought you were dead. That you'd been shot."

Hilde pointed.

Then Sofie saw.

Nine bodies remained tied to one of the great linden trees that had grown in the cathedral square for years. None moved. All had gunshot wounds in the center of their chests and bloodstains spreading over their torsos.

"What happened, Hilde?"

"The prophet made us shoot those people!"

"You *shot* a person, Hilde?" Sofie stared into her sister's eyes. She couldn't believe Hilde could kill anyone.

"The prophet made us. He said that if we didn't do it, it was a sign of disbelief that angered God, and we would die with the other enemies of the Father. Matthys only had seven prisoners at first, but that woman from inside the church became the eighth, and then when one of the men refused to pick up an arquebus and fire, they tied him to the tree and shot him for lacking the true faith, too. Oh, Sofie, what have I done?"

Sofie didn't know what to say. She pulled Hilde in and gave her another hug that lasted for a very long time while more tears fell. Both women continued crying all the way home.

Chapter 15

Münster

March of 1534

"Sofie, can I talk with you?" a voice shouted through the door to Sofie's home.

Sofie moved toward the door like her limbs were wood. It was the day after her imprisonment in St. Lambert's Cathedral.

"Who is it?" she grunted.

"Sofie, don't you know my voice by now?"

"Rudolf, go away. I don't want to talk to you."

"We need to talk, Sofie."

"No, we don't. Go away."

"I know what happened at St. Lambert's yesterday, and I have things I need to tell you."

Sofie threw open the door. Rudolf stood there in the pale morning sunlight, dressed considerably less foppishly than usual. Just a linen shirt, brown, with a green velvet vest over the top.

"What."

"Sofie, your eyes are red. Really red."

"I only slept an hour or two last night. Rudolf, what is it?" She almost added, *after what I saw yesterday, anyone who associates with the prophets is no friend of mine.* But remembering what happened to the woman in St. Lambert's who said just that, Sofie decided to hold her tongue.

"Things weren't supposed to happen that way, Sofie. I never thought anyone would die."

"Well, they did."

"But they weren't supposed to."

"How do you know?"

"My father talks to Bernhard Knipperdollinck often because of their status in the guilds. Knipperdollinck said the ungodly were supposed to be sent out of Münster, not killed."

"Tell that to Hilde. She cried all night over what Matthys made her do. She'll probably cry all day today, too," Sofie said sharply as she drew her arm back to slam the door.

"Wait! I'm not done," he shouted. "I was there outside St. Lambert's when the shootings happened."

"So what?"

"I begged Enoch not to include Hilde. Begged. I told him she was too young, too young to understand why the Father was angry. He replied that in the days to come, even the children would stand in judgment over the Lord's enemies, and that all was as the Father wished. Then I pleaded with him again not to include Hilde. I got on my knees, Sofie. Ask Hilde if you don't believe me."

Sofie stood with her arm out in the air. Her fingers rested on the door. "Thank you, Rudolf," she whispered at last.

"It might not be much comfort," he added after a moment, "but I'll be back this afternoon with bread from my family. Since no one has money of their own now, there's no one to pay them for the bread they bake. But people still must eat, and they don't want the bread to spoil, so we figured we'll make sure our neighbors don't go hungry."

"Tell your family thank you," Sofie whispered again as Rudolf bowed. Then he turned and walked in the direction of his family's bakery.

Three days after Rudolf's visit, Sofie stood on the inner walls of Münster, her uncle's arm around her shoulder. She hadn't been on the walls since the siege began. Below her, in the common dining room where Heinrich ate on days when he was on duty, a reader droned verses from the Old Testament while the last few members of Heinrich's shift finished chewing their bread, bacon, and eggs and prepared to take their watch.

"I wanted to show you a few things, Sofie," Heinrich told her.

From where she stood, Sofie could see the besieging army of Bishop von Waldeck. Its campfires, tents, horses, and men dotted the plain outside the city's walls. "How many soldiers are there again, Uncle?"

"We've counted about two thousand."

"It doesn't look like that many to me."

"That's because they're spread out all around the city. When you look in any one direction, you only see some of them."

"What are those buildings that look like small towers, Uncle?"

"We call those blockhouses."

"What are they for?"

"To watch us, and to give the besiegers shelter if we try to break out and attack them."

"Have we done that?"

"Several times now. We call our breakouts sorties. Some of our men ride out on horseback to try to burn down the blockhouses and disrupt the construction of the trenches you see going between the blockhouses."

"What are the trenches for?"

"The earth walls in front of them give shelter to the soldiers behind them, and they're good against horses because horses have a hard time jumping over both the wall and the trench on the other side."

"It sounds like the bishop's men know what they're doing."

"They're professional soldiers, yes. *Landsknechts* is the word for mercenaries like these."

Sofie looked quickly to her left and right. "And do our men know what they're doing?" she whispered.

Heinrich also lowered his voice. "Some of them do, yes. In fact, that's why I brought you to the walls today. My commanding officer, Eding, wants me to relay to you that in case of an attack on the walls, you have a job. You must race to the wells and pass buckets as part of the fire brigade should anything catch on fire during an attack."

"That doesn't sound too bad."

"I know you can do it."

"Will the bishop attack soon, do you think, Uncle?"

"I doubt it. Not right now, at least. It's hard for landsknechts to assault cities with good walls like ours. I doubt he'll try until more men arrive to help. We're in little danger for now."

"And will more men arrive?"

"No one knows, Sofie. But for the moment, the small number of besiegers helps us. We have men who pass through the enemy's lines at night to gather food from the surrounding countryside. They don't have enough soldiers to prevent us from doing so. I've gone myself a couple times. Ways still exist to get through the enemy's lines if you know what you're doing."

"Is that part of why no one seems too scared that our city is surrounded?"

This question brought on another of Heinrich's pauses while he sighed. At last, he whispered, "Yes, partly. But the soldiers serve as a useful tool for the prophets, Sofie. You remember how part of their prophecy is that the army of Antichrist will lay siege to the New Jerusalem?"

Sofie nodded.

"This is their proof. While those troops remain out there, people in the city believe everything that happens to them is part of God's plan for Münster. As long as the soldiers look like they're prepared for war, many people take that as confirmation that what the prophets say is true. It's another tool for them to keep up the morale of the townspeople."

"How do you know so much about military tactics, Uncle Heinrich?" Sofie was very impressed that her uncle seemed to know about military things but couldn't figure out where he would have gained such knowledge. Not while making cabinets, for sure.

Just as he opened his mouth to answer, Heinrich closed it again and pointed toward the cathedral square. "Speaking of fire, what's that, Sofie? Can you tell?"

She turned and followed his finger. "There's a lot of smoke coming from the square, for sure. Are we under attack?"

"No, there's no attack, or horns would sound to warn everyone. But all that gray and black smoke means something's burning. Will you go and find out what it is?"

Sofie hesitated, saying nothing.

"What's the matter, Sofie, aren't you curious?"

"Yes, of course I am, but my last trip to the cathedral square didn't go well, Uncle."

Heinrich sighed deeply and closed his eyes for a moment. "I'm so sorry, Sofie. I wasn't thinking clearly when I asked you that."

Sofie set her jaw. "I'll go. I know what I'll do."

Within ten minutes, Sofie stood in front of the Schweren family's bakery. Rudolf's oldest brother, Karl, came out to meet her. He had on the cloth apron stained with flour one would expect a baker to wear. Karl stood about average in height and had thick, curly brown hair. Sofie thought he had a handsome face.

"Sofie Gresbeck, I don't get to see you as often as I'd like anymore." He bowed and gave her a friendly hug.

"You're right, Karl. You work so much at the bakery these days that you and your friends don't have the chance to tease me while I play in the streets anymore."

He laughed and blushed. Karl was nearly five years older than Sofie, and when she'd first come to stay with Heinrich in 1525, he'd teased her a little about her funny accent. All in good nature, of course. Karl was among the gentlest souls Sofie knew. It made her wonder how Rudolf had turned out so different.

"And I've spent most of the years since then trying to make that up to you," he replied.

"You have, it's true, but I need your help with one more thing, Karl."

"Name it."

Minutes later, Sofie and Karl were lying on the roof of the bakery, peering over the peak of the roof to see into the cathedral square. The bakery faced the marketplace, but from the roof Sofie could see over the intervening houses between it and the square.

"My God," Karl said. "Look at the smoke. I was so busy baking I didn't see it or smell it."

"What have they done?"

It was, in fact, a rhetorical question because Sofie could see the answer for herself.

Like ants, men swarmed back and forth from the bonfire to St. Lambert's Cathedral and the smaller St. James's Church next to it. Whenever the ants came out, they carried paintings, tapestries, holy icons, and books. All these went onto the fire.

Already the bonfire was many yards wide. Sofie watched as the gray and black ashes that once were the pages of books floated by on the light breeze.

"They're burning everything," Sofie moaned. "Everything that a person can move and carry."

"Some of those paintings were beautiful works of art. The icons, too. All those small, painted figures of people and scenes from the Bible. But why, Sofie?"

"Is that John of Leiden down there directing things?" Sofie asked Karl.

"It looks like it, yeah. More of the work of the prophets. Are they going to destroy everything?"

"How much do you know about the prophets, Karl?"

Instead of answering Sofie's question directly, Karl rumbled, "If my brother had any part in this . . ."

"He didn't this time, Karl. He came to my house again this morning to deliver some bread."

"Rudolf told me about the other day, Sofie. I'm so sorry that happened to Hilde."

Sofie still couldn't bring herself to talk about it, so she gave Karl a hug of thanks instead. Then she asked, "Karl, how are you getting by without your middle brother?"

"I heard from him the other day. An old family friend smuggled a letter from him into the city. He still plans to return to Münster once everything calms down. I was surprised he chose to leave at the end of February, but maybe he was the smart one."

"I hope that you're wrong. But maybe you're right. It's hard to be sure about anything anymore."

Then Karl said, "Look. People are gathering around John of Leiden. I want to hear what he says."

"I can't go to the cathedral square again today, Karl. I just can't."

"I'll go, then. You wait here, and when he's finished, I'll come back and let you know what's going on."

"Thank you so much, Karl," Sofie said with another grateful hug.

An hour later, Sofie and Karl sat in Brigitte's house. Sofie knew her neighbor would want the latest news.

"They burned everything, Brigitte. The paintings, the icons, everything. But what struck me most," Karl said as he stopped to sigh, frown, and slowly shake his head, "was what happened with the books. You know St. Lambert's was also the town's library, and all the old manuscripts saved over the generations were there, right? Not just printed books, but hand-written manuscripts that went back centuries."

"Such a shame," Brigitte said while shaking her own head slowly. "What harm can old books be?"

"I also heard John of Leiden say to also burn all the documents that kept records of who owned property in the city."

"And we know what the next step will be from that," Brigitte announced. "Already, we must hold money in common. Or, should I say, the prophets hold our money for us in common. The rest of our goods, maybe even our homes, will be next."

Karl chewed his lip for a moment over this possibility, then said, "The thing was, though, that John's henchmen had this weird look on their faces the whole time. Call it delight, elation, rapture, I don't know the exact word that fits, but most of them just beamed in joy the whole time. Like they took pride in destroying everything older than the New Jerusalem. But then John started sermonizing, and that was almost as scary."

"What did he say now?"

"John of Leiden harangued everyone about how the Father despised the learned for their pride and boastfulness. The Father would curse them for their vanity and ambition in seeking to imitate God."

"What rubbish," Brigitte exclaimed. "Did he say people couldn't eat fruit, either, because the trees in the cathedral square were all the Tree of Knowledge like in the Book of Genesis?"

"But that's not all. John went on at length about how the unlearned were the chosen people of the Father. It was they, he said, who would redeem the entire world and rule in the New Jerusalem because the words of man hadn't corrupted them. God loved most the pure and simple folk who believed in God's word and followed it without question."

"You mean, the prophets love most the fools who follow their teachings without question."

"Those words did cross my mind, Brigitte, yes."

While she and Sofie shook their heads, Karl continued, "And here's the last thing he told everyone—"

Before Karl could repeat John of Leiden's words, the trumpets sounded in the street, and the voice of a crier reached the three discontented souls in Brigitte's home.

"The prophet Enoch has received a revelation from the Father. The Father abhors the pretensions to knowledge of the so-called scholar. All the knowledge of the past is of no use in the New Jerusalem, and all who cling to the teachings of the world will not enter the New Jerusalem. Therefore, Enoch commands that tomorrow, God's faithful must bring all books other than the Bible to the cathedral square and cast them into the fire. All the teachings of this world of sin and unbelief must perish in the flames of righteousness!"

Then the crier moved on to repeat the decree a bit farther down the street. Sofie saw Karl clench his hands, and his face grew redder with each moment.

"I'm gonna whip that boy," he growled.

The crier's voice, of course, was Rudolf's.

As Karl rose to storm out, Brigitte took him by the arm, "Karl, don't. Save your anger. We'll need all the calm heads we can find in the days to come. If you storm out in anger now and strike Rudolf, the prophets will use that against you. They'll hold you up as an example of the prosperous and vain world of sin they're here to deliver God's chosen people from. You see that, don't you? In the eyes of the people of Münster, you'll be exactly what this proclamation is trying to rid the city of."

Karl yanked his arm from Brigitte's grasp, took two quick steps toward the door, but then stopped. He ran both hands through his curly hair, and then Sofie saw Karl untense his shoulders while he slowly turned around.

"You're right." A deep breath. "Yes, what you say is true. It's just hard when your own brother is such a fool."

"Besides, you never told us the last thing the prophet said earlier today."

"I don't need to. You just heard it from Enoch's obedient mouthpiece."

Chapter 16

Amsterdam

March of 1534

Bartholomew Bookbinder looked into the eyes of the newly baptized apostles surrounding him. "Fellow believers, you've been given the seal of holy baptism. God will protect and watch over you as you spread his word to the people of this city. We know that Christ will return. The day is at hand. Already Münster rises as the New Jerusalem. However, since we do not already dwell in the New Jerusalem, our souls are in danger unless we make our way to the new City of God."

"What signs can you offer us?" Claus Baesser, the owner of the house where Bookbinder held his meeting, questioned. "We want to believe, but you ask much in requesting we leave our homes and travel to Westphalia."

As he spoke, Baesser rose and paced in front of his blazing fireplace. He and Bookbinder had chosen to hold the meeting at night, the better to escape unwanted eyes. The combination of the fire and all the men crowded into Baesser's house made the room entirely too warm, but Bookbinder paid that no heed.

"I would quote the Lord's words that blessed is he who has not seen, but still believes," Bookbinder said with a kindly smile, "but you are right. Leaving one's home is no light undertaking. Yet, the Lord calls us to Münster for Christ's return."

"I'm ready to go," a rough-hewn man standing behind Baesser proclaimed. "There's nothing for me here, just more poverty while I lay paving stones until I die without a guilder to my name."

"Yes!" another man called out. "We've been baptized, and I've felt the Holy Spirit come upon me!"

"But how do we know Münster really is the New Jerusalem?" another man cried out, his face scrunched up doubtfully.

Bookbinder held up his hands for calm. "Let me share with you some letters that will assuage your doubts."

"Letters?" the last man responded with a hint of disdain. "Unless they're from God Himself, what good will letters do?"

"They are from the prophet Elijah."

"I heard he'd been killed," a man at the back of the house shouted.

"No, he's not dead. Elijah waits, imprisoned in Strasbourg, just as he foretold. But he's not dead. At least, he was very much alive when I spoke to him last."

"You've seen Elijah?" Baesser asked.

"I have. I've just returned from Strasbourg, in fact. I went there to see Elijah and free him from his shackles."

"What happened?"

"I disguised myself as a Lutheran preacher who intended to dispute Elijah and return him to the Lutheran fold. Once in his presence, I informed him of my intent to spring him free from prison."

"Where is he, then?"

"He would not escape. Elijah claimed he must remain in prison to fulfil the scriptures, and that when Christ returned, his chains would fall away, just as they did for Paul and Silas. He did, however, bid me to return the next day, when he wrote several letters to encourage the faithful. I've brought some of them."

With a flourish, Bookbinder produced several parchment documents from one of his saddlebags. He passed them around for inspection. It was dim inside because Baesser had drawn all the curtains to disguise the Anabaptist gathering, but the few literate men in the crowd hunched over the documents by candlelight or firelight and read them to their fellows. Soon, all were nodding.

"The Lord's prophet has spoken," even Baesser admitted at last. "If Münster is to be the New Jerusalem, we must prepare and debark in haste. We have no time to lose. The events have begun."

"The Master of Barges on the Rhine is a fellow apostle," Bookbinder told the gathering. "He will take you up the river, and you can travel overland to Münster from there. Now, I must go and gather the apostles from Leiden and other nearby towns. The Lord be with you, my fellow believers."

Chapter 17

Münster

April of 1534

"Are you well, Sofie? To tell you the truth, you don't look so good."

"I don't know, Kurt. I don't sleep very well anymore. Do you?"

"Depends. Some nights it's bad. Others, it's not."

While they strolled through what used to be the busy marketplace, Kurt took Sofie's hand. He didn't do that often, but she didn't object.

"So many of the shops aren't open anymore, Kurt."

"Well, it *is* Easter."

"You know what I mean. They weren't open yesterday, and they won't be open tomorrow, either. Most people can't get enough materials to work with while the city stays under siege, and even if people had money of their own, they'd spend it on food. My uncle hasn't made a new cabinet in two weeks."

"It'll be fine, Sofie. We'll make it through if we stick together."

Sofie turned to face Kurt and looked into his eyes.

He smiled. "I thought it was my turn to cheer you up for once. Did it work?"

"It helped a little," Sofie smiled back as she relaxed her shoulders. She hadn't even realized how tense she'd become while looking at the empty marketplace.

"Sofie, Kurt, come with me. Quick!"

The voice that haunted Sofie. How did he always turn up at such a poor time? She rolled her eyes to Kurt while trying to keep her smile as she turned to face Rudolf. Sofie expected him to say something rude or demeaning to Kurt when he ran up, but instead, Rudolf took them by the hand and led them away from the marketplace, down Salt Street toward St. Servatius's Gate, on the southeast section of the city's walls. Rudolf tugged at them like a child anxious to share a wonderous discovery with his best friend.

"Rudolf, why must we do this?" Sofie asked in frustration when he finally let go of her arm.

"The prophet Enoch is setting forth to battle Antichrist and free the city from the siege! We must go and see it."

"Wait," Kurt demanded as he stopped walking. "Say that again."

"Enoch plans to deliver the city. Today. It's Easter, and he foretold that the New Jerusalem would begin on Easter Sunday."

"Rudolf, what's happened? What else have you managed to learn that we don't know about?" Sofie questioned as she, too, stopped and stood next to Kurt.

"Oh, that's right, you weren't at the wedding last night. A friend of my father, another baker, Albert Geistehovel, got married, so I was there. Both of the great prophets, John of Leiden and Enoch, also attended."

"Geistehovel lives in my section of town," Kurt stated.

Rudolf, wrapped up in the memory, ignored him. "Enoch's wife Divara came, too, and we all sat at the wedding feast in Geistehovel's home. Albert had just served an excellently prepared roast to go with our red wine when Enoch received the Holy Spirit. He sat still for what must've been an hour. The only time he moved was to clap his hands gently, nod his head, or sigh like someone who'd just lost a brother. It was eerie. No one else at the feast moved or said anything, either, which was even more eerie. They just watched him."

Neither Kurt nor Sofie had anything to say. They just stood and waited for Rudolf to finish the story.

"After the hour was up, Matthys sighed and said, 'O Father, not as I will but as you will.' Next, he stood up, took each person at the banquet by the hand, gave them the kiss of peace, and told them, 'God's peace be with you all.'"

"Isn't that what Jesus said right before he died on the Cross?" Kurt asked. "In one of the gospels? Matthew, maybe?"

"I don't know. Finally, he said that tomorrow, meaning today, he'd go forth to deliver the city but would die in the battle. It was necessary to fulfil the prophecies and allow the New Jerusalem to reign forever. That's what's happening now. If we don't hurry, we'll miss it! Come on!"

When Rudolf left them to run to the walls and watch, Kurt turned to Sofie. A few people drifted by them on Salt Street, also headed for the walls.

"Looks like we'll miss the party if we don't go," he told her.

"I don't mind. This party stopped being any fun a long time ago."

"I know, Sofie, but maybe, if Matthys leads the people into battle and they're defeated, maybe everyone will come to their senses, and the party will finally be over."

"What's come over you today, Kurt? That's two optimistic things you've said in one day."

"Can I do three optimistic things?" Without waiting for Sofie to answer, he leaned in and gave her a kiss.

It took Sofie by surprise, and at first, she tried to pull away, but then she realized how good it felt when Kurt took her by the shoulders, held her, and pressed his lips to hers. After a few moments, he backed away and looked her in the eyes. "How do you feel now?"

Sofie knew she blushed badly. "That was wonderful, Kurt. But is now the time? I thought we were going to watch a battle?"

"If this is the start of the New Jerusalem like the prophets claim, I didn't want the world to end without you knowing I love you."

"You don't really believe that'll happen, do you?"

"The New Jerusalem? Nah. I'm not betting on it, at any rate. But I do love you, Sofie, and if today isn't the end of time, and things get worse in the days to come, I want to spend as many of them as possible with you. I was hoping you felt the same."

"I do, Kurt. Wait, are you proposing?" Sofie felt the color return to her cheeks as her heartrate accelerated.

"Hmm, well, I didn't mean to. I suppose I could've chosen certain words better. But I do want to see you whenever I can."

Sofie took a deep breath. "I want to see you, too. It's just that . . ." Sofie's voice trailed off as she scuffed the cobblestones with her toe.

"It's just that what?"

Before she could answer, horns blared, and a cheer went up from the city walls.

"I'll tell you more later, Kurt. Promise. We might as well see if the New Jerusalem will begin today while we have a chance, though, right?" Even with all the emotions running through her, Sofie managed to crack a grin at her last bit of sarcasm.

Hand in hand, they walked to the inner wall. They arrived just in time to hear the trumpets sound again and watch John Matthys and his men parade through the outer gate on horseback. Picking up speed, they trotted toward the bishop's mercenaries, sunlight glinting from their armor and weapons as they advanced. A fair distance existed, a couple hundred yards, between the city walls and the blockhouses of the mercenaries. Sofie noticed another tall figure riding beside Matthys. Must be the other great prophet, John of Leiden.

She furrowed her brow. "Where is everyone?" she asked Kurt. "They're charging the bishop's lines with only fifteen men!"

"You're right, Sofie. What on earth are they doing? Look! Already the bishop's pike men are lining up to receive the charge."

By now, the charging attackers had closed most of the distance separating the two forces. Before Kurt could say anything more, a burst of gunfire erupted from the arquebusiers manning the bishop's trenches. The flash of gunpowder was terrific, and Sofie recoiled and hid her face at the sound. She'd never seen a firearm go off before. However, to her surprise, when she looked up again, only one of the charging riders had gone down in the volley. Next, she saw the men on horseback raise their own arquebuses and return fire at the trenches. Sofie didn't know if they'd hit any opponents—the dirt piled in front of the trench blocked her view. That, and the smoke from the discharged gunpowder soon clouded the battlefield in a murky haze.

When the breeze blew some of the smoke clear, Sofie caught a glimpse of when the two sides met. She shuddered at the collision of horsemen and pikes. The pikes threw some of the riders from their horses while others charged through the line, swinging their sabers at the heads of the pikemen. Soon, the two groups fought hand-to-hand with weapons, and from her distance, Sofie couldn't make out what was happening.

Before long, though, a shout went up, and all Sofie saw was a lone rider galloping back toward St. Servatius's Gate. The gaunt man with the long, black beard. John of Leiden.

In his wake, Sofie and Kurt watched the mercenaries advance to within fifty yards of the gate. They marched in two lines. At fifty yards the front rank parted, and men from the second rank stepped into the gap.

Everyone around Sofie gasped, and many wailed or moaned hysterically. There, with a pike stuck through his chest, was John

Matthys. Enoch, the Lord's prophet, hung from the pike, limbs twitching and mouth gasping as he somehow clung to life.

One of the mercenaries in the front row then drew his sword and, in a single blow, severed the head from the body, torrents of blood spurting. Four more slashes removed Matthys's arms and legs, with equally gory consequences.

Next, four mercenaries picked up the severed limbs, which still dripped fresh blood, and hit each other playfully with them. Sofie hid her face in her hands. She felt Kurt put his arm around her shoulders and squeeze.

Meanwhile, the captain of the mercenaries planted Matthys's head on a pike and stuck the pike into the soft earth. He and his companions jeered at the people of Münster, although, absorbed in grief, no one could make out the obscenities.

"Let's go, Kurt, I don't want to watch anymore," Sofie stammered through her hands.

At some level, she'd always understood that people die in war. Her own parents had. But seeing it with her own eyes was different. And the sight of soldiers mutilating a body and hitting each other with the body parts was too much for her nerves. Somehow, it was worse than the field of blackened bodies she'd seen as a young girl during the Peasants' War. Everyone was dead by the time she reached the field of battle that day. It was another feeling altogether watching blood spurt from a body that had been alive moments prior.

By the time Sofie and Kurt staggered down from the city's inner wall, a crowd had gathered in the courtyard of Nichting's Monastery, which stood next to St. Servatius's Church. Sofie and Kurt meant to pass by and go home, but they got stuck in the enormous crowd gathered around John of Leiden. Then, John raised his voice and addressed the throng. Sofie couldn't fail to notice that Bernhard Knipperdollinck stood at John's side.

"Dear brothers and sisters, you shouldn't be despondent because our prophet Enoch is dead. For God will raise up another who will be even higher and greater than John Matthys was! For it is God's will that he should die in this way. His time had come. It is not without reason that God has brought it about that he should die in this way. The purpose was that you should not hold God's prophets above God Himself. The Father is mightier than John Matthys was. What John Matthys did and prophesied, he did through God. So, God can certainly raise for us another prophet through whom He will reveal His will."

Then Knipperdollinck stepped up beside John. "John of Leiden rode against the armies of Antichrist! John alone survived the battle and did not perish amidst the Lord's foes. The meaning of this is clear. The Father calls John as his new prophet!"

From various spots in the crowd, men and women cheered and chanted John's name. Others shouted from the steps of the monastery, beseeching John to be their prophet. Surrounding the crowd, several armed soldiers did likewise, raising their swords to the heavens while they cheered and cried out John's name.

Waving his arms for quiet, John of Leiden spoke again. "Everything that is unrighteous and is still in sin must be stamped out, since the example is ready. You have entered into the Apostolic Church, and you are holy. Holy is the Lord, and you are His folk. Now that the example is ready, it shall spread over the entire world, just as it began here in this holy city. Soon, God will show us a sign that we are His holy family and that His people hold the fate of the ungodly in their hands!"

Another round of cheers erupted for God's new prophet, John of Leiden. Having heard enough, Sofie and Kurt pushed to the edge of the crowd and walked toward Sofie's house.

"Do you believe that?" Kurt asked her when they were inside and safe from eavesdroppers.

"It's like a bad dream, Kurt, but we never seem to wake up. Now we have a new prophet. Will he be better or worse than the old one, I wonder?"

"I'm almost sure things will get worse, Sofie."

She considered teasing him about being more positive but couldn't find the heart.

"Do you think John of Leiden set Matthys up, Sofie?"

"It *is* strange that he's the only one who survived the, what do you call it? The sortie?"

"Strange indeed. And notice how his lackey Knipperdollinck was there to acclaim him to the people afterward. Next thing you know, he'll be the king."

"And John is married to Knipperdollinck's daughter."

"Sounds to me like Knipperdollinck is angling for influence, Sofie."

Sofie put her arms around Kurt and embraced him for several moments. "I'm just so tired, Kurt. So tired of all these strange things happening. How do other people stand it all?"

"I know you're scared, Sofie. Who wouldn't be after what happened to you at the cathedral? But that's the point of everything, in a way, I think."

"What do you mean?"

"If everyone's scared of the prophets, they won't speak out against them, especially if the prophets have the soldiers on their side."

Chapter 18

Bishop Franz von Waldeck poked at the roast duck on his platter while he savored another draught of wine. White Riesling, an excellent vintage. He rubbed his palm over his growing paunch and belched in contentment. Then he adjusted the fur cap on his increasingly bald head while he shivered. It had been a damp day, and cool, with consistent rain throughout, and the bishop's joints ached. At age forty-three, even good food couldn't make that go away. He was on his way from Osnabrück to Münster to oversee the siege of Münster personally, and he'd asked his captains to meet him here to discuss their plans.

As bothersome as his aches were, von Waldeck was about to begin on the roast pork that accompanied the duck when a knock came at his door. "Enter," he called with all the imperiousness he could muster.

The man who walked through the door looked much like von Waldeck—long, dark hair, stringy strands covering his ears, and a thick face with a mustache curled above his upper lip. At fifty-seven, he was half a brother and half a father figure to Franz.

"Ah, it's you, brother. Come in, Herman. What news have you?"

Then, another man entered right behind Herman, Archbishop of Wied. It was Duke John of the principality of Cleves-Jülich, his crest—a golden shield on a red field, with eight fleurs-de-lis sprouting from the shield in the pattern of a compass—prominent across his chest. Duke John had an entirely different aspect from Franz's brother. His face was almost triangular, and at the point of the triangle Duke John sported an equally triangular brown beard. At age forty-five, his hairline had just begun to recede.

"I have good news," Duke John began.

"And I have horrible news," Herman finished.

Franz von Waldeck held up his right hand, palm out, in a gesture of calm. "And I have news as well. Who shall start?"

Duke John stepped forward. "I will."

Von Waldeck signaled him to go ahead. He liked Duke John. Sometimes. Although John's reputation was as a very moderate man who considered all points of view before reaching a decision, once he'd made up his mind, he was decisive and relentless. His only real drawback was his forgiving nature and desire to avoid confrontation unless someone forced his hand.

Duke John began. "About one week ago, I intercepted a convoy of barges heading up the Rhine when they passed into Cleves. Finding the presence of thirty-six barges on the river at once rare in the extreme, I questioned the captain as to their destination. Under, shall we say, exceptional duress, he confessed his passengers planned to debark at Moers and then walk to Münster. On board, I found many pamphlets of Anabaptist origin."

"What did you do next?" the bishop inquired as his face brightened.

"I informed them they would go no farther and sent most of the people home. Although I detained their leaders for a time and questioned them, they knew nothing except that they'd received the call that Münster was the New Jerusalem and that they must go to Münster with all haste. I also uncovered a series of reprinted letters from Melchior Hoffmann, the raving preacher imprisoned in Strasbourg. It appears he's made a convert of one of his jailors or has some other accomplice because he's written several missives to friends in the Netherlands."

At this news, the bishop's visage darkened considerably. "You . . . sent them home?"

"Yes. These were simple townsmen and villagers from Brabant. They were no soldiers, no revolutionaries. So, I sent them back whence they came."

Von Waldeck clenched and unclenched his fists.

"Why are you angry, Bishop? The threat is averted."

"Have you not heard?"

"Heard what?"

"Duke John, Emperor Charles apparently feels more alarm than you do over these so-called harmless adult baptizers. He's declared Anabaptism punishable by death throughout the empire."

Duke John blanched. "I was not aware of such an edict."

"You were not aware, or were disinclined to enforce?"

"Perhaps, Bishop von Waldeck, you'll reconsider those words. Do you really think I would order the death of more than three thousand people solely for following their conscience? The situation in Münster is serious, yes. Alarming, even. But I'll not have the blood of thousands on my hands who have, as yet, committed no violent act, simply to help you get your bishopric back and punish a small handful of preachers who've claimed fantastic visions."

"But Duke John, these orders do not come from me. They come from the emperor himself."

"And like I just told you, I've yet to receive word of these orders. Until now. Were it not for the Imperial Recess of Speyer that obliges me to provide assistance in situations such as this, I'd not even be here. You'll further note, Bishop, that not all your neighbors have answered your call for help. Presumably, Emperor Charles is more concerned about their refusal to honor his proclamation than about one of the few princes who did."

By now, von Waldeck's face had turned a peculiar and dark shade of red, and he rose to shout at Duke John when his brother laid a hand on his shoulder.

"Perhaps, brother, you should hear my news before responding? Now is not the time for rashness."

Still glaring at Duke John, Franz von Waldeck slowly reseated himself.

"This is the situation within Münster. The prophet John Matthys is dead. His head rests on a pike in view of St. Servatius's Gate."

"This is excellent news," von Waldeck growled. "Why did you say your news was horrible?"

"My spies in the city inform me that the man known as John of Leiden now directs events inside the city."

"And what do you know of this John of Leiden, brother?"

"He's already proven himself a much more astute opponent than his predecessor. So astute, in fact, that he's already bribed two hundred of our mercenaries over to his side. They marched into the city just three days ago."

"What?" Now the color of von Waldeck's faced surpassed red and bordered on purple.

"Did I not tell you that employing mercenaries was a risky move? They fight for the highest bidder, especially when not paid regularly."

"But I promised them their money at the end of April! And where did the prophets of Münster get enough money to bribe two hundred of our soldiers?"

"I can't say where the money came from. Nonetheless, those mercenaries now fight for the Anabaptists. Whose literature, I'll add, we found in the blockhouse of the turncoats. Might I suggest, brother, raising the siege until more troops arrive and we can fully invest the city? Our numbers were too few to surround the city completely at the end of February. Perhaps, when our numbers are greater and our success assured, the risk of desertion will diminish."

"Nonsense! I'll not raise the siege. Thanks to our 'allies' such as Duke John here, more people will stream into the city if I do so, and our foes will multiply. Instead, send out messengers to the hesitant princes. Remind them of their duty to the empire and the edict of Emperor Charles. As soon as enough men are here, we'll take the city by storm. Then our mercenaries will get all the loot they can carry."

"As you desire, brother. In the meantime, I'll recruit more spies and see what more I can learn about this John of Leiden."

Chapter 19

Münster

May of 1534

It was the sunniest and warmest day of the year so far, but Sofie almost shivered while she waited in the cathedral square with Kurt and Hilde.

"I don't want to be here, Kurt."

"Neither do I, Sofie. But I think we'd better, and your uncle will want to hear what happened."

"Can it be true? Is John of Leiden dead like the rumors hold?"

"Dead? What are you talking about? When did that rumor start?"

"Three days ago. In my neighborhood, the rumor is that three days ago John of Leiden went running through the streets naked, collapsed, and died on the spot."

"Nonsense, Sofie. I heard that he fell to the ground in a trance and has spent the last three days in prayer and fasting."

"I heard that one of the mercenaries did him in," Hilde added.

For the first time since she'd shot one of the nonbelievers, Hilde had emerged from Uncle Heinrich's house today. Sofie's compassion for her younger sister had only grown over the past weeks. It had taken nearly two days for Brigitte, Heinrich, and her to convince Hilde that she wasn't a murderer, she wasn't going to Hell for breaking one of God's commandments, and that she must eat something. Hilde had vomited twice before she managed to keep anything down.

How Hilde had found the courage to come with her to the cathedral square today, Sofie didn't know, but she was glad to have both Hilde and Kurt by her side for the prophet's latest announcement. Assuming the rumors were false, and he was alive.

Just as she was about to respond to her sister, the trumpets blared. Sofie's shoulders sagged, and her gaze fell when she saw John of Leiden walk to the stage in the center of the square. Alas, he lived.

Sofie could see tears form in Hilde eyes.

"I just want this to be over," Hilde whimpered quietly.

Sofie saw Hilde's arms were shaking visibly. She put a hand on her sister to steady her. "Keep up your courage, Hilde. You're tough, and you'll make it through whatever happens. Remember, we're here to get news for Uncle Heinrich while he's on guard duty."

John's personal guards flanked him like always. Bernhard Knipperdollinck and Bernard Rothmann walked behind him. Only this time, twelve other men followed behind the prophet and his preachers, also escorted by guards. All were well-dressed, and Sofie recognized some as prominent townspeople.

John of Leiden raised his arms in his usual style, elevated above his shoulders, palms to the sky, and the crowd quieted. Through his great dark beard, John's powerful voice carried to the edges of the cathedral square.

"I have summoned the Elect today, the successors of the Israelites of the Old Testament, God's holy people, for much has befallen God's kingdom of late. For the past three days, I've prayed to the Father. I've taken no food and no rest but have spent the time beseeching the Father for signs and for the Father to make plain His will to me. You, the Elect gathered to hear God's Word, must make His commands known throughout the New Jerusalem.

"God is satisfied with His holy people. He wishes for His people to be a holy folk. Everything that is unrighteousness and still in sin must be stamped out, since the example is ready. You have entered into the Apostolic Church, and you are holy. Holy is the Lord, and you're His folk. Now that the example is ready, it shall spread over the entire world, just as it began here in this holy city."

"Father, O Father, give love, give love!" one person in the front of the crowd shouted.

"Yes, the Father will give us His love. He has marked us as His holy folk. Already, two hundred of Antichrist's soldiers have repented of their sins and joined the people of God. Did I not say to you that He would give signs of His approval? This is the first! Just as these two hundred have abandoned sin and become members of the New Jerusalem, so eventually will all the world follow. These two hundred are only the beginning!"

The crowd cheered and exalted the Father with praises and shouts of thanksgiving before John quieted them again.

"However, the Father has also commanded me that because we've now entered a new age, we must live as the faithful Israelites lived of old. They, too, were God's chosen people until they denied Christ and fell into sin. We've taken up their mantle as God's Elect, and we cannot turn from the path they abandoned, lest we, too, share the fate of the ungodly.

"Therefore, God commanded me that twelve Elders shall rule the New Jerusalem, as the Israelites of the Old Testament were ruled. These are the twelve Elders of the New Jerusalem!"

Twelve men, the same who'd entered the cathedral square in John of Leiden's wake, now moved to the front of the stage.

John stepped through their line to continue his speech.

"I am but the spokesman of the Elders. God has chosen me to play this role in the New Jerusalem. Our new laws shall be the laws of ancient Israel. They will strengthen the New Jerusalem by making sure the unrepentant will be unable to make any excuses for their crimes against the Elect, and by seeing to the needs of any weak and aged people who live amongst us. For behold, the Father has given the twelve Elders the right to bring justice to His kingdom and punish the ungodly!"

With a flourish, all twelve Elders drew swords from their waists. Although some of them looked uncertain of how to hold and wield their weapon, the blades gleamed in the sun as each man knelt upon his left knee and laid the sword across his right, heads down in a gesture of submission. John took a knee alongside them.

"Very clever," Kurt whispered to Sofie.

"What do you mean, Kurt?"

"The twelve Elders. I see three members of the town council among the elders, three of the leading guild members, two preachers, and one nobleman. The last three must be some of the immigrants from the Netherlands."

"He's chosen Elders from all the groups who used to have a say in the city's government."

"Exactly, Sofie. The twelve Elders are a new government but run by most of the same people as the old government. Change the name but keep the same people, as long as they're loyal to the prophet. Before all this is over, John will be king. Mark my words."

"It'll never go that far, will it? I can't believe people will stand for that, after all they did to get rid of Bishop von Waldeck. How could they forget so quickly?"

Kurt tilted his head to the side and tapped his forehead with one finger.

Meanwhile, John rose from his knee and resumed his address. "These swords are the Lord's Swords of Justice. You are the true people of God, the Elect, and the sword shall be brought to bear against our enemies. Against God's enemies. Still, every evil, every sin, must be eradicated from our midst. There must be no impurity in the New Jerusalem, no dissension amidst the chosen of the Father."

At this, Bernhard Knipperdollinck stepped forward and stood beside John of Leiden on the stage. Like the last time Sofie had seen him, he wore the rich robes of a guild master, white cloth colored in scarlet and gold. He also drew a sword after a glance from the prophet.

"The righteous must wield the sword established by God in order to terrify the wicked and protect the good. Bernhard Knipperdollinck, the Lord has revealed to me that you shall wield the Sword of Judgment. He has given you the wisdom and authority to decide the fate of the guilty and the wicked. Death shall be the punishment for all crimes against God's Elect. Brother Bernhard, what are the crimes punishable by death?"

Knipperdollinck stood tall, shoulders thrust forward and head held high. "The first crime is blasphemy against God and His prophet. The second is disrespect for the Lord's Elders and the government they've established for the New Jerusalem. Third, all children must respect their parents, and fourth, all wives must respect their husbands as the Lord's appointed leaders of the household. Fifth, because marriage is sacred to the Lord, adultery is punishable by death, as is fornication. The only valid marriage shall be marriage between two of the Elect. Next, because the Lord abhors greed and dishonesty, avarice, theft, fraudulent business transactions, and lying shall all be punishable by death. The eleventh crime is gossiping. Rumors only sow dissension among the Elect. Likewise, being quarrelsome bears the punishment of death. Finally, and most gravely of all, sedition against the Lord, His Elders, or the people of the New Jerusalem brings death. This is the Father's will."

"Thirteen new commandments," Kurt muttered to Sofie.

"The Old Testament gave us ten to start with, and we haven't done very well with keeping those," Sofie agreed. "How can we do better with thirteen more?"

John of Leiden stepped forward. "Do not be troubled at heart, people of God. The Father desires to have a holy people, and if you prove yourselves holy in the Father's eyes, the New Jerusalem shall spread over the earth, and all of you shall stand in righteousness over the sinful and the enemies of God. The Father merely wishes you to know His will so you will not sin or reject the Father in unbelief.

"Also know that the Father hears your prayers. I know that some of you who are craftsmen have been worried about how you shall support yourself when God's people hold all money in common. Fear not! The Lord provides for His people. Continue to go to work and produce goods. The Elders shall pay you a fair wage for your work in the form of whatever goods you require. They shall distribute the work of your hands to the people of the New Jerusalem according to need.

"Because the Lord wants you to know that you are His people, He has also commanded that tomorrow be a feast day in the New Jerusalem. Each of you shall gather at the gate nearest your home, and all shall celebrate God's love for His people. Now, go and spread the good news throughout the city!"

"Holding a public feast in a city that's under siege? I've never heard the like in stupidity," Brigitte whispered to Sofie while they sat at the banquet table on May 4, 1534. The day was nearly as warm as yesterday had been. "Bishop von Waldeck's forces now number nearly four thousand troops, and his noose around the city tightens. What will the prophet think of next? Will he turn cobblestones into bread?"

Sofie wanted to laugh, but with the Scripture Readers pacing up and down the aisles of tables, repeating their assigned verses for all to hear, she judged it unwise to draw attention to herself, worried the Readers might notice. She just smiled to her friend and patted Brigitte's hand instead. Sofie wasn't sure if the Readers also spied for the Elders and the deacons, but she didn't want to draw their notice until she learned the truth. When she scanned the banquet, it didn't take her long to find Rudolf among the Readers, droning out scripture that no one listened to.

Meanwhile, she and Brigitte continued to eat the roasted pork, bread, and cheese provided for the feast, which they washed down with mediocre beer.

"And have you cleansed yourself from sin and put aside all unrighteousness and idolatry, my dear?" Brigitte asked with a wink between mouthfuls.

"Absolutely. My soul is pure, and it sparkles with the love of the Father," Sofie winked back.

"I've been told the Elders will attend the banquets and request that any who still have money should bring it forth, and that all with quarrels with each other should come and arrive at forgiveness of their dispute."

"How do you know so much?"

"I'm an acquaintance of Engelbert Eding, just like your uncle is. I've always found it possible to get him to speak his mind when given the proper inducement."

"Wine? Brigitte!" Sofie gave a mock gasp, which sounded very strange when she croaked it in a whisper.

Her friend grinned. "Never. Just company one day when I came to visit him after his shift on the walls. His wife is a rather distant woman who keeps her head buried in the scriptures for much of the day. I don't gather he gets a lot of attention at home. So, I just provide a little chaste companionship for the poor man now and then."

"And in return he tells you things. Very sensible."

"Not to mention I'm just being a decent neighbor. Speaking of, Hilde isn't with you today."

"No. She made it through the gathering in the cathedral square yesterday but said she felt poorly this morning and wouldn't join us."

"I don't blame her. The poor thing."

"I'm not sure what'll happen to her, Brigitte. I know she has nightmares. They've woken me up several times since that day in St. Lambert's. I don't tell Hilde, though. She doesn't need more to worry about."

"You do look tired, Sofie. Are you well yourself?"

"I think so. I hope so." A pause, followed by a long sigh and a nervous glance. "Well, to be honest, I don't really know, Brigitte. How can anyone predict the future right now? When will," Sofie paused again and looked around carefully, then lowered her voice further, "when will the prophet and the Elders realize that we are surrounded, and more enemies arrive every week?"

Brigitte nodded while she leaned in close to Sofie's ear. "They feel emboldened because some mercenaries deserted to our side, I'm sure. And here's something else Engelbert let slip to me. The prophet and his preachers like Rothmann have sent out messengers to recruit more Anabaptists to Münster. They're hoping more people will arrive and help them lift the siege."

Sofie stiffened at this news of more Anabaptists potentially arriving. It was the last thing she wanted to hear, and she wasn't sure how much more bad news her nerves could withstand.

She was going to respond with something uncharacteristically pessimistic when Sofie overheard one of the Elders questioning some of the banqueters nearby. She knew the man. Henry Rode.

Sofie didn't know very much about Rode other than his name, but he'd been on the city council before all the Anabaptist madness began. That's how she knew who he was. At present, Rode was busy questioning an elderly woman seated near Sofie and Brigitte. Sofie didn't know the older woman and wondered if she'd always lived in Münster.

"Face forward, and don't say anything," Brigitte whispered in Sofie's ear.

"Why?" she whispered back.

Brigitte just put her index finger to her lips and shook her head.

Meanwhile, Rode's voice rose. He had a gravelly voice that sounded distinctly unnerving to Sofie.

"What is your faith, woman? What do you believe in?"

"I believe in God," she answered in a voice that seemed neither afraid nor confident.

"What truths do you hold about Mary and the saints?"

"I believe that Mary was a pure maiden, a virgin, and that she was the mother of Christ. The saints are people who have suffered for God's sake."

"And do you keep icons of the saints in your home, woman?"

"I do," she stated without hesitation.

"You ungodly woman!" Rode's harsh voice grated. "You dare to blaspheme the Father with idols! You are an abomination in the Father's sight!"

Sofie thought back to the day when she and Karl Schweren watched the Anabaptists burning icons along with the books in the cathedral square. This wasn't likely to end well.

With a scowl, Rode raised his voice to address all who could hear. "Listen, dear brothers and sisters. This devil of a woman has idols in her home! She is not worthy of coming to the Lord's table and holding this supper with us."

Everyone nearby stopped eating and looked up.

"The prophet has spoken. The Father has spoken. Such unbelief is the stain of sin creeping in amongst God's Elect. Will you repent of these idols, woman?"

"I have nothing of which to repent. Icons are not offensive to God."

Rode's scowl grew deeper and Sofie watched the color come into his cheeks. Between gritted teeth, he said, "Then you leave me no choice. You must go to the Rosendale and await judgement. You are unworthy to eat with God's people."

Two men with swords, who'd been standing some distance behind Rode as he questioned the banqueters, now stepped forward at his sign. The woman, however, shrugged their hands off her shoulders.

"I don't need an escort of knaves. I know the way."

Still no one in the area spoke. Sofie looked to Brigitte. Again, her neighbor put a finger to her lips and shook her head.

Next, Sofie saw Rode take a few steps and question another onlooker. "Do you believe this supper is a real supper, in the way Christ supped with His disciples?"

"Yes," came the answer from another voice Sofie didn't recognize. Although the response was neutral, she heard a tinge of fear.

"And are you willing, as Christ was, to suffer for God's sake, even to suffer fire, water, or the sword?"

"Yes," came the monotone response once again.

"Then you are blessed in the Father's sight."

Boots scraping the cobblestones, Henry Rode strode down the row of tables to question more banqueteers.

Sofie heard Brigitte exhale audibly. "The poor woman."

"What's the Rosendale?" Sofie replied.

"It's where the nuns used to live. Before they either accepted baptism or left the city. The Church of Our Dear Lady. I'm not sure why it's called the Rosendale now."

"Will she be killed, Brigitte?"

Sofie's friend just shrugged her shoulders. Then, she said, "More importantly for you, it's crucial you stay away from Henry Rode. As far away as you can."

"Why?"

"He and your uncle aren't on good terms. Or even speaking terms. I don't know if he'll try to do anything to you, now that he's an Elder, but I'd avoid him whenever I could if I were you."

"So much for all the faithful forgiving their disputes, right, Brigitte?"

"Indeed."

The two women continued eating. When they'd nearly finished, Henry Rode reached the front of the gathering and clapped for attention. As he did, the Readers put down their books and began bringing around loaves of flatbread to each table.

"Brothers and sisters, you've been called to this feast so that we may share a meal in holy fellowship, just as Christ did with His disciples. You will all do for us just as we do for you first. Just as Jesus led the disciples, so the Father wishes that you shall follow His Elders. First, let us break bread together."

On cue, each of the readers broke off a piece of the flatbread and ate it. Next, they did the same for all the people nearby, breaking them chunks of bread and handing it to each person in turn. A glass of wine followed the flatbread.

Once everyone had finished, Rode called out, "Dear brothers and sisters, go in the name of the Lord, and God's peace be with you. Let us sing a hymn of praise to the Father."

Sofie knew what was coming. "A Mighty Fortress Is Our God." It had become the unofficial hymn of the New Jerusalem.

Just as the hymn began, however, and everyone was about to sing the first verse, they heard the drumming begin outside the city walls.

Brigitte's eyes went wide. "The bishop's men are gathering to attack. The city's under assault!"

"I'm on the fire brigade," Sofie said as she rose from her wooden bench. "I've got to get to the well, just in case something catches fire."

She was ready to move out in good order, and to Sofie's great surprise, many of the other people around her didn't panic, either. It was true that the deacons and other Anabaptist leaders had drilled the people on what to do for the last two months, and the mercenaries who'd deserted to Münster's side gave the people additional discipline and training, but that was only practice. Sofie had always wondered what would happen during a real attack.

She just hoped that discipline, and Münster's defenses, were enough. If the mercenaries breached Münster's double walls and got inside, it would be a bloodbath.

Chapter 20

Münster

June of 1534

Heinrich Gresbeck crawled along the friable earth, staying low and out of the firelight. Around him, campfires shed fitful illumination while the mercenaries sang bawdy songs and bragged of their prowess with weapons and women, their shouts and boasts mingling with those of their fellows.

He wasn't sure if sneaking around the mercenary camp was a good idea, but last night he'd decided he must try. Heinrich's nieces were eating a bit less every week, so he had to do something. The Elder of the New Jerusalem who lived in Heinrich's district, Henry Rode, was an old enemy who, Heinrich believed, had reduced his family's share of the food distribution. The risk, however, was that making foraging trips outside the city walls had become more dangerous with each passing week. As more mercenaries arrived to besiege the city, the gaps in their lines and trenches grew smaller, and the risk of trying to sneak through rose.

After Bishop von Waldeck's assault in early May had failed miserably, his forces easily defeated by the height of Münster's walls and by a lack of numbers to carry through the assault, von Waldeck had resumed his siege while waiting for more men. Heinrich had hoped he'd give up after such a substantial defeat, but it appeared the bishop was as stubborn as he was militarily inept.

Heinrich sighed quietly. The longer the siege lasted, the greater the possibility von Waldeck would gain sympathy from the surrounding princes. If he convinced them the Anabaptists in Münster were a threat to their own lands, a repeat of the Peasants' War, the greater the odds they'd send men and money. This lowered the odds that anyone in Münster would make it through the siege alive. Münster's best hope was that the bishop would run out of money and willpower before everyone in the city starved.

Heinrich steeled himself. He could not fail. Sofie and Hilde needed him to succeed. So, he waited calmly, not more than one hundred feet from scores of men who would kill him without hesitation and put his head on a pike for all in Münster to see, including his nieces.

Heinrich waited because if the landsknechts followed standard procedure, they'd change their watch at the end of the hour, at midnight. Right before midnight was when he'd make his move. The soldiers on guard right now would be tired and unwary, just waiting for their relief. The people of Münster had continued fighting sorties since the beheading of John Matthys but had always sortied during daylight, never at night. If Heinrich darted through just before the new watch showed up to take their positions, he stood a good chance of passing unseen. Then, he simply had to do the same in reverse when sneaking back into Münster with whatever food he could forage in the darkness.

Still, thinking of the sorties made him shake his head slowly. In a way, each one was necessary. Some had even succeeded in capturing livestock and ammunition from the mercenaries. But each time, more of the able-bodied men of Münster suffered wounds or death. Münster now had, by Heinrich's guess, nearly three times as many women as men.

But that didn't matter tonight. Eluding capture to scavenge food mattered. He'd done this about a dozen times since the siege began, but his heartbeat still pounded in his ears while he waited, muscles taut and tense.

When Heinrich judged that midnight had nearly arrived, he crawled forward on his stomach, a few feet at a time. This was the perfect route to pass unnoticed. The river that supplied Münster with water, the Aa, flowed to Heinrich's left, its babble just enough to cover up sounds. Plus, the mercenaries couldn't dig their trenches all the way to the river because they'd fill up with water. This route was how Heinrich got through their blockade most nights.

The end line of the trenches was to his right. Only one campfire to skirt, and he'd be past the besiegers. When Heinrich looked up, however, he saw that the bishop's troops had now thrown up a second trench a few hundred feet behind the first. How had he missed that when reconnoitering his route from the city walls yesterday?

Well, one more obstacle to get around. No point in turning back now. Presumably, the men standing guard here were less aware than those on the front line. That was Heinrich's best hope, in any case.

Then, Heinrich realized his worst fears. He saw a shadowy figure leave the second line of trenches and crawl in his direction.

He didn't know if the approaching stranger had spotted him. Heinrich hoped not. He resolved to stay low, quiet, and motionless. Maybe the figure was from the city, too, and was foraging as Heinrich was.

The shadow crept closer. It veered neither right nor left but made straight for him. Heinrich inched his palms under his shoulders, arms in pushup position, so he could jump up and make a run for it.

Heinrich couldn't believe his ill luck. The mercenaries had dug a new line of trenches in this sector in a single day! If the approaching figure spotted him, all the man had to do was call an alarm, and Heinrich's opponents had him surrounded. A glance around told him that diving into the river would be his best chance of survival, if worst came to worst.

By now the mysterious figure was only twenty-five feet distant. Heinrich wasn't armed. The Anabaptists had control of the weapons in the city; when the watchmen left their posts on the walls, all the weapons went into a communal armory. It hadn't bothered Heinrich before—his hope was in stealth, not force.

Heinrich tasted blood. He realized it was from biting his lip too hard. The shadow was only ten feet away now. Heinrich knew it had spotted him. He pushed to one knee to make a sprint for the Aa.

"Heinrich, don't run!" the shadow called to him quietly.

He crouched back down and turned his head. It couldn't be.

"Get down, stupid!" the man whispered again. "They'll see you!"

Heinrich dropped on his chest and waited until the shadow reached him. "Herman Ramers," he whispered into the night. "What on earth are you doing here? And how did you know it was me?"

"Follow me, and I'll tell you," Herman said, tugging Heinrich's sleeve and crawling back whence he'd come.

Half an hour later, safely hidden in the forest to the north of the city, Heinrich Gresbeck embraced his old friend.

"You almost got us both killed, standing up to run like that," Herman scolded him. In the fitful moonlight, Heinrich could see the scar from an old knife wound still marred his friend's right cheek. He also noticed the heavy beard Herman used to wear was gone.

"I thought you were the guard and you'd spotted me."

"Well, I am the guard, and I did spot you, but only because I knew how to look for you. I figured you'd go that way the next time you went foraging."

"You taught me well. The river conceals sound, and then I need only stay low and quiet. But the question, Herman, is why were you looking for me?"

"I wanted to talk with you, of course."

"Well, here we are. Out with it. I still need to find some food for my nieces tonight before sneaking back into the city."

Herman took a moment. He blew the air out of both cheeks and rubbed his hands. It was June, but the nights could still be chilly, and tonight was one of those nights. Rubbing his hand over his mouth, he sighed. "This whole thing has gotten out of control, Heinrich. We both know it."

"True. I can't believe you joined von Waldeck's army, though."

"It pays. Soldiering is what I'm good at. It's more exciting than being a carpenter, anyway. Soldiering is what you used to be good at, too."

"But you lived in the city for years, Herman. Now you're helping to starve out the people who used to be your neighbors. That's not like you. You're a good soldier, and as ruthless as you need to be in war, but I never figured you'd turn mercenary against your old friends."

"That, Heinrich, is why I was hoping I'd find you."

"You want me to join you? Is that it? You know I can't. My nieces live with me. I won't abandon them."

"No, no," Herman said with a gentle touch on Heinrich's shoulder. "That isn't what I meant. I know you won't abandon your girls, and I'd never expect you to. The reason I wanted to find you is so we can discuss a plan to end the siege with as few deaths as possible."

"I was hoping von Waldeck would give up after his first attack flopped so spectacularly."

"That's because you don't know the man. He's stubborn. Stubborn, and willing to pay any price to get his bishopric back."

"I realize that now."

"And I, Heinrich, I was hoping that after Matthys made that foolish attack on Easter and got his head cut off, the Anabaptists would lose heart at the loss of their prophet, and their morale would fall apart. But that hasn't happened, either."

"No. John of Leiden now leads the Anabaptists. He's taken Matthys's place as the chief prophet. He's just as ruthless and egotistical as Matthys, but smarter and even more cunning. I don't know if you remember much about him, seeing that you were one of the people who left in that horrible February snowstorm, but the man is convinced he's God's right hand."

"We learned just how cunning John of Leiden is when he bribed two hundred of our men to change sides." Herman sighed again. "That's why we must do something, Heinrich. The madness must end, or thousands of people will die. We're both seasoned soldiers, even if it's been a little while for you. We know how war works. If von Waldeck triumphs, I fear he'll put most of Münster to the sword in retribution for all that's happened."

"If there's anyone left in the city by that time. John has proclaimed the time has come to kill the ungodly, wherever he finds them. He's prescribed death as the punishment for any behavior he deems sinful. Knipperdollinck is his executioner."

"How does he get people to go along with his plans?"

"The Anabaptists control all the gates and all the weapons. As long as John keeps his bodyguard loyal, he can rule the city through the combination of force, terror, and appealing to fear."

Herman closed his eyes, laced his fingers behind his neck, and then bowed his head. "He isn't going to give up until he's destroyed everything, then?"

"That's how it looks to me, Herman. John of Leiden believes God speaks to him, and he's destined to bring the return of Christ.

It appears both you and I have leaders who can't be reasoned with."

Herman sat in thought for a long time in the near blackness of the forest, elbows on knees. Finally, he said, "What if we didn't?"

"What do you mean?"

"What if we did away with both von Waldeck and John of Leiden? The bishop's brother, Herman of Wied, is an archbishop and, from all I've heard, a much more patient and merciful man than Franz is. If he became the leader of the bishop's army and had someone from Münster who was in his right mind to negotiate with . . ."

"They just might reach a settlement where thousands don't have to die," Heinrich finished his friend's sentence. But then he shook his head sadly. "I don't know if you can get that close to the bishop, Herman, but I can't get that close to John. He has a bodyguard that goes with him everywhere."

"So does von Waldeck. That's why we've got to use some cunning of our own, Heinrich."

"What do you have in mind?" Heinrich asked wearily as he rubbed his eyes and stretched his neck.

"I'll tell you about it while we find some food for your girls."

Two days later, Heinrich Gresbeck and Herman Ramers strode nervously to the doors of St. Lambert's Cathedral, where John of Leiden had resided since becoming the Father's prophet and the spokesman of the twelve Elders of the New Jerusalem. It was an overcast day, reasonably warm, but not sunny yet.

"You sure this is gonna work?" Heinrich whispered.

"No. But I'm willing to try it, anyway. You've got your lines down?"

"Yeah."

"Let's just hope you know as much about John of Leiden as you think you do. If what you've told me about his character is true, this just might work."

Although he nodded gravely, Heinrich raised his fist and knocked on the cathedral doors with what he hoped sounded like confidence.

Immediately, the door opened, and a man in armor and a halberd emerged. His bearded face showed neither friendliness nor hostility. "What is it, brother?" he asked after glancing at Heinrich's neck and seeing his copper emblem.

"I seek permission to speak with the prophet. This man," Heinrich patted Herman on his shoulder, "has returned from spying on Bishop von Waldeck's forces and has important information about the armies of Antichrist."

"Is that so?" the guard wondered, now turning to study Herman Ramers. "He does not bear the sign of adult baptism," he finished skeptically.

Heinrich instantly realized they'd forgotten to get Herman a copper disc to wear around his neck like all the Anabaptists wore.

"I was never given one, brother," Herman put in cheerfully. "My mission as a spy began before you handed them out, and I've been away from the city since that time. May I please have one?"

Rather than respond, the soldier gave a short whistle. Another armed guard emerged, sword in hand.

"Why, then, brother, haven't you requested one from your deacon?" the guard said suspiciously, fingering the shaft of his halberd.

"I didn't know of the law until you mentioned it just now. I've only arrived back in the city within the hour and need to see John of Leiden without delay!" Herman bluffed. "I have news that will help lift the siege and allow us to prevail over the ungodly!"

The guard looked to his companion, who shrugged.

"Will you allow Antichrist to triumph just because I don't wear a copper token? My news is a matter of urgency!" Herman frowned and crossed his arms.

Finally, the guard lowered his weapon and waved them inside.

As they strode through the murky light toward John of Leiden at the other end of the cathedral's sanctuary, Heinrich whispered, "Nice improvisation."

"I've been ordered around by enough officers to know how to talk to an enlisted man," Herman replied with a wink.

When the two men reached John of Leiden, they saw him sitting in the bishop's chair, which he'd moved next to the pulpit. At his elbow was a glass of red wine and an empty plate. Another pair of armed guards flanked the prophet.

Heinrich bowed deeply. Herman followed his lead. Heinrich said, "Brother John, my apologies for the intrusion, but I have news of the enemy's actions that is of considerable value," Heinrich stated in his best soldier's voice.

"Indeed? And who are you?"

"Heinrich Gresbeck. I serve under Deacon Engelbert as a watchman at St. Ludger's Gate. I was among those who first stormed the walls in that sector of the city."

"A true member of the Elect," John of Leiden said as he rose from the bishop's chair. "Without doubt, the Father will number you among his chosen people when the Son returns to lay claim to his earthly kingdom."

Heinrich noted the booming voice John used in public was gone, replaced by a quiet, calm tone that was, if he had to put a word to it, calculating.

John paced for a few moments, looking at his guests every few steps. "And who is your companion? He is not among the Elect."

Herman stepped forward. "My apologies, Brother John. But my news cannot wait."

"All that happens, happens as the Father wills it. Time is without importance. To dwell in the New Jerusalem without being one of God's Elect, however, is punishable by death."

When John said this, the armed guards at his side stiffened and regarded the petitioners with a new seriousness.

Heinrich glanced at Herman, but his friend's face showed no strain or nervousness. Nor did he tense his muscles or show fear. Instead, Herman replied, in the most earnest and sincere voice he could fake, "In February, Brother John, I went forth as a spy to learn the plans of Antichrist. I've only just returned to the New Jerusalem. I've not had time to acquire a token to show I number among the true believers."

"A spy, you say?"

"Yes, brother."

"For what purpose? Your mission lasted more than three months?"

"Yes. Enoch sent me forth to infiltrate the councils of Bishop von Waldeck. He is a suspicious man, the bishop. Suspicious, and wary of outsiders. It took some time to gain his trust."

"Enoch never mentioned such a mission to me while he lived. I fear you may be lying. And surely, one of the Elect such as Brother Heinrich knows the penalty for lying to God's prophet." John gave a slight nod, and his guards descended the short flight of stairs to take Heinrich and Herman by the arm. God's prophet turned to walk away.

Heinrich was amazed that his friend stood calmly and didn't flinch. He also knew, however, that he and Herman had only one toss of the dice left before John decided they were traitors. He decided to take the toss.

"Enoch prophesied the arrival of the bishop's army and the siege of the city, did he not?" Heinrich asked John as the soldiers turned to lead them away.

John of Leiden stopped and turned his shoulders. "He did."

"And have all his prophecies thus far come to pass?"

"They have."

"When the two hundred mercenaries deserted to our ranks, who do you think convinced them to desert the bishop?"

John cocked his head to the side.

"This man, Herman Ramers, is the one who delivered them to us. He's the one who distributed Brother Bernard Rothmann's tracts, and the money that purchased their loyalty, to the captain of the men who've joined our side. He did all this under Bishop von Waldeck's nose. Surely, he's shown he belongs among the Elect?"

Now John of Leiden stared at his pair of guests intently. Slowly, a smile spread across his face. "You are the one who persuaded the mercenaries of our righteousness?"

"This man is the key to the fulfillment of the prophecy," Heinrich went on. "The Father works through him to bring about Christ's return to Münster."

"And how did you enter the city? How were you able to return from your mission without passing through the city gates? The captains of each gate inform me of all who enter or leave the city. No one is supposed to do either unless they bear the sign of the Elect."

"I was on guard at the time, Brother John," Heinrich continued. "When Herman appeared at my gate not one hour ago, it was like a miracle."

Without warning, the space inside the cathedral brightened. The sun broke through the morning clouds, and the light coming through the high, stained-glass windows of St. Lambert's cast the entire sanctuary into a dazzling, polychromatic brilliance of light.

"A miracle, you say?" John said as his face brightened.

"An angel of the Lord brought me to Brother Heinrich's gate," Herman put in. "The angel brought me back to Münster, so I can describe the state of Antichrist's forces in time for us to defeat them."

John smiled. "Go on, then, Brother Herman. If the Father brought you here in such haste, surely, He has plans for you. Speak."

Heinrich felt the grip of John's bodyguard leave his arm, although the men remained nearby.

Herman bowed again. "The state of von Waldeck's army is as follows, Brother John. Its morale hangs upon a thread. Although the bishop did not lift his siege after you threw back his assault last month, the mercenaries are a fickle army. We learned as much when the plan to bribe them worked so brilliantly."

"It merely fulfilled the Father's will."

"And that is why your daring plan met with such success, of course," Herman said in the most soothing voice he possessed. He saw John smile again. "Because their morale is low, I believe that if we can cause them another setback, the mercenaries will break camp and lift the siege. It will be like the pebble that starts the avalanche in the mountains."

"And," Heinrich put in, "once we have the Lord's enemies on the run, once the ungodly see our righteousness, many will join our ranks. The rest we must hunt down as they flee the city."

John of Leiden scratched his chin through his immense beard. "And you can accomplish this?" he asked Herman.

Herman bowed his head a moment. "Not on my own, Brother John. Bishop von Waldeck has many bodyguards and takes many precautions to protect his person."

John scowled.

"But he has other weaknesses," Herman offered.

"Such as?"

"Women, Brother John. The bishop, as one would expect of a servant of Antichrist, has given himself to debauchery and fornication. If we can find a woman brave enough, who loves the Father enough to undertake a mission on His behalf, I can get her close enough to Bishop von Waldeck that she could do away with the bishop in some fashion. With your enemy suddenly leaderless, I believe many of the troops will disperse, especially if the bishop no longer lives to provide them their pay."

John of Leiden again scratched his chin. "I like this plan," he said at last. "I believe it is God's will that you arrived today, and we must serve God and carry out His will." Then, John turned to one of his bodyguards. "Summon Bernhard Knipperdollinck. Together we shall choose the woman to execute Brother Herman's scheme."

"Yes. I shall summon Brother Bernhard immediately."

"I want the two of you to return here in one hour," John of Leiden told the co-conspirators. "Together, we shall work the Lord's will and fulfill the next part of the prophecy."

Heinrich and Herman bowed, turned, and then walked away. Once safely outside the cathedral, Heinrich finally saw the sweat bead on his friend's brow. Herman sighed in relief and then gave a weary smile.

"An *angel* brought you to my gate?" Heinrich said incredulously.

"You told me John was mystical and believed in signs from God. I figured it couldn't hurt, and our plan was in trouble at that point. Then, the sun came out and the cathedral lit up. That couldn't have been better timing."

Heinrich conceded that might be true.

"But why, Heinrich, why oh why did you tell John that I'd bribed the mercenaries and their captain? All John needs to do is ask their captain if that's true, and he'll unveil me as a fake. I don't know if I can think of another miracle that will save us then."

"Oh, that won't be a problem."

"How do you know?"

"John of Leiden had Bernhard Knipperdollinck shoot the captain of the mercenaries about a week ago."

For the first time in hours, Herman laughed. His shoulders relaxed, and Heinrich saw the stored-up tension drain from his face. "Good thinking, Heinrich, good thinking. Can I ask what happened?"

"The captain—whose name was Gerard Schmoester, in case you need to know the name of the man you supposedly bribed— and three companions barged into someone's house after getting drunk. The man of the house wasn't home, but his wife was. They demanded the wife tap a keg, so they could continue drinking, and then insulted her and roughed her up a little when she wouldn't do it. The next day she complained to the Elders, claiming the mercenaries had broken the laws of the New Jerusalem. She called on several neighbors who had heard everything and corroborated her story, as if her bruises weren't proof enough."

"Then what?"

"John of Leiden had the mercenaries arrested and brought to the cathedral square. Each one begged for mercy, saying they'd been drinking. They pleaded to work every day in the city canal as their punishment."

"That's hard work, dredging the sediment out of the canal."

"Sure is, Herman. I think they thought that would prove their remorse. John got to one knee and prayed to the Father. When his eyes opened and he stood up, he proclaimed that the door of mercy was open for some but not for all. Because the woman told John that Schmoester was the one who'd hit her, the door of mercy slammed closed for him. John made Schomoester's friends tie him to a linden tree in the cathedral square, and then Knipperdollinck shot and killed him. We won't have to worry about him disproving our story."

"I do feel better. Even though I thought you were nuts when you said it, I understand now."

"What we need to do in the next hour, though, Herman, is decide how things work from here. You say you can introduce a woman into the bishop's presence to kill him?"

"I think that can be managed, yes. Everything I said about the bishop's sexual habits is true, from what I hear. If the woman keeps her cool, she just might pull it off."

"Then what?"

"That's where you and I come in, Heinrich."

Chapter 21

Münster

June 16 of 1534

"Sofie and Kurt Boetmester, I now pronounce you man and wife."

At the preacher's words, Sofie and Kurt leaned in for a gentle kiss. She had tears in her eyes. Sofie cried tears of love, but also fear, sadness, and uncertainty over what lay ahead.

Kurt saw them. He knew why Sofie cried, and he hugged his new wife deeply. "I know you're scared," he whispered in her ear as gently as he could. "But I love you and want you by my side, come what may."

"And I love you, too," she whispered back. "I always dreamed of being married. I just never thought I'd get married like this."

"It isn't what I imagined the day would look like, either, but I'm still happy to be with you, Sofie."

It felt strange to Kurt that he was the optimistic one for a change, but he knew he needed to act like a husband now that he was one. That meant standing by Sofie in happiness and sorrow like he'd just vowed to do. Oddly, this made him feel upbeat rather than worried. He concluded love must be a powerful emotion indeed to make him go against his nature like this. But he'd do anything for Sofie.

Even still, Kurt couldn't help but feel some sadness of his own. A person's wedding day was supposed to be a great celebration—the happiest day of their life, perhaps. But not in the New Jerusalem.

Instead, less than two weeks ago, the prophet had stated that all men in Münster of eligible age must marry. John of Leiden cited the verse from the Book of Genesis commanding that the faithful should "increase and multiply" and claimed the Father had revealed to him that this was of the greatest importance. Any man who ignored the Father's command and had not married by the end of June faced execution.

After that, it hadn't taken much courage to propose marriage to Sofie. She'd accepted, of course, and Kurt knew she'd done so both out of love and out of fear of what might happen to him if she said no.

So, it came as no surprise to Kurt that her hands shook even as he embraced her on their wedding day. Kurt regretted nothing, except that he couldn't give Sofie the wedding she deserved—no dancing, no music, and no feasting with friends and relatives. At least Sofie's Uncle Heinrich had saved his deceased wife's wedding dress, so Sofie had one to wear today. Still, that was the only outward sign of their marriage. That, and a paper signed and witnessed by the preacher that they now lived in holy matrimony among the Elect of God's kingdom.

"What do we do now?" Sofie asked while the pair descended the steps from the altar of St. Lambert's Cathedral.

Pausing to look Sofie in the face, Kurt shrugged. "Go home, I guess."

"It just feels like there should be more than this, Kurt. Our wedding day is supposed to be joyous and happy, but I don't feel anything. I mean, I love you, and I want to be your wife, laws or not. But shouldn't we feel like something special just happened?"

"We're married. That's special."

"But there's no one here but us, Hilde, Uncle Heinrich, and Brigitte. Shouldn't there be singing, and dancing, and music all night long? A banquet? Something that makes today stand out as different from all the others? People with whom to share the memory? I mean, what'll we tell our children someday? Do we tell them we got married, hugged a few people, and then went home with a piece of paper?"

"I don't know what to tell you, Sofie. I wish it could be like that. A big party, lots of guests, and all the rest. But it isn't."

"That's what I always dreamed would happen on my wedding day. What do you do when the thing you've always wished for happens, but not in the way you dreamed it? Does that make your dream a lie?"

"I'll make it up to you tonight," he said, hoping but uncertain he could meet her expectations. As if either of them knew what to expect on their first night being married, anyway.

Sofie shook her head slowly and then said, "You know I don't mean that. I thought when I got married, I'd at least be moving to a new home. But I'm going back to my uncle's house, instead."

"Let's hope it's a temporary thing, Sofie. Your uncle, or I guess I should say our uncle now, is living with Brigitte and her children, and I'm living with you and Hilde. We all agreed it would be best to have a man living in both houses, especially since it's now a crime to lock your doors in the New Jerusalem."

"Heinrich and Brigitte are getting married tomorrow. I'm happy for them. Ever since the plague killed Aunt Liese, I'd always hoped they'd get married, and now they are. So, maybe one good thing happened because of this crazy law."

"Just one, Sofie?"

She kissed him gently again and wiped the wetness from her cheek, but Kurt saw her eyes grow watery once more. "I'm so sorry, Kurt. I didn't mean it to come out like that. So many things are happening I can't think straight today. Please forgive me."

"There's nothing to forgive, Sofie. I just need you to get your optimism back, all right? You know how I am. Most days I don't have enough optimism for both of us," he said with a hopeful smile. "You're better at that than I am."

She smiled back, although weakly. "You're right, Kurt. Someday, we'll look back on this day with joy and happiness, even though I didn't get a big party. I've got you, and that's worth a lot."

"Now, I suppose it's time we go to our little party at home. Can I have the first dance tonight?"

"Tonight, and every night, Kurt."

Even as Sofie and Kurt walked down the aisle and out the cathedral's double doors into the June sunshine, their immediate family trailing behind them, a figure in the shadows watched silently. One uninvited guest had sneaked into the wedding ceremony. Cheeks flushed in jealousy, the figure brooded and clenched a fist. This wasn't how his plan was supposed to work.

Then, a thin smile. The story wasn't over. Not yet. Now that all the laws of the New Jerusalem carried a death sentence for those who violated them, any number of things could happen to turn the tables. It was just a matter of directing events toward the desired conclusion.

The same night that Sofie and Kurt became husband and wife, June 16, 1534, two figures crept silently beneath the walls of Münster.

"You sure you're ready?" Herman Ramers asked the woman at his side.

His partner nodded.

"Let's go over the plan again, Heille. No matter what happens on our way toward the bishop's trenches, don't lose sight of me, and don't make a sound. Got it? The moon is out, even if it's only a half moon, so let's hope light won't be a problem."

Heille Feicken nodded again.

"You've got your pack with the fancy dress, other clothes, and the rest of your gear?"

"Of course."

"Good. Tomorrow evening is the bishop's birthday. You can bet wine and beer will flow freely. Tonight, we'll get behind von Waldeck's lines, and then tomorrow evening I'll present you to him. We'll claim you can show him how to sneak into the city, and then you offer him your first gift. Then, if all goes as planned, you offer him your second gift."

"Yes, yes, everything is ready."

Herman looked over his partner again. "You know what'll happen if they catch you?"

"The Father wishes me to prove my faith by taking this mission. How can I say no? Whatever they might do to me, the same thing will happen to you once they remember you brought me into the camp."

"Like you said, the Father wishes it. I serve the Father and His holy people. If God is with us, who can stand against us?" Herman said, repeating the line John of Leiden had used when he anointed them for their mission. "Once we get to a safe spot tonight, I'll go and find the bishop's brother, Herman of Wied, to set up your meeting with the bishop tomorrow. I'll tell him you wish to report on all the doings inside the city in exchange for your safety. Then, once you and the bishop are alone tomorrow night, you can do the deed."

What Herman didn't tell Heille was that when he spoke with the archbishop, he'd also deliver a letter written at Heinrich's house last night.

The letter mentioned nothing of the plot to kill the archbishop's brother Franz, of course, but did mention that he, Herman Ramers, had gained access to Münster. Herman also mentioned that he'd met with John of Leiden and that John believed the Anabaptists were destined to spread over the world. The letter painted John as supremely confident of divinely assisted success, as indeed he was. Ramers's letter also suggested feigning lifting the siege to draw out John's forces in pursuit, followed by a surprise attack that would surround John and his bodyguard and capture him while leaving most of the townspeople alive.

Herman Ramers hoped the archbishop would listen to his counsel. He believed Herman von Waldeck a moderate man who preferred to minimize bloodshed, unlike his brother Franz. Ramers also knew that Duke John of Cleves-Jülich inclined in the same direction. If Franz von Waldeck were dead, perhaps those two would see the wisdom of his plan.

It was a lot of hoping, true. But worth it for the chance to save the lives of his fellow soldiers and the lives of the townspeople who used to be his neighbors.

As for Herman Ramers, his plan was that as soon as he introduced Heille Feicken into the bishop's presence, he'd sneak out of the camp again, steal a horse, and ride as far from Münster as he could. If the plan he and Heinrich had devised happened to work, he'd hear of it eventually and come back later to claim his reward. If it didn't, no one in Westphalia would ever see his face again. He'd go to France first. Herman spoke tolerable French, and King Francis always needed more experienced soldiers for his wars.

Although the odds seemed slight, when Herman looked at Heille, he concluded she just might pull off her mission. Although she was a few years beyond youthful beauty, she had a very pretty face, long brown hair, a buxom figure, and had shown no outward signs of anxiety so far. Heille was attractive enough to catch the bishop's eye, but she didn't stick out by being awkward or saying rash things. Maybe, just maybe, she could do it.

Heille said, "After I kill von Waldeck like Judith killed Holofernes, either with my poison or with my dagger, the armies of Antichrist will be leaderless. God's faithful people will march forth to victory."

"Amen. Now, let's get moving."

Chapter 22

Münster

July of 1534

Heinrich Gresbeck, now Captain of the Night Watch at St. Ludger's Gate, stood forlornly on the outer walls of Münster in the pale dawn, leaning on his halberd. The cool breeze stirred the ripped elbow of his doublet, which hung loosely from his increasingly slight frame. Although Heinrich tried to make sure Sofie and Hilde always ate before he did, Hilde especially, he had to eat something or else risk falling asleep from exhaustion while on watch. That crime, like every other new law in Münster, bore the penalty of death.

The sun would be up in moments, but for now, the patches of clouds glowed with deep pink and purple hues. It was such a peaceful, sublime scene, Heinrich thought. Quiet, too, except for the roosters. Until he lowered his gaze from the clouds to the plains below.

Already, he could see it emerge from the gray shadows. Heille Feicken's head on a pike, right next to the skull of John Matthys. The rest of Heille's headless body lay strapped to a wheel planted beside the pikes. The body was upside down. Heinrich took this as conclusive proof that the plan he and Herman Ramers concocted had failed. Heinrich just hoped that Herman was now hundreds of miles from Münster. It seemed likely, or else he'd see his friend's head impaled on a pike, too.

In one respect, however, Heinrich was thankful he was on watch this morning. Not only was the last watch of the night the quietest, when very little ever happened, but if the enemy hadn't made any sudden movements during the night, it wasn't likely an attack would take place the next day, either. So, once the sun was up, and he could confirm everything looked just as it had the day before, that usually signaled a quiet day ahead.

Taking this watch also gave Heinrich an excuse to go home to Brigitte and sleep through today's summons to the cathedral square. The watch was exempt from any summons. He trusted that Sofie and Kurt would attend and bring him the news, however strange it was, afterward.

He sighed again. Life in Brigitte's house wasn't so bad, if only they had a little more to eat. Heinrich liked a lot of things about his new wife. Brigitte was smart, resourceful, and just a little on the feisty side. He liked that combination. If Brigitte were a man, she'd have made a good soldier with traits like that. Most important in the present, she shared Heinrich's view of making sure the health of the girls came first. After Heinrich watched her treat Sofie and Hilde just like she did her own children, he realized that Brigitte didn't have a selfish bone in her body.

True, she tossed and turned all night in bed, and that was taking time to adjust to. And Brigitte seemed unconcerned with what her own children were up to at any given time, always trusting they'd be home at some point. That went against Heinrich's nature. All things considered, though, he liked Brigitte and was happy with her.

As he stared off at the enemy camp and saw everything remained in the same place it'd been yesterday, Heinrich yawned.

He and Brigitte agreed on one other important thing. The night of their marriage, Heinrich told her he would've asked her for her hand years ago, except that part of him felt like he'd be dishonoring Liese if he did. He'd always liked Brigitte, after all, and was grateful to have her for his neighbor, but he probably never would've asked her to wed if not for the Anabaptists making marriage mandatory.

To his surprise, she'd said she understood, and that she felt much the same after losing her own husband to the plague. That made things easier between them. They also agreed that if Münster ever came to its senses, and if they managed to make it out of the present pickle alive, they'd consider making the marriage permanent at that point. In the meantime, they'd play their roles and hope things didn't grow too much worse.

A couple hours after the sun broke the horizon, Engelbert Eding arrived on the walls with a handful of men to relieve Heinrich's watch of its duties.

"Good morning, Deacon," Heinrich said quietly in the warm, clear morning air.

"Good morning to you, Captain. Nothing to report, I take it."

"Nothing unusual, no. Although, to be honest, I'm a little uneasy."

"How so? You've got good judgment, Heinrich Gresbeck. If you're uneasy, then I'm uneasy."

"Well, Engelbert, have you noticed the bishop's forces seem to have increased their cannon barrages lately?"

"I have, yes. We repair the damage to the walls every night, at the prophet's instructions. The women of the city bring up the stone, and our stonemasons repair whatever damage the cannonballs do. So far, however, the bishop hasn't tried to follow up any of the cannon attacks. I presume that's either because the damage is too slight, or he's probing for a weak spot in our walls."

"That may be true, Engelbert, but I'm not sure. Normally, a cannon barrage precedes infantry attack. If the cannons can punch a hole in the walls that's wide enough, then the infantry advances and storms the breach. But the landsknechts outside the walls aren't even bothering to form up."

"Because they know our walls are too strong, and they lack the numbers to storm the city, I hope."

Heinrich's face lit up. "That's it! You've got it!"

Eding gave Heinrich a dull look. "What do you mean? There's nothing special about what I just said. Everyone can see that for themselves."

"No, Engelbert, that's not what I mean. You're right that the city walls are too strong, and our enemies lack the strength to storm them right now. But that doesn't mean they aren't up to something. Do you know what a sapper is, Engelbert?"

"A sapper?"

"People who tunnel underground. They build a tunnel underneath the enemy's fortifications, put a bunch of gunpowder in the tunnel, and then light it off. The explosion wrecks the city walls and collapses them from below. That may be what von Waldeck's men are up to!"

"Does that work?"

"Not always. You need good mining engineers to make sure the tunnel is deep enough to get under the moat and that it ends up right underneath the enemy walls. But the Saar Valley isn't far away. Von Waldeck could easily have hired some people with mining expertise over the past several months."

"What are the countermeasures, Heinrich?"

"I can't think of any good ones, really. You can dig a tunnel of your own where you think the enemy is and try to break into their system of tunnels and collapse them. It's exceptionally dangerous to do that, though. Really, the best defense is to hope they don't set off the explosion in the right spot, or it's too deep underground to do any real damage. Usually that's a safe bet, too, but you never know. I'd better inform John of Leiden and the Elders."

"It'll have to wait. You can't go tell them now."

"Why not, Engelbert?"

"John of Leiden is getting married today. Right about now, in fact."

"What? Married? He's got a wife. Knipperdollinck's daughter. Has she died?"

"He's taking a second wife. Divara, the widow of John Matthys."

"You're kidding. Two wives? What's going on, Engelbert? You're a deacon. What have I missed that a captain of the watch needs to know about?"

"Today, John of Leiden plans to pronounce polygamy legal in the New Jerusalem."

Sofie and Kurt Boetmester stood in the audience, speechless. They'd just witnessed John of Leiden take Divara, the widow of John Matthys, as his wife. His second wife. Now, he stood to address the gathering in the cathedral square, the teenage beauty at his side. As usual, a bodyguard surrounded John and the twelve Elders. Sofie noticed that Bernhard Knipperdollinck was not present at the gathering. Not a surprise, considering the circumstances.

At first, Sofie had assumed something had happened to Diana Knipperdollinck, and that was why the prophet had taken another wife. But there she was, standing and watching the proceedings with a neutral look on her face. John of Leiden hadn't announced a divorce from Diana, either. He simply had two wives now.

John spoke to the onlookers. Like usual, his voice boomed over the hushed, shocked gathering. "Brothers and sisters, today is the dawn of a new era in God's Kingdom. The Father deems the time has come for his Elect to grow, increase, and spread over the world. The patriarchs of the Old Testament lived according to

God's will. Like in the Old Testament, twelve Elders rule the New Jerusalem. Likewise, the Father desires that his people should take as many wives as they desire, just as the patriarchs of the Old Testament did."

Before he could say anything more, astonishment rippled through the crowd. Everyone began speaking to their neighbors.

"I don't believe it," Sofie gasped to Kurt.

"That can't be true," he replied quietly. "It's absurd. Stupid. An abomination." When Sofie looked in her husband's face, he quickly said, "Don't worry, Sofie. Never. I'm not taking another wife any more than you're taking another husband. No matter what anyone says."

Sofie gave him a kiss and a hug. When she pulled back, however, she saw something new in Kurt's eyes. Like part of his thoughts were far away. "Kurt?"

He blinked a couple times. "Don't worry, Sofie. I'm just in shock."

Before Sofie had time to think about where she'd seen that look before, the gunshot brought the entire crowd to silence.

Sofie's eyes darted to the stage to see who the Elders had killed now for displeasing the Father, but instead she saw the arquebus pointed to the sky, the puff of gunpowder expanding around the bodyguard who'd fired. John of Leiden held up his arms for calm.

"All womenfolk, virgins, maidens, and widows, all those who are marriageable, should all take husbands without delay. The wives whose husbands have fled the city and abandoned them here should likewise take other husbands, since your old husbands are godless and have fled from the Word of God and don't number among God's Elect. To those sisters, I say that for so long did you live in heathendom in your marriage, it was not a real marriage.

"The Lord has proclaimed that we must be fruitful and multiply and that His people shall cover the earth. Therefore, each man who has a wife who is no longer fruitful should take a younger wife who is. If she becomes fruitful, the man shall have nothing to do with the woman until she delivers the child. However, if the man is unable to stay away from women during that time, he should take another wife, and so follow the Father's command. In this fashion shall we increase the world, in accordance with the Father's wishes.

"The Father also desires, however, that each husband must honor each of his wives and live with them without the blush of sin. The Lord wishes for His people to increase, but we must maintain the godliness of the Elect. Brothers, if you wish to please the Father and take additional wives, you should send word to the sister or go alone into her house, and you should ask for her hand in marriage. If it's the case that her spirit doesn't attest to her willingness to have a husband, or if she's betrothed to someone else, then you should leave her alone and go to someone else. For as long as God puts this in her mind and her spirit then attests to it, then it's God's will that she should then get someone else who God assigns to her.

"Dear brothers and sisters, when the brother works to get a Christian sister, so that they both wish to become a married couple, they should pray to God for three days that it should be His will that he take her and that he may live with her, that this may be God's pleasure, that it should be for His praise and for His glory, and that he may increase the world with her and all the women whom you get."

The longer John spoke, the more bizarre he sounded to Sofie. Some of the smatterings of conversation she heard around her indicated that others in the crowd thought he'd gone nuts, too. At least none of this would change her life. She was married already, and Hilde was far too young to think about marriage, just fourteen years old. Sofie just prayed that the craziness would be over before her sister was old enough to get more involved in it than she'd already become.

Still John of Leiden went on. "Just as the patriarchs of the Old Testament ruled in the name of the Lord, so it shall be within the families of the New Jerusalem. All wives must refer to their husbands as 'lord.'"

Try as she might, Sofie couldn't envision that Brigitte would ever say that to her uncle.

John paused in his proclamations for a moment while one of the Elders, Conrad Kruse, whispered something in the prophet's ear. After nodding a few times, John continued.

"All God's Elect will be cared for in the New Jerusalem. The Father wishes for all His people to know the love and support of a family. Therefore, the Father has also revealed that all old women and widows in the city must choose a guardian. Although this man shall not be their lawful husband, the guardian shall watch over his wards as if he were a husband. He shall be responsible for them, and they shall also refer to him as their lord. The lord must instruct the old women and the widows, provide for their nurturing in the faith, and be their keeper.

"Should either party fail to see to their duties, the lord to take care and instruct his wards, or the widows and old women to give obedience to their lord, they shall face punishment according to the laws of the New Jerusalem.

"The hour of the Father's return draws near. Soon, we will sweep away the ungodly and replace them with God's holy people and spread over the earth. Go, now, and live out the Father's commands for his people!"

"Well, what do you make of that?" Kurt asked Sofie as John of Leiden retreated from the stage, his rich fur cape flaring behind him. The twelve Elders and their guards fell into step behind the prophet.

"I'm glad I've got a husband who loves me, and I won't have to face all of this lunacy, that's what I think. But why, Kurt?"

"What do you mean?"

"Why the last part? The part about widows and older women having to take a guardian. I don't get it."

"I don't understand very much that's happened lately, Sofie. I just don't see how it can work to have more than one wife. And I don't plan to find out," he told her with a kiss and an arm around Sofie's shoulder as they turned and left the cathedral square.

"Thank you, my lo—." Sofie winced. "Sorry, Kurt, I just can't say it."

"You know I would never ask you to," he replied with his handsomest smile.

Sofie smiled back. Another reason to love her husband.

Chapter 23

Münster

July of 1534

Franz von Waldeck belched as he dined on another plate of roast chicken served with lemons and pepper. The lemons, just arrived from Spain, offered a nice contrast to the otherwise spicy dish. Around him, his comrades in arms sat eating their fill. Duke John of Cleves-Jülich and Franz's brother Herman sipped from silver goblets filled with white wine as they discussed strategy to bring the siege to its conclusion.

Franz began. "I believe it's time, gentlemen, to finish what we've started and bring this entire affair to its overdue climax. In two days, we shall mass our cannons and open a breach in Münster's walls. Our numbers are greater than in May. Great enough, I judge, to follow up a breach with a coordinated assault. I want you to make sure the mercenaries under your command are ready."

Herman chewed his lip at this news. Duke John opened his mouth to speak but thought better of it.

"Something you wish to say, my duke?" the bishop asked while he wiped his mouth with his bushy beard.

John of sighed, looked at the bishop, and then looked down again. "No, I believe not," he muttered at last, without looking up.

"Good. In my plan, you'll provide the diversion. We'll place some token cannons in your lines and have you fire them off and make a lot of noise like something's afoot in your district. Even you should be capable of that. While your diversion happens, I'll take the best landsknechts from my forces, and the best from Herman's, and we'll give the southeastern walls a good pummeling before storming them and capturing the city."

"Brother, if I may," Herman put in. "Why are you confident of victory now? Could we not let the siege do its work? That would cost no lives on our side, while assaulting the city will surely cost many."

"That is true, brother Herman. But we have lives to spare. The more mercenaries who die, the fewer of them we must pay from the spoils of victory. Besides, surely the defenders are low in morale by now. They're fully surrounded, and the skull of their chief prophet rests firmly affixed to a pike within view of the city. What do your spies have to say on that matter?"

Herman returned to chewing his lip for a moment, then replied. "They report that John of Leiden has declared polygamy God's will. The city foments with outrage even as we speak."

"You see, our timing is perfect. God will smile not on those Anabaptist heretics who defile God's holy commands, but on us, the true believers of His holy church. This is a sign that it's our time to attack and claim the victory! Now, go and make your preparations."

His commanders gone, Franz von Waldeck crossed his arms and frowned. He hadn't told either Duke John or his brother of the letter he'd received from Emperor Charles that morning. Fresh forces, imperial soldiers under the command of Count Wirich of Falkenstein, were on their way to aid in the siege. This was wonderful news except for one detail. Charles had also commanded von Waldeck to turn over control of the siege to the count. This, the bishop could not abide. Münster was his city, in his bishopric. He'd not be beholden to the emperor, or Count Wirich, or anyone else for that matter, if it were in his power to avoid it. So, the attack would go forward tomorrow. With any luck, he would sit on the bishop's throne in St. Lambert's and present Count Wirich with John of Leiden's head when the count arrived at Münster.

Outside Franz von Waldeck's great tent, its banners and pennants sagging in the still July air, Duke John took Archbishop Herman von Waldeck aside in the fading evening light.

"Herman, what kind of unchristian revenge has entered your brother's mind? Do you agree with me that this attack is likely to be fruitless?"

Herman nodded, although he said nothing.

"Then why not say so? Your brother might listen to you, rather than sending these soldiers to their deaths so rashly."

"He might, but I doubt it. Franz is not himself. Even less so, as the days pass. I believe that when that woman, Heille Feicken, attempted to poison him and he nearly drank the poisoned wine, that sent him over the edge. Whether time and gentle persuasion can bring him back, God only knows."

"What of the letter you shared with me, Herman? The letter from Herman Ramers recommending luring John of Leiden into a trap but sparing the town itself?"

"What of it?"

"Isn't the idea worth a try? I cannot believe that every single resident of Münster has lost their minds within months. Surely, opposition to the Anabaptists remains in the city. Didn't your own spies report that people are outraged over this polygamy proclamation?"

"They are. But John, if the people of the city had it in their power to reclaim their city from the fanatics who lead it, wouldn't they have done so by now? Either the people stand more solidly behind their leaders than you believe, or their leaders have deprived them of the power to make a change. Either way, however much I abhor bloodshed, I fear we may see some before Münster is back in our hands."

Now it was John's turn to chew his lip. "This is not a good idea," he said at last. "No good will come of it. If we attack and fail a second time, will it not strengthen the morale of Münster's defenders? That would only reinforce the authority of their leaders. And that, I fear, will undo all the work of our siege these past months."

"You speak truly, John, but I know one thing that you don't."

The duke's eyebrows arched.

"For several days now, we've been tunneling under the city walls in the southeast section near St. Ludger's Gate. Sappers. The plan is to explode the walls from below at the same time our cannons attack. My brother is confident the combination will create enough chaos to allow our men to storm the city."

"And what do you think of this plan, Herman?"

The archbishop shrugged. "It doesn't matter what I think. The outcome rests in God's hands now."

Chapter 24

Sofie and Kurt walked through the nearly deserted marketplace the next morning, just as the brilliant sun rose above the rooftops of Münster. It promised to be a very warm day. The light glinted off cobwebs that lined some of the shops and booths where Münster's craftsmen used to sell their goods. Although people like Uncle Heinrich and Kurt still made cabinets when they had supplies of wood, all trade and commerce went through the deacons now. Whatever people produced, they surrendered to the deacons, who paid the makers in kind, rather than in coin.

"I'm glad we took the long way home, Kurt," Sofie began. "Whenever I go through the cathedral square now, I just shiver in fear. It's worth it to me to go around."

"I understand," Kurt said as they walked out of the marketplace and south down St. Ludger's Street. "And I don't blame you, after what happened to Hilde." As Kurt walked, he scratched his head.

"I'm just glad your mother had some spare stockings stowed in your family home for us to use. Mine are passable, but Hilde has nearly worn hers out, and they're full of holes. I'm so worried about her, Kurt. I know we both try to slip her some extra food whenever we can, but we're all getting so thin. My stomach rumbles at me every day. I'm sure hers does, too."

"Wait, what's this?" Kurt stopped walking and scratched his head again.

"What's the matter? I don't see anything unusual, Kurt."

"Look at this." He held out his hand to her.

"Kurt! That's your hair! Turn around."

Kurt complied.

"I see a small patch in the back, Kurt. Is that where you just scratched?"

"Yeah, I think so."

"How can your hair be falling out? You're way too young for that."

"I don't know, Sofie. Maybe it's all the strain and pressure getting to me. My dad, Big John, always joked that he's bald because raising Conrad and me made him that way, but maybe it's not a joke after all."

"Oh, Kurt. What'll we do?"

"It's only hair, Sofie," Kurt tried to shrug as he resumed walking. "Losing some hair isn't going to kill me."

Not knowing what to say, Sofie continued in silence, taking Kurt's arm in hers. Right now, she just wanted to get home, sit down, give Hilde the stockings, and try to figure out why some of Kurt's hair was falling out in tufts.

Just before she reached her door, however, Karl Schweren, Rudolf's older brother, came bursting out of his family's house. His eyes wide, he ran up to Sofie and Kurt and grabbed Sofie's shoulders. His breath came in ragged gasps. Sofie saw tears.

"Karl, what's wrong? What's happened?"

"They came about an hour ago. It's Hilde. She's taken. I've been running around looking for you ever since."

"She's gone? Where did she go? We told her to stay put in the house while we got the stockings from Kurt's house."

Now the tears came freely. "No, Sofie, not gone. Taken." Weakly, he let go of Sofie's shirt.

"By whom?" Kurt demanded.

"John of Leiden."

Sofie froze.

Karl spluttered out the rest of the story even as he broke down. "I'm so sorry, Sofie. I just got home for a break from baking when I saw John carry your sister out of the house, and I demanded to know what he was doing. He told me God wanted him to marry Hilde, and that she was to be one of his wives."

Unsteady, Sofie fell to her knees. "How can that be? She's only fourteen!" Kurt tried to console her by taking her shoulders, but she shook his hands off.

"I tried to stop them, Sofie. I did. But John's guards were with him, and they threatened me with death if I opposed the Father's will. I couldn't stop them, Sofie."

"We've got to get her back. We can't let this happen," Kurt stated.

Sofie put her hands to her temples and screamed.

Both Kurt and Karl stood motionless. They'd never seen Sofie like this before. Again, Kurt attempted to comfort her with a hand on her shoulder.

Sofie, however, had already risen to her feet and taken off toward St. Lambert's Cathedral at a sprint. Kurt and Karl ran after her.

Moments later, when Sofie ran into the marketplace and prepared to turn left into the cathedral square, a crowd exploded from the other direction, from the cathedral square into the marketplace. Instantly, it engulfed Sofie in the mass of bodies as it surged toward the city council building at the northern end of the marketplace. When Kurt and Karl reached the marketplace a few seconds after Sofie had, they couldn't see her.

"Where?" Kurt shouted while he bounced on his toes, trying to find his wife in the throng. Karl did the same.

"There!" Karl shouted, pointing. "She's at the front of the crowd! See her on the steps to the city council building?"

Without another word, both young men joined the mob in the hope of rescuing Sofie.

Once Sofie saw what was going on, however, rescue was the last thing on her mind.

A man she recognized, Henry Mollenhecke, a locksmith from her neighborhood, directed the crowd toward the basement of the city council building. Pulling out the key and turning it in the lock, he threw open the door and shouted, "In with the traitors!"

Sofie watched as the mob tossed first John of Leiden, then Bernhard Knipperdollinck, and then the rest of the twelve Elders into the basement, below the street and out of sight. Bernard Rothmann landed in the makeshift dungeon as well, along with about a dozen other men whom Sofie didn't recognize but figured were prominent Anabaptists.

Only when Sofie emerged back on the street was she reunited with Kurt and Karl.

"Sofie! What's happened?" Kurt shouted, so Sofie could hear him over the cheering crowd.

"An uprising, I think," she shouted back. "John of Leiden, Knipperdollinck, Rothmann, and the Elders are all prisoners in the city council basement! This could be our chance!"

Before anyone could say anything more, Henry Mollenhecke shouted for quiet, his voice booming through the marketplace. Hands cupped in supplication, he shouted to the assembly, "O God in Heaven, look down here and punish the great wrong that's taking place in this city, and whoever is wrong, may you punish him!"

Then Mollenhecke lowered his hands and shouted to everyone. "We have the betrayers in our hands. Half of us will stay here to guard the prisoners. The rest must go to St. Servatius's Gate and

St. Maurice's Gate. Open the gates, take the white flag, so you can meet the bishop under parley, and lead his troops into the city. We'll hand over the Anabaptist leaders in exchange for restoring the bishop and ending the siege. Now go! Quickly!"

At this signal, a portion of the crowd marched directly east, toward St. Maurice's Gate, and another portion southeast, toward St. Servatius's Gate. Although all the weapons remained locked in the common storehouses administered by the deacons, Sofie saw that the rebels wielded makeshift arms—kitchen knives, cleavers like butchers used, wooden clubs made from furniture, scythes for cutting wheat, blacksmith's hammers, and other improvised tools and farm implements.

Sofie didn't know if it'd be enough. The soldiers at the gates had armor, swords, and pikes. She looked at Kurt and Karl. "What'll we do?"

"Do we even know if the bishop will accept the offer?" Karl wondered.

"And what about Hilde? Where is she?"

"Are we with the rebels?" Kurt asked. "I think we should be. It's our best chance."

Sofie looked at her husband. "Did you know about this?"

"Just rumors. I didn't know whether to believe them. If I'd known they were true, I'd have told you."

"I think we should stay together, whatever we do," Sofie replied. "But we need to move quickly."

"But we're needed in three places," Karl countered. "We need to rescue Hilde if we can, but they'll probably need help to storm the gates and to watch the prisoners here, too. It won't be long before the city council gets word of what's happened and tries to liberate the prisoners."

"It'll all be for nothing if we can't get the gates open and make a deal with Bishop von Waldeck," Kurt said. "I think we need to do that."

"But I want to find my sister and make sure she's safe. That's what most important to me," Sofie pleaded.

"But both those things will be for nothing if John of Leiden escapes and regains control of the city," Karl answered. "If he's freed, Hilde will still be in danger, and the city will fight back against von Waldeck. What'll we do? We have too many choices."

For several moments, all three stood looking at each other. It was true; all three choices were interdependent. If any of the three went poorly, all would go poorly.

Finally, Kurt spoke. "I think we should do what's in our hearts. There's danger no matter what we do. But we've got to go now, or else it won't matter what we choose."

"Then I'm going to the cathedral to get Hilde back," Sofie said. "My sister's already been through enough."

"I'm going to stay here and stand with Henry Mollenhecke," Karl told the others. "He lives in our neighborhood, and my family has known him for years. Henry is an honorable man, but he'll need all the help he can get here."

"I'm going to go to St. Servatius's Gate," Kurt sighed. "At least one of the gates must be opened, or nothing else matters."

Sofie looked in her husband's eyes. "I love you," she said as she reached in for a hug.

Kurt put both his hands on her neck and gently pulled Sofie in for a deep kiss. "I *will* see you again," he said. Then, he was off to the gate.

It wasn't long before Karl Schweren's fears came true. Herman Tilbeck, Master of the City, marched toward the city council building with a mass of soldiers at his back. It looked to Karl as if he commanded seven or eight hundred men. Many were the recent immigrants from the Netherlands, identified by their clothing, and most of the mercenaries who'd defected marched with Tilbeck, too. Karl looked around. Enough of the rebels had gone to the gates that the defenders numbered only two hundred or so. How had Tilbeck rallied so many men so quickly? Had someone betrayed the rebels?

Tilbeck stepped forward. Mollenhecke went out into the now glaring sunlight to meet him. Karl thought them an interesting contrast. Tilbeck wore the rich robes and doublet of the wealthy, dyed a deep blue with scarlet trim. Mollenhecke, however, had on the brown leather jerkin and soot-stained hose of a craftsman and laborer. Tilbeck spoke first.

"It's over, Henry. Give up the prisoners. On behalf of the city council of Münster, I demand your surrender."

Mollenhecke didn't respond at first. Instead, he looked Tilbeck up and down. Karl realized he was playing for time, hoping against hope that relief would come from the gates before a fight began.

"Herman Tilbeck. I see you're happy to be someone else's tool, like always."

"Now, now, Henry. There's no need for petty insults," Tilbeck replied, fingering the cloth hat he wore and, Karl noted, had refused to remove in Mollenhecke's presence, a sign of measured disrespect for someone Tilbeck considered beneath him.

"I see you've got the dregs of the city at your back, Tilbeck. Nothing's changed in that respect."

"And the city holds a lot of dregs, to be sure. But at least they're loyal to their leaders and know how to follow orders from their betters. A lesson that others still need to learn, it seems."

"Blind obedience is no virtue."

"Ah, but it can be. Now, enough of the games, Henry. Are you going to give up, or must things get rough?"

"You know the answer to that."

"Very well, then, I suppose the dregs will have to prove their worth. Where shall I place the pike displaying your head when things are over?"

"Right next to yours, Tilbeck. Right next to yours."

And with that, the battle of the marketplace began.

Kurt Boetmester already was reconsidering his decision to leave Sofie. Not because of fear. He'd been scared most of the time for weeks now. But he'd vowed to stand by her, come what may. And the rebels had to open at least one gate. If they didn't, their rebellion would fail. As Kurt ran toward St. Servatius's Gate, he pledged to himself he'd never leave Sofie again.

It didn't take long to arrive—the gate was southeast of the marketplace, and Salt Street ran directly to the gate. Kurt realized, belatedly, that he had no weapon, but that didn't frighten him. At least one person would be down by the time he got there, and he'd scavenge a weapon that way. What did frighten him, however, was that it might not matter what weapon he ended up with because he had no training in how to use anything more dangerous than a wood chisel.

Once Kurt got to the gate of the inner wall, he paused a split-second to survey the fight. It looked promising. Although inferior in weaponry, the rebels outnumbered the gate guards considerably, and Kurt saw several men on both sides already bleeding and lying upon the cobblestones.

He snatched up the nearest weapon he could find and entered the fray. It was just the leg of someone's table, but Kurt didn't mind. It gave him reach, and he was familiar with wood.

Nearby, a rebel was engaged with one of the Anabaptist guards. He was on his back while the guard straddled his body. Although he'd lost his helmet, the guard had wrapped both hands around the windpipe of the rebel beneath him. Kurt wound up and delivered a tremendous blow to the head of the guard, knocking the man out cold.

He extended his hand to help his fellow rebel back to his feet. Kurt didn't know the man, but as he rose, he thanked Kurt. Then, he pointed and yelled, "Look! An opening! We can get to the winch that opens the inner gate!"

Kurt saw it was true. The masses of bodies had parted in the melee, clearing a path to the gatehouse.

"Come on, brother!" the man yelled, and he stumbled toward the apparatus that would raise the gate.

Kurt followed. He could see the man's wounds. A crimson stain spread down his left leg, causing him to stagger toward their objective at a limping run.

They reached the winch at the same time. The injured man pulled on the iron wheel with all his might while Kurt assisted.

Slowly, agonizingly slowly, the heavy iron gate inched upward. Beyond it, Kurt could see the wooden bridge leading to the gate on the outer walls.

Soon, a third pair of hands joined them, and Kurt was aware of several more bodies massing near the gate. They'd done it! Looking around, Kurt saw the rebels had subdued or killed all the guards at the inner gate.

With another heave, they raised the gate above shoulder height, and the waiting rebels ducked under it and then surged forward to storm the outer gatehouse. Some now wielded swords they'd taken from the defeated Anabaptists. As they charged, Kurt heard the report from several arquebuses fill the balmy morning air. When he looked again, three rebels were down on the causeway, blood spurting from wounds where lead balls had entered their bodies.

"Come on," his companion grunted. "Just a little higher, and then we can join them."

Kurt leaned into it and strained. They raised the gate until it was about eight feet off the ground, two-thirds of the way up.

"That'll do," his new friend gasped in relief as he locked the gate in place. "Let's go!"

Picking his table leg back up, Kurt ran onto the causeway, his veins pulsing with energy and excitement as he emerged into the bright July sun. Another blast rent the air as more arquebuses fired from above him. Kurt felt the air stir as a lead ball whizzed past his ear, but miraculously, the defenders did not hit him. Sweat stung his eyes. Kurt wiped it away.

Just a short distance ahead all was chaos. No one had much room to maneuver on the causeway because it was only about twenty feet wide. So, the scene in front of the outer gatehouse was one of bodies compacted together. Fists punched, legs kicked, fingers tried to rake eyes, hands grasped for throats, and men tripped and fell over each other.

When he arrived at the melee, Kurt couldn't believe his luck. Just as he prepared to charge, table leg in front of him like a lance, a gap parted in the mass of humanity, and he leapt through it.

There it was. The winch to the outer gate. Kurt leapt to grab it and hauled down with all his strength. The gate rose an inch, then fell back. He needed help. Taking up his table leg, he jumped back into the fray just in time to whack the arm of an Anabaptist who'd raised his sword to strike. The man cried out, then curled on the wooden causeway, writhing in pain, his arm probably broken.

"Thanks, friend," the rebel he rescued said.

"Come on, it's heavy, I need help, but we can do it," Kurt replied as he pulled the man up and pointed to the winch for the outer gate.

Together, they strained to get the gate up. It rose a few inches at a time, but soon, the gate was up to the height of a man's waist. They'd almost done it!

"Heave!" Kurt panted, muscles straining.

"I'm try—" A blow to the back of the head cut off the words.

As the rebel crumpled to the stone floor of the gatehouse, Kurt just had time to see a man step from behind the body. A young man wearing a brightly striped doublet of green and yellow.

"You—" was all Kurt had time to say. Even as he released the winch to defend himself, the young man drew back his right arm and then lunged.

Kurt felt the dagger enter his chest and pierce his lungs. The stab of pain stopped him in place as his mouth opened wordlessly.

Stepping forward, the young man twisted the dagger in deeper. "Now I'll take back what should've been mine."

Kurt tried to respond, but the words gurgled and died in his throat.

His opponent drew out the dagger and then used it to slash Kurt's neck. Kurt sank to his knees as he watched the blood cascade down the front of his body, then fell on his face.

The last thing Kurt Boetmester remembered in life was a familiar voice hissing in his ear, "You stole Sofie from me. Now I'm taking her back."

Kurt never even felt it when his body splashed unceremoniously into the moat that surrounded Münster, there to sink with dozens of other dying and dead men.

Sofie's hair flew wildly behind her as she ran up to the double doors of St. Lambert's Cathedral. Wiping her tear-streaked face with her sleeve, she paused just a moment, took a breath to steady herself, and then pulled open one of the heavy doors. It took all her strength, but once she'd cracked it sufficiently, she raced inside.

The sanctuary, brightly lit by light streaming through the windows, stood empty and silent. No sign of Hilde, or anyone else, anywhere. When the cathedral door shut behind her, the sound echoed softly through the lofty vault of the church.

"Where?" Sofie whispered. The tears were on the verge of returning as she ran down the aisle toward the altar, looking this way and that frantically.

"This is where John lives. Hilde and the other wives must be here somewhere," she whispered to herself again. "They aren't with John at the city council building, so they must be here."

Sofie stopped, stood still, and listened. Nothing. "I'll find Hilde if I have to search every room in St. Lambert's," she said out loud.

Looking through the jagged glass shards that remained of the window on the third floor of the city council hall, Karl watched in dread as the Anabaptists inexorably dragged a cannon into the marketplace square. With injured and bleeding men all around him, things looked dire.

Henry Mollenhecke croaked out orders from beside Karl. "Prepare for a last sortie," he said to those gathered around him. "I'll lead it." When Karl looked at his neighbor, he saw that Henry's right arm hung uselessly at his side, and every time he spoke, Henry winced in pain from a blow to the ribs he'd suffered. His hair, matted with blood and dirt, was disheveled, and he used his sword like a cane in order to keep himself upright. He couldn't charge anywhere, much less into the hostile crowd now encircling the city council building.

"Stay here, Henry. You're wounded," another of the rebels, whom Karl recognized as Derek Buttermans, said to his leader, stating the obvious. Derek had injuries, too. Blood caked his face from a deep gash near his scalp.

"Nonsense. I'm leading the attack," Henry grunted. "This was my plan, and I'll see it through, for good or ill. Ill being the more likely, it appears. But, if we can just buy a little more time, it's possible that our men have opened a gate and the bishop's troops are on their way to relieve the city."

"I'll go up to the roof and have a look," Derek informed his leader.

"Stay here. They'll shoot at you."

"They'll shoot at me if I stay, too."

It was true enough, Karl knew. Every now and then, the Anabaptists let fire with an arquebus volley. The guns were slow to reload between shots, and Karl didn't know how much ammunition the besiegers had left, but apparently, they hadn't run out yet. The city council building had very few windows left intact, and broken glass littered the floor.

This left Karl sad. Not because he cared about the building itself, but glass was uncommon and expensive. Only a few buildings in town had glass windows. To him, it seemed a shame to destroy something so rare and beautiful.

While Derek Buttermans clambered up to the roof, another of the rebels spoke to Mollenhecke. "Henry, let someone else lead. No one doubts your bravery. We just don't want to see you killed like that."

"I have a feeling I'm going to be killed in any case. Whether quickly now or slowly from my injuries, I don't think it matters," he wheezed in reply. "If John of Leiden's lackeys don't shoot me today, they'll hang me tomorrow. Might as well get it over with."

"Don't give up hope yet, Henry. We don't know what's happened at the walls. Why don't you stay here and create a diversion for us? We've got a few arquebuses left here. You give them a volley to draw their attention."

"Get ready!" another defender yelled out. "They're coming!"

Karl Schweren looked down as the crowd surged toward the front door of the city council building. They carried a workbench taken from the marketplace in front of them like a battering ram while they charged. In an instant, the handful of defenders on the bottom floor who still had lead balls for their arquebuses let fire. Two of the attackers went down, but it wasn't enough to disrupt the charge.

Mollenhecke spoke. "Steady, men. Get ready." A pause. "Now!"

On command, half a dozen of the defenders on the third floor, Karl included, opened the grates of several foot stoves and dumped the contents out the window, their glowing coals dropping on the attackers. Instantly, Karl heard the screams of people scalded and seared by the red-hot chunks. A cheer went up when the attackers dropped their workbench and withdrew.

"How much coal do we have left?" Henry Mollenhecke asked his comrades.

"Enough to repel one or two more attacks, Henry, but that's it."

He shook his head. "It won't be enough. See if you can find anything else around here that'll burn hot enough to make coals."

Suddenly, Buttermans returned from his foray onto the roof. Karl looked to see what he'd say but knew the answer even before Buttermans opened his mouth.

"It doesn't look good, Henry. I can't see the gates themselves because of the distance and the arquebus smoke hanging in the air, but I didn't see any troops marching into the city to relieve us. It appears both gates remain closed. I'm sorry, my friend, but I think we're on our own." He fell silent and looked at the floor.

Mollenhecke sighed. "We've failed, then. God has truly abandoned Münster."

Karl looked around while no one spoke for several moments. For a battle, it was eerie how quiet and still the third floor of the council building had become.

Finally, Mollenhecke spoke in the dull monotone of a man who knows he's beaten. "I will not surrender. Tilbeck knows I'm the leader of the rebellion, and I plan to go down fighting. It doesn't matter to me if I die now or tomorrow. I've tried to do what I thought was right. God have mercy on my soul."

Then, he looked each of his co-conspirators in the face. "If you wish to surrender and ask for your lives, I'll not fault you. It's been an honor, my brothers. I'll see you again at Heaven's Gate." With that, he limped toward the stairs, leaving his companions to decide how to face death.

A few followed instantly. Others shuffled their feet. A couple of men took a knee and prayed for guidance. Karl was just about to follow Mollenhecke when the cannon blast boomed. When the ball shattered the third floor of the building and the roof came down on top of him, Karl's world went dark.

Hilde leaped into her sister's arms. "Sofie! You found me! What's happening out there?"

"I've been looking for you for more than an hour, Hilde! The cathedral is empty. I never even thought to come next door to St. James's Church until I realized that truly no one was there."

"The prophet made us take shelter here when the mob came to capture him," Hilde told her sister.

Looking past Hilde, Sofie saw that Dianna Knipperdollinck, Divara, and two other women who she presumed must also be John of Leiden's wives stood huddled around the altar of St. James's sanctuary.

"He hasn't harmed you, has he?" Sofie asked while she hugged Hilde again.

"No, Sofie. Almost as soon as John took me out of the house, the men came armed to arrest him. Then Dianna led us over here. We've been hiding ever since, waiting for news. What's going on?"

"Some people in town have led a rebellion. They took John and the Elders to the city council building and locked them in the cellar there. Others went to storm the city gates and let the bishop's army inside the city. I don't know if they've succeeded."

"So, we aren't safe, yet?"

"I don't know anything else, Hilde. I just came to find you and see if you were safe."

"I'm fine, Sofie. But now, I'm scared again. What if soldiers come here? Who'll protect us then?"

"Maybe you should come home with me, Hilde. I really don't know where the safest place is, but I want you to be with me."

"My newest wife isn't going anywhere," stated a grim voice. It came from the open doors to the church behind Sofie. "God's Elect have triumphed over Satan's minions, and righteousness reigns in Münster once more."

Sofie turned to see John of Leiden. Although dirt encrusted his rich robes, he still stood tall, looming over both Sofie and Hilde as he advanced, bodyguards behind him. He had a new person beside him as well whom Sofie didn't recognize. A short man who walked with a limp.

Sofie's heart fell. The rebellion had failed. What had happened to Kurt and Karl? She tried to hide her fear but felt frozen in place, her shoulders tightening and tensing. Now, John of Leiden stood directly in front of her, his gaunt form towering over Sofie and Hilde.

"And how, my child, do you know of the plans of the rebels?"

"I-I saw them for myself w-when I went looking for Hilde," Sofie told him. It wasn't a complete lie, just the truth with a little twist. "W-When I saw things were getting dangerous, I wanted to find my s-sister and make sure she was safe."

"And for that, I thank you," he said with the hint of a smile. "Making sure the prophet's family is safe and cared for was a godly act on your part."

Sofie was about to fall to her knees and beg on Hilde's behalf when the trumpets sounded and the cannons boomed. All the people in St. James's Church huddled or covered their heads at the sound. All, that is, except John of Leiden.

"What's happening?" Divara shouted in a hysterical voice from where she knelt behind Sofie. "What's going on?"

"The city is under attack by Antichrist," John stated flatly. "I will lead the Elect forward to triumph. Stay here, my precious wives, where you'll be safe. Men, this way."

"Do not worry, my lord," the short man with the limp said to John of Leiden. "You shall triumph over the soldiers of Antichrist and deliver the New Jerusalem into its glory. I've foreseen this, just as I foresaw your escape from the dungeon a mere hour ago."

"And what else have you foreseen, Johann Dusentscher?"

"Soon, this nightmare will be over, and you will reign victorious over the New Jerusalem as God's king on Earth."

"And so it shall be, according to the will of the Father." With that, John of Leiden strode quickly from the church, followed by his guards and the limping Dusentscher, their boots echoing softly on the marble floor as they marched away.

God's king on Earth, Sofie repeated to herself. Then, it occurred to her that she already lived in a kingdom. A nightmare kingdom.

"Sofie, please stay here with me. I'm so frightened," Hilde whimpered.

"I'm not going anywhere, Hilde. I'm staying right here with you this time, no matter what."

"Keep up your fire, boys. Give it to 'em," Heinrich Gresbeck called to his men as Bishop von Waldeck's mercenaries advanced on Münster's outer wall with their scaling ladders.

The volleys of gunfire were, admittedly, a largely futile exercise. The arquebuses at his men's disposal weren't particularly accurate weapons. It was chance, as much as accuracy, that determined how many of the bishop's soldiers his men would hit. Add to that the fact that arquebuses took about a minute to reload between shots, and the guns' efficacy as weapons of war was altogether questionable in Heinrich's eyes.

Heinrich looked to his right, where the cannon bombardment had done considerable damage to the outer wall. Although townspeople were already at work bringing up stone and dirt fill to repair the wall, the cannon blasts had leveled a section near the gatehouse guarding the approach to Heinrich's gate. The rubble filled in the moat in places. The mercenaries would be able to bring their ladders directly to the outer wall where Heinrich stood.

And Münster faced a lot more mercenaries this time than it had in May.

Heinrich wasn't about to panic, however. He was an officer, and officers had to lead by example. So, he stood tall and waved his sword, directing the aim of his men. Meanwhile, he looked at the pot of oil now heated to a boil behind him. Should any of the mercenaries be so foolish as to try to go through the gate rather than over the wall, they would lose their skin. Literally.

The shout from below signaled to Heinrich that the ladders were coming up. At the same time, the attackers opened fire with their own arquebuses to provide cover for those climbing the ladders.

"Draw weapons, men! And push the ladders back down!" Heinrich shouted, although his men hardly needed the reminder.

Although the defenders largely succeeded in repelling the ladders, a few of the mercenaries reached the city ramparts. Then, the real fighting began. Heinrich Gresbeck took a deep breath, even as his heartbeat raced and the perspiration dripped down his body. It'd been a while since he'd done this.

Just as one attacker reached the top rung of the ladder and prepared to jump down onto the parapet, Heinrich gave him a hard kick in the chest. The splash of the man falling into the moat below followed momentarily.

The next man up swung his sword weakly to keep Heinrich at bay until he was over the wall. Seeing that his opponent had landed off balance, however, Heinrich swung his own sword, slashing downward. It connected with the man's shoulder, and he screamed as the blade pierced his body.

Withdrawing his blade, Heinrich was about to duck under the sword thrust of another opponent when a lead ball from an arquebus struck him in the upper right side of his chest.

Staggering backward as his weapon fell from his hand, Heinrich clutched at his wound even as the blood began to flow through his fingers.

He gasped for breath. Then, the ground exploded, and everything tilted to a crazy angle, knocking Heinrich from his feet.

As his shoulders and head hit the stone beneath him, the last thing to cross Heinrich's mind was to wonder why no one had listened to him when he'd warned them about sappers.

That evening, as the smoke from the battle began to lift over the city, a young man in a green and yellow striped doublet sat alone, his back to Münster's inner wall. Rudolf Schweren looked at his shaking hands, the rest of his body motionless. The hands that had killed two people just hours before. Including the husband of the woman he loved.

What have I done? he asked himself over and over. *What have I done?* Now that the rush of battle had left him, all Rudolf had was a hollow feeling that penetrated deep into his soul. Things should never have gone this far. *What have I done?*

Chapter 25

Münster

August of 1534

Tears streamed down Sofie's face at the coronation assembly in the cathedral square.

She'd wanted to wear mourning clothes today to show her outrage, but Brigitte had talked her out of such foolishness.

In the days after the uprising and the attack by Bishop von Waldeck, her husband's body had not been found. Sofie knew Kurt was dead. Drowned in the city moat, most likely. His unidentifiable bones would surface next time the city authorities dredged the moat.

After John of Leiden, or, as he was now known, the King of the New Jerusalem, had pried Sofie away from Hilde and forced her to go home, Sofie hadn't left the house for three days, other than to go next door to Brigitte's home and check on her uncle. After the second visit, she and Brigitte had agreed that Sofie should also move in and stay with Brigitte, since she was alone without Kurt or Hilde. Sofie hadn't reappeared in public until today.

Heinrich had nearly died in the attack on the city. Once the battle was over and his men pulled his body from the rubble of the outer gate, they patched up the wound to his chest. Although he still cried out in pain at times when he shifted in bed, it was her uncle's delirium that troubled Sofie the most. At times, he couldn't recognize her face, and at other times he refused food, claiming it was a poison. But then, after a few hours, he'd appear normal and eat voraciously after saying how hungry he was. Sofie couldn't understand what had happened to his mind.

That left Sofie and Brigitte on their own to mind Brigitte's children and tend to Heinrich. All the children, by now, had lost enough weight that their clothes hung limply from their bodies. Sofie knew she'd look the same if she could see herself in a mirror.

Brigitte stood beside Sofie, left arm around her shoulder while they listened to the coronation.

"Do you want to leave?" Brigitte asked her young friend. A trickle of sweat rolled down her cheek from the sultry August heat.

"I'm only here because I want to talk to Hilde after the ceremony, if I can," Sofie responded, wiping her own sweat from her forehead. "I don't care about the rest anymore."

"Just tell me if you need to go, darling. If it's too much, I understand."

Sofie leaned into her friend's side and gave her a squeeze.

"Can you believe it, though?" Brigitte whispered again. "How many women are there in Divara's Court?"

For the first time, Sofie looked closely at the center of the cathedral square and took in the details. The makeshift wooden stage that the prophets had always used to make their proclamations was gone. In its place, John of Leiden now sat on a gilded throne. Draped over the throne was scarlet cloth shining with gold thread. Behind the throne, on its own pedestal, was a wooden globe pierced by two swords, and a wooden cross behind it. The inscription on the cross read "One king of righteousness over all."

All around the king's throne were benches where the Elders sat. Except, they weren't Elders any longer. Now, the men were the king's court. Knipperdollinck sat in attendance, the Sword of Judgment in his hands. Bernard Rothmann was now the king's Royal Orator. Herman Tilbeck, the man who had recaptured the city council building and rescued John and the Elders, claimed the title of Master of Court. The king had four royal councilors, too, although Henry Redeker was the only one whom Sofie knew by name. Gerard Reynning was the king's Master of the Treasury, and he sat along with his guard, Magnus Kohuss. Gerard's brother Herman was the Wheat Master of the court. Sofie saw other officials, too, arrayed on benches facing the king, but didn't know their names.

To King John's right stood a young boy, the king's page, holding aloft a large Bible opened to some chapter from the Old Testament. To John's left was another page holding up a naked sword.

King John himself wore rich robes of silk, satin, and velvet and had gold and silver chains draped around his neck. The sunlight reflected off the numerous gold rings he wore on his hands. Sofie saw he'd shortened his beard. Now it was merely a few inches long, rather than stretching to the middle of his chest. The king gripped a gilded scepter in his right hand.

Queen Divara, King John's second wife, sat next to him on a gilded throne of her own. Sofie noticed that Diana Knipperdollinck now sat in lesser position, grouped around the beautiful young queen along with six other young women, Hilde included. Queen Divara, like the king, wore beautiful robes of scarlet and gold. She sat on a silk pillow. While the king's other wives also wore dresses of fine satin, their dresses were of one color only, scarlet, and their chairs lacked gilding.

To Sofie's eyes, all the king's new wives had two things in common. All were uncommonly attractive, and all appeared younger than twenty years old. She couldn't be certain, but Sofie judged another of the king's eight wives to be even younger than her sister was.

Presently, the King of the New Jerusalem arose to address the assembly. When he stood up, Sofie noticed that one of his gold necklaces had the same emblem as the pedestal—a globe pierced by two swords.

At his side stood the limping prophet, Johann Dusentscher.

"Who is that, Brigitte?" Sofie whispered. "I know his name is Johann, but nothing else about him."

"I believe he's a goldsmith," Brigitte answered. "But I haven't heard much about him, either."

"Being a goldsmith would explain the king's new attire, I suppose."

"Quite so."

Dusentscher spoke first. To Sofie's surprise, he had a loud voice that carried well in the open air of the cathedral square.

"People of the New Jerusalem, we gather here today at Mount Zion as God's chosen people. Just as God delivered Brother John from captivity, so has God delivered His Elect from our enemies without."

A great cheer went up. Brigitte leaned in and said to Sofie through the noise, "Most of the bishop's forces have left. After we threw back their second attack, most of the mercenaries abandoned von Waldeck and struck camp. I suppose they got tired of sitting around digging trenches and then storming the walls of a well-prepared city. I hear there's even a bit of food trickling into Münster again through all the gaps in the lines of the besiegers."

Sofie supposed she should be thankful for that but wasn't sure if she was. The loosening of the siege wouldn't bring her husband back or free her sister from the clutches of the madman who was about to be crowned king. Meanwhile, Dusentscher resumed.

"Most Christian brothers, just as the Israelites of the Old Testament had a king, so God desires His chosen people to have a king. The Father has revealed to me that John of Leiden, a man of

God and a saintly prophet, will be king across the entire Earth. He will be lord of emperors, kings, and princes and all the powers of the world. He will be over every ruler, and no ruler will be over him. He will hold the scepter and throne of his father David until God the Father returns and reclaims His Kingdom."

Having spoken, Dusentscher limped to where the former Elders sat and took the Sword of Justice from the nearest of them. He then handed the sword to John, stating, "Receive the Sword of Justice and along with it all power, so that with it you will make all the peoples of the Earth subordinate to yourself."

King John took the sword and held it in his left hand, keeping his scepter in his right. Then Dusentscher stooped to the foot of the throne, held up an urn, and from it poured oil into his hand. Next, he dripped some of the oil on John of Leiden's forehead and called out, "You are king of the new temple and God's people. By the favor of God, you are King of the New Zion." Dusentscher ended his role by placing a thin, golden circlet atop John of Leiden's head.

At this, King John slowly raised both arms aloft until they stretched toward Heaven. As he did, a roar rose from the assembled throng. Then the king lowered himself to his knees, setting down the sword and scepter in a gesture of supplication, and remained in that posture for several moments.

Finally, the king stood and addressed his subjects. When King John spoke, it was the same voice that he'd used so many times when addressing the people of Münster—commanding, rich, full, and with the ever-present hint of God's wrath.

"In like manner was David, a humble shepherd, anointed by the prophet, at God's command, as King of Israel. God often acts in this way, and whoever resists the will of God calls down God's wrath upon himself. Now I am given power over all the nations of the Earth, and the right to use the sword to the confusion of the wicked and in defense of the righteous. So, let none in this city stain themselves with crime or resist the will of God, or else he shall without delay be put to death with the sword. Shame on those who resist the will of the Heavenly Father! Though they were all to join together and oppose me, I shall still reign, not only over the New Jerusalem but over the whole world, for my Father will have it so. My kingdom which begins now shall endure for a thousand years and know no downfall!

"Now God has chosen me as a king over the whole world. But I say to you, dear brothers and sisters, I would much rather be a swineherd and much rather hold the plough or dig ditches than be such a king. What I do, I must do, for God has chosen me for this. Dear brothers and sisters, let us thank God for this."

With that, the king led the crowd in singing Münster's adopted hymn, "A Mighty Fortress Is Our God," followed by another picked for the occasion, "To God on High Alone Be Glory." When the hymns concluded, the court retired, King John leading the procession through the cathedral square toward St. Lambert's Cathedral.

Sofie tried to make eye contact with Hilde but failed. She could see her sister's face, however, and it showed alternating looks of fear and resignation.

"I want to go now, Brigitte," Sofie finally whispered. "I can't take this anymore."

"That's a good idea, Sofie. It doesn't appear you'll get to speak with Hilde today, after all."

"I just want to know that she's not suffering, Brigitte. If he's hurt her . . ." Sofie finished, her fists clenched while color came into her cheeks.

"Not now, Sofie, not now," Brigitte admonished quietly. "Wait until we get back to the house."

Then Sofie was crying again. "I just can't take the pressure anymore. When will it stop?"

Brigitte guided her young friend home, all the while whispering soothing words in Sofie's ears.

Sofie Gresbeck wasn't the only one in the cathedral square that day who cried bitter tears, however. Rudolf Schweren stood by himself, off to the side of the great gathering, while King John received his crown and addressed his subjects.

Next to Rudolf was the freshly turned earth of a mass grave, the final, unconsecrated resting place of the forty-seven rebels put to death for their occupation of the city council house during the uprising.

His older brother Karl was among them. Karl had survived the attack that liberated John of Leiden, barely. But John ordered his death immediately thereafter.

Rudolf couldn't even look at the king or his court. He'd fought for them. Held St. Servatius's Gate for the New Jerusalem. Rudolf killed two rebels with his own hands, even. But during the trial of the rebels, no one would hear his pleas for mercy on behalf of Karl. Instead, John of Leiden forced Rudolf to watch while one of the Elders shot his brother in the chest and another slashed Karl's body with a dagger until the flesh fell off in chunks.

While John's lackeys hacked Karl's body to pieces, other rebels had received mercy. The hypocrite Rothmann had preached to them in St. John's Monastery, Knipperdollinck declared that the door of mercy had cracked open, and they'd lived. Rudolf didn't understand why.

His plan had seemed perfect. Once the Anabaptists made marriage compulsory in the New Jerusalem, he'd planned to ask for Sofie's hand. But Kurt Boetmester, the pathetic cabinetmaker's journeyman, had beat him to it. Rudolf had been sure Sofie would learn to love him in time. That's why he'd tried so hard to gain favor with the Anabaptists—to protect Sofie and make sure she'd be safe, loved, and cared for in the new world dawning in Münster.

But the uprising had wrecked everything. He hadn't planned to kill Kurt that morning. Never wanted him to die at all, in fact. It was mere chance that Rudolf was on duty on the walls when the revolt started and chance again that it was Kurt who broke through and was trying to lift the outer gate. True, he'd gloated as Kurt lay dying, but that was the rush of victory and of having killed someone taking over his emotions. Before the siege began, Rudolf had never held a weapon in his life, and the energy of the battle carried away his ability to think clearly. Now, he never wanted to wield a weapon again, unless it was the sword that pierced the heart of John of Leiden.

No, he'd never wanted to see Kurt Boetmester dead. In his plan, he would scheme to have Sofie and Kurt's marriage declared invalid and gain Sofie's hand for himself that way.

Rudolf couldn't stand the thought that harm might come to Sofie. He'd been smitten with her for years. But she'd never returned his feelings. Still, he tried to remain devoted to her. Time and again in July, he'd put off finding a bride, even though Münster now had several women for every man, because he wanted her, and her alone. When he'd pleaded and begged for John Matthys to spare Hilde the ordeal of executing that man in the cathedral square, he'd meant every word of it, because all he wanted to do was spare Sofie and Hilde pain.

Rudolf would never lift a finger for John again. As if things couldn't get worse, John had admitted Johann Dusentscher into his circle of advisors. Rudolf knew Johann. All too well. He'd gambled against Johann before all the madness in Münster began and usually beaten him, too, even though Dusentscher was a liar and a cheater. Now, it seemed, he'd lied and schemed his way into the confidence of the king.

Rudolf didn't know what he'd do now. He wasn't sure if he could ever ask Sofie to be his wife after he'd killed her husband. She'd never find out that he was Kurt's killer, but inside, Rudolf would always know the truth. Besides, she'd never say yes to him anyway, and even though he probably could compel Sofie to be his bride, he loved her too much to force her. Try as he might, he'd never been able to impress Sofie, even when times were normal. Rudolf didn't believe he could do better now.

Finally, Rudolf threw up his hands and stalked from the cathedral square, kicking at the cobblestones in the street as he trudged home alone. He loved Sofie, but she didn't love him. So be it. He made up his mind he'd devote himself to protecting her as if she did. And that started with making sure John of Leiden never went near her again.

Chapter 26

Bernard Rothmann sat at his wooden desk in a quiet corner of St. Lambert's Cathedral, tapping his quill on the edge of the inkwell, the only other sound the splatter of rain falling outside in the dreary afternoon. Quiet corners of the cathedral were not easy to find. Now that King John had fifteen wives, the clamor could be well-nigh universal some days.

Brow furrowed, Rothmann bit his lip. The New Jerusalem had yet to reach its glory. The halcyon feeling of destiny and euphoria he'd had at the second defeat of Bishop von Waldeck's mercenaries had been incredible. But it only lasted about a few weeks, until new soldiers under the command of Count Wirich of Falkenstein arrived at Münster.

These, Rothmann mused, were no flighty mercenaries who would desert after a defeat. Rather, Wirich commanded hardened imperial troops who'd seen action against real soldiers, if their behavior so far was any indication of their training and experience. Immediately upon arrival, they'd built new trenches and built them closer to Münster's walls, then connected them with blockhouses at much tighter intervals than the previous besiegers had. Watchfires burned all night up and down their lines, and they kept up an intermittent cannon barrage after dark as well, making it harder for the defenders to get regular sleep.

In retrospect, the best course would have been to follow up the bishop's defeat in early August with a counterattack to capture von Waldeck once most of his forces had left him. However, that hadn't happened. Instead, John of Leiden had held his own coronation, and Count Wirich's forces had dug in outside the city a few days later, unopposed.

Rothmann took a moment to sip from his wine cup and chew some of the bread and cheese laid before him. He knew to pace himself, however. No need to spoil his appetite for the salted pork and roast chicken that he'd share with the king and his court this evening.

Not capturing the bishop was a setback. Not a fatal setback, however. It might turn out quite the opposite, in fact. What better sign could God give his Elect than to deliver them from such dire circumstances and lead them to unconditional victory? And so would it be, if the Elect did not falter upon the way.

This realization brought Rothmann's eye to the document he'd completed yesterday, his latest testament and statement of the faith of the Anabaptists. Adult baptism remained the core of the faith. No one could number among the Elect by infant baptism alone. Accepting baptism was a statement of sincerity and love for God that only an adult could make. The same held true regarding the community of goods. Christ's apostles had shared their possessions in common. God's followers must do the same.

But his recent Bible readings had taught Rothmann so much more. It was clear that all human history, from the temptation of Adam and Eve down to the present, was a series of falls engineered by Satan. Always, Satan would tempt God's people, and because of Original Sin and human frailty, the seduction always worked. Clearly, this was one part of Satan's undying effort to overthrow the Word of God. The first fall had come when Adam and Eve had consumed the forbidden fruit in the Garden of Eden. Other falls had followed, like the Great Flood.

Always, however, God, in His mercy, had restored His chosen people. The replenishment of the Earth by Noah and his family after the Flood had been one such restoration. Christ's arrival on Earth and His death on the Cross had been the latest restoration. Christ had provided God's people with the New Testament and eleven apostles, so that this restoration would be a final one.

But that hadn't happened. Again, the Elect had fallen into error, tempted by Satan's wiles. And that, Rothmann realized, was the key. How did Satan corrupt God's people into sin in age after age? Through appeals to their vanity. By offering them greater knowledge in imitation of God, just as he'd done to Adam and Eve. After puffing up the pride of man, and then filling man's head with false teachings, Satan had only to stand back and watch as these so-called learned scholars led God's people away from His truth.

That was why the New Jerusalem would be different, Rothmann knew. Only the unlearned and the poor could resist Satan's temptations because only they remained uncorrupted by vanity, pride, covetousness, and all the other things the Father had warned against through Moses on Mount Sinai. God's Elect had fallen deeply in the centuries since the death of Christ. They had one last chance at restitution because this final restitution, the one taking place in Münster, would be eternal.

Dipping the quill into the ink, Rothmann set about doing his part to assure the deliverance of the Elect and the favor of the Father. The king and his court had decided it was time to summon all true believers to Münster for a final battle with Antichrist. Tomorrow, Rothmann would anoint the apostles who would carry the summons to all the empire. Even now, they prepared to set forth. Today, it was Rothmann's job to write the words that would rally all believers throughout the lands to Münster.

Taking another sip of wine, he began.

Brothers and sisters in Christ, greetings.

Amongst us God—to whom be eternal praise and thanks—has restored community, as it was in the beginning and as befits the Saints of God. We hope, too, that amongst us community is as vigorous and glorious, and is by God's grace observed with as pure a heart, as at any time before. For not only have we put our belongings into a common pool under the care of deacons, and live from it according to our needs, we praise God through Christ with one heart and mind and are eager to help one another with every kind of service. And accordingly, everything which has served the purpose of self-seeking and private property, such as buying and selling, working for money, taking interest and practicing usury— even at the expense of unbelievers—or eating and drinking the sweat of the poor (that is, making one's own people and fellow-creatures work so that one can grow fat) and indeed everything which offends against love—all such things are abolished amongst us by the power of love and community.

Knowing that God now desires to abolish such abominations, we would die rather than turn to them. We know that such sacrifices are pleasing to the Lord. And indeed, no Christian or Saint can satisfy God if he does not live in such a community or at least desire with all his heart to live in it.

The poorest among us, who used to be despised as beggars, now go about dressed as finely as the highest and most distinguished. By God's grace they have become as rich as the burgomasters and the richest in town."

As the rain continued falling and the daylight waned into twilight, Rothmann continued writing the words that would draw all God's Elect to Münster for a final confrontation with the unbelievers and their leader, Antichrist.

The next day, Sofie and Brigitte sat huddled at Brigitte's table.

"Is that all of the onion soup, Aunt Brigitte?"

"I'm trying my best to save it, Sofie. I don't know when we'll get more."

"But I'm so hungry," Sofie stated as she pulled the wool shawl around her shoulders. It was a cold and misty October evening, and the soup hadn't done much to warm her. "I'm just so hungry."

"I know, dear. Whenever I go to the deacons to get our share, though, the portions get smaller every week. I picked all the apples off my apple tree two months ago because people were taking them, but we don't have many of them left now."

Sofie sighed and nodded. "How are your boys doing? I don't see Rolf go out to play much anymore."

"No. He's taken to scavenging for whatever food he can find. That's what he spends most of his time doing lately. Whatever he finds, he splits with his brother and sister."

"Brigitte, may I ask you something?"

"Of course."

"Did you want to marry Heinrich? I mean, if it hadn't been for the Anabaptists, would you have?" When she saw her aunt hesitate, Sofie added, "I'm glad that you did."

Brigitte gave a smile, but it was a decidedly nervous smile.

"Is something wrong, Aunt Brigitte? Was it a bad time to ask?"

"I'm sorry, Sofie. I knew you'd ask me that question someday. It's just that I feel bad because I've never figured out how to answer it very well, even though I knew it was coming."

"How come you can't answer it?"

"Sofie, did your uncle ever tell you what he did between arriving in Münster and marrying Liese?"

Sofie knit her brows and thought for a long while. "No, I guess I don't remember him ever telling me much about that," she conceded. "Has he told you?"

"Only because I asked him a few evenings after our forced marriage. I told him I needed to know. He agreed."

"Well, what did he say?" Sofie asked, now sitting up straight with her hands gripping the table.

"This is what Heinrich told me. In 1521, a war broke out across Europe. France fought on one side, the Empire, Spain, and England on the other. It started when King Charles of Spain gained election as the Holy Roman Emperor. France's king, Francis, felt threatened because Charles now ruled lands on both sides of his kingdom, so he allied with the Republic of Venice, and the two sides fought for several years. For more than a year, your uncle was a soldier in that war, fighting against the French."

Sofie's eyes were wide. "I never knew about that."

"It makes sense, though, doesn't it Sofie? Why do you think the Anabaptists made Heinrich a watch captain? He knows military tactics. Your uncle said he was a spy and an aide for one of the commanders because he could draw accurate maps of the terrain he saw from memory. It's also where he learned to read and write."

"My goodness. No wonder he always seems to know what the bishop's men are trying to do."

"Absolutely. But there's more, Sofie. Do you want to hear about it?"

Sofie nodded.

"Are you sure?"

Sofie nodded again. But more slowly. She stared intently at her aunt.

"When the war began in 1521, your uncle joined the imperial army, which invaded northern France. They razed two cities to the ground, Ardres and Mouzon, before encountering French resistance. Do you know what that means, Sofie?"

She shook her head. Brigitte noted a hint of doubt in Sofie's tightening smile while Sofie crossed her arms and sat back in her chair.

"They burned everything down after looting the towns. Many old people, women, and children died, either from soldiers robbing them or from the flames afterward."

"But my uncle didn't rob anyone, did he?"

Brigitte nodded slowly. "It's how he got the money to become a cabinetmaker."

Sofie let out a little gasp. She couldn't believe her uncle had done that. The same uncle who enjoyed singing and who was so kind to her all her years growing up.

"After that, your uncle traveled to the south and fought in a battle at a place called Bicocca. He served under a mercenary leader named George Frundsberg. His side won that battle, too, and they did more looting around the countryside."

"And he stole from people again?"

"No, not the second time. Heinrich told me that after that second campaign, he'd had enough of war and fighting. He came back here to Münster, married Liese, and never touched a weapon again. Until all this Anabaptist madness began."

"I don't know what to say, Brigitte. I never knew any of that."

"Now you understand why I never had a good answer to your first question?"

"Yes."

"I was always suspicious that he'd done something he didn't want to remember during the year or so when he left Münster. Heinrich told me he still has black dreams about those days. When he married Liese, he'd hoped they'd go away, and for a while they did. But when she died, he had no one to help him forget at night. The dreams came back. It's why he's been so taciturn and quiet the past few years. The images flood back to him, and he spends hours at night waiting for them to go away."

"I wonder how come he never told me."

"He didn't want you to worry about him. Heinrich only ever wanted to make up for what he'd done by helping you and Hilde grow up happy and without fear. But that's why I'd always hesitated at the thought of being his wife. I always guessed he had a reason why he never said anything about that year of his life when I was around."

"But it's good he told you the truth, right?"

"Yes, Sofie, it is. Don't worry. Your uncle and I are going to take care of you the best we can. I still think he's an honorable man, and I'm happy to be his wife." Brigitte smiled warmly, rose, and then collected the wooden soup bowls as she reassured her new niece.

"I'm just happy he felt strong enough to walk the streets today. He's seeming more like his old self every day. His injuries seem to be improving." Sofie smiled, too, got up, and then gave her aunt a fierce hug.

Before she could say anything else, however, a soft knock came at Brigitte's door. "I'll see who it is," Sofie said because Brigitte had both her hands full.

When she opened the door, Rudolf was there. But it wasn't the same Rudolf she'd grown accustomed to seeing. Instead of bouncing on his toes with his smug grin, he'd already retreated several feet from the door after knocking. He stood, hands behind his back, looking down at the street. "May I come in, Sofie?" he asked very quietly.

"Yes, I suppose so. It's been quite a while since we've talked, hasn't it, Rudolf?"

"It has. Here, I brought this for you," he said quickly, holding forth a fresh loaf of bread while he came inside. "Please, take it."

"Are you allowed to do that? I thought the deacons gave out all the food now."

"They do. I baked this special for you, though. No one knows but my father."

"That's very kind of you, Rudolf," Brigitte stated.

"I'll bring you more whenever I can."

"Won't that put you in danger if someone finds out, Rudolf?" Sofie inquired.

"I don't want my neighbors to go hungry."

Sofie noted Rudolf hadn't answered her question. This was strange behavior indeed. Usually, he was direct. Annoyingly direct. Was he trying to set her up for something? Trying to trick her into revealing something she shouldn't?

Looking in Rudolf's eyes, though, Sofie didn't sense that. She didn't know what to make of her neighbor's timid posture and earnest expression because it was so unusual to see him that way.

Finally, when he continued to stand and shuffle his feet, she decided to just ask. "What's wrong, Rudolf? You don't seem yourself."

He still didn't look Sofie or Brigitte in the face. "The king will proclaim new laws today. I wanted to make sure you knew about them ahead of time," he claimed, his voice barely above a whisper.

"New laws?" Brigitte asked skeptically. "We don't have enough already?"

"These ones are about clothing, Miss Brigitte. According to the prophet Dusentscher, the Father said to him that Christian brothers can own no more than one coat, two pairs of hose, two doublets, and three shirts. Christian sisters are an abomination to the Father if they possess more than one chemise, one dress, one pelt, two collars, two pairs of sleeves, two pairs of hose, and four shirts. All the rest must go to the deacons. A wagon will come by within days to take away the extra clothing and bedding. Those of the Elect who are in need will receive the clothes."

"How can that be pleasing to the Father? Does He wish His Elect to disappear before next spring because they froze to death during the winter?"

"The king also declared that all the old names must pass away. He's renamed the streets, the gates, and everything else in

Münster. Parents must even bring their newborn children to him, so that he can name them according to the Father's will."

Sofie and Brigitte merely shook their heads. Brigitte asked, "What next? Will the king decide that living in houses during the winter displeases the Father?"

"Brigitte!" Sofie gasped. She couldn't believe her aunt would say something against the king in Rudolf's presence.

He had no visible reaction to the remark, however. Instead, he continued in his morose tone, "You've heard the news already, then, Miss Brigitte?"

"The news of what?"

"From this day forward, all who wish may live in the houses of others if those houses are not occupied."

Stunned, no one spoke for several moments. What was there to say? The king had spoken.

"I think I'll go home now," Rudolf finally said, although he said it as if going home was a punishment.

"Rudolf, you still haven't answered my question," Sofie insisted. "You aren't yourself today. What's happened?"

"I'll be back with more bread whenever I can," he said, and then he turned and left.

"What do you make of that, Aunt Brigitte?" Sofie wondered aloud. "Something's happened, even if Rudolf won't say what it is."

"Of course, it has. You don't think I would have blasphemed the king if the old Rudolf were here, do you?"

"But what? What's different about him?"

"That's a harder question to answer, but I'll wager Karl's death had something to do with the change."

Sofie blushed because she knew she should have thought of that. She'd gone to look for Karl in the days after the failed rebellion, only to learn from Karl's father that he'd died for his role defending the city council building.

"Do you think Rudolf blames me for that?" she asked, the sudden recognition causing her pulse to race.

"No. I think he blames himself, somehow. Do you think he'd bring us food if he blamed you for his brother's death?"

"Maybe he's setting me up for something. I think he's capable of that."

"But why, Sofie? He has friends among the Anabaptists. If he wanted to punish you, all he needs to do is accuse you of something in front of them, and that would be the end for you. Besides, Rudolf would have done that long ago if he ever meant to. We both know he isn't the patient type."

"Then what's caused his new attitude?"

"I don't know for sure, but I'll bet it's linked to Karl in some way."

Sofie was about to agree when Brigitte's door opened again, and Uncle Heinrich walked through, patters of rain blotched on his overcoat and glistening in his hair. Sofie opened her mouth to ask him how his walk had been, but then she saw the tears.

"I saw Hilde today," he sobbed as he sat at the table and wrapped his head in his arms.

"You saw Hilde?" Sofie gasped. No one in the family had spoken with Hilde since she'd become one of the king's wives. The king did not allow his wives to visit their families or receive visitors without the king or queen's permission, and seldom did they give that permission.

Seeing her uncle's tears caused the fear to ignite in Sofie's guts. "What's happened to her?"

Finally, Heinrich managed to raise his head. "I went to see her by pretending I was ready to return to duty on the walls, so I could get into the presence of King John and his court."

"But you aren't ready," Brigitte protested. "Today was your first day out of the house since your head injury."

"I know. And I wasn't going to walk very far. But I just wanted to see Hilde so much. I tried to think of a plan. That was what I came up with."

"But if you saw Hilde, why are you so sad? Something's happened to her, hasn't it?" Sofie almost bawled the words, her heart was so frightened. She'd seen her uncle quiet and withdrawn hundreds of times, but she couldn't remember ever seeing him cry.

"Yes."

"But what, Uncle?"

"I saw her, but it wasn't her. Her face . . ." Again, Heinrich put his head in his arms.

Instinctively, Sofie and Brigitte both put their hands on his shoulders to reassure him.

"Take your time," Brigitte soothed, although when Sofie looked in Brigitte's face, she saw that her aunt's lips and chin trembled and the tendons in her neck stood out. Sofie imagined that she looked about the same.

It seemed an hour to Sofie, but finally Heinrich gathered himself and raised his head.

"When I went to report to King John and tell him I'd be able to resume my watch soon, he was pleased. So pleased, in fact, that I decided to risk it and ask if I could visit with Hilde for a little while. To my surprise, the king agreed. But when I met her in the room she shares with two of King John's other wives, she jumped into my arms and cried into my neck. Luckily, we were the only ones in the room."

"Is she safe?" Sofie couldn't help interrupting.

"You would hardly recognize her, Sofie," Heinrich said, voice cracking while he struggled to regain control of himself and continue. At last, he did. "She cut her hair. It's so short now, you might take her for a boy if you didn't know better. But it was her face. All scarred and scratched, like an animal had attacked her. When I asked her why she looked like that, I thought she'd say that she'd been in a fight with one of John's other wives. But that's not what she said. Hilde did it to herself. She thought if she made herself ugly John would get tired of her and divorce her."

Now, it was Sofie's turn to break down. She couldn't imagine how bad her treatment must be for Hilde to cut her own face.

"But that wasn't the worst. Hilde told me other things. Terrible things. She said that one of King John's wives is only twelve years old. One night, the king tried to lie down with her, but because she was so young, she began to bleed, and no one could stop it. They took her to a doctor, the only female doctor in Münster. The doctor saved the girl's life, but now she walks with a limp and is always in pain. The king has not visited her at night again. Because this poor girl and Hilde sleep in the same room, that's where Hilde got the idea to mar her face. She did it for her own protection."

Sofie looked up. Even Brigitte had tears streaming down her face now. Brigitte was about to say something when they heard the trumpet blasts in the street.

Chapter 27

Münster

October of 1534

The trumpeter blew three deafening blasts, each lasting about ten seconds. Then, Sofie heard a crier in the street announce, "The Trumpet of the Lord sounds its call. All people of the New Jerusalem must assemble on Mount Zion within the hour. Arm yourselves. Take weapons from the storehouses. Today, we go forward against the armies of Antichrist! Today, we march to victory!"

Then the Trumpet of the Lord sounded three more times.

Sofie, Brigitte, and Heinrich just looked at each other, bewildered.

"I'll go," Heinrich said at last.

"You can't," Brigitte responded. "You can barely walk a straight line."

"I just told King John I was nearly fit to return to duty. How can I not go after that? Perhaps my plan wasn't such a good one, after all."

"We'll go together," Sofie stated. It wasn't a request. "We have to. The herald said all in the New Jerusalem must assemble. And I won't be separated from what family I have left."

Wordlessly, Heinrich and Brigitte assented. If the soldiers of the New Jerusalem were about to march forth to war, Heinrich knew, it wouldn't matter who went and who stayed. He'd spoken with Deacon Engelbert Eding two days ago when Eding came to check on his recovery. The deacon said that a vast force of imperial soldiers surrounded the city, possibly ten thousand. If Münster opened its gates and gave battle in the open field, everything would be over before nightfall.

Within the hour, Sofie, Heinrich, and Brigitte stood, waiting, in the packed cathedral square. The clouds remained dark and gray, and rain splattered upon the gathering in brief, light showers. Sofie judged it could rain harder at any time. At least the wind was light.

Then more trumpets sounded, and King John arrived with his retinue of advisors and bodyguards. Sofie thought the king's court larger than ever. Heinrich noted that all now rode on horseback.

"Apparently, the armies of the New Jerusalem created a cavalry squadron while I was recuperating," he quipped to Brigitte.

"They did," she replied. "If it's as effective against the nonbelievers as it is at keeping order in the New Jerusalem, perhaps we have a chance."

Heinrich smiled wryly, knowing the people of Münster still had no chance.

After a few moments of trotting around the square in his majesty, King John dismounted and took up his seat on his throne, his wife Divara beside him on her silk pillow. Sofie saw that no other wives attended. She didn't know if she was happy or sad about that. Getting a chance to see Hilde was the first thing on her mind, but now she was scared because of what her uncle had told her Hilde had done to herself.

Like he always had since becoming king, John wore a velvet overcoat adorned with golden and silver chains. His gold crown rested upon his head, and his left hand gripped his scepter. Divara also had a crown and a velvet dress, the same deep purple as John's overcoat.

"People of the New Jerusalem," John exclaimed, "the hour of deliverance is at hand! Today, we go forward to smite the foe!"

A few people shouted acclamations but to Sofie's ears the response seemed decidedly muted.

Undeterred, John continued. "In moments, we will form ranks and march to victory, men in the front, women and children behind. You may be in fear, for our enemies are many, but do not be. The Father has given me power over all. The hosts of Gog and Magog will flee or perish by the sword. For the Father has revealed that our strength shall be as thunder. Five of you will kill one hundred of the enemy, and ten of you together will kill one thousand. The armies of Antichrist will flee before you or die where they stand, and together we shall march forth to the Promised Land.

"Do not burden yourself with worldly goods, food, or other vanities. God will see to it that his Elect suffer neither hunger, nor thirst, nor fatigue on our journey. Indeed, He shall bear His people up with a host of angels. Now, my people, form ranks."

John drew his sword as he mounted his horse, smiling and confident while he sat tall in the saddle.

The square burst into commotion and confusion. People milled aimlessly, unsure even of the gate to which they were to march.

Heinrich looked at his niece and his wife. "I love you, Sofie," he said while he gave her a last embrace. "If you survive, tell Hilde I love her, too."

"She knows that, Uncle. Hilde knows. And so do I."

Smiling, Heinrich wiped away the tear that had formed in one eye. Looking Brigitte in the face, he said, "I'm glad I've spent the past few months with you. When you watch your children grow up, make sure they know I loved them, too."

For once, Brigitte was speechless.

Dimly, Sofie heard one of the king's cavalrymen ride by and call out, "Form up, soldier!"

Heinrich nodded, set his jaw, and walked forward slowly and unsteadily toward the front line of townspeople. It appeared the king meant to lead them out of the city to the northwest, through either Jew Fields Gate or Cross Gate.

Sofie ran forward to give him another hug. "Please, tell them you can't fight. Pretend you're wounded. Do something, just don't leave me."

When she looked up, to her surprise, Heinrich smiled at her. "I've done the best I could with you and your sister, Sofie, even if my best left a lot to be desired. When you have children of your own someday, please tell them my name. Here, at the end, I go to battle for the last time with a clear conscience. Farewell."

He slipped from Sofie's arms and walked toward the soldiers now amassing in the northwest corner of the square.

"You've got to let him go, Sofie," Brigitte said softly. "Please, stay with me. I'm frightened, and I need your company."

When she looked up, Sofie saw the cavalry wheel until they ringed the cathedral square, their weapons—swords, lances, and arquebuses—drawn. She didn't know anything about cavalry, but she assumed they would lead the charge against Antichrist. They were the fastest, after all.

At the exit to the square, King John sat astride his mount, naked sword glistening with raindrops. Just then, the sun broke from its cover and shone from the blade. The king smiled.

Then, the sword dropped to his side. "People of the New Jerusalem, God's Chosen," he shouted into the still air, "the Father is well pleased with His people. He wished to test the loyalty of His Elect, as He tested the loyalty of Job in days gone by. You have passed the test, and God rejoices at the steadfastness of His people."

Sofie just looked at Brigitte. "What on earth does that mean?"

Brigitte just shrugged and nodded in the king's direction.

John spoke again. "People of God, the Father loves you. You are His Chosen People. Being satisfied of your love for Him, God now commands that you shall be rewarded for your loyalty with a great feast!"

Still Sofie looked at her aunt, uncomprehending.

Sensing the confusion, the king shouted again, "Dear brothers, we will not march out and leave the New Jerusalem empty and let the godless come back into the city. This is not the will of God. Today was nothing more than a temptation of you as to what you would do by the Father, whether you would be obedient. Now, dear brothers, let each one take his wives and set himself down at the table of the Lord. Set your arms beside you and be joyful with the Lord!"

Suddenly, Sofie felt her eyes go gray, her muscles relax, and her body slump to the ground.

Chapter 28

Münster

October of 1534

When Sofie's vision returned, she rested upon her back on a wooden bench. Intermittent raindrops splashed on her face while she blinked herself awake.

"Sofie, please wake up and hear me."

Sofie shook her head gently. The voice sounded so far away.

"Sofie, are you all right, child?" the voice said again.

Then Sofie realized the voice belonged to Brigitte. She also had her hand on Sofie's forehead.

"I think so," she stammered. Then, "What happened to me?"

"You fainted, Sofie. And now your head feels very warm."

She blinked again. Yes, for sure, her head felt warm. A headache had formed, too. She sat up slowly, with Brigitte's help.

"I think I must have been overwhelmed by everything," she told her aunt cautiously. "I remember hearing the attack was cancelled and that a feast would happen instead, and I suppose the relief and shock was too much for me. If I did anything after that, I don't remember it."

"You were only unconscious for a few minutes, Sofie. I've only just had time to get you over to this bench you're resting on."

"Wait. Where's my uncle?"

"I'm right here, too," Heinrich's voice called from behind Sofie. "You're a grown woman. It took two of us to get you onto the bench."

Sofie sighed in relief, although her head still hurt. She rubbed her eyes and then tried to massage the pain out of her forehead.

She was still trying to clear her head a short time later when the food arrived. Headache or no headache, she ate like someone who hadn't eaten in days. After she'd wolfed some food and looked around, Sofie realized she wasn't the only one acting that way.

Then, she, Heinrich, and Brigitte heard a commotion. Near where they sat, a handful of the king's soldiers dragged a man between the tables, hauling him toward the king's throne. The man wore a dirty blue and yellow loose-sleeved doublet with slashes in the upper arms—the uniform of one of the mercenaries who'd defected several months prior.

Most eyes in the crowd followed the mercenary until he knelt before King John. Sofie was close enough to the throne to see that the man's body quivered as he knelt. The king rose while Bernhard Knipperdollinck, Bernard Rothmann, and the rest of his court watched.

"Luke Hotmaker, you stand accused of attempting to defect to the enemy while on watch. The eyes of the New Jerusalem are upon you. Speak the truth, and the door of mercy may open."

"It's not true, my king. I only sought to leave the city long enough to forage for food and test the enemy's defenses. I planned to return after midnight. It's the honest truth, my lord."

"And yet, I'm told you had money with you."

"It was to bribe the enemy in case of my capture. Please, sire, you must believe me!"

The king closed his eyes and stood still for some time, hands clasped in front of his head, face turned upward to the heavens. At last, he looked down on the kneeling figure of Luke Hotmaker.

"I have asked the Father for guidance. The Father has proclaimed that the door of mercy stands shut. God is angry with you for staining the New Jerusalem with sin." The king turned his back and moved to sit down.

Hotmaker rose, took two steps, and then knelt again at the king's feet. "No, sire, it can't be. Please, pray for my soul again—"

Before he could finish, Knipperdollinck swung the Sword of Judgment, and Hotmaker's head fell at King John's feet. As blood spurted everywhere, his body slumped to the ground.

"Call out the other prisoners!" Knipperdollinck said to the guards.

Momentarily, they returned with three women in hand. Again, all knelt at the king's feet, awaiting judgment.

Soon, the guards read out their crimes. The first stood accused of denying her new husband his marital rights and not addressing her husband as "my lord," the second, of having more than one husband, and the third woman had denounced Bernard Rothmann's preaching in public, labeling it blasphemy. All three found the door of mercy closed, and soon, all three perished, their heads resting at King John's feet courtesy of Knipperdollinck's sword.

Then, the king rose once more to address the faithful, stepping around the growing pool of blood near his throne as he did so. "All who sin against God's truth do not belong among the Elect. Their lack of faith is an abomination to the Father. All who persist in sin and do not turn to righteousness will be summoned and sentenced to death. I shall extirpate them from the New Jerusalem, and all memory of them shall disappear forever, erased and forgotten as though they had never lived. Even beyond the grave they shall find no mercy as they descend to the dungeons of Hell."

King John turned and made a beckoning motion with his right hand. About twenty-five members of his court stepped forward.

"I don't recognize any of those men," Sofie whispered to her uncle.

"I don't, either. Probably because they're all immigrants from the Netherlands who've arrived within the past year. Look how well they're dressed," he whispered back. "They owe everything to the king, and so they stand by him."

"But all is not lost for the Elect of God," the king continued. "The Father is pleased by the faithfulness of all gathered here today. He has blessed our actions and our words. Although He did not call us to march forth and give battle today, that time is nigh. But first, we must gather all true believers to the New Jerusalem. These men are the new prophets of the Lord, His new disciples. Marked with the seal of baptism, today we shall bless them to go forth throughout all the lands and call God's people home."

The audience sat quietly, or perhaps in shock after seeing four more beheadings. One after another the new prophets who would make disciples of all nations stepped forward to the king and received a blessing from Rothmann, who also anointed each with oil.

After all the apostles had received their blessing (Sofie counted twenty-six of them), each knelt in prayer. At the same time, various Anabaptist preachers circulated through the crowd, handing out bits of flatbread to each person in the cathedral square.

King John mounted his throne and spoke again. "Thus, the people of the New Jerusalem celebrate Holy Communion together, in Christian fellowship, as one body of believers. Truly, this is a blessed people."

Then Johann Dusentscher spoke from beside the king. "God has revealed to His prophet that these disciples shall set out for the cities of Soest, Osnabrück, Warendorf, and Coesfield first. Disciples, are you ready to depart with the Lord's blessing?"

When the first group stood and nodded in affirmation, Dusentscher said, "You dear brothers, I say to you as the Word of the Lord that you're to march into Warendorf in broad daylight, and to walk into the city and proclaim God's peace to them. If they won't accept the peace, then the city will sink down on the spot and burn up in hellfire."

Sofie listened as Dusentscher gave the same instructions to the other groups of disciples bound for Soest, Osnabrück, and Coesfield.

"He's just condemned those men to their death," Sofie heard her uncle whisper to Brigitte. "Even if they get past the trenches and blockhouses, by now all of the Holy Roman Empire must know what's happening in Münster. The city authorities will arrest these men on the spot, and probably kill them within days."

Brigitte shook her head slowly. "How many more must die before people come to their senses?"

Heinrich just shrugged and chewed his food. He'd tried once to concoct a plan with Herman Ramers to end the siege. But his plan had failed. Perhaps it was time to try another. He'd been working on one while laid up with his injuries. All he needed was to find a new accomplice.

That night, the prophet Henricus stood with King John, Bernhard Knipperdollinck, and Bernard Rothmann.

"Brother Henricus, we have a special mission for you," Knipperdollinck began.

"Anything to serve the Father," replied Henricus, his shaggy, long brown hair falling over his broad shoulders.

Rothmann stepped forward. "You will not go to Coesfield as we told the crowd in the cathedral square today. The New Jerusalem needs more men, more true believers. So, we're sending you to Deventer instead."

"In the Netherlands?"

"Yes. Your task will be to assemble the brothers there and lead them back to the New Jerusalem. Here," Rothmann extended a heavy cloth sack to Henricus. "This is money to finance the return journey of all the true believers you can muster. Two hundred-fifty

Spanish gold coins. Tell them to bring all the food and weapons they can. We also have this for you."

Knipperdollinck brought forth a large white banner emblazoned in gold with the symbol of the New Jerusalem: the earth with two swords passing through it and the Cross rising behind it.

"When you reach Deventer, unfurl this banner to rally the faithful," Rothmann told him. "Then march back here immediately. Make all haste. Upon your return, send a single messenger into the city to alert us. Then, when you near the bishop's trenches, unfurl the banner, and the king will sally forth to open a way for all of you to come into the city. If our timing is right, we'll take the besiegers by surprise. We'll attack from the front, you attack from the rear, and after we've inflicted severe losses on the bishop, we'll bring you into the city. We should be able to capture some of their supply wagons in the process."

"If it's the Lord's will, I shall not fail."

"You will not fail," King John stated flatly. "Were you to march out of the city gates right now and walk directly to the bishop's blockhouses and announce your mission, still, you could not fail, for the Father smiles on you. The godless lack the power to hinder you or prevent your success."

"Amen," said Henricus with a submissive bow.

The next day, Henricus stood before Bishop Franz von Waldeck and military commander Count Wirich V of Falkenstein in their command tent. A warm fire burned in the center of the tent, which also shielded Henricus from the bitter wind outside. Count Wirich's banner, a medium-blue field with a white wagon wheel in the center, fluttered behind the count.

The count dressed in black armor, which contrasted with the red-brown hair and beard on his balding head. Henricus also noted that Wirich's son and heir, Phillip, sat at his father's side. The young man looked to be about twenty years old, which surprised

Henricus given that he was the count's first son, and the count appeared to be nearly sixty.

"Welcome back, Henricus. What news can you bring us from Münster?" Count Wirich asked.

"All goes as planned, my lord. Yesterday, King John and his fool Dusentscher anointed me as an apostle to go forth and convert the city of Coesfield. Somehow," Henricus said with a broad grin, "your men managed to capture me while the rest of the apostles sneaked away. I seem to be the victim of ill luck in that regard," he finished sarcastically.

"Yes, funny how these things sometimes don't go the way one expects," the count said with sarcasm of his own in the firm, assured, deep voice of one used to giving orders. "Thanks to you, we've already sent messengers ahead to Soest, Osnabrück, Warendorf, and Coesfield. The authorities there will arrest the other so-called apostles on sight."

"Will they be killed?" Henricus asked. His face betrayed neither joy nor sadness at the prospect, only curiosity.

"Perhaps. I care little, so long as the authorities torture the missionaries and get intelligence from them first. Since that is why we sent you into Münster as a spy in the first place, Henricus, tell us what you know."

"Certainly, my lord. The population suffers. Although to my knowledge none have starved yet, morale sinks daily and resentment toward King John rises."

"To the point where an internal rebellion is imminent?"

"I think not. King John and his court continue to dine in sumptuous fashion, which alienates some of the townspeople, but the king now maintains a squadron of cavalry to enforce his will. Because of that, and because his most loyal retainers are immigrants from the Netherlands who owe everything to him, he maintains enough of a faithful following that any attempt at rebellion remains suicidal. The uprising of July failed, and I believe the opposition remains cowed by that failure and the force at John's command."

"It's a strange thing," the count observed, "that faith can convince so many to remain docile, even though it goes against their interests and may cost them their lives. Faith combined with fear, that is. I take it the city defenses remain as stout as ever?"

"They do, Count Wirich. The population remains well-organized and alert. Any damage done by your cannons is repaired within a day, and any direct assault on the city will result in severe casualties to the attacker."

"Then we must continue our siege until conditions become more favorable. For that, I have a plan."

"Does it involve my services?"

"Only indirectly, my good Henricus. One of my associates in the siege, Philip, the Landgrave of Hesse, came up with the idea of printing pamphlets and catapulting them into the city. These will encourage the citizens of Münster to desert their posts and come over to our side in exchange for lenient treatment. What if we were to add a statement from you to these pamphlets?"

"A statement concerning what, my lord?"

"The king anointed you as a prophet of God, correct?"

"He did."

"If you were to make plain that you've been a spy all along, and are a false prophet, perhaps that will diminish morale in Münster still further and cause more desertions. What do you think?"

"I'll get to work writing such a statement without delay, Count Wirich. All I require is a quill and parchment to get the words into form."

That said, Henricus departed the tent. He felt it inconvenient to burden either the bishop or the count with the knowledge that, while he'd dutifully turned over all two hundred Spanish gold coins that he'd been given for his journey by King John, fifty more gold coins had appeared by God's grace, and he'd hidden and locked them in his personal trunk of clothes and other supplies.

Count Wirich turned to the bishop. "I know such maneuvers try your patience. But I see no need to rush things. The people of the city cannot escape. In time, they will starve, as surely as you and I sit here. This trick with Henricus will sap their numbers and their will yet further. I still hold out hope that, given enough time and suffering, the people of Münster will do our work for us."

"All it costs us is money," von Waldeck countered sourly. "Lots of money. That's why I prefer a more direct approach."

"An interesting outlook for a bishop."

"A bishop who's sat in the same spot for seven months, Count Wirich. A bishop who is impatient to bring these recalcitrant sinners and traitors to heel and resume the Lord's work."

"What the spy Henricus said about the city's defenses is no doubt accurate. I believe you can speak from experience about the futility of open assault."

"We have twice the numbers now I had at my disposal in early August."

"Which still won't be enough, in my judgment. This isn't like my campaigns against the Ottomans of days gone by. The Ottomans like to come out and fight in the open, wheeling their cavalry just out of your reach while showering you with arrows. This is more like to when Christian II of Denmark employed me to help him claim the throne of Sweden."

"And after doing so, Christian immediately massacred the leading nobles of Sweden, thus ensuring an uprising against his rule."

"I advised him not to kill so many opponents. A handful of beheadings, as opposed to dozens, would have sufficed in my eyes, but I'm a general, not a royal councilor. That's also why, when he attempted to reclaim his throne in 1531 and inquired about my services, I was indisposed to fight on his behalf once more."

"Was that before or after you began taking up with Protestants like Sybille of Cleves and Johann Frederick of Saxony?" von Waldeck questioned, a very serious look in his eye.

"I was an escort, not a convert."

"Both Martin Luther and Phillip Melancton attended the marriage."

"And proved to be fine fellows, too, if I may say. But if," and here, the count's eyes narrowed and his voice dropped, "you make another comment that even suggests I may have motives here beyond capturing a city full of delusional fanatics, perhaps I'll withdraw my men and let you have another crack at the city walls with what's left."

Bishop von Waldeck continued to look Count Wirich in the eyes but had no response.

"We must have patience, my dear Bishop. Münster will fall, and its people will die. It's only a question of how they choose to die and how long they can postpone their deaths."

Chapter 29

Heinrich had returned to his position as Captain of the Watch in early November, but this was one of those nights he wished he hadn't. The wind blew from the north without mercy, bits of snow flew sideways into his face, and even the watch fires burning on Münster's walls made little difference against the freezing chill. He blew on his hands while he paced the watch, but even with his thick mittens, it wasn't enough to keep them warm. Absentmindedly, he crumpled up the latest propaganda paper launched into the city by Phillip of Hesse from its basket and tossed it to the flames. Immediately after the first pamphlet barrage in October revealing Henricus as a false prophet, King John had made possessing or reading the pamphlets punishable by death. So, now Heinrich used them to keep the fire going.

He joined one of his men in stamping his boots to keep the blood flowing in his feet. The man, who went by the name Little Hans, had on the colorful uniform of the landsknechts who'd defected earlier in the year. By now, however, the sleeves were tattered under the stained fur cloak that Little Hans had wrapped around his body. They were the only two on this section of the wall.

"Ghastly night, isn't it, Captain? I almost wish the bishop's men would do something. It might be better than freezing our bones up here. But I imagine they're hunkered down inside their tents waiting for the storm to blow over, just like we are. Or should be, anyway."

"I suspect you're right, Little Hans," Heinrich said with a smile. "It's not a night to do anything but huddle by the fire. Yet, here we are."

"Here we are," Little Hans replied with a sniffle.

Heinrich wasn't sure if the sniffle was sadness or just the weather. Come to think of it, he didn't know that much about Hans, other than that he went by Little Hans. But Hans was the quiet type who generally stayed off to himself. Dependable, but calm and quiet. *Not really the traits of a mercenary soldier*, Heinrich thought, but much like himself.

"Say, Hans, why is it that people call you Little Hans?" Heinrich asked after a moment. "Most grown men wouldn't want that name, I'd guess, but you don't seem to mind." It couldn't be because of size. Little Hans stood about average in height and was on the burly side. At least, he had been before the food got scarce.

"My father was Big Hans. Therefore, I'm Little Hans."

"Is he still alive?"

"No. He died when I was nineteen. That's when I left my home, Nijmwegen, in the Netherlands and set out to see the world. We lived on Long Street, so I grew up with people calling me Little Hans of Longstreet."

Inside, Heinrich laughed. That sounded familiar. Although it wasn't the answer he expected coming from a quiet guy like Little Hans, he could certainly sympathize.

"So, how did you get here, then? You didn't make it too far out into the world if you came to Münster unless you stopped here on the way home."

Little Hans laughed. "I wasn't a very good traveler. I'm not the quickest at picking up new languages, for one thing, and it got a little lonely traveling by myself. So, I did the next best thing."

"Became a soldier?"

"It took care of the lonely part, and I still get to travel."

Heinrich laughed again, out loud this time. "Yes, I suppose that's true. Well, we've got that in common. I was a landsknecht once myself."

"Really?"

"I fought in the war against France that started in 1521. Didn't care much for being a soldier, though, and I decided to come here and settle down after my time was up. My plan worked, too, until our present difficulties began."

"I hope I live long enough to get to choose a place to settle down," Little Hans said quietly.

"What do you mean?"

"I'd rather not die here. I haven't seen my sister in a couple years, and I'd like to see her again before the end. Don't take that as a sign of cowardice, though, Captain. I'll fight when it comes to it."

Heinrich nodded in the flickering firelight, the misty vapors billowing out whenever he exhaled shredded away by the wind. "That makes sense to me. And no, I don't think you're a coward. Wanting to see your family again isn't a sign of weakness. At least, not to me. Can I ask, though, why you came over to our side and deserted von Waldeck? Surely, you know that if the bishop's men ever get into the city, they'll show no mercy toward you."

"Yeah, you're probably right about that. I just happened to be drunk when our captain decided to defect, so, I went with him."

"I've never seen you drink beer, though, Little Hans. Not even once."

"Experience is a hard teacher, Captain. I did something stupid. As soon as I realized it was stupid, I made up my mind not to drink anymore. A little late on my part, perhaps, but I hope to live long enough to profit from the lesson I learned."

Heinrich patted Little Hans on the shoulder. "Don't we all."

Bernard Rothmann stared blankly at the wall of his study, trying to blink some clarity into his mind. The night was far gone, his study freezing cold, and he could barely keep his eyes open. But he had to finish for the sake of the salvation of the New Jerusalem.

He'd spent all night writing his third and last statement of faith on behalf of God's people. Rothmann looked down at the document, written out in his smooth, flowing cursive script. Beautiful words, such beautiful words of God's truth.

He lifted the parchment from his writing desk and extended the top right corner toward the flame of one of his candles. It was good work, he thought, for someone just nicknamed "Stutenberent" earlier that day. Stutenberent! White Bread Bernie! After all he'd done to bring about the New Jerusalem and God's return to His people on Earth, the only thing people would remember him for was handing out communion bread.

Just as the first yellow flame licked the corner of his third testament, Rothmann pulled the paper back. No, he'd not give the fools who advised King John that much satisfaction. This testament was his proof that he was right. When the flames of Hell engulfed Johann Dusentscher and the king's other false councilors, his words would protect him from sharing the limping prophet's fate. Rothmann dropped the parchment back to his writing desk and sighed.

Why didn't King John march out and throw back God's enemies? The time was right. The Age of the Apostles was over. That had been the time for preaching, spreading the gospel, and bringing people to Christ through conversion and persuasion. An age of martyrs and saints, when God allowed the godless to carry out their persecution of His Church in fulfillment of the words of scripture. Rothmann knew that the Age of the Apostles was a time of waiting, when God's faithful suffered patiently while the number of Saints grew and reached its appointed total.

But that time had ended. The Age of Vengeance had arrived. Now, God's apostles would unsheathe their swords and turn the wickedness of the godless back upon them tenfold. Indeed, as he'd written in his testament, it was time to "let fall the apostolic weapons and take up the armor of David." God's Chosen would fight Satan's minions "not only with the humble weapons of the apostles for suffering but also with the glorious armor of David for vengeance."

There must be no hesitation. God had made one Earth. He had one Chosen People. There could only be one king.

Both the Old Testament prophets and the apostles themselves had foreseen this day. The books of Deuteronomy, Isaiah, Jeremiah, Daniel, Ezekiel, Joel, Micah, Zechariah, Malachi, Matthew, Luke, Acts, Romans, and Thessalonians all referred to this transition from one age to another. The captivity in Babylon endured by the Israelites was but a model, a prediction, of the entire history of God's Church. Now the Elect would shake off the chains thrown around them by Antichrist and emerge from their own captivity. Just as the biblical David had cleared the way for Solomon, the new David, John of Leiden, would clear the way for Christ's return.

It all seemed so clear to Rothmann. And yet, something was wrong. None of the apostles sent out in October had returned. Not one. Henricus had elected to endure eternal hellfire and revealed himself as a false prophet, but Rothmann expected that false prophets would emerge at times. That was the way of history. But no one had come to the relief of the New Jerusalem.

Rothmann blamed Dusentscher, for he believed the man to be another false preacher. It was curious, suspicious, in fact, that he'd only arisen as a prophet during the summer. After men like Rothmann, John of Leiden, John Matthys, and Bernhard Knipperdollinck had taken all the risks to establish the New Jerusalem, then Johann had limped into the picture, coming from nowhere, as it were.

Perhaps the presence of another false prophet among God's faithful was what had prevented the success of the apostles. Yes, that must be it. Rothmann himself had written in October, "The mouth of the godless must be stopped on Earth. All evil, and everything the heavenly Father has not planted must be rooted out and done away with." This meant that Rothmann had to find a way to expose or eliminate this false prophet. Yet, Dusentscher stood high in King John's favor. Rothmann must think further about how to uproot this thorn bush in the garden of the New Jerusalem.

Until this happened, the Elect couldn't carry out the Lord's plans. As he'd written, "The glory of all the Saints is to wreak vengeance. Revenge without mercy must be taken upon all who are not marked with the Sign." Then, but only then, could God's Saints live free of the oppression of the unrighteous. When the Saints had risen and their vengeance was complete, then God's people would live in peace. Earthly rulers, all the princes and the mighty, would disappear, and all the beautiful things they owned would be available to all. And yet, God's people would hold such things as jewels and riches to be as cheap as mud or stone, for no one would be above his neighbor, and all would hold everything in common, as the Scriptures demanded.

Rothmann knew it was up to him, perhaps up to him alone, to clear the path for the Lord's return. But not tonight. It was time for some rest at last. Picking up his work, Rothmann scanned the final paragraph one last time, making sure he'd made his call to action sufficiently urgent.

There may be those who think that God Himself will come down from Heaven with His angels to avenge Himself on the godless, and who confidently wait for it. No, dear brother. He will come, that is true. But the vengeance must first be carried out by God's servants who will properly repay the unrighteous godless as God has commanded them. God will be with His people and will give them iron horns and bronze claws against their enemies. For very soon we, who are covenanted with the Lord, must be His instruments to attack the godless on the day which the Lord has prepared. Thus, God's strong arm will be with us, and He will display His glorious power in His people who have so long been despised and cast out before the world. It is as Malachi says: You shall tread the wicked to death, for they will be dust under your feet on the day which I make, says the Lord of Hosts.

Bernard Rothmann smiled. Perfect.

Slowly, Hilde dragged herself from under the soft linen blankets where she slept. With the morning light shining through the high window of the room in St. Lambert's Cathedral she shared with two of John's other wives, she crawled to the mirror.

Hilde didn't know the woman who looked back at her. Her dark hair, once long and lustrous before she cut it short, lay matted and tangled on her head. Some of the scratches she'd given herself on her face had healed, but with others she'd cut herself too deeply, leaving scars. But neither of those things concerned her most today. Instead, it was the bruises to her right cheek and eye socket. Hilde sighed and blinked rapidly, hoping her black and purple splotches would look better after she'd cleared the sleep from her eyes. But they didn't. All she managed to do was make herself look at her eyes in the mirror. Bloodshot. It was the price of being too scared to sleep at night.

Hilde didn't cry. She'd given that up weeks ago. Crying didn't help or make things any better. All it accomplished was to make her look weaker in Queen Divara's eyes and more pitiful to King John.

Not pitiful enough to dismiss her as his wife, however. Instead, he'd had Divara slap her until she stopped crying, stating that she brought dishonor on him when she wept. After a few days, Hilde stopped. Now, almost any movement from Queen Divara caused her to flinch involuntarily.

That was the cause of her present facial injury. When King John had bidden Hilde to bring his drinking cup to the table last night, the queen had dropped a carrot on her plate just as Hilde approached. Her sudden movement caused Hilde to fumble the wine to the floor. A blow to the side of her face from the king had been her punishment.

Many mornings, Hilde awoke and felt ready to vomit. Her mouth hurt, and sometimes her stomach cramped, too. Lately, she'd added occasional dizziness and intense headaches to her list of maladies.

When she'd first become one of King John's wives, Hilde had prayed to God nightly to ease her troubles. But after a couple weeks, when those troubles only increased, she'd stopped praying, too. Besides, what kind of god would make someone like John of Leiden a king?

So, Hilde sat on the chilled stone floor and shivered, her breath puffing out in front of her in the morning cold. She wished that she could talk to one of the other wives she slept beside, but she couldn't. The older of them, Victoria, would squeal to Queen Divara should Hilde dare to tell her anything. The other, Rose, was the twelve-year-old girl who'd almost died after King John forced himself upon her. Now, in her terror, Rose rarely spoke to anyone.

In fact, Hilde had only spoken to Rose once since the day Rose had had to rush to the doctor. That was two days ago. In whispers, they'd made a pact. If there ever came a time when they both were in the kitchen by themselves, they'd grab the longest knives they could find and end their misery together.

Hilde just hoped that that day came soon. For both their sakes.

When Heinrich woke in the middle of the morning and came to the table, he found Brigitte sitting there, head in her hands.

"How is Sofie doing this morning?" he asked his wife quietly.

"She's working hard at her weaving."

"Sofie puts so much pressure on herself. Since the king decreed that having excess clothing was an abomination to the Father, she's worked harder than ever to make more for us and replace what the burgomaster took away. I'm just happy she had some wool stored to work with."

"Sofie told me it's almost gone. When she finishes the shirt she's working on now, that'll be it."

Heinrich made a sour face. "How about food?"

"Likewise, it's almost gone. Rudolf continues to bring us bread when he can, but even that's becoming less frequent."

"You've been working on him whenever he comes over, right?"

"Of course, Heinrich, just like we planned. He's been a different man ever since his brother's death this summer. I've never gotten him to admit as much, or explain why, but I think he's changed."

"Changed enough that we might bring him into our plans?"

Brigitte hesitated. She opened her mouth to answer but then closed it.

Heinrich blew air from his mouth while he sighed. "Not yet, then. If you aren't convinced, then I'm not convinced."

"I want to say yes, Heinrich, but I just can't do it. I want to. Rudolf still has the favor of some of the king's council. If we could get him to cooperate with us, we might use him to get some news about Hilde. None of us have seen her since you did back in October."

"Just keep working on Rudolf. If things get desperate, we might have to take a chance on him."

"Have you had better luck finding an accomplice?"

"Maybe. I've got one man in mind who might have potential. I don't think he's ready to turn yet, however. I'm going to need more time to sound him out."

"Heinrich, how much more time do you think we have?"

He shrugged. "I doubt the besiegers will do anything rash in the next month or two. It's hard to dig trenches when the ground is frozen, so I don't foresee that they'll try to get any closer to the walls. If they didn't attack last fall, I doubt they will in the early spring, either. Their numbers haven't gotten any greater, and it appears that two unsuccessful attacks have made them more cautious. But there's been one new development I haven't mentioned to you before, Brigitte."

"Oh?"

"I'm sorry I didn't tell you earlier, but it just struck me why it might be important. I've seen new banners flying in the bishop's camp. A blue field with a white wagon wheel."

"Why does that matter?"

"Remember when I finally admitted the details about my early career as a soldier?"

"Of course, Heinrich."

"I fought against the French, but some of the other troops of the Holy Roman Empire fought in the southeast against the Ottomans. Rumors reached us in France about the exploits of a commander named Count Wirich of Falkenstein. My memory is hazy, but I seem to recall that he killed a great number of Ottoman soldiers in his campaign. I think that was his standard."

"How does that change things for us?"

"I'm working on that, Brigitte. Perhaps it's time I make one more trip over the walls and do some eavesdropping on the bishop's men. Perhaps I'll learn something useful. It's unlikely, but it's the best I can think of right now."

"You remember what happened in October to the last man who tried that. Knipperdollinck cut his head off. Is it worth the risk, Heinrich?"

"Everything is a risk now. If I'm killed quickly by the sword, or slowly by hunger, I die either way. And you and Sofie will, too, if you and I can't unravel this knot of questions."

"Maybe I can help you."

Heinrich and Brigitte looked up to see Sofie standing on the edge of the room.

"How long have you been standing there?" Brigitte asked.

"A while. I've heard everything, and I want to do my part to help."

Sofie braced herself for her uncle's anger and reproach for listening in on Brigitte and him.

Instead, he smiled and beckoned her to the table. "You have a plan?" Heinrich asked his niece.

She sat down. "I do. What if I married Rudolf?"

Sofie's statement hung in the air for several moments.

Finally, Brigitte spoke. "But you don't like him at all."

Sofie looked down. "That's true. Even the new Rudolf is still not enough to make me like him very much. But you said it would help if he were on our side. If he were my husband, we might be able to win him over."

Again, silence reigned while everyone considered the importance of this step.

This time, Heinrich broke the stillness. "You realize, Sofie, that even if our plan works, and we survive the siege, he'll be your husband for life?"

"It's better than seeing you and Brigitte suffer and maybe die. Plus, you said he might be able to help us find out about Hilde. If it helps Hilde, then maybe I should do it."

"I don't think either I or your uncle can tell you what to do, Sofie," Brigitte stated carefully. "This has to be your decision, and your decision alone. All I ask is that you don't do anything rashly. The city isn't going to fall tomorrow. Take some time and think it through."

The next evening, Heinrich's shoes made a tiny crunching sound when he dropped to the ground. Hunched over, he half walked and half crawled forward, making for a point in the lines of the besiegers directly between two watchfires. When he got close enough to hear voices, Heinrich dropped to his stomach and pulled himself forward with his elbows. First one, then the other, he edged nearer to the first line of trenches.

The weather had warmed a bit since the storm, so the ground was half-thawed mud, but Heinrich couldn't help that. In fact, Heinrich realized, the dirtier his clothes were, the better he'd blend in. It was still cloudy. That would also help. No moonlight to reveal his position.

As Heinrich inched closer, he saw men posted as guards in the weak firelight. They looked out from their trenches now and then, but this far after midnight, Heinrich guessed they cared more about staying warm than watching for intruders. He couldn't blame them. No forays, sorties, or foraging missions coming from Münster had bothered them for days, so they had no reason to expect tonight to be any different. The only way they'd know someone had listened to them was when they saw the trail his body made in the mud later in the morning.

While he waited and listened in the slim hope he might overhear something useful, Heinrich thought about his nieces. He'd heard nothing from Hilde. No messages, no public appearances, nothing. King John kept St. Lambert's ringed with armed guards. Heinrich saw no way to get to her, which scared him to the core. Hilde could be dead, and no one would know a thing about it. He just prayed that wasn't true.

Sofie, however, was another matter. Heinrich didn't know what to make of her suggestion regarding Rudolf yesterday. He only wanted Sofie to be happy. That's why he'd almost tried to talk her out of it then and there. But Heinrich conceded that her idea had some merit. However he'd acquired them, Rudolf had connections with the Anabaptist leadership. Heinrich had never heard him complain about being hungry, and he didn't look like he'd lost weight in the way most other Münsterites had during the past months. If Sofie's choice was between marrying Rudolf and surviving, or having nothing to do with him and starving, it wasn't that tough a decision.

With a shiver Heinrich realized how morose that thought was. Had it really become a matter of life or death? It was one thing to say that to Brigitte and Sofie to emphasize the gravity of the situation, but another to know in his heart that things really were that dire. Heinrich closed his eyes in thought and then conceded that things had nearly reached that point. After all, that's why he lay huddled and shivering in the mud tonight, enemy soldiers less than fifty feet away. Heinrich admitted to himself he wouldn't be here if he had any reasonable hope that the people of Münster were going to survive by holding to their present course.

With that thought to further chill his heart, Heinrich lay there in the mire, hoping against hope to learn something beneficial that would make his choices clearer. He wished that Sofie didn't have to make such momentous decisions when she'd only just turned twenty years old.

Almost three hours later, shortly before dawn, Heinrich pulled himself back over the outer wall of Münster, safely away from the mercenaries. Shivers wracked his body from the chill air and almost-frozen mud clinging to his clothes, shivers that even his strenuous climb up the wall hadn't gotten rid of. More than anything, he needed to get indoors and find a fire.

To Heinrich's dismay, several men from the watch stood there waiting for him.

"Going somewhere, Captain Gresbeck?"

"Had a good talk with the bishop's soldiers, did we?" another asked.

A third man stated, "Deacon Eding said to beware of the bishop's spies. It looks like we found one."

"Hardly," Heinrich grunted. "Spies don't climb over walls looking like I do. Their job is to blend in, not to stand out."

"A likely story," the first man stated in sarcasm.

"But a true one. If I were a spy, I wouldn't have had to crawl on my stomach to get to the enemy's lines. They would've let me pass standing up. And fed me, too. I'm starving." Heinrich shivered again.

"Perhaps you'd like to tell it to the deacon himself. He can judge."

"If you insist." Heinrich had no doubt Eding would listen to him. Most of the time, he listened to whomever spoke last.

"That won't be necessary," a new voice called out.

Heinrich looked to the new speaker. Rudolf.

"I have instructions from King John himself to bring Heinrich Gresbeck to St. Lambert's Cathedral. He's anxious to speak with his captain of the watch about the captain's recent activities."

When Heinrich saw the two guards flanking Rudolf finger their swords, he bowed his head and followed. It appeared his luck had run out.

Chapter 30

Near Groningen, the Netherlands, Holy Roman Empire

March of 1535

The Duke of Gelderland, Charles II, waited astride his horse as the rain misted down upon him and his soldiers. The tiny raindrops swirled in the light breeze before gently landing. Charles hated to see his banners, with their alternating scarlet and gold chevrons, damp and slack. In his mind, it just didn't make for a stirring cavalry charge unless they billowed in a fresh breeze. Regardless, a cavalry charge was what was about to happen.

"All is ready, sir," Maarten van Rossum, Charles's field marshal, said. "Shall I order the infantry forward to engage the enemy?"

Charles didn't reply. He just looked out at his foes as they marched raggedly across the open plain toward him, still about half a mile distant. He adjusted his plumed hat and rubbed his stubbled chin while a few raindrops fell from his metal armor.

"Sir?" van Rossum repeated while Charles waited.

"It's not a *bad* day for killing heretics, I suppose," Charles finally said to his subordinate with the full red beard. "What does their leader call himself again?"

"Christ, the Son of God."

"Indeed. How humble of him."

"He won't defile the Son of God's name much longer after you give the order to advance, my lord."

"You've performed brilliantly these past months, Maarten. If only I'd had your services at the Battle of Béthune in 1487, perhaps we would have carried the day."

Van Rossum smiled. He'd been nine years old when that battle in France took place.

"Still, I'm getting too old for this sort of thing," Charles continued. "Killing peasants and artisans while you command professional soldiers doesn't hold much glory, does it?"

"It beats the alternatives, does it not?"

At last Charles smiled and laughed. "Yes, I suppose it does. Given how much Emperor Charles hates me, the last thing I want is for a peasant rebellion to get out of hand to the point where he decides to send troops and interfere. Were it not for this trouble in Münster distracting him, we'd probably be at war with Emperor Charles again right now."

"Well, then, let us treat these Anabaptists marching toward us as practice for the emperor's forces, then."

Charles laughed again. "Well put. Practice, it is. Tell me again how you tricked them into coming out to meet us today, Maarten."

"When Count Wirich of Falkenstein sent word to you that John of Leiden had dispatched missionaries to stir up the Anabaptists throughout the empire, it gave me an idea. I obtained a few copies of Bernard Rothmann's pamphlets, printed more of them, but added a section stating that King John himself would march out to meet any Anabaptists going to Münster and that together they'd drive all the ungodly from the face of the Earth. I encouraged any

Anabaptist reading the pamphlet to set out for Münster without delay."

"Clever, Maarten, very clever. Still, part of me wishes we could do this without so much bloodshed. Perhaps these poor fools deserve it for being gullible and falling for this Anabaptist nonsense, but I'd rather save the lead shot for Emperor Charles's men."

"I've always said that burning and torching is the jewel of war. Dead bodies won't come back to fight you another day."

"True enough, Maarten, true enough. But it's also true that dead bodies can't go back to their daily lives and pay taxes when the war is over."

"Shall I change tactics, then, sir? The plan calls for the infantry to advance and skirmish with the enemy briefly, then feign a retreat. When that draws our opponent into pursuit, the infantry will turn and hold its ground while our cavalry swoops in from both flanks and cuts them to pieces. The battle will be over in one hour."

"No, keep the plan. Just pass the word for the cavalry not to kill everyone. When our opponents panic and try to flee in all directions, let some of them get away. We need a victory that's decisive enough that we'll see no further Anabaptist uprisings, but that's all."

"As you wish, my lord."

"Oh, and Maarten, after it's over, feel free to inform Count Wirich of the complete annihilation of our foes."

"Sir?"

"I can't let him think that Antoine of Lalaing has outdone me when it comes to putting down peasant unrest."

Van Rossum laughed. Antoine of Lalaing was Emperor Charles's Imperial Stadtholder, or governor, in the Netherlands and a rival of the Duke Charles he served.

"I'll write him that their bodies blacken the ground while the carrion birds feast upon the corpses," van Rossum replied. "My reputation should ensure he believes the tale."

As it turned out, van Rossum was wrong about the length of the battle. Rather than being over in an hour, his victory was complete within twenty minutes.

At the same time Duke Charles II of Gelderland plotted the destruction of Groningen's Anabaptists, Antoine of Lalaing, likewise seated on horseback, looked through the light rain at the burning monastery before him. Would this stupidity ever end?

Not more than a week ago, he'd intercepted three boatloads of Anabaptist sympathizers trying to sail and row up the Ijssel River. A message from Count Wirich of Falkenstein had arrived mentioning that the crazed leaders of Münster were sending out missionaries to promote a general uprising of Anabaptists in the Holy Roman Empire. Thanks to this tip, Antoine had gathered what forces he could and sent out spies in the towns where he knew Anabaptists dwelt. Once his spies told him of the three vessels on the Ijssel, Antoine had hurried to halt their progress. He'd pounded the ships with cannon fire until all three had sunk, drowning most of the people on board. Those who could swim and tried to crawl out of the river his soldiers had butchered.

Now, here he was, looking at St. Plechelm's Monastery. Inside were a rumored eight hundred Anabaptists who had taken cover at his approach. Twice already, his mercenaries had charged the old monastery, confident of easy victory against simple townspeople. Both times, those inside had fought back fanatically, and his men had fallen back. So, Antoine decided to use cannon to blow holes in the monastery's walls.

He supposed he could've just laid siege to the place. The Anabaptists couldn't have that much food inside, not with eight hundred people sheltering within. But his soldiers, angry over their unexpected repulses, thirsted for blood. Antoine would give it to them. The coat of arms of his family was a red field with white checkered diamonds, and the blood of the Anabaptists would soon run like the red on his banners.

While Antoine waited, another boom of cannons filled the air, and another section of the monastery's outer wall crumbled.

"Shall I order the men to advance once more?" his marshal inquired.

"No, no more direct attacks for now. Just keep up your fire until the flames force our prey out into the open. When they finally come out, then you can order our men forward. Give no quarter. Exterminate them to the last."

"You wish to take no prisoners to interrogate, then?"

"Not this time. My spies report we may see more uprisings. Perhaps at Minden, and perhaps even in Amsterdam. The more harshly we deal with these rebels, the better the chances that others will think twice before rebelling."

"I see, sir. I'll pass your orders to all our men."

"Have you seen this?" Antoine held out a scrap of paper for his subordinate. "It's the proclamation made by these rebels when they took up arms. Note the part that states their goal: 'To kill all monks and priests and all rulers who live in the world, for our king alone is the rightful ruler.' That is what we're up against here, and that is why they all must die."

Chapter 31

Münster

March of 1535

"Bishop von Waldeck, Count Wirich, I must see you immediately," the breathless courier panted as he hurried into the tent where the commander of the siege conversed with the bishop.

"You've come from Worms?" Count Wirich said, noting the man's livery. It was a black double-headed eagle on a yellow field. The emblem of Charles, the Holy Roman Emperor.

"Yes. I carry the emperor's latest decree about Münster." With a bow, the man handed over the parchment document sealed with the insignia of Emperor Charles. "The Imperial Diet at Worms met, and Emperor Charles sends its decision."

Count Wirich broke the seal and read silently. Once finished, he handed it to Bishop von Waldeck with a faint smile.

Von Waldeck read the document as well. "At last!" he crowed.

"This is excellent news," Count Wirich said calmly. "Every single ruler in the empire has voted funds to help recapture the city. Some have pledged troops as well. Within a month, our resources will double."

"Did you read the last lines?" von Waldeck inquired. "If Münster continues to resist, we are to pull down its walls, raze the city to the ground, and exterminate its people."

"Yes, I read those instructions," the count answered as he licked his lips.

"My king, I fear we have another false prophet amongst us," Bernard Rothmann said to John of Leiden in the sanctuary of St. Lambert's Cathedral, which had become the king's audience hall.

John's eyebrows rose. "Can you name the man?"

"I can, although it pains me greatly to speak the name, sire."

"Brother Rothmann, you are the King's Royal Orator. Always you've served me, and the Father, loyally. You have nothing to fear. Speak."

"My lord, I believe that Johann Dusentscher has been bearing false witness to the Elect of God."

The king frowned hard. "Say it is not so, Brother Rothmann. I find that hard to believe."

"That is why I hesitated, my liege. I know he serves as the chief prophet of the Father, but I beg you to distance yourself from his false counsel."

"What evidence have you for this accusation? Surely, you've not forgotten that when the July rebellion against the Father resulted in our imprisonment, it was Brother Johann who prophesied our deliverance."

"I know he predicted that we would be redeemed, as Paul and Silas were, and our lives spared. But consider, my king, the other things that have happened since July. Before July arrived, all events pointed to the establishment of the New Jerusalem here in Münster. The Elect gained control of the city, and we defeated an attack by the bishop's men with ease. We established the community of goods and then polygamy. The two hundred mercenaries, won over by our righteousness, deserted and entered the city. Everything pointed to the victory of the Lord's people. We went from success to success."

"What you say is true so far, Brother Rothmann. Continue."

"Now think of what's befallen the Elect since July. We've become trapped in the city. The armies facing us have grown. Even though we defeated the bishop's second attack, we did so only with great effort. The people now go hungry. Most damning of all, none of the apostles we sent out to convert or destroy the other towns of Westphalia succeeded in their missions. The other cities of Westphalia have not perished in flame, nor have they sunk in damnation. No relief has come to us. Finally, although it pains me to say it, my lord, I fear that some of the people of the New Jerusalem lose faith. How could this happen, if not for a false prophet who has displeased the Father and brought these sufferings upon us?"

King John stared ahead for a considerable time. Twice, he worked his mouth as if ready to answer, but didn't. Finally, he turned to Rothmann. "This is a most serious accusation, Brother Rothmann. Yet, one cannot deny that your words are a true description of the past year. Perhaps some bit of truth is in them."

"What is to be done about the false prophet Dusentscher, then?"

"I shall send for him and ask him to answer for what you've said. Have you carried out your other duties as Royal Orator, Brother Rothmann?"

"Yes, my king. Tomorrow morning, my messengers will call for the whole people of God to assemble and learn that our deliverance is near. I only hope that we've regained the Father's approval by then so that the words will prove true."

That said, Rothmann spun on his heel and left the king's presence.

Only when he'd returned to his quarters a minute later did he let his breath out fully. Part of him had feared that King John would become angry and strike him down on the spot. The fact that he'd listened was a promising development. But Rothmann knew he had nothing to lose at this point, and so, truly he had nothing to fear. Either King John would eliminate the false prophet Dusentscher, and the New Jerusalem would witness Christ's return, or God would smite the city into ruin for its lack of the true faith. And if the second event happened and Rothmann perished, he knew God would soon welcome him into the Kingdom of Heaven.

Jost Kalle stepped through the ruins of what had been the Church of Our Dear Lady, his stomach grumbling all the while in hunger. The first blush of dawn brightened the horizon. The convent built alongside the parish church likewise stood in ruins, everything gutted save the foundations of the church's steeple tower and the outer walls of the sanctuary. Stumbling over some of the charred remains of pews and the broken shards of stained-glass windows, Jost approached where the altar had once stood, running his hand through his haggard beard and unkempt hair. He hoped his eyes weren't too bloodshot from lack of sleep.

He found a middle-aged woman kneeling there, praying, and knelt alongside her. He saw the trails from the tears that streaked the dirt on her face, although she wasn't crying at present. The woman appeared almost waifish, she was so thin.

"Hello, sister," Jost said as he dropped his wiry body to one knee. The woman nodded in return but didn't respond.

Jost closed his eyes and prayed for a few moments, and then looked over at the woman again. Finally, he ventured to ask, "You were a nun here, weren't you? Before the king ordered most of the churches and convents destroyed."

She nodded again, then said, "I spent twenty-seven years of my life in this convent, serving God. Twenty-seven years destroyed in a matter of days. But I still like to come here and pray just before dawn, like I used to. I always found it a quiet and peaceful time to talk to God."

"It's a tragedy," Jost agreed. "What's happened in Münster is a tragedy. The people suffer daily while the king and his court feasts on bread, beer, and pork. Now, I hear that the people must slaughter all their horses to provide more meat."

"I wouldn't know about that. Our convent didn't own horses."

Jost gave a little laugh. "Me, neither. Stonemasons don't have much need for them, I suppose, any more than nuns do."

"You're a stonemason by trade?"

"Yes. I spend most of my time inspecting the walls of the city after the bishop's cannons score a hit. If the cannonballs damage the walls, I help repair them."

"It sounds as though you have much work to do. What brings you here to what's left of my church, then?"

"Well, sister, we masons have a great deal of work to do, and it makes one very hungry. But without any meat to eat at home, I find it hard to sustain myself."

"Perhaps you should pray with me, then, and hope that God will hear our pleas."

"An excellent idea. You begin. You have more practice than I do."

While the woman whispered her prayer in the still air of the gray morning light, Jost stood and reached into his torn and ragged shirt. She stopped.

"It works better if you kneel and are still," she told him without turning around or standing herself. "God listens to the penitent and humble."

"Of course. I'm sorry. Go on." Jost knelt again.

When the woman resumed her petition, Jost stood once more.

"Please, be still," she sighed in exasperation. "Or go on your way and leave me to my morning prayers."

"Just make sure you ask God's forgiveness on my behalf," Jost said as he brought the short wooden club down on the nun's skull. Soundlessly, she crumpled to the ground, unconscious. After a few more blows, he felt for a pulse. Nothing.

Jost looked up at the sky through the opening where the church's ceiling had once been. He still had time to hide the woman's body before the sun came up. That night, he'd return with his oldest son and they would drag the body back to their home, salt down the woman's flesh, and in the days to come they would eat from the corpse until it was gone. His heart shuddered at what he'd just done, and what he was about to do, but Jost had no choice. It was that or starve himself. Jost had tried to eat leather, bark from trees, and even sawdust, but nothing filled his stomach. It was this or watch him and his children die of hunger.

Sofie and Brigitte trudged to the cathedral square, heads down. Although it was a fair enough day, pale sunshine but cool, Sofie shivered like she was walking to the gallows. Perhaps, in a way, she was. Only an hour before, the king's criers had marched through Münster's streets, calling everyone to the cathedral square once more to hear of their impending deliverance.

Beside her, Brigitte stumbled and fell to one knee. Slowly, unsteadily, she got back on her feet with Sofie's help. "I'm sorry, Sofie, just a loose cobblestone."

Sofie didn't buy it. "You don't look well, Brigitte. Is something wrong?"

"Just let me rest a moment," Sofie's aunt replied, going back down on her right knee. "I just feel so weak sometimes, and I see these gray spots in front of my eyes."

"That's because you need to eat more. Are you going to use that cane I found for you? It might help."

"A woman my age shouldn't walk with a cane. I'll be fine. Just give me a second."

Sofie helped her aunt back to her feet. This time she kept her balance. "Most women your age eat more than one meal per day, Brigitte."

"I just wish Heinrich were here to help me."

It took far longer than it used to, but eventually, Sofie and Brigitte reached the cathedral square. To save energy, both sat down while they waited for the king's appearance.

He didn't come out of St. Lambert's immediately. After a few minutes of sitting quietly, Sofie felt a tug on her shoulder. She turned. "Oh, Rudolf, it's you. I was wondering when you'd find me."

"We must move quickly. This way."

"Brigitte, I'll meet you at home afterward. Are you sure you're well?" Sofie asked.

"Yes, I think so. Just sitting here has revived me. You go along now."

"Hurry, Sofie. Before it's too late," Rudolf pleaded in her ear.

Sofie walked behind Rudolf as they headed for the outskirts of the gathering crowd. She tried to move casually even though her guts twisted and fear gnawed at her. Finally, Rudolf stopped and crouched down. Sofie noted they stood directly behind St. James's Church.

"Hilde's in there?"

"She should be, yes. Now that Queen Divara is pregnant, all the king's wives have moved in here, so things will be quieter. Once the queen comes out to attend today's royal audience in the square, you'll sneak in."

"How? Won't someone see me?"

"I bribed the lone guard who'll be left inside with two loaves of fresh bread." Just for a moment, Rudolf had his old, smug grin again.

For once, Sofie grinned back.

Before she could say anything else, a trumpet sounded, and King John emerged from St. Lambert's front double doors. He looked regal as always, today's robes alternating scarlet and deep blue. The king's crown and gold chains flashed whenever they caught the sunlight. Like usual, Knipperdollinck, Rothmann, Dusentscher, and the rest of the king's court followed him forward.

As he approached his throne in the middle of the square, John's mounted guards fanned out around the grounds. Few horses remained alive in Münster, but these looked strong and healthy.

When the front door of St. James's Church opened and the queen emerged, dressed as elegantly as the king and in the same colors, Rudolf crept to one of the church's side doors and knocked. Momentarily, it opened, and Sofie stole inside.

Rudolf smiled again. He'd done his part. Now, to get back to Brigitte, so he could help her get home safely. He walked calmly through the crowd, back to where she sat.

While Rothmann, the Royal Orator, announced the king, Rudolf sat down by his neighbor. "She's inside," he said quietly.

Brigitte nodded. "Thank you, Rudolf. You're sure it will work?"

"No, nothing's for sure, but Sofie's odds are good. How's your husband?"

"Heinrich is back on duty tonight. The men who found him climbing the walls back in December have been stationed elsewhere in the city."

"The Lord works in mysterious ways sometimes," Rudolf said with a broad smile.

"I won't ask how many strings you pulled to make that happen but thank you."

"All the strings I had left, I'm afraid. I persuaded Englebert Eding that your husband was scouting out the enemy, looking for weak spots in their defenses."

"Which is what he was doing, in a manner of speaking."

"Yes, my conscience is more than clear on that matter, even if not on all matters. But I doubt I could intervene again if things came to that."

"Hopefully, they won't. Just tell me one thing, Rudolf."

"Yes?"

"I don't get it. Sofie and I have both known for years that you are in love with her."

Rudolf's face reddened. "Yes, I was. And I still am."

"Yet, when she proposed that you two get married in January, you turned her down."

"I did."

"Why?"

Rudolf dropped his eyes and worked his mouth for a moment. "It has to do with those other matters upon which my conscience isn't as clear," he said at last, barely loud enough for Brigitte to hear him above the milling crowd.

The king had begun his address to the people of the New Jerusalem, but neither paid any attention to him. Brigitte's attention stayed riveted on Rudolf, who seemed to be making an unusually close examination of the cobblestones.

Finally, he continued. "Yes, it's true that for years I hoped to make Sofie my wife one day. I thought that by becoming prosperous, getting the newest, nicest clothes, and trying to rise in social standing I could win her favor. But when she married Kurt, it dawned on me in time that she didn't want those things. She just wanted someone who made her happy. For years, I thought I wasn't doing enough to impress her when, really, I was trying to do too much."

"That's very noble of you to admit, Rudolf, but it still doesn't explain why you turned her down two months ago. It seems to me that you've put all that behind you."

Again, Rudolf paused for a good while. He took a deep breath and continued. "But that isn't all. When the Anabaptists came to Münster, I got involved with them. Partly because of real enthusiasm for their teachings, but I know now that that was a mistake."

"You weren't the only one to make that mistake."

"No, but I supported them with more enthusiasm than most, and it took me far too long to see the hardship they caused for most people. Again, I did it partly to impress Sofie with what kind of figure I could cut in the town. But look where that's led me. Nowhere good.

"My mistakes with Sofie also helped me realize that I wasn't nearly the man I thought I was. Over the past months, I've learned that stepping on other people to get ahead of them isn't the right way to live. I've also admitted to myself that I was on the wrong side back in July. I should have stood with my brother Karl. If any of us manage to survive what's going on, maybe I'll think about Sofie's proposal again. But until then, I know I'm not worthy of Sofie."

Brigitte put her hand on Rudolf's shoulder and squeezed. He didn't dare tell her about certain other things he'd done in the service of the Anabaptists. No one could ever know those things.

Brigitte was about to compliment him again when the crowd cheered King John, so she decided she might as well listen in on what he said. After all, when the king spoke, it was the law of the New Jerusalem.

But he hadn't said anything. Instead, the king held aloft a tiny baby in his arms.

"The king's son, Newborn," Rudolf said.

"He named his son Newborn? What kind of a name is that?"

Rudolf shrugged.

Then, King John spoke. "This is a sign of the Father's favor. Never, since the birth of Christ himself, has a child like this been born into the world. The people of God have seen no such king since Christ's time on Earth. One day, this baby will grow and become king over all the world, just as the New Jerusalem shall spread over all the world."

Again, the crowd cheered, although Brigitte noted a pause between the king's words and the response, as if the people cheered because decorum required it.

After a few moments of this, King John handed his child back to its mother, Diana Knipperdollinck, who for once had gotten to leave her sheltered life and appear in public. When he turned to face the crowd again, however, his face had turned grave and serious.

"People of the New Jerusalem, it has come to my attention that serious crimes have been committed by some of the Elect. I hear words of doubt about the deliverance of our city from the hands of our enemies. Some of you hoped, as I did, that the apostles sent forth last October would bring relief to the city."

When the king paused a moment, several in the crowd around Brigitte and Rudolf murmured. Brigitte took this as confirmation of the king's words.

Growing still more grave, if that were possible, King John continued. "The lack of relief is due to our lack of faith. We were wrong to put our hopes in the hands of outsiders. We were wrong to put our faith in those not yet baptized into the Elect. This is not who we should rely on. God will certainly relieve us when it's our time.

"If our faith is true, God will certainly come to our aid. For I have seen visions, people of the New Jerusalem. Visions granted to me by the Father. In the Old Testament, an angel with a fiery sword delivered the Israelites. The same God who delivered his people of old still lives today. Then, I saw this city, the New Jerusalem, going around in a circle. This has great portent. It's a sign from the Father that we're still going to march around the world, and that I'm still going to be king over the world and lord over it.

"Some of you may wonder, however, why this hasn't happened yet. You may wonder why some of us suffer. I will tell you the reason. False prophets and betrayers like Henricus have arisen to sabotage the Father's will. I expected this. The pits and snares of Satan are many. It is our task, as the people of God, to find these spreaders of falsehoods and destroy them. As Brother Rothmann has written, only then will the path be straight for Christ's return.

"Today is a day of great joy. The Father has seen fit to grant me a son to rule after my appointed time. But the Father has also seen fit to reveal a betrayer amongst us. Bring forth the man!"

A silence fell over the crowd. Bernard Rothmann licked his lips in anticipation. Soon, however, his smile turned to a frown. King John's bodyguards did not move to seize Johann Dusentscher. Instead, they brought forward Claus Northorn, a man who had once been a burgher in Münster before the Anabaptists seized power.

But this was different. Instead of dragging Northorn in front of the king to have his punishment pronounced, some of the king's men wheeled forward a wooden frame that looked like an oversized ladder. A rack. Stretched upon the rack was Claus Northorn, hands and ankles bound securely. Even from where she sat, Brigitte could see the perspiration dripping from Northorn's face and arms as his limbs spasmed with fatigue.

Once the torture rack stopped near the king but in view of all the crowd, Bernhard Knipperdollinck stepped forward. "Claus Northorn, to your eternal damnation, you have sought to betray the New Jerusalem. Now you must face the punishment decreed by the Father."

Northorn croaked something in response, but his voice was too quiet for Brigitte to hear. She thought he said, "I am innocent," but couldn't be sure.

Knipperdollinck continued while waving a piece of paper for all to see. "I hold in my hand the note you wrote asking another of the Elect, Nicholas Snider, to join you in defecting to the enemy and betraying the city into Bishop von Waldeck's hands. However, Brother Nicholas revealed your betrayal to the king. In the process, he has earned a place of favor in the eyes of the Father. You are condemned of treason, Claus Northorn, and you must die."

While he spoke the last line, Knipperdollinck turned the wheel on the rack. Northorn's body stretched farther. He screamed in pain.

Knipperdollinck continued. "Your memory shall be blotted out, as if you'd never lived." Another crank of the wheel. Another scream. Now, anyone could see the perspiration streaming off Northorn's body.

"Once you die, the Great Serpent himself, Satan, will embrace you into his following. Everlasting pain shall be your fate." With a final turn of the wheel, everyone in the audience heard several sickening snaps. Claus Northorn screamed again, and then went on screaming as the rack tore his limbs from their sockets.

At a nod from Knipperdollinck, some of the king's guards cut down Northorn from the rack, holding him upright even as he tried to slump to the ground. Knipperdollinck drew forth the Sword of Judgment.

Before he could strike, however, King John intervened, taking the sword for himself. With a quick stroke, he parted Northorn's head from his body.

But that was not the end. Retrieving the Sword of Judgement from the king, Knipperdollinck continued hewing at Northorn's body, not stopping until he'd hacked the arms and legs of the corpse into a dozen pieces. Finally, he plunged the blade into Northorn's chest, cutting flesh from the cavity until one of the king's bodyguards pulled out the dead man's heart. He threw it on the ground, and Knipperdollinck stomped upon it.

All in the crowd were silent at the macabre scene. They'd seen several executions before, but nothing this gruesome. At last, the king spoke. "Take a section of this sinner's arms and legs. Take one to each gate as a reminder for the guards to remain watchful for betrayal. Hang the head from a pole in the cathedral's bell tower.

"This is the fate that awaits those who betray the Father. But, people of the New Jerusalem, God has revealed one more vision to me. He will deliver the city by Easter. If Christ has not returned to lead his people to victory by Easter, you shall do to me just as I've done to this traitor. This is the will of the Father."

288

While King John held forth outside, inside the church of St. James Hilde leaped into Sofie's embrace.

"Hilde!"

"Quiet, Sofie, they'll hear," Hilde said while finally releasing her sister.

"Who?" Sofie asked, reducing her voice to a whisper. She saw that Hilde's hair had grown back part of the way, but she also saw the pink and white scars on her sister's face from the wounds Hilde had inflicted upon herself. Sofie tried not to cry.

Hilde looked around nervously and then said, "The other queens." Then she extended her arms to hug Sofie once more.

In the process, Sofie saw her sister's bare forearms. "Hilde! What have you done?" Scars crisscrossed the pale flesh, some older, some that appeared very recent.

Hilde looked to the floor, and then put her head on her older sister's shoulder. "I was so scared, Sofie. I didn't think I'd ever see you again. I almost . . ." the words trailed away. Hilde was scared to say what they both knew.

"Didn't the king take pity on you when he saw that?"

"No. He told me he saw holy writing in the lines. A message from God. That I was special, and that the Father had a plan for me."

Still on the edge of tears, Sofie hugged her sister again and shook her head. All she could say through the sniffles was, "It's that bad, then?"

"Being the king's wife is a nightmare. Most of the king's wives hate each other and everyone's jealous of everyone else. Either they're trying to gain more favor from King John, or they're scared and would rather die than stay here."

Tears formed in Sofie's eyes, even though she tried to stop them, knowing which of the two groups her sister fell into. "I've got to get you out of here, then, Hilde."

Hilde stepped back, eyes flicking around wildly. "No, you can't. He'll know, and then you won't be safe, either."

"Hilde, you don't understand. We've got a plan. Uncle Heinrich, Brigitte, and I are working on a plan to get out of the city. But we won't go without you."

"No, Sofie," Hilde's eyes grew wider while she shook her head violently. "Someone already tried that. Rose tried to sneak away, but the king found out."

"Where is she now?"

"Buried in an unmarked grave. You need to leave without me."

"I'll never do that, Hilde. Neither will Uncle Heinrich."

"You must. Forget about me, Sofie. I'll be fine."

"But you aren't fine. How many times have you tried to cut your wrists?"

Before Hilde could answer, the young women heard booted footsteps moving down the hallway in their direction.

Hilde hid behind her sister as the guard who'd let Sofie inside appeared.

"I think you'd best be leaving," he whispered to Sofie. "The ceremony outside will be over soon."

Sofie kissed her sister's forehead and took her by the hand. "Just hold on, Hilde, and don't give up. I'll come back for you."

As the guard gently pulled Sofie from her sister's grasp, she looked at Hilde's scarred face once more. But Hilde's look had already turned ashen while she backed away.

Chapter 32

Münster

May of 1535

The news passed through the streets of Münster like a shock wave.

Rudolf Schweren sprinted down St. Ludger's Street, racing to bring the tidings to Sofie and Brigitte. When he arrived, he found Sofie, Brigitte, and Brigitte's children all at home.

Rudolf almost knocked the door from its hinges while bursting through. "Have you heard? What do you think?" he gasped.

Blank stares.

"The king has just made another proclamation. We're free to leave the city!"

"What?" everyone shouted at once.

"Yes! King John has just proclaimed that any of his people who are faithless and wish to choose eternal damnation rather than the rewards of Heaven can leave the city. But only today. By supper time, the gates of the city will close once more. And anyone who leaves can only take with them the clothes on their back. Everything else must stay in the city."

"We must get ready immediately, then," Brigitte stated. "This might be our last chance to get out before hunger kills us."

"Yes, I agree," Rudolf panted. "I heard King John myself. He said this was the only time the gates would open. He also said that because he was a merciful king, he'd let the unbelievers go, rather than kill them, but anyone who tried to leave after this must die."

"Then I say we go before he changes his mind. Remember his Easter prophecy? King John said he'd be beheaded if the city wasn't delivered by Easter, but then he changed his mind and said his death was only a spiritual one, and that it had purified him to lead God's Elect to victory over the unrighteous."

"Yes, and then he followed that up with three days of feasting and a parody of a Catholic Mass at which he said he could change the stones into bread."

"Speaking of," Brigitte asked Rudolf, "I don't suppose you have any more bread for us to eat before we go? The only reason we're still alive is because of you sharing with us, and my boys catching frogs and other critters to eat. If it weren't for that, we'd have starved like the family down the street who Deacon Eding found rotting in their beds last week."

Rudolf crossed himself in memory of his elderly neighbors who had starved to death, but then shook his head. "The bread is gone. I have no more ingredients to bake with."

Then, both noticed Sofie hadn't moved or spoken.

"Sofie, aren't you going to get ready?" Rudolf asked.

"I'm not leaving."

"But this is our last chance. We have to."

"I'm not leaving without Hilde. You can go. But I'll share the fate of my sister."

It was Brigitte who broke down and begged Sofie to reconsider. "Sofie, you have to come with us. If we become separated now, I just couldn't bear it. We have to stick together."

Sofie rose from her chair unsteadily and patted her aunt's shoulder. "You should go, Brigitte. Take your children. They shouldn't have to starve and die because of the mistakes of adults. But I'm staying."

"Sofie, my heart tells me you'll die if you don't come with us," Brigitte answered. "I know you love your sister but how do you plan to help her if you stay? You can't get to her. None of us can."

"Sofie doesn't need to," came a quiet voice from the doorway. All looked. It was Hilde.

"Hilde!" Sofie cried, running to the door to hug her younger sister. After holding the embrace for several seconds, she let go and took Hilde by the shoulders. "How did you get here?" Then Sofie noticed the fresh blood caked on her sister's left arm. "What happened now?"

"It's fine, Sofie, really it is."

"But you're bleeding again. Did you . . ." Sofie's voice trailed off, not daring to think her sister had cut her own wrists again, and unsure if the others present should know how many times Hilde had tried already.

Hilde gave a small smile. "No, not this time, Sofie. Earlier this morning, a crazed man came before King John. I didn't recognize who he was, but he said, 'Lord King, I've got to feed!' Then he leapt at me, grabbed my arm, and bit me. It hurt horribly, but the king's guards killed him."

"But how did you get here?" Brigitte wondered.

Again, Hilde gave a tiny smile. "The attack turned out to be a blessing in disguise. The whole time, the king didn't move. Once the crazed man was dead, John just sat in silence. Finally, he said that the attack was a sign from the Father. King John said the attack meant that his wives would suffer if they stayed by his side. So, he gave all of us permission to leave if we wished. All except Queen Divara and Diana Knipperdollinck, the mother of his son."

"Just like that, you got to leave?" Brigitte exclaimed.

"Yes, just like that. After months of being his prisoner, he decided to let us walk away if we wanted to. I also suspect he may be running short on food, and he was getting rid of extra mouths.

Our meals have been lighter of late. So, the man who bit my arm may have been only a convenient excuse. But in any case, here I am."

"That settles it, then," Sofie said. "It's time for all of us to get out of here at last, while we still have strength."

"Where's Uncle?" Hilde wondered.

"My goodness, you're right!" Sofie exclaimed. "We can't leave without him."

"He'd want us to go," Brigitte told the young women.

"How do you know?" they both replied.

"Many nights the past few months we've talked about this together in bed," Brigitte answered. "He's Captain of the Watch. Heinrich can't just leave his post; the Anabaptists will never allow it. But every time the thought came up, he told me that if the chance ever presented itself, to go without him. He'd sneak away later and join us as soon as he was able."

"Can he do that?" Hilde wondered.

Then Brigitte remembered Hilde hadn't heard the revelations Heinrich had given about his past life as a soldier. "Yes, I believe he can. At least, if anyone is capable of it, he is," she told Hilde.

"But how do you know?"

"Once we've found someplace safe, I'll explain how I know."

"What can we take with us?" Sofie wondered. "Rudolf, you said we're only allowed to take what we can carry?"

"Not even that. Just the clothes you're wearing. But don't wear nice clothes."

"Why not?"

"I overhead one guard say that the deacons had orders to confiscate any good clothing people were wearing and make them trade it for old, worn-out clothing."

"Well, I think we can manage that."

"Here's something we haven't thought of, though," Rudolf added. "What'll prevent us from starving once we leave the city? If all we have is clothes and no money, what'll we do? Fall on our knees and beg Bishop von Waldeck for a home? I can't see how we're going to get far once we pass the city gate."

"We have money," Sofie told him.

"But the deacons confiscated all of it."

"No, not all of it. Being a cabinetmaker has its benefits. Heinrich hid a small sum of money before the deacons came around. In fact, the chair your hand rests on has some coins hidden in the leg. We haven't spent them all these months because nothing costs money."

Rudolf produced his lopsided grin that Sofie hated so much, but right now it was a welcome sight. But a frown soon replaced it. "That still won't help us. The deacons will find it when we leave."

"Not if I have anything to say about it," Brigitte told everyone. "Not only will we benefit from Heinrich's craftiness, but don't forget, I'm a seamstress. My first husband was a tailor. I can sew those coins into our old clothes so inconspicuously that no one will know they're there."

Finally, Sofie smiled. "Let's go, then. We'll trust to Uncle Heinrich's talents to join us as soon as he's able."

It took some time for Brigitte to perform her work, but by late afternoon, the bedraggled troupe struggled and limped toward St. Ludger's Gate. Still, they stood among the very last to arrive because of the delay. A stream of people wanted to depart; hundreds at this gate alone, it looked like to Sofie. Most were already through the gatehouse and into the open space between Münster and the besieging troops. Sofie and her companions still had to wait quite a while to get to the gate itself, however. So many people meant to leave that the guards had to hold the rest while they searched those passing through the gate.

They'd been in line for about half an hour, in fact, but it was almost their turn; only a few people remained ahead of them. As Sofie looked at the people around her, it was hard to believe her eyes. Some were so skinny from hunger that they held up their pants with their hands. One older man looked like nothing but ashen skin pasted over thin bones. She wasn't sure how he could even move because his muscles were so shriveled. Sofie also saw young children, their bellies distended from eating moss, leather, and who-knew-what other things even less edible. These people simply stumbled forward in the lines, their movements achingly slow and deliberate. Still, it was an orderly line. Sofie supposed that was because no one had the energy left to push or cut in front of anyone else.

Finally, the moment came and Sofie reached the front of the line. Freedom and salvation were within her reach. Sofie saw the frowning guard nearest her motion her forward. She took a step in the worn, brown, dirty dress with all the holes that she'd nearly worn out last year. Brigitte had done her work perfectly. The coins hidden in her clothing made no sound when she moved.

Even as she stepped forward, a hand yanked her back with force.

"No!" Heinrich barked at Sofie. "You can't go. I won't let you. How can you embarrass me like that? A captain of the watch can't stand back and watch his family betray him!" To emphasize his point, he shook Sofie by her shoulders and tossed her away from the gate. She stumbled to the ground. Another person stepped forward to take her place and endure a search by the guards. Several other members of the crowd shuffled between Sofie and escape.

"Uncle, what are you doing?" she cried, tears already forming. She'd put so much hope in the escape plan, and now her own uncle had torn it away from her!

He leaned in close and spoke softly. "Sofie, you must play along. I'll explain later, but for now, pretend. You must trust me." Then, Heinrich resumed shouting for the benefit of whomever was watching. "My own niece, letting down her faith and going against the Father!" He shook her again.

Then, Heinrich saw Brigitte, her children, Rudolf, and Hilde gather around him. Hilde! His heart almost broke on the spot at the sight of his younger niece free at last. He'd have to find out how she escaped from King John as soon as he could. But now was not the time.

Heinrich walked to his wife, grabbed her by the hair at the back of her head, and yanked her close. "Forgive me. Just do what I say," he whispered to her, even as Brigitte whimpered from the sudden pain at her scalp. Then, out loud, he yelled, "And my own wife! Betraying me and the Elect of God! Come with me. Now!"

He dragged Brigitte by the arm toward the stair leading to the top of the city walls. Sofie came after, leading Hilde by the hand. Hilde's whole body shook visibly. Rudolf brought up the rear, leading Brigette's three children, hand in hand with them to make a chain.

When they reached the ramparts, Brigitte reached back to slap Heinrich, but he caught her arm midway. Again, he pulled her close. "I had to. Watch. You'll see why in a moment."

She just stepped back, cheeks flushed bright red, and seethed.

"Uncle, how could you!" Hilde shouted as she stepped to Heinrich, fists balled.

Heinrich just engulfed his niece in a hug, pinning her arms at the shoulder in the process. Then he saw Hilde bare her teeth. She bit his arm.

"Hilde!" Sofie shouted. She pulled her sister away as Heinrich recoiled.

"He betrayed us!" Hilde shouted at her. "He's one of them!"

Sofie held back Hilde from rushing at their uncle again. She'd become so weak from hunger, however, that Hilde was about to break free when a trumpet sounded outside the city. Everyone's head turned to see what was happening.

Simultaneously, the city gate grated closed. It was the sound of despair driving a sword through Sofie's heart. Their last chance of escape was over.

But that wasn't the reason for the trumpet call. When Sofie had a chance to look out over the walls and see all the bishop's soldiers encamped in the field beyond, she gasped. There were so many now!

As the refugees from Münster walked into the open space beyond the city walls and up to the trenches of the soldiers, the trumpets sounded again, and men boiled out of the blockhouses nearby, like ants leaving their burrow after someone stepped on it.

The townspeople outside the walls fell to their knees, arms raised to the sky in gratitude for their salvation. Sofie was too far away to hear or see them distinctly, but she could imagine the tearful faces and joyful voices of people who had just escaped a living nightmare. She still wanted to know why she wasn't among them.

Just as Sofie turned to ask Heinrich, the soldiers opened fire with their arquebuses, and then they drew swords and charged.

Everyone on the walls, whether the assigned watchmen or the people like Sofie who were there to see what would happen, gasped. Sunlight glinted from metal in the May sunshine as swords arced and sliced through the warm spring air.

At first, the refugees bunched together in panic, the people in front backing away while the people in the rear pressed forward. After a few moments, however, the crowd scrambled in every direction. When it did, another round of arquebus fire pierced the air, and a few more of the townspeople dropped to the ground, grasping at wounds or screaming and writhing in pain.

Then the imperial soldiers waded through the helpless, unarmed crowd, hewing and hacking at whomever was nearest. Soon, though, Sofie saw they had a method to their actions. Nearly all the people down on the ground were men. The soldiers paid no attention to the women or children in the throng, passing them by as if invisible.

The massacre didn't take long. When Sofie looked farther along the city walls, she could see the scene repeated at the other gate that was within her field of vision, St. Tilgen's. There, too, the soldiers surrounded the fleeing townspeople and cut the men to shreds.

When the smoke from the arquebuses cleared and Sofie had a chance to take in the scene in front of her again, she gasped. Three things were happening at once. A few of the besiegers walked around the bloodied field, stabbing any man who was down until he ceased moving. As if starving men posed any threat. Already, Sofie saw some of the troops mounting severed heads on pikes. Another group had seized all the refugee children, forcing and herding them into the blockhouses.

That left the women. It didn't look to Sofie as if the soldiers had killed many of them, yet they prevented the women from following their children at sword point. Finally, the soldiers returned to their blockhouses, leaving the women where they stood, trapped in the field between the trenches and the city's walls.

"What's going to happen now?" Brigitte whispered to Heinrich.

"Nothing will happen. The soldiers will leave the women there."

"To die of hunger?"

"Yes. Unless Münster opens its gates and allows them back, and I don't think that's going to happen."

"So, they'll have to sit out there, with no place to go, in the cold at night, until they starve or die some other way?"

"Now you see why I wouldn't let you join them, don't you?"

"You knew this would happen, Heinrich?"

"Yes. I overheard some of the mercenaries talking about it the night in December I sneaked over the walls. One of them said the order had come down to show no mercy to anyone in the city."

"I'm so sorry, Heinrich."

"For what?"

"For a moment, when you grabbed me by the hair and shouted at me, I really did think you'd betrayed us. I shouldn't have doubted you."

Somehow, Heinrich found his smile. "You just haven't been married to me long enough yet, I guess."

Brigitte smiled, too.

Heinrich continued. "I suppose I should have passed along the information I learned to the rest of you, but I never imagined King John would permit anyone to leave the city. All the literature that Philip of Hesse has fired into the city encouraging people to desert, we've had to burn. I never saw this coming."

Brigitte gave her husband a hug, and Sofie and Hilde joined.

"Now, Hilde, you need to tell me everything about your escape," Heinrich said. "That was the first thing I thought of when I saw you, and I can't tell you how much it hurt me that I couldn't ask you right away."

"I'd be happy to stay here with you and tell you about it, Uncle."

Sofie cleared her throat. "So, I guess there's nothing to do, then, except go home and starve, is there?" That brought everyone back to the grim reality of what they faced in the weeks ahead. Sofie no longer thought months ahead. That was pointless. She wasn't going to live that long.

Chapter 33

Münster

June 23, 1535

"I think all is ready," Heinrich said with an air of resignation. "This is the last chance. I'm ready."

Seated at Brigitte's table, Sofie looked at the man with her uncle, Little Hans of Longstreet. He was a reasonably handsome young man a few years older than she. His beard, untrimmed for many months, brushed his chest, and he was now thin and gaunt, with hollow eyes. Little Hans just nodded at Heinrich's pronouncement.

"Thanks to Little Hans' luck, we have two landsknecht's uniforms. Right after we go on our watch at midnight, we'll lower ourselves over Münster's walls. Most of the time, we're the only two on guard in our section, so no one should see us until it's too late. Then we'll sneak into the trenches, pretend to be members of the night watch for the besiegers, and then report to Count Wirich our scheme to betray the city when our watch is over."

"How did you get an extra uniform again?" Hilde wondered.

Little Hans spoke for the first time. "I won a game of chance two nights ago. I bet my boots against his extra uniform."

"And how do you know the enemy commander is Count Wirich?" Brigitte questioned.

"I'm almost certain that his standard flies alongside that of Bishop von Waldeck. I just hope we find the right trenches in time tonight. If the trench we infiltrate has German landsknechts, I'll do the talking. If they're from the Netherlands, Little Hans will."

"I'm from there. Nijmwegen," Little Hans said in explanation.

Heinrich nodded. "Rudolf, you know your role?"

"Yes. In two nights, I'll be at St. Ludger's Gate with my father to create a distraction while you lead the attackers closer. We've scrounged together a few last bits of flour for baking, and we'll hand out bread. Everyone is so hungry now, it's almost certain they'll let down their guard to eat. There's almost no moon, either. That'll help you approach unseen. Then, once the gate is open and you're inside, Father and I run straight here to make sure no one harms Sofie, Brigitte, and Hilde."

"Good. That settles it, then. Wish us luck," Heinrich said while he kissed his wife and two nieces. Not for the last time, he hoped.

Shortly after midnight, Heinrich and Little Hans got on their stomachs and maneuvered their way, pulling themselves along by the elbows, toward the trenches ringing Münster.

"That smell," Little Hans whispered.

"I know. It's the decaying bodies of the women who starved to death out here between the walls and the blockhouses."

"Hearing them beg for death night after night was the most pitiful thing I've ever heard, Heinrich."

"And one of the cruelest things I've ever seen. The king should've allowed them to return to the city, for mercy's sake, but he declared that the gates of mercy had shut forever. And the bishop's men wouldn't kill them to end their suffering. This whole thing turned into a tragedy long ago. That's why we can't fail. We have to end it, or else everyone in Münster will die."

"How long do you think we should wait, Heinrich? We want to sneak through the lines, find Count Wirich's tent, and hope he'll listen to our plan in exchange for not killing us."

"There should be one more change of the watch before the sun comes up. I've observed from the walls for months, and the besiegers change the watch every four hours. At midnight, and then at four in the morning. When that happens, we'll scale the earthworks in front of the trenches and try to disappear in the darkness and sneak to the count's tent that way. It's our best shot to avoid being captured and killed by the besiegers."

"So, we'll lie low for about three more hours," Little Hans said. "At least it's June, and we won't have to lie in freezing mud."

Somehow, Heinrich and Little Hans managed to stay awake until the changing of the guard. When that time came, they heard movement in the trenches, Heinrich gave a nod, and then they inched forward on elbows and knees until reaching the wall of earth thrown up in front of the first line of trenches.

"Now or never," Heinrich whispered. He cupped his hands to give Little Hans a boost. Hans jumped and got his body astride the top of the earthwork. He looked up and down the trench. No one around yet. They had a chance if they moved quickly.

Hans reached his hand down, caught Heinrich's, and pulled him up. Then they both toppled down the other side of the dirt wall and into the trench.

Right atop the body of a soldier sleeping in the trench. The darkness had hidden him from Little Hans' view. Startled from his rest, the man sat up and went wide-eyed. Heinrich tried to put a hand over the watchman's mouth, but he gave a shout before Heinrich could silence him.

In moments, Heinrich and Little Hans heard boots running toward them and saw the torches approaching from both sides. The game was up.

Heinrich leapt and tried to clamber out of the trench to escape into the shadows. When he got both feet under him, however, he looked up to see two men with arquebuses leveled at his chest.

"That's far enough," one of them growled.

"Just shoot him," the other said.

"No, he looks like one of us."

"He's not. I've never seen him before."

While the two landsknechts discussed his fate, Heinrich noticed that a handful of other men, presumably the next watch, had come out from the blockhouses and surrounded him and Little Hans of Longstreet. They leveled their pikes all around the two men.

The first man spoke again. "We want to take this man prisoner and hear what he'll say. I'm tired of this siege. Maybe he'll know something useful."

Finally, Heinrich gathered the nerve to say something. "I ask you, my dear landsknechts, to take us prisoner because we, too, were landsknechts, and I ask that we be granted an interview in front of your captain."

"I still say we shoot him. Those are our orders," the second captor retorted.

"Orders, yes, but this man is unarmed. He's no threat. Look how skinny he is. Besides, dead people can't give us any information about what's happening inside the city."

"I'm following my orders," the second man claimed, and he leveled his gun at Heinrich's chest.

"That'll be enough, Lars," came a new voice.

Heinrich and Little Hans looked toward the blockhouse, where a man walked toward them, rubbing the sleep from his eyes. Heinrich noticed the captain's insignia on the new man's arm.

"We have a prisoner. I don't want to kill him," the first man told his captain. "At least, not without seeing what he knows first."

"Our orders are to kill everyone, aren't they, Captain Lichtherte?" Lars asked.

"They are, but let the man speak first. Give him a chance to convince us why we shouldn't run him through where he stands," Captain Lichtherte stated.

Heinrich replied, "Thank you, Captain. I am Heinrich Gresbeck, and this is Little Hans of Longstreet. We are, as you've realized, defectors from Münster. We wanted you to capture us, so that you can bring us before Count Wirich and Bishop von Waldeck."

"How did you know Count Wirich now leads our forces?"

"I'm an experienced soldier. I recognized his banner."

"Not bad. Well, Heinrich Gresbeck, what else have you to say for yourself and Hans here?"

"I just ask that you hear a word from me. Münster suffers greatly. The people are on the verge of starvation. Some already have died from hunger and weakness. Little Hans and I have been at work on a plan to betray the city and bring the siege to an end. We have men inside the city who will help. So, I tried my luck and decided to turn myself in to you. It's better than starving to death in a city with no hope."

"If the people of Münster starve, then they'll open the gates to us soon," the captain responded.

"No, sir, I don't think so. King John, as John of Leiden refers to himself, won't hear of surrender. He still believes the Lord will come to the city's relief if its people are true. And you'll be here several more months if that's the case. I take it, Captain, your men would really rather take their pay and return to their homes than wait several more months, or risk themselves assaulting the city."

Lichtherte rubbed his chin between his thumb and forefinger.

Heinrich decided to play all his cards and hope. "I was a captain of the watch on the city walls. I know where they are weakest, where they are strongest, and where a breakthrough can be effected. Imagine the credit you and your men will get if you are the one who captures the man who can end the siege."

The captain said nothing in reply. He continued scratching at his chin while studying Heinrich and Little Hans. Finally, he announced, "Give these men some food. Watch over them. At first light, we'll take them to the count. He'll decide their fate." Then, looking at Heinrich and Little Hans, he added, "You've passed the first test. If you're as good as your word, the count may let you live. Then again, he may not."

A few hours later, Captain Lichtherte, flanked by several of his men, ushered Heinrich and Little Hans into the presence of Count Wirich of Falkenstein.

"So, these are the prisoners who claim they can offer the city into our hands?" the count asked his captain.

"Yes, commander. We caught them in the early hours this morning. They claim they meant to surrender to you."

"Well, let's at least hear what they have to say before we kill them like all the others from Münster. Speak, landsknecht!"

"Yes, my lord. It's an honor to finally meet the man who killed so many Turks at Vienna. Your efforts to help Christian II regain his throne are legendary, too."

Count Wirich smiled. "You have military experience?"

"I fought against the French at Ardres and Mouzon back in 1521. I was also with George Frundsberg at Bicocca the next year."

"One of the empire's most talented soldiers before his death, even if he was a mercenary at heart."

"Yes, my lord, he won many battles, and I was fortunate to serve under him."

"Prove to me you were at Bicocca, landsknecht. Tell me of the details of the battle."

"My lord, I was among those who helped set the field of battle. I knew that the advance of the Swiss and French would stall if we could get them into a confined space where the firepower of our arquebusiers could take its toll. So, I advised Prospero Colonna to set up a defensive position behind the sunken road. It offered protection from the Swiss pikes while our Imperial soldiers held their ground."

"You were a scout, then, landsknecht?"

"Yes, I was. Then, once we'd bottled up the Swiss mercenaries, I was with Frundsberg when we attacked the enemy's flank, forcing the Swiss and the French back and carrying the day."

"And was that Lautrec's left flank, or his right?"

"His left flank, sire," Heinrich stated without hesitation. "To charge on Lautrec's right would've been foolhardy. That land was too marshy."

At last, Count Wirich flashed a real smile. "You *were* there, then."

"Yes, Count Wirich. Frundsberg liked me because I could remember terrain and draw him accurate maps from memory."

"And you can do the same of Münster?"

"Of course. I've lived there for more than a decade. I know every street, gate, and landmark. Because I was a captain of the watch, I know which sections of the walls are strongest, which are weakest, and where the least attentive and most incompetent men stand guard. I also have friends on the inside of the walls who've sworn to help me. I can deliver the city to you with minimal loss. But if that is to happen, it must be soon. Tomorrow night, in fact."

"And why is that?"

"I don't believe my family will survive much longer than two more days."

Chapter 34

Münster

July 25, 1535

As soon as the booming of the cannons reached them, Heinrich, Little Hans of Longstreet, and their companions gathered their supplies. Count Wirich had assigned the men he judged his crack troops to carry out Heinrich's plan. Captain Lenz of Horst was their officer. He was, Heinrich thought, the classic military man, and a good leader. Although his face bore scars from who-knew-how-many battles, he stood tall, gave each soldier detailed instructions of what to do, had been over the plans with Heinrich and his junior officers several times, and exuded confidence.

The company's gear consisted of eight scaling ladders and two wooden gangways to bridge the moats guarding the city walls.

"How long do we wait, again?" one of the soldiers asked.

"Twenty minutes," Heinrich answered. "That will give the diversionary attacks time to draw the attention of the defenders toward Jew Fields Gate, Cross Gate, Our Dear Lady's Gate, and New Bridge Gate on the north and west sides of the city. They'll think the attacks are there. That's when we rush to the walls with our ladders, ropes, and scaling gear. With any luck, the sliver of moon will stay behind the clouds, the sound of the cannon and the first alarm will confuse any additional alarms, and my friends on the inside will keep the watch distracted long enough that we can get over the walls and open the gates. Then, we light a fire to show the rest of the men hiding in the trenches and blockhouses that it's time to advance and that the way is open."

"The count will have your head if this fails," Captain Lenz told Heinrich.

"Of course, he will. That's why we aren't going to fail. He'll have yours if your men aren't quick or tough enough." Heinrich didn't know if this was true, but he remembered from his time with George Frundsberg that casting doubt on a soldier's abilities, desire, fighting spirit, and manhood was a good way to motivate them.

"Just watch it, Gresbeck," Lenz growled back. "My men are tough. They won't fail. I'm more worried about an old-timer like you letting us down."

Works every time, Heinrich thought to himself.

"You're sure the gangplanks are long enough to bridge the moat?" Count Wirich's chief engineer, his Trench Master, asked Heinrich.

"I've crossed the moat dozens of times. The planks are long enough."

The minutes dragged by, but at last, twenty minutes were up. It was eleven at night.

"Move out," Lenz called quietly. "We approach at a light run. No talking and no lights. Send the word down the line."

While the junior officers relayed the captain's instructions, Heinrich noted with satisfaction that yesterday, Count Wirich had ordered all the sutlers in his camp to stop distributing alcohol to the soldiers. A wise move from an experienced commander. At least all the men he was alongside were sober. Now, it was time to see if they were competent.

To Heinrich, it felt like the approach to the walls and St. Ludger's Gate took another twenty minutes, even if it was more like three.

He got to the outer moat. No alarm yet. Heinrich dropped into the water.

Wow! The water was still cold, even in June. Heinrich spluttered but didn't cry out.

Without speaking, Heinrich motioned with a shaking arm, and the men brought up one of the gangplanks. He grabbed the end and swam for the other side.

Heinrich's instructions on the length of the plank were perfect. When he reached the far side of the moat, he set the iron hooks attached to the gangplank into the ground to secure the crossing. The troops advanced with their ladders, set them against the walls, and began climbing.

When the first wave reached the tops of their ladders and dropped onto the wall beyond, finally, the alarm went up. Heinrich sighed in relief. With any luck at all, the alarm was too late.

He watched from the cold water as all the soldiers scaled the ladders, and then he pulled himself up and followed. As he did, the defenders managed to tip two of the ladders backward. Heinrich watched as the men climbing them splashed into the water below.

When Heinrich reached the top of the wall, the fight had just finished. The first set of walls was theirs. A few bodies lay dead on the parapet. A few other of the watchmen had surrendered. Quickly, Heinrich descended to the gatehouse. Rudolf and his father stood there, as planned, arms up in surrender. Sofie stood with them. That was not part of Heinrich's plan.

"Sofie, what are you doing? You're supposed to be at home, safe." He turned to Rudolf. "Why did you bring her here?"

"It was my idea, Uncle," Sofie said.

"But why?"

"To help Rudolf. He only had enough to make two loaves of bread. That wouldn't distract all the guards. So, it was my idea to come along and pretend I was interested in finding a new husband, and that I admired the guards on the walls because you were one and always talked about how handsome your men are."

"It worked beautifully, too, if I may say," Rudolf put in. "Your men got to the top of the wall before anyone saw them."

"It's lucky for you she was here," Captain Lenz said, coming up to Heinrich. "If it hadn't been for her, my boys might've mistaken these two for more guards."

"But they're wearing fancy clothes, just like I told you they would be." That had been part of Heinrich's plan. Rudolf and his father would wear Rudolf's gaudiest doublets, so the troops would know they were accomplices and not kill them.

"It's almost midnight," Lenz said by way of explanation. "It's hard to see flashy clothes when it's dark and you think someone might try to kill you."

Even as Captain Lenz spoke and Heinrich stood there shivering in his drenched clothes, Heinrich saw the soldiers open the outer gate to bring in the ladders to scale the inner walls. Looking up, however, Heinrich saw that the defenders on the inner walls had rallied to the alarm, at least a few of them, and had gathered on the parapet above the gate.

"All right, we've got more fighting to do here. Let's get it over with," Lenz barked as his men carried their ladders across the causeway to the inner wall.

Just then, a blast of gunfire from the arquebusiers on the parapet rent the night air. A lead ball struck Heinrich on the left side of his chest, near the shoulder. He went down while blood spread over his torso.

"Uncle!" Sofie cried.

Rudolf and his father gathered around Heinrich, too. "Is it bad, Mr. Gresbeck?" Rudolf said, his voice rising and shaking.

Before he could make sense of what had just happened to him, Heinrich saw a gray veil drop over his eyes, and spots of blackness began intensifying and clouding out his vision.

"Help. Help Brigitte and Hilde," he managed to croak out before his head drooped back and his eyes shut.

"No!" Sofie screamed. "No, it can't be!" she cried again. Sofie grabbed her hair, shook her head wildly, and then repeated "It can't be," over and over.

"Sofie, you heard your uncle. We've got to get back to your house," Rudolf said, trying to take Sofie by her shoulders and guide her away.

"No!" she shouted again, shrugging off Rudolf's hands and trying to prop up her uncle's sagging body.

Rudolf's father knelt by Sofie and put his finger's to Heinrich's wrist. "Sofie," he said as gently as he could, "Heinrich isn't dead. I can feel his pulse. Go with Rudolf. I will stay here and watch over Heinrich. Your sister will need you."

"Will he die?" Sofie sobbed.

"I can't say. But unless you want Hilde and Brigitte to suffer the same fate, you need to go. I'll watch him."

"Look, Sofie!" Rudolf shouted, trying to get through to her. "The inner gate is opening! The soldiers captured the inner gatehouse! That means they'll signal their comrades to invade the city. We have to get to your home."

Just then, Little Hans of Longstreet staggered over to the people kneeling around Heinrich. Rudolf saw that Little Hans had tied a cloth bandage around his upper right leg.

"I'm fine," he stammered to everyone. "Time to complete my part in the plan. I'll go with you to your house and keep you under guard, so no other soldiers will break in and hurt you. Heinrich and I were supposed to guard you together, but it looks like it'll be just me. I'll try to grab an arquebus on the way."

"Sofie, please go. I'll stay and watch over Heinrich," Rudolf's father repeated.

"You're wounded," Rudolf stated to Little Hans.

"A little. I can walk, though. Sofie, Rudolf, let's go."

Little Hans saw Sofie set her jaw. He told her, "We have to. You know that. Mr. Schweren will take care of your uncle if it's possible. I know it sounds harsh, Sofie, but his sacrifice will be meaningless if you and your family don't survive. Your sister needs you right now."

That broke through to Sofie at last. Slowly, she released her hair, and then she took a deep breath. "You're right. Let's go."

Sofie and Rudolf ran ahead while Little Hans limped behind. They were too weak to travel very quickly, however, so it seemed as though it was a mile just to reach Brigitte's home. When they reached it, panting and staggering, they pulled open the door and lunged inside, only to find Brigitte crying while her children gathered around her.

"What's wrong?" Sofie asked. Then, she knew. "Where's Hilde?"

"She left," Brigitte said, looking up. "When she heard the alarms and the fighting begin, she left before I could stop her. She didn't say where."

"Oh, no. How will we find her?" Rudolf wondered. "If she panicked and ran out, she could be anywhere by now."

"Rolf tried to follow her, but he couldn't keep up and lost sight of her," Brigitte cried miserably.

That's when Little Hans arrived. True to his word, Sofie saw, he'd acquired an arquebus to help defend the home.

But when Brigitte looked up and saw him, she said, "Where's Heinrich?"

No one spoke. As Brigitte looked from face to face, Sofie knew she had to say it. "He's been shot, Aunt Brigitte. Rudolf's father is with him now."

"He's dying, then?"

"No one knows. He was alive when we left to come protect you, Hilde, and your children."

"But our plan has failed, Sofie. Your sister left, and we can't find her."

At that point, the shouting in the streets began. Everyone heard the clash of metal on metal that signaled hand-to-hand combat between the defenders of the city and the attacking soldiers. The end had arrived. Somewhere, Hilde was out there.

Brigitte put her head in her hands. "The last thing I heard her say was that she owed it to the rose. But I don't know what that means. What do roses have to do with anything?"

"I've got it!" Sofie called. "Hilde wasn't talking about flowers. She owes it to Rose. Rose was another of King John's wives."

"But what does it mean?" Brigitte asked plaintively.

"It means I know where she's gone. Rudolf, we must go save my sister."

Instantly, Sofie was back in the street. She felt like she was slogging through mud as she tried to run toward St. Lambert's Cathedral. Her legs were so weak from lack of food, she couldn't get them to move as fast as her mind thought they should be able to.

By the time she reached the marketplace, she stumbled out of weakness and fell to the ground, scraping her right knee until the blood ran. Rudolf tried to pick her up, but she fell back.

"Where are we going, Sofie?"

"To St. Lambert's. Hilde wants to kill John of Leiden."

"But she'll never get past all his guards."

"I know. That's why we must stop her before she tries. But I'm just so weak, Rudolf. I don't know if I can run any farther."

"The fighting is behind us. For now. But the troops will be here soon enough. They're trained soldiers who've eaten regularly for months. The townspeople won't be able to stand up to them in their weakened condition. Here, try again to stand."

This time, Sofie got to her feet, but she hobbled and staggered out of the marketplace and into the cathedral square. On her way to the cathedral, she noticed someone had already knocked over the king's throne. Somehow, that sight gave her a bit of hope.

While she and Rudolf plodded toward the cathedral's doors, Sofie said to Rudolf, "The guards at the front door are gone."

"At least we won't have to make up a reason to get inside."

"But what if Hilde's gone, too?"

Rudolf had no answer for that. "Let's just keep going, Sofie. We've almost reached the church. Do you hear that?"

Sofie could hear it. The sounds of battle. Much closer again. She wasn't moving fast enough.

When she reached the stairs out front, Sofie felt so exhausted, she literally picked up her legs one at a time to put them on the next step. Heaving for breath, she reached the top step and stumbled through one of the cathedral's double doors. Thankfully, the door rested open a crack. Sofie didn't know if she could've opened something that heavy on her own, or even with Rudolf's help.

When she pulled herself inside, all was chaos as armed men ran back and forth, grabbing weapons and trying to get organized. The inside of the cathedral was eerie at night, Sofie realized. Although several chandeliers hung from the ceiling, with many lit candles in each, the light wasn't enough to do more than bathe the interior of St. Lambert's in a murky gray. Complete darkness concealed the edges of the sanctuary.

She and Rudolf wandered toward the altar. None of the guards took any notice of them in the dim half-light.

Then, Sofie saw John of Leiden emerge into the sanctuary, Queen Divara alongside him, carrying the king's tiny son. They mounted the steps toward the altar, where the bishop's seat rested. Only then did Sofie notice a shadow emerge from behind the altar where it had hidden itself. After coming a few steps closer, Sofie had no doubt. The shadow was Hilde.

"My king, what shall we do?" Hilde cried as she approached John.

"We shall fight to the last man. The Lord will deliver His people," the king replied as he fastened the leather belt at his waist. Sofie couldn't help but notice the king was the picture of full health while most people she knew were little more than skeletons.

"Please, help me! I'm so frightened!" Hilde exclaimed, stepping closer.

"Hilde, we're here!" Sofie called out while she and Rudolf tried to get to her sister. They'd almost reached the steps leading to the altar where Hilde and John stood.

When the king turned to look at who'd spoken, Hilde drew Brigitte's cutting knife from behind her back and lunged at John of Leiden. Just as he turned back toward Hilde, the blade flashed briefly in the fitful candlelight, and Hilde drove it into the king's side. Then, she pulled the knife down and twisted. He clutched at the wound, blood running through his hands. Hilde stepped back.

The king did not go down, however. Rather, he drew out the knife even as Queen Divara screamed.

Sofie's mind tried to process everything, but she froze for a moment, and then she heard a nearby guard yell, "She attacked the king! Kill the woman!"

At the same instant, the cathedral doors burst open, and a group of men in the uniforms of the landsknechts poured through.

When Sofie looked back at Hilde, she was backing away even as King John gripped the knife and slashed at her, slicing her forearm as Hilde raised her arms in defense. Hilde screeched in pain.

Sofie lunged forward. She meant to jump on the king's back and wrap her arms around his throat, but in her weakened state she only managed to get him in a loose hug from behind.

John of Leiden threw back one elbow and connected with Sofie's forehead. She tried to clear the flashes of color from her eyes even as she hit the floor, stunned. Blinking, trying to regain her senses, Sofie saw one of the king's guards advance on her, raise his sword, and swing it down. The iron blade, gray in the sanctuary's twilight, arced toward her neck.

It sliced directly into Rudolf's chest as he stepped in front of Sofie to receive the blow. He screamed and fell to the ground beside her.

The guard just growled, withdrew his blade from Rudolf's already spasming body, and raised it to strike again. Sofie put up her right arm in a useless gesture to ward off the next blow.

The sword began its remorseless descent. But then Sofie's attacker went stiff, even as the blast of an arquebus rent the cathedral's sacred space. Sofie saw blood gurgle from his mouth, and he dropped his weapon and fell on his side.

Instinctively, Sofie got to her feet to find Hilde. She saw that Hilde had taken cover behind the altar again, both forearms bleeding freely now. The king, meanwhile, let her go and jumped down into the fray as the charge of the landsknechts reached the front of the sanctuary and engaged his personal guards.

Hilde motioned Sofie over. "This way," she said, pointing. "I know how to get out the back from here. We still have a chance to get away and hide from the soldiers."

"Both your arms are bleeding, Hilde."

"It's not that bad. He didn't slice me that deep."

Sofie looked her sister in the face. She didn't know if her doubtful look registered in the gloaming.

"Trust me, Sofie. I've got practice at this."

Then Sofie looked back at Rudolf. He'd fallen with his back to where she was now. It was impossible to tell if he was alive or dead. "We can't leave him there," she told Hilde.

"Hurry, come with me!"

Hilde crawled to where Rudolf's body rested and grabbed one arm. She motioned Sofie to help. Together, one lunge at a time, they dragged him to the door behind the altar that led to the room where the priests stored the sacred vessels of the church.

The room was utterly dark, so the women bumped what sounded like chalices and silver candlesticks to the floor as they stumbled toward the back.

"Don't worry about that," Hilde told her sister. "The sight of silver will slow down the soldiers, I'll bet."

Even as the young women heard the screams of dying men behind them, Hilde pulled open a door and the trio fell into the cathedral square at the back of the church. Although Sofie heard the battle around her everywhere, they were the only ones in the shadows behind the cathedral. It was very dark.

Then, Rudolf coughed, spitting blood.

"Rudolf! You're alive!" Sofie cried.

"Not for much longer, I'm afraid," he sputtered in response, his voice little more than a whisper. "The wound is mortal."

"You can't die. I won't lose you and my uncle on the same day."

"Too . . . too late for that now."

"But you gave yourself up for me, Rudolf."

"I owed it to you."

"What do you mean?"

"I wish . . . wish I had time left . . . to explain."

"Explain what?"

Rudolf managed to shake his head. "I'll get to . . . get to see Karl again soon. Promise me . . ." another cough of blood.

"Promise what?" Sofie pleaded, tears falling freely now.

"Bury me . . . next to him . . . if you can. Sofie, I . . ."

"What, Rudolf? What is it?"

But it was too late. Rudolf died in Sofie's arms, hidden deep in the shadows of the cathedral. She closed his eyes, kissed him on the forehead, and let his body rest on the ground, hands folded over his chest.

Hilde put her bleeding arms around her sister's shoulders and squeezed. "It's over, Sofie. It's finally over." Then, Hilde sobbed. "The nightmare is over at last."

Sofie just held her there while the minutes passed. Then, she helped her sister bandage her arms, since the blood had stopped oozing from the wounds.

The sisters sat in place for a long time, their backs to the cathedral's outside wall. Sofie had no idea how long they stayed, arms over each other's shoulders, while the sounds of combat nearby rent the air around them. Somehow, no one found them in the dark shadows where they hid.

Eventually, Sofie and Hilde realized that the sounds of battle had died down. Sofie helped Hilde to her feet. "I think we can go home now, Hilde."

Chapter 35

Münster

March of 1536

Sofie, Hilde, Brigitte, and Heinrich stood in the cathedral square, just as they'd done so many times over the past few years. Wispy strands of fog drifted by on the raw morning wind. A chill hung in the air, and the macabre scene in front of them did nothing to dispel it.

"I wish that Little Hans would have stayed in the city for a while longer, Heinrich. He seemed a very decent fellow," Brigitte told her husband.

"Agreed."

"We'd have nothing if it weren't for him. The night you two led the attack on the city, he shot one soldier who came to my house, and then fought off two more with his sword. I'm very sorry to see him go."

"Me, too, but it's easy to understand why he wanted to go home to Nijmwegen. He told me he'd had enough of soldiering, and that maybe following in the family business was a good idea, after all."

Brigitte hugged her husband.

Sofie, meanwhile, looked up at the three cages that hung, creaking and dangling at the end of long chains, from St. Lambert's Cathedral. One held the bones of John of Leiden, his rotten, dead flesh long since picked clean by the crows. Bernhard Knipperdollinck's lifeless bones were in the cage beside it, with Herman Tilbeck's remains in the third iron-banded prison.

"Uncle, did the bishop and the count really torture those three men?" Hilde asked when silence descended on the conversation.

"With red-hot branding irons. They led John of Leiden around in a cage for several months, like a bear, then tortured all three men before locking them up and letting them starve to death in their cages. The tongs they used hang from that tree over there." Heinrich pointed to the metal implements still on public display. "The story has it that John never even cried out in pain while they branded him."

"And all the other Anabaptist leaders are dead, too?" Sofie wondered.

"As far as I know," Heinrich answered. "Rothmann died in the fighting. Dusentscher, too. In fact, many men in the city perished the night of the attack, and most of the rest the count's men beheaded afterward, as a warning to the rest of the empire. They cut off the queen's head, too. I never heard what happened to the king's infant son."

"I suppose that's the same reason the count decided to destroy Münster's walls, isn't it, Uncle?" Sofie stated.

"Yes. He felt the need to send a message of what happens to anyone who rebels."

"How long do you think they'll leave the cages there?" Brigitte wondered.

"Bishop von Waldeck said they should hang there until the Second Coming," Heinrich answered with a nervous laugh. "The joke seemed in poor taste to me, but I suppose he was still sore after all the trouble Münster caused him."

"Are you all ready to go?" Brigitte asked everyone. "I think I've seen enough."

"If I never see Münster again, it'll be fine with me," Hilde added.

Sofie looked at her poor younger sister's face. Some of the scars she had given herself last year had faded and Sofie could barely see them now. Others, however, would never heal all the way. Whether the same was true of the scars on her sister's heart, Sofie didn't know. Only time would tell.

"Yes, everything is ready," Heinrich said after a moment. "The wagon to load our goods will be by this afternoon. It isn't very far to Osnabrück from here. It's a nice town to start over, yet large enough that I'm sure it has room for one more cabinetmaker. And one more seamstress," he added, smiling at his wife.

"I wish the whole last three years had been a dream," Hilde said wistfully. "But we lived through a nightmare. In every way."

"Even nightmares end, Hilde. At least, I hope so," Sofie told her sister, and then added a hug.

Hilde looked at Sofie and smiled briefly but didn't respond.

"Let's be on our way, then," Brigitte announced. "No use reliving the bad times any more often than we have to."

"You all go along. I've got one thing to do first, and then I'll follow," Sofie told them.

After everyone else left, Sofie walked to the mass grave in the cathedral square, the one where Karl Schweren's body lay. Rudolf's body didn't rest beside that of his brother, as requested. The people who'd died last June had their own mass grave outside the city. But in Sofie's heart, Rudolf rested there with his older brother who'd always been kind to her. And so did Kurt. No one had ever found Kurt's body after his death. So, Sofie pretended he lay there, too.

She stood for a while, saying nothing, not moving, and then took a deep breath. "I'm not very good at this," Sofie said quietly, to the air, "so, I don't know exactly how to say what I'm thinking.

But I know I wouldn't be alive today if not for the three of you. I also know you had things you wanted to say to me, things you wanted to tell me, all of you, but now you'll never have the chance.

"For you, Karl, thank you for being so kind to me for so many years. I always looked up to you, and it breaks my heart I'll never get to see the man you should have become. Your father is very proud of you. He talks about you all the time, even today."

Sofie paused a moment to wipe a stray tear from her cheek. "And you, Rudolf, I guess we had a strange relationship. Our paths always crossed, but never entwined. Maybe that's how it was meant to be. For most of my life, I wanted nothing more than to stay away from you. Maybe I was wrong about that. Perhaps it just took crazy things to happen to bring out the best in you. I don't know. But I'm going to believe that's true. When I think back on you, I'm going to remember the person you were the last year of your life. I'll remember that person and believe that's who you would've been if you'd lived. It's the best way I have to honor what you sacrificed for me."

A long pause followed. Sofie blinked her eyes several times, trying to keep more tears at bay, so she could finish.

"Kurt, you were all I ever wanted. The man I wanted to marry since I was seventeen. I got my wish, but it didn't turn out the way my dreams told me it would. Maybe things never do. I thought I'd get to spend my whole life with you, and that we'd grow old together with children all around us. That's become my nightmare. It's what the Anabaptists took away from me. Sometimes, I wake up in the night and imagine you're still beside me. I guess your memory always will be. To me, you'll always be the young man I fell in love with. Goodbye, my husband."

Sofie turned and started home. Just saying the words out loud helped a little. She breathed deeply, inhaling the damp morning air, but couldn't bring herself to smile.

She walked out of the cathedral square and through the marketplace, her head down. Even though merchants and commerce had returned to the market months ago, Sofie had too many memories of this route that she wanted to avoid. So, she stared at the cobblestones while she walked on.

Finally, the door to her house came into view. Her family waited inside. Rudolf's father came through the door, helping load possessions into the wagon for the move to Osnabrück. Finally, Sofie managed a smile at the thought of a new life. She'd always been the optimist, and Kurt the pessimist, before Münster's descent into madness. Sofie decided to get that mindset back. It's what Kurt would have wanted her to do. What her family needed her to do. Most importantly, deep down, she knew it was what she needed to do.

It was the only way to put the nightmare behind her, the only way to get back what the Anabaptists stole from her. Sofie meant to reclaim her life. If she didn't, that meant that John of Leiden still haunted her, even in death. Sofie couldn't allow him to continue terrorizing her like that. Moving on was the best way of fighting back against what he'd done to ruin so many lives.

Sofie walked inside. Hilde was the first to see her.

"All ready, Sofie?"

"Yes. I'm ready for whatever comes our way, Hilde."

"It feels strange moving from our home that we've had for so long, but where we're going can't be worse than where we've been, can it?"

"No, Hilde. No, it can't. I'm going to make sure of that. We both are. You, me, Uncle Heinrich, and Aunt Brigitte."

"All of us, together," Hilde agreed.

"Together. For us, and for our future."

I'd like to thank everyone who purchases *The Nightmare Kingdom* for reading my book. If you enjoyed it, I would be grateful if you'd leave a short review of the book on whatever website you purchased it from. Favorable reader reviews are very important to authors like me. They help tremendously in attracting new readers and spreading the word about existing books that you think others will enjoy.

Thank you!

If you want updates on future books, please join my Reader's Club mailing list at www.robbauerbooks.com.

Author's Note

If one is so inclined, they can go to Münster today and still see the three cages mentioned in chapter 35. They still hang from St. Lambert's Cathedral.

About the Author

I'm Rob Bauer, author of historical fiction and nonfiction books and owner of Rob Bauer Books. I hold a PhD in American History and was a Distinguished Doctoral Fellow at the University of Arkansas.

My fiction has two purposes—entertaining readers and explaining historical injustice. Although I enjoy adventure and humorous books as much as the next reader, I'd like my books to stand for something a little bigger. All my studies in history put me in a position to do that. Whether I'm writing about how racism damages the individual psyche, the deportation of the Métis people of Montana, the South's prison labor system, or the utter terror of the Belgian Congo, with my books you'll find yourself in powerful historical stories.

I also write nonfiction about baseball history because I've always loved the game, its history, and its lore. I sometimes joke that baseball may be the one thing in life I truly understand. Although I love the statistical side of the game, if you don't, never fear because my histories go light on the statistics and heavy on what baseball was like in the past. They're stories about baseball, but stories with a point.

The history blog on my website offers posts on a variety of interesting historical figures and events. I'd love to have you follow along.

When I'm not working on my next story or writing project, I enjoy spending time at the beach. And, oh yeah, I still read a history book or two. When I'm not watching baseball.

Acknowledgments

I also want to thank the people who helped make this book possible, especially Jim Soular for his help with editing. Thank you to E.M. Bosso, Amber Daniels, David Mitchell, and Brigitte Baake for reading and making suggestions. I appreciate your help in making this story into the best I could write.

Made in the USA
Middletown, DE
14 February 2022